DEBORAH GRACE WHITE

# A Splintered Land

## HEARTSONG BOOK ONE

*For Constance and Alora*
*To friendships across oceans...*
*Thanks for cheering this series on!*

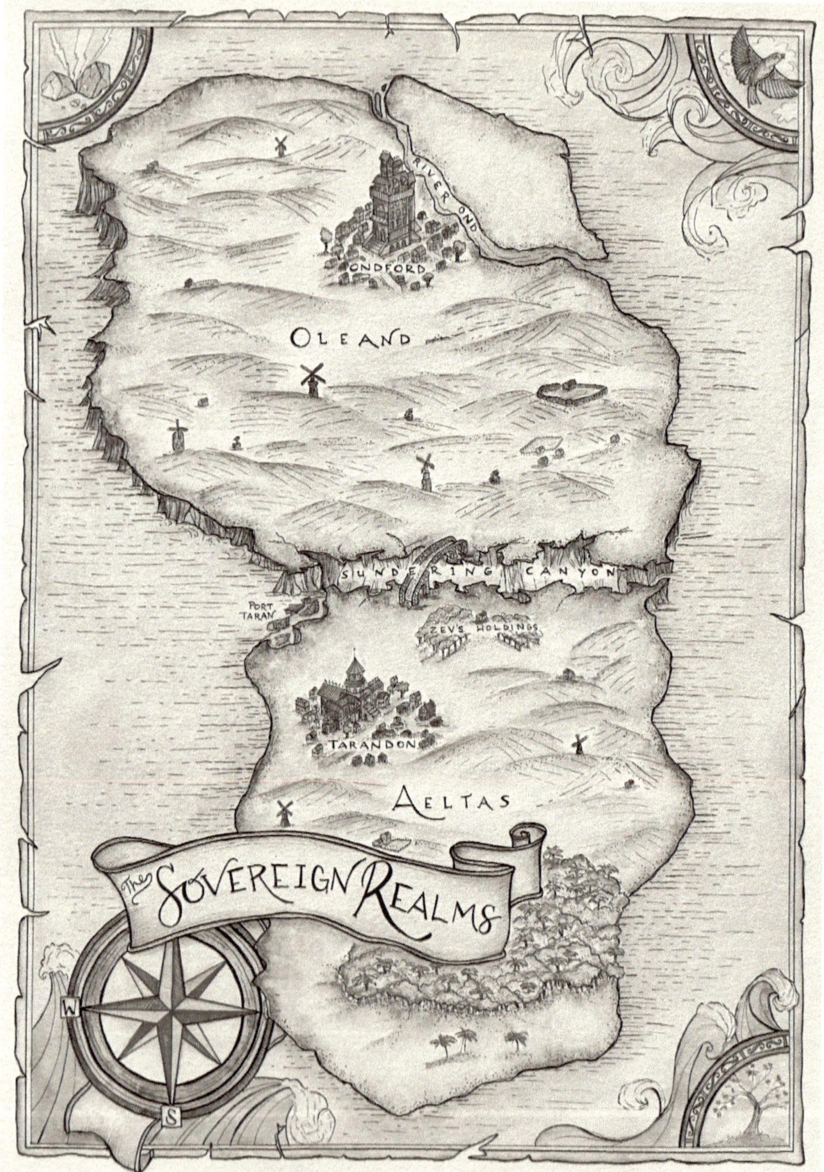
RIVER OND
ONDFORD
OLEAND
SUNDERING CANYON
PORT TARAN
ZEV'S HOLDINGS
TARANDON
AELTAS
The Sovereign Realms
W
S

*Marieke*

Marieke knocked at the door, reminding herself sternly that there was no need for her surge of nerves at being summoned to the Head Instructor's office. She was no longer a student at the Academy of Song. He didn't have power now to get her in trouble.

Not that she'd been a troublesome student. All of her instructors had only had one complaint about her—she asked too many questions.

Smiling slightly at the memory of all the long-suffering comments she'd had on that particular flaw, she pushed the door open. The Head Instructor looked up from his desk, beckoning her in.

"Marieke," he said with a smile. "Thank you for coming so quickly."

"It's my pleasure, Instructor Rafael," she said, nodding her head respectfully. "It was nice to have an excuse to come back. I'm still not used to the fact that I don't live here anymore."

The Head Instructor smiled vaguely. "Are you enjoying your summer break? I was pleasantly surprised to learn that you were still in Ondford. I'd understood that your family didn't live here in the capital."

"They don't," Marieke confirmed. "They live on the eastern coast. I went back for a brief visit after graduation, but I confess I was eager to be back in the capital. I've been staying with a friend while I figure out what comes next for me, now I've graduated from the academy."

"Which brings me nicely to the reason I asked you to come see me today," the Head Instructor said.

Marieke sat straighter in her chair, trying not to look too eager. She couldn't help but hope that he'd called her to offer her a position—either at the Academy of Song, or the Council of Singers, of which the Head Instructor was a member—even though it felt presumptuous. After all, she was only just eighteen, and although she'd given a good account of herself at the academy, she had no family connections to recommend her for further advancement.

"I've been asked to consider a graduate for an opportunity," Instructor Rafael went on. "And you came immediately to my mind."

"I'm flattered, sir," said Marieke quickly.

She saw a slight smile cross his face. "You should wait until you hear all the details before deciding that," he said. "I think it would be a good opportunity for you, but you may well not agree."

Marieke frowned inquisitively, and the older man leaned back in his chair.

"The request comes from the Oleandan ambassador to Aeltas."

Marieke raised her eyebrows. She hadn't expected the conversation to relate to Aeltas, the country to the south of Oleand. "The ambassador? He lives in Tarandon, presumably?"

The Head Instructor nodded at this mention of the Aeltan capital. "Yes, but he's been back in Ondford to meet with the Council of Singers."

Marieke nodded politely, taking note of the shrewdness with which Instructor Rafael looked her over.

"I'll be frank with you, Marieke, because you're a sensible girl. It's not a matter for public discussion, but the ambassador attended the council at our request, to discuss the deteriorating state of our land."

Marieke stilled, her interest fully caught. It was an open secret that their country of Oleand was becoming more arid, the landscape notably more barren and dry than it had been in her childhood. It was the topic of constant mutterings and complaints, from the marketplaces to social events. Not being from the city herself, and needing to travel across farmland to go between her home and the academy during every break, Marieke had good reason to know that the landscape really was changing. But she'd never before heard it acknowledged by anyone official. In fact, discussion of the so-called problem had always been nipped in the bud at the academy, with the instructors accusing the students of rumormongering.

As usual, questions burned inside her, but she was smart enough not to blurt them out this time. Clearly the Head Instructor had more to tell her, and she'd be wisest to wait for it.

"It seems," he went on, sounding like the next words cost him pain, "that Aeltas is not experiencing a similar phenomenon. The ambassador confirms it."

Marieke sat back, intrigued by this information. She'd assumed that if the land itself was affected, it would apply to all of the Sovereign Realms.

"Why would that be?" she asked slowly.

Instructor Rafael sighed, interlacing his fingers in a gesture that made him look especially scholarly. "Many theories have been proposed. None provide satisfactory explanation, in my opinion." He pinned her with a look. "Further research can only benefit the deliberation process, which is why the ambassador has requested the expedition."

"Expedition?" Marieke repeated, finding herself leaning forward once again.

The Head Instructor nodded. "The ambassador has secured an invitation from the Aeltan Council of Singers for an Oleandan group to travel to the Aeltan capital to see if we can learn from anything they might be doing differently."

Marieke reflected that it must have tasted bitter for the Council of Singers to ask their Aeltan counterparts to let them study their approach and learn from them. The successful running of a unified and strong Oleand was the chief pride of the council—it had been in all the generations since the singers first rose up and overthrew the corrupt, magic-less monarchs who'd once ruled Oleand with their despotism. No doubt the Aeltan singers, who by all accounts prided themselves on the same feat, took pleasure from this admission that they were having more success managing their own country.

"Most of the delegation is assembled," Instructor Rafael went on. "But the ambassador asked in particular for a recent graduate to be added. His hope is that you can observe some of the processes of the Aeltan Academy of Song and give a student's perspective on whether they're training their singers differently."

Marieke nodded slowly. "Does that mean that the council suspects there may be a magical cause of the changing landscape? That the general exercise of magic across the country might be having an unintended effect?"

"We aren't ruling out any possible explanations," said Instructor Rafael noncommittally. His face suddenly relaxed into a smile that was a little weary. "But your mind is clearly sharp enough to grasp the type of investigation we wish to undertake in Aeltas. Are you willing to join the expedition?"

Marieke's response rose to her lips, but she held it back a moment, not wanting to seem too eager. She understood why the Head Instructor had cautioned her she might not like the assignment. Many Oleandans thought poorly of Aeltas, and from all she knew, the feeling was mutual. It was especially strong in those of higher status, who had more personal stake in the pride of their own country. Marieke, on the other hand, was a singer born unexpectedly to simple country folk whose line hadn't seen any magic-carriers for generations. She was astute enough to know that this lowly status was probably a large factor in her being chosen for the trip. She was less likely to turn her nose up at the offer.

But she wasn't offended. She had no intention of turning her nose up at anything. She'd never been to Aeltas—never imagined she'd have the opportunity to go there. And to her, leaving Oleand sounded like an adventure too rare to be missed. Together, the two countries formed the entire continent of the Sovereign Realms. Oleand occupied the northern half of the land mass, Aeltas the southern, a long way from her home on Oleand's northeastern coast.

And to be personally selected by the Head Instructor...it was an honor she couldn't refuse, not if she wanted to make something of herself. She'd learned in her two years at the academy that while she might share the ability of every other singer to pull the ever-present magic from the ground and channel it into usable power through her song, she didn't share the same opportunities as those who'd been born into established families of singers, who'd spent generations building up their name in the community.

"I'm more than willing," she said, trying to sound dignified. "I'd be delighted."

"Excellent. I apologize for the short notice, but the delegation leaves in only a few days."

Marieke nodded compliantly. The Head Instructor seemed genuinely pleased with her acceptance, which bolstered her.

"Honestly, I'm just relieved I was called in here for good news," she said, adding with a chuckle, "I was nervous it would be bad news when I got called to the Head's office. I had to remind myself I'm not a student anymore, and you can't kick me out of the academy."

Instructor Rafael smiled indulgently. "You were an excellent student, Marieke. I wouldn't be recommending you for this position if you weren't. I don't think you ever needed to worry about being *kicked out*, as you phrase it."

"Not unless you can get kicked out for asking too many questions," Marieke joked.

The Head Instructor's response surprised her. His gaze became strangely searching as his smile faded, and he didn't immediately answer.

"I meant no offense," said Marieke cautiously, confused as to what in her words had prompted the change in his demeanor. He was looking at her as though he suspected a hidden meaning behind her words, but she hadn't intended one.

He nodded slowly in acknowledgment of the half-apology. "There's nothing wrong with asking questions, Marieke. In fact, it's an important part of how any student learns."

The tone in which he said it made Marieke sure there was a *but* coming. She had to wait for several painful seconds before her instinct was proved correct.

"But discretion is important. No student would ever be expelled from the academy just for a simple question. But we must ask ourselves honestly what attitude is behind our questions. There's wisdom in being mindful of the context and company in which you voice things." He gave another nod. "You would do well to be conscious of that when you're in Aeltas."

"Yes, sir," said Marieke meekly. She remained utterly confused. Her words had been intended to be light and humorous. And yet, for a moment, she'd really thought he was reconsidering the wisdom of selecting her for the diplomatic trip.

After another tense moment, Instructor Rafael seemed to relax. He gave her another smile, the expression once again a little weary.

"I'd best let you go, then. If you leave your directions with my assistant, someone will be in touch with the details. I'm sure you'll have preparations of your own to make."

Marieke excused herself gratefully, torn between elation at the unexpected chance to represent Oleand on a diplomatic mission, and unease at the strange sternness she'd provoked in the Head Instructor. She still had no idea how she'd managed it.

It didn't matter, though. All that mattered was that she'd been given a chance to prove herself. She didn't intend to waste it.

~

Marieke pressed her face against the carriage window, straining to see ahead. But as usual, all she could see was the farmland past which the vehicle was trundling. It had been unchanging for the two and a half days since they'd departed the capital. And she'd long since observed that this southern farmland looked much the same as that in the north—that was to say, not nearly lush enough for the time of year. Even the uncultivated land looked scrubby and bare, in spite of the temperate weather.

"You're leaving a grimy mark on the window again." The long-suffering comment came from her carriage companion.

"No, I'm not," said Marieke, but she sat back quickly. At about fifteen years older than her, Solomon didn't have the intimidating presence of someone like the Head Instructor. But he was an assistant instructor all the same, and she didn't care to make too much of a fool of herself. Especially when he'd been the only one in the delegation to voluntarily climb into the carriage with the overly talkative singing graduate that morning.

"Let me guess?" Solomon asked good-naturedly. "Still nothing to see?"

Marieke grimaced. "I thought they said we'd reach the canyon by noon."

"Around noon, is what they said," Solomon corrected. "And we should interpret that very loosely. I'm sure it won't be long now, though."

He sounded absent, his eyes already straying back to the tome he was examining, and Marieke studied him curiously.

"Aren't you a little excited? Curious, at the very least? I mean...Sundering Canyon! It's the stuff of legends."

Solomon shut the book with a sigh, apparently accepting that he was going to be forced into conversation for a while.

"I'm a little curious," he acknowledged. "It's supposed to be quite a fascinating phenomenon. Certainly magical in origin."

Marieke nodded eagerly. She'd learned enough history at the academy to know that there had been no canyon back in the days when Oleand and Aeltas had been kingdoms. It was only after the monarchies ended that the huge ravine had splintered the land, stretching all the way from the west coast to the east.

"It could hardly be naturally occurring," she agreed. "Not when it appeared right along the border like that."

"Being caused by magic doesn't mean it's not naturally occurring," said Solomon, his tone slipping to that of an instructor teaching students. "Magic *is* nature. It comes from the ground itself."

Marieke had become comfortable enough during their journey together to direct a pointed look at him. "It can hardly be called natural if the magic in question was directed intentionally by a singer. That's like saying that a chiseled sculpture is naturally occurring because the tool used by the sculptor was made of materials that once came from the ground."

Solomon snorted. "How could Sundering Canyon have been intentionally created by a singer? To split the whole land like that, coast to coast...not even all the singers of the original alliance could harness that much magic. And their collective songcraft gave them enough magic to overpower two corrupt monarchies in one fell swoop."

"Thank you, Instructor, for the history lesson," said Marieke meekly.

Solomon eyed her, clearly smart enough not to be convinced by her docile response. "History isn't my area of instruction," he told her with asperity.

She just grinned, unabashed. "And yet you still have that teaching tone perfected." She felt the carriage slowing and leaned excitedly against the window again. "I think we might be arriving!"

The carriage came fully to a stop, and Marieke pushed the door open. Solomon followed her out more slowly, the morning's hours of travel apparently not enough to make him want to leave his reading.

Ignoring the protest of the carriage driver, Marieke hurried forward along their line of vehicles, all of which had pulled to a stop. She caught her breath at the sight that awaited her in front of the first carriage. About ten yards ahead, the ground fell abruptly away. The ravine yawned widely enough that she had to squint to see the far side and continued as far as the eye could see to both left and right.

Sundering Canyon.

Marieke moved forward more slowly, peering down into the canyon. She caught a flash of motion and heard the sounds of water. Apparently there was a river down there. But she could also see rocky ground, a long, long way down.

"Marieke!"

The sharp voice drew her up, and she looked sheepishly back at the head of the squadron of official guards who accompanied the delegation.

"Sorry," she said. "I was just so curious to see the canyon!"

"It's a hole in the ground," the man said, unimpressed. "Not worth risking your life to see."

Marieke thought he was being dramatic—it wasn't as though she was teetering on the edge. But she moved further back compliantly.

"Why are you out of your carriage?" the guard asked, his eyes scanning the row to where Solomon still stood next to their vehicle.

"We've arrived," Marieke said blankly. "I wanted to see."

"We haven't arrived anywhere," said the guard in exasperation. "We're only at the border. We'll be crossing straight over."

Marieke followed his gaze back to the road, her eyes widening with excitement as she caught sight of the point where the road curved upward and became an enormous bridge that spanned the chasm. It was an impressive feat, the stone structure almost seeming to hover over the empty space, with supporting beams only in place about a third of the way from each side of the canyon.

"Oh, I didn't realize we were continuing on immediately," she said. She frowned as she realized there was no traffic coming along the bridge that might have required them to wait. "Why did we all stop?"

The guard fingered the hilt of his sword, looking slightly ill-at-ease. "The delegation head is speaking with the toll-keepers."

Marieke frowned as her eyes found the familiar figure of the delegation leader, Isabel. She was a senior member of the Council of Singers, the council's only representative on the trip. She was deep in conversation with a man who'd emerged from a small stone building near the point where the road turned into the bridge.

Disregarding the head guard, Marieke hurried forward, curiosity getting the better of her. Isabel looked over as she approached, a frown marring her brow.

"Is everything all right, Councilor?" Marieke asked.

"I hope so, Miss," said the toll-keeper, looking anxious. His eyes flicked over the row of vehicles. "There's been some shifting this week, and that's a lot of carriages. The group who crossed over yesterday for the market already tested it more than I'd like."

"Everything is fine," said the councilor repressively.

"I dunno." The toll-keeper still sounded unconvinced. "I've been working here twenty years, and I swear it's never been as bad as it has the last few months. We have to get the singers out to repair it practically every few weeks."

"Some of us in the group are singers," Isabel reminded him. "If we sense any weakness in the enchantments holding the bridge up, we'll stop. But the bridge is the only way across Sundering Canyon, yes?"

The toll-keeper acknowledged it, and the delegation leader gave a brisk nod.

"Then we have no choice but to continue." Her eagle eyes found Marieke again. "What are you doing out of your carriage, Marieke? You'll hold up the group."

"Sorry," said Marieke, following Isabel back to the vehicles.

She bit her lip, not sure whether the older woman felt as confident as she claimed, or was just faking it for her benefit. Despite her talk of singers in the group, they only had Isabel, Solomon, Marieke, and one of the guards.

"It seems we need to keep a closer eye on you," the councilor said wryly. "I'll have the trained guard join you and Solomon in your carriage. My carriage will go at the front, and yours can bring up the rear. The bridge is held up in part by magic, and as you've just heard, the structure has been weakened by shifting in the canyon of late. Be on the alert for anything amiss."

Marieke nodded, hurrying back toward Solomon. She knew what Isabel meant by *the trained guard*. Obviously the guards were all highly trained in their role, but the councilor meant the one trained in songcraft. Marieke had long since noticed that singers tended to think only those born with the capacity to sing to be truly trainable in any useful skill.

Kaine, the guard in question, climbed into the carriage soon after she and Solomon had re-entered it. Before long, the vehicle trundled into motion, falling into a new position at the very back of the group. Kaine began to hum, the sound soon turning into a soft song. The words fascinated Marieke. She hadn't studied combat at the academy, and hadn't learned any song quite like this one. She could feel the magic that passed up from the ground below and into the guard before snaking outward. It wasn't flowing in a torrent. It felt more like questing fingers. Judging by the song's words, which sounded like a military chant, the purpose of the enchantment was to act as a magical scout, searching for signs of danger.

As they reached the bridge, the guard's song went quiet, his expression troubled.

"What is it?" Marieke asked.

He shrugged ruefully. "There's just so much danger involved in crossing a gorge on a narrow, unstable bridge, it's hard to identify whether it's anything new or specific triggering my sentry song."

"It's not that unstable, is it?" Solomon asked nervously. He screwed his eyes shut as he concentrated. "I can feel the magic that coats it. The supporting enchantments are definitely still in place."

Marieke frowned, her own senses picking up the presence of magic as well. She pressed her cheek against the carriage window, once again wishing she could see forward. And this time, it wasn't just because she wanted to know how the carriages in front were faring. It was also because the view to the side, of the massive drop into the ravine, was making her dizzy.

"I don't hear any screams, so I think the carriages ahead are progressing without an issue," she said.

"Deeply reassuring." Solomon's voice was sarcastic, and Marieke flashed him a grin as she raised her own voice in a quiet song of assessment.

"It feels...different, doesn't it?" she said after a moment. "The magic here is more chaotic than anything I've felt in the city."

"Well, it is Sundering Canyon," Kaine pointed out reasonably. "The most volatile place in the Sovereign Realms, both geographically and magically."

Marieke nodded slowly, feeling a different change with her ordinary senses. "The carriage is moving downward now. We must have passed the top of the curve, which means we're more than halfway across." She pressed one eye to the window again. "In fact, I think the front carriage has reached the Aeltan side."

The words had barely left her mouth when two things happened at once. The second—a sudden, ear-splitting crack— was so dramatic that her mind almost missed the sensation that had come right before it.

A rush of magic, potent and out of control, speeding from the canyon itself up toward their vehicle.

The carriage lurched violently, and the door against which Marieke had been leaning was flung open. With a scream, she grasped at the side, her mind barely comprehending that she was now dangling from a crazily leaning carriage over the ravine itself, no stone bridge beneath her flailing legs.

"Mari!" Solomon lunged forward, but Kaine stopped him with a shout and a hand on his chest.

"You'll destabilize the—"

The warning was too late, the carriage already slipping further into the enormous hole that had opened below it. Marieke's terrified eyes saw that a whole section of bridge had simply fallen away, right underneath their carriage.

The poor horse was whinnying in terror, the driver shouting as he tried to bring the animal under control. The guard braced himself against the far side of the carriage for balance as he reached a hand toward Marieke. She heard his voice raised in a fierce song, and saw a rope snake its way out of a storage chest and toward her hand.

She reached for it desperately, her fingers just grasping it as the horse finally lost its head. It lurched forward, the front wheel of the carriage miraculously gripping on a jagged edge of stone and jumping up onto the secure part of the bridge.

But the jolt was too violent for Marieke's weakening grip. As one hand closed around the rope, the door of the carriage was yanked out of her other hand. She dropped like a stone, too terrified to even scream as the rope, secured to nothing, fell with her.

# TWO

## Marieke

For a fraction of a second, Marieke's mind was completely blank of anything but knowledge of her impending death. But it was no quick fall and sudden impact. The canyon was deep—too deep at this highest point of the bridge for her to even see the bottom—and it took only a moment for her will to survive to reassert itself.

Almost before she decided to act, she heard her own voice, the song issuing out on instinct. There were no words—she didn't have the time or thoughts to form them—but a trained singer didn't need to tell the magic what to do with words. Had she been planning it, she would probably have tried to pull magic from the ground above, but her mind was too panicked to plan. As she called for magic with her wordless song, she felt a torrent of power rush up from the canyon below. It was far stronger than the magic she'd felt at ground level, and her voice grasped onto it eagerly.

She still held the rope in her hand, and she sent the magic coiling around it. The strands of power tugged the rope taut, pulling the other end out from her hand. There was no time to think of a plan. She could see the ground speeding rapidly toward her, the sides of the canyon narrowing. Desperately, she sent the end of the rope toward a gorse bush protruding from the rocky slope slightly above her. It tangled in the branches, Marieke trying frantically with her song to direct the rope to tie itself into one of the sturdy knots her father had taught her back in her coastal home.

Her fingers would have been defter than the magic, but she succeeded in getting the rope to secure itself somewhat to the bush by the time it pulled taut again. Her hands were still wrapped around the other end of it, and she was yanked up sharply, her song cutting off in a cry of pain as her hands slid down the rope, the rough threads burning. With no control over her motion, she swung sideways, slamming violently into the canyon wall below the gorse bush.

The breath was knocked out of her completely, and she had barely enough awareness left to realize that the impact had pulled the rope free of her clumsy knot. She was falling again, but this time only briefly before her back thudded into the ground. She lay prone for a moment, still winded and gasping to take in air. She'd been incredibly lucky to be so close to the bottom of the ravine when the rope gave way. And to land on a patch of ground which, while not exactly flat, wasn't ridged enough to impale her.

She couldn't seem to fully catch her breath, but her immediate panic ebbed enough for her to become aware of a sharp pain. She raised her shaking hands before her eyes. They were raw and bleeding, huge welts bearing testimony to her desperate attempts to hang on to the rope.

Slowly, wincing, she sat up. Her back was aching, and her elbows, which seemed to have hit the ground first, were bruised and scratched. But she could move everything, so nothing seemed broken. And when she gingerly felt her head, she was relieved to find no sign of injury there.

Yes, all things considered, she'd been very lucky.

But she was still in quite a fix, she realized as she peered upward. She could barely make out the thin line of the bridge above, and she knew no one up there would be able to see her. Perhaps she could alert them to her survival with a song.

But when she tried to raise her voice, nothing emerged. She was completely winded from the fall, even speech not yet possible.

Groaning, Marieke pushed herself to her feet. How was she going to get out of the canyon without her song? One glance at the sheer cliffs on either side showed that it would be no simple feat to climb them. Especially with a death-defying fall awaiting any misstep. She leaned down with a wince, collecting the rope and coiling it around her shoulder. Perhaps there was a goat track or something. There must be some way out.

She'd barely gone two steps, however, when she suddenly went still. She could have sworn she'd heard movement in the rocks nearby. Did creatures live down here? Marieke peered around her, painfully aware that she was defenseless without her songcraft. Perhaps she should have studied combat at the academy after all.

Even if she couldn't sing, she could still sense magic, and she relaxed a little when she felt no sign of any enchantment nearby. Power swirled beneath her feet, the magic in the ravine stronger and more responsive than that up on the normal ground level. But it was untapped magic, not directed to any purpose. It was no help to her without her voice, but it was no danger to her either.

She'd let her guard down too soon. Just as she started back into motion, something launched itself from the side of the canyon. Marieke barely had time to spin before it was on her, the impact flattening her weakened body once more to the canyon floor. She tried to cry out as her arms were seized, but no sound came. The gray object had looked like falling rock, but it was definitely human arms that grappled with her. She couldn't get a good look at her assailant, but she did manage to get in one kick that elicited a grunt of pain. She thought she caught a flash of metal and began to struggle more desperately when a sharp voice caused her attacker to pause.

"Gorgon! What are you doing?"

Marieke, now pinned on her stomach, swung her head around with a painful effort to see the new arrival who'd spoken. A middle-aged woman loomed above the struggling pair. Her eyes—as gray as the hairs that streaked her brown braid and the garments that swathed her slight form—were fixed on whoever or whatever was sitting on Marieke.

"Who is that? Get off her!"

"She snuck in here, intent on mischief."

The voice of her assailant sounded frustrated but, to Marieke's relief, he got off. Shaking her head in denial of the accusation, she clambered to her feet. She was confronted by not only the two speakers, but half a dozen others gathered behind the woman. They were all clad in the same gray, practical clothes. It wasn't hard to see why the young man had blended in with the rocks around him. Marieke eyed him uneasily. Perhaps she'd imagined the flash of a blade, because she saw no sign of a weapon on him now.

"Who are you?" The woman's harsh voice reclaimed Marieke's attention, her eyes narrowed in suspicion. "How did you get down here?"

Marieke tried to speak, but only a rasp came out. Drawing in a breath, she pointed above and mimed falling.

"You fell?" The woman raised an eyebrow. "How did you survive?" Her eyes traveled to the rope now tangled messily around Marieke. "Were you trying to climb down here? You must have gotten a long way down before falling if you survived so unharmed."

Marieke gave no reply, suddenly realizing that it might not be wise to expose to these strangers that she was an Oleandan singer and had saved herself with magic. They were presumably Aeltans, although why they chose to be down in the ravine, she couldn't imagine.

"Why don't you speak?" the woman demanded. "Are you mute?"

Marieke raised her hands in a futile gesture, unsure how to explain that her inability to speak was temporary. At least, she hoped it was.

"Bring her with us," the woman said curtly. "We'll get to the bottom of it as we go."

"But she's a stranger!" The protest came from the one who'd pinned Marieke. "We can't take her with us!"

"We're nowhere near base," said the older woman dismissively. "She'll see nothing that could hurt us. I'll see to that." She scowled at him. "If you wanted her to be ignorant of our presence, you should have remained hidden. I know you have the skills, Gorgon. Why did you reveal yourself?"

"She was a threat." The answer was unconvincing, and Marieke noticed that he wouldn't meet the older woman's eye.

She gestured insistently, trying again to communicate that she was no threat. Everyone ignored her. At a signal from the woman, a man stepped forward and grabbed Marieke by the shoulders. She made an impulse decision not to resist. So far the woman didn't seem to mean her harm, and without her voice, she was hopelessly outnumbered.

"What's wrong with you, Gorgon?" the new man complained, as he tied Marieke's hands with her own rope. "This is the third time in two weeks you've been out where you're not supposed to be. Why are you obsessed with watching the bridge?"

"I'm not," said Gorgon sulkily. "I wasn't even looking at the bridge. I was just scouting. Routine."

"Nothing routine about attacking strangers," the woman said sternly. "Especially coming from you, Gorgon. You're always adamant we leave no sign of our presence behind." She shot a piercing look in Marieke's direction. "I for one don't mind the surface people being reminded that we're still down here. They can pretend to have forgotten us, but the swine in power know perfectly well there are still monarchists in the so-called Sovereign Realms."

Marieke, being pushed along in the group's wake, raised her eyes to the speaker, causing her feet to stumble over the uneven path. Monarchists? What did she mean? As in...people loyal to the royals of the old days? Surely that was impossible after so long. Who was left for them to be loyal to? And why *would* they be loyal to the despotic overlords of the past, when they'd had generations to see the wisdom and stability with which the Council of Singers governed the land?

At least, in Oleand. Maybe Aeltas was a different story, Marieke reasoned with herself. Although...wasn't Aeltas the kingdom that was continuing to thrive, while Oleand began to decline for reasons no one could identify?

She closed her eyes for a moment, overwhelmed as much by her confusion as by the aches in her body. Her breathing was still shallow and labored, her lungs feeling compressed. The brisk pace at which she was being pushed to walk wasn't helping.

What had she stumbled into? And how was she going to get herself out, and back to the world above? She had a sinking feeling that the delegation had probably assumed that she'd died in the fall. They would continue to Tarandon without her. No one knew the fix she was in. No help was coming.

She would just have to help herself.

A thin trail of water was now running along one side of the canyon on the southern edge, and Marieke followed as the group stepped over it and into a crevice that opened into the side of the cliff. To Marieke's surprise, the small chasm gave way to a large cavern as soon as they stepped through. It took her eyes a moment to adjust, but when they did, she saw that a number of tunnels snaked away through the side of the mountain.

"Probably best to blindfold her," said the woman. She pulled a gray kerchief from her hair and handed it to the man still guarding Marieke. "Use this."

Marieke tried again to use her voice, but her breath was still far too short. Not that she would likely have gained anything from protesting. She saw Gorgon glancing furtively at her before the blindfold was wound swiftly and deftly around her face, completely blocking her vision. She was spun several times, and then pushed forward. From the way the air seemed to close around her, she guessed they were going down one of the tunnels, but she had no idea which one.

The next ten minutes were misery. Every inch of Marieke ached, and her chest still felt tight and strained. She thought that if she could lie down for an extended period, she might be able to catch her breath and hopefully regain her voice, but that seemed unlikely. She reflected idly that she was probably in Aeltas now, or at least under it. It wasn't quite how she'd expected to enter the southern country.

When she was at last pulled roughly to a stop, she bent double, trying to draw deeper breaths.

"Take off the blindfold," said the woman briskly.

Someone ripped it off, and Marieke blinked in the flickering light of the torches set into the walls. She was standing in a cavern of decent size, this one much more established than the entrance cavern. It was even furnished, although sparsely. The woman had said they weren't close to their base, so this must be somewhere else. How big was this community, and how many dwellings or meeting places did they have? Marieke felt as though she'd wandered into a dream—she'd never heard rumors either of monarchists or of people dwelling in Sundering Canyon.

"Now, let's have a chat," said the older woman, seating herself in a chair. She gestured for Marieke to do the same, and Marieke did her best to navigate awkwardly into the indicated seat.

"Check her for weapons, and if she's clean, undo her hands," said the woman impatiently.

The man who'd bound Marieke checked her roughly, then gave an affirmative grunt. To her great relief, her bruised and bloodied hands were released from the ropes.

"Now, are you mute?" the woman asked.

Marieke shook her head.

"Faking?"

She shook her head again, exasperated this time. What was the point of that question? She wasn't exactly going to admit if she was faking.

A smile flickered across the stranger's face, as if she could guess what Marieke was thinking. Then her expression sobered as she looked Marieke over.

"Winded by the fall?" she guessed.

Marika nodded eagerly.

"Hm." The woman studied her. "It might just be that. Might be something more. The magic down here sometimes does strange things to outsiders." She accepted a tankard from one of her companions, taking a pull before adding, "Or so I'm told."

Marieke frowned, wondering uneasily if there was any truth to the theory. Surely her voice would come back?

The stranger leaned forward, resting one elbow on the table between them. "My name is Svetlana. I suppose you can't tell me what you call yourself, can you?"

Marieke bit her lip then, struck with a sudden inspiration, mimicked writing with a quill on the table.

The older woman sighed. "You can write, can you? Well, good for you, but that doesn't do us any good. None of us can read."

Marieke slumped back in her chair. After a moment, she lifted her hands, using one arm to create the bridge and moving the fingers of the other hand along it in a walking motion.

"If you were trying to cross the bridge," said Svetlana, unconvinced, "how did you end up down here and alive?"

Marieke just shrugged.

With another sigh, Svetlana's eyes passed over her. "You don't look in the best shape. I suppose we'd better bind up those hands, if nothing else."

She cast her eyes around the cavern, and following her gaze, Marieke saw that they were alone for the moment.

"You'll have to excuse Gorgon," the other woman said. "No idea why the boy is so over-enthusiastic lately." She pinned her shrewd gaze on Marieke. "Not that I'm saying he was wrong to call you a threat. I don't trust you, not by a long shot. Wait here. We'll get your hands seen to, and then we can find you a quiet spot to wait while we figure out where you really came from."

Marieke's mind whirled as Svetlana stood. She recognized the description for what it was. She was to become this group's captive, for an unspecified length of time. She had to get out before they had a chance to throw her into some kind of prison cave. She had to rejoin the delegation before her death was accepted and reported back to her family.

Her would-be captor disappeared through a roughly hewn doorway, and Marieke cast her eyes about in search of an escape. She was fairly sure she knew which tunnel they'd come through, but would that help her? For all she knew, the trail she'd been led on while blindfolded was a labyrinth. And if this wasn't their main base, she might be risking losing her way in an abandoned tunnel system. The very fact that Svetlana had left her unattended suggested that she had no great fear of the captive escaping on her own.

"Pst."

Marieke looked up, suspicion overtaking her instantly when she caught sight of Gorgon lurking in a doorway on the far side of the cavern from where the group had entered.

"Come this way," Gorgon said.

Marieke narrowed her eyes at him. Did he think she'd forgotten that he attacked her last time?

He just shrugged. "You don't have to, but they'll lock you up if you stay."

Marieke hesitated. She didn't trust him at all, but she'd reached the same conclusion herself about the leader's plans for her. She'd never been one to sit still, and she thought she preferred to take her chances with the likely duplicitous youth rather than the imprisonment that certainly loomed with the capable woman. Now she'd seen him properly, she realized he was younger than she'd first thought, probably no older than her. And her hands were free this time.

Hoping she wouldn't regret the impulsive decision, she pushed herself to her feet and strode toward him. He turned before she even reached him, hurrying down the passage and out of sight.

Marieke followed, her footsteps sounding loud in the muffled closeness of the tunnel.

"This passage leads up and out," Gorgon said. "You'll see."

In seeming confirmation of his words, the ground began to slant steadily upward. Soon, they were curving back toward the ravine, probably walking right above the cavern where the woman had left Marieke. Glad as she was to be moving toward the surface, Marieke's unease grew with every step. She could think of no reason why Gorgon would suddenly want to help her. He must intend treachery, which meant she needed to keep her wits about her.

Much sooner than she expected, Marieke felt a draft, and caught a hint of sunlight ahead. She hurried forward, already spooked by her time underground and eager to reach fresh air. The path emerged, not at the top of the ravine, but halfway up its side, in a roughly carved staircase that zigzagged its way upward against the cliff itself.

She'd just drawn in a deep, relieved breath when Gorgon stopped abruptly. Alert to his movements, Marieke pulled instantly to a halt, falling back a couple of steps to put distance between them. As he whirled around, the venomous look on his face told her that her instinct had been right.

"I heard you when you were falling," he hissed. "You're a singer."

Marieke shifted her feet to a more stable position. She didn't know much about combat, but she was aware that it wasn't good that her opponent had the higher ground.

"And the canyon has taken your voice, hasn't it?" Gorgon sneered. "This is where the magic of the kingdoms is at its strongest and least corrupted, and it chose to strip you of the voice you've trained into a weapon of control and deception. What more evidence do you need that the land is against your kind?" His eyes hardened. "*I* don't need more."

He lunged forward, but Marieke was ready for him. She dodged to the side, pressing herself against the cliff and kicking out as he passed. She caught him in the stomach, and he let out a growl, steadying himself just in time. Marieke seized her opening, darting upward and gaining the advantage he'd held a moment before. But she didn't attempt to flee up the staircase. He was too close behind her, he'd catch her before she reached the top for sure.

She heard him cursing, and cast around desperately for a non-magical means of help. A loose rock clattered under her foot, and she bent to scoop it up. By the time she straightened, Gorgon was rushing at her, his arms extended. There could be no doubt that he intended to send her over the edge. They were only halfway up the cliff face, but it was still plenty high enough for a fall to be fatal, especially now she had no rope and no voice.

She held out one arm to fend him off, grasping the rock with the other. Her new position made all the difference, and she knew a moment of temptation as they struggled. She thought that if she put all her strength into it, she could probably throw him off the edge, as he clearly hoped to do to her.

But she banished the thought. She was no killer, and she still didn't pretend to understand what was behind his antagonism. Bringing the rock up with a swift motion, she slammed it into the side of his head with all her force. He let out a cry and fell back a step, but she pursued him, repeating the gesture. This time, her blow was enough to knock him out. He crumpled, only her grip keeping him from toppling into the ravine.

Heart hammering, Marieke laid him down on the stairway, leaning close enough to feel his breath on her face. He was alive, his chest rising and falling steadily. That was a relief, but it also meant she would be wise not to linger. His unconsciousness could be momentary for all she knew.

Dropping the rock, she sprinted up the staircase. It wasn't long before the rush of energy ebbed, and she had to slow her pace. There was still so much of the canyon to climb.

Her mind raced faster than her feet as she traversed the rough path. If she'd been back at the academy, she would be earning her reputation a hundredfold right now. She'd never in her life had so many unanswered questions. She doubted even the self-proclaimed monarchists could answer them all. They obviously had their own fractures—otherwise why would Gorgon have been at such pains to hide his violent intentions from the others?

She was most of the way up, her breath coming in pants, when she was dismayed to see the route ahead blocked by a rockfall. She realized with alarm that Gorgon had brought her on a dead path, not one that would truly take her up to freedom. She should have realized it, but the blow hit her hard, having thought she was so close to escape.

She craned her neck, peering upward. The top of the ravine looked close. Surely she could make it. She clambered up and over the rocks, moving more cautiously now. If only she had her rope. Or, better yet, her song. But her voice still came out as a harsh rasp, not strong enough to draw magic to it.

Marieke reached the top of the rockfall, swallowing as she studied the short stretch of sheer cliff between her and the land above. She'd climbed cliffs higher than that back home on the coast. But there, a fall would have meant being dunked in the ocean, not plummeting to her certain death.

Still, it was upward or back to a prison and an uncertain future. If she even made it past Gorgon, who may well be stirring by now. Steeling herself, Marieke began to scale the cliff, her fingers sweaty as they searched for handholds. She was still bruised from her earlier fall, and her limbs shook with the effort of holding her weight. Twice a foot slipped from beneath her, and she barely managed to cling on, her heart racing and her breath coming in sobs. She was so close. Having survived one impossible fall, was she really going to lose her life to another?

She was little more than a body length from the top when she stopped moving. Fear rose within her at her predicament, but she couldn't deny the truth. She was stuck, with nothing above but flat rock, no handholds in sight. She didn't dare glance down to look for a way of retreat. She knew that if she saw the sheer drop beneath her, panic would overtake her completely.

It was already doing its best to claim her. The longer she hovered, stuck in position, the more violently her limbs shook. She could see no way out, and her voice still refused to obey her. Gripping her last remaining handhold with one hand, she curled the other into a fist and slammed it against the rock face, half in an attempt to make a hole she could cling to, half out of blind desperation. The hammering of her fist was the only thing anchoring her to reality, as if her body was trying to convince her mind that her heart was still beating, steadily, rhythmically, determined to keep living.

Even if her mind knew perfectly well that her grip was weakening with every passing beat, the horrifying end more inevitable by the second.

# THREE

## Zev

Zevadiah slapped the reins idly against the horse's flank, urging the creature to pick up the pace a little. It had been a long morning, and he was eager to be home.

"Well, that market was a waste of time," commented his companion from beside him.

Zev grunted in acknowledgment of his brother's words. "Not sure what we expected, really."

"Well, I expected that the Oleandans would have *something* interesting," Azai reasoned. "I mean, they're from a whole different country. Everyone makes such a fuss of how rare it is to have a shared market—you'd think they'd bring some variety."

Zev wasn't convinced. "I think the shared markets are nothing more than a show. The Councils of Singers want us all to think there's more cooperation between the countries than there is."

Azai leaned over the side of the cart, spitting onto the ground at this mention of the country's leadership. Zev ignored the dramatic gesture. It wasn't that he disagreed with his brother's views. But personally, he didn't see the point in spitting and cursing fate.

Whatever fate did or didn't have to do with it.

"Why are we going this way?" Azai asked, frowning as he took note of the path down which Zev was directing the horse. "Isn't the other way more direct?"

"Probably," said Zev placidly. "But I like going near the canyon. It's more picturesque."

Azai shot him a look. "Thinking of popping in on our dear friends the monarchists?"

Zev snorted. "Sure, let's pay them a visit, shall we? Have a chat over a pint of ale, perhaps?"

The two brothers chuckled, but the humor was thin for Zev. He felt pained when he thought of the well-intentioned but misguided group of outcasts who lived down in the ravine. He'd heard the rumors that the bridge between Aeltas and Oleand was weakening, and he'd even wondered if they might have something to do with that. It seemed unlikely, but he couldn't shake the suspicion that the process wasn't entirely natural. Why they would think killing random travelers would help their cause, he couldn't imagine.

He heard the smart clopping of hooves behind them, and directed the horse to the side of the path. Azai gave him a long-suffering look, which he ignored. Their lumbering cart was far from nimble, and Zev was in the habit of letting any other travelers past.

A horse came alongside before long, but to Zev's surprise, the rider pulled up.

"Afternoon!" he said, his face alight with the excitement of gossip.

"Afternoon," chorused the brothers, both studying the newcomer curiously. It was normal for passersby to greet one another, but not usually to stop.

"Have you heard the news?" the man asked eagerly.

"About the market?" Azai asked. "Yes, we've just come from there."

"No, no, not the market." The man waved this inconsequential guess away with a hand. "About the bridge."

"What about it?" Zev asked sharply, some premonition stirring within him at this mention of the very topic he'd just been silently pondering.

"There's been an accident," the man said, clearly pleased to have met someone unaware of the tale. "Not more than an hour ago. A group was crossing from Oleand, and a whole section of the bridge just cracked and fell away."

"Who was crossing?" Azai asked sharply. "Our people?"

The man shook his head reassuringly. "No, no, they were Oleandans, coming from the north."

Azai sat back in relief, but Zev's frown didn't soften. "Was anyone hurt?"

The man nodded, his features dropping into an unconvincingly somber expression. "Apparently a girl fell right out of one of the carriages and into the ravine. Tragic."

"She died?" Azai asked, startled.

The man gave a dry laugh. "I think we can safely assume so. It's caused a bit of a stir. Apparently they were part of some official delegation. I heard something about the Oleandan ambassador, but I didn't get the details."

"What caused the bridge to break?" Zev asked, his heart all the heavier for being the only one in the conversation who seemed to consider the news bad.

The stranger shrugged. "Who knows? What's been causing it to weaken all this time? Anyway," he gave his horse a nudge with his boot, "I'd best be off. Afternoon to you both."

And he trotted away down the road, no doubt to look for more travelers with whom to share his sensational news.

Azai gave a low whistle. "So it's finally falling apart. Do you think the bridge will crumble altogether?"

"At this rate, it's only a matter of time," Zev said.

Azai shook his head. "What would happen then? Would we just have no contact with Oleand? I mean, we don't really need them, do we? By all accounts, their country is the one slowly dying, while ours is doing just fine." He smirked slightly as he nudged Zev's shoulder. "For some reason."

"It's not a joking matter, Azai," Zev said sharply. "None of it is."

"Oleand's issues aren't our problem," Azai argued.

"I agree," said Zev. "But they affect Aeltas, and that makes them our problem."

He steered the cart along the narrow path as it wound closer to the edge of Sundering Canyon. The ravine came into sight, steep and harsh and clearly unnatural. Not that it looked unnatural, exactly. It just *felt* it in a way that was impossible to explain. Zev only knew that ever since the first time he'd seen it, he'd always found the gaping chasm unsettling, as if a hole had been torn in his own body rather than in the land under his feet.

"There it is," Azai commented. "It's a long way down, isn't it? Wouldn't be a nice way to go."

Zev grunted, preferring not to dwell on the fate of the unknown girl. He could only hope her end had been quick, although the fall would certainly have taken long enough for her to feel the terror of her impending death.

Moved by some morbid instinct, he pulled the horse up, the carriage trundling slowly along as the path passed closest to the ravine. He found himself wanting to linger when peace of mind would be best served by moving quickly on.

"What's that?" he asked suddenly.

"What's what?" Azai seemed confused.

"That sound," Zev insisted. "Do you hear it? Like a dull, persistent thumping."

Azai squinted as he listened, before his face relaxed back to its previous expression. "No. I don't hear anything."

"I do," said Zev. He pulled the horse off to the side of the road, straining his ears in the silence. "It's faint, but it's persistent."

"Zev," his brother protested, as he handed over the reins. "What are you doing? We've already missed lunch, now we're in danger of missing dinner—let's go home."

Zev ignored him as he swung himself down from the carriage. He couldn't explain why he was so determined to find the source of the noise. He just knew that he wasn't going anywhere until he'd identified it.

"Are you having one of your mystical moments again?" Azai called after him, with the mocking tone only a sibling could master. "Because I don't care how much the land speaks to you, I'm not missing my dinner for it!"

Again Zev ignored his brother's words, although they were more accurate than Azai imagined. The thumping really did feel like the land trying to communicate with him, like some message of import was passing through the ground itself. Zev had these moments sometimes, and he'd learned not to ignore them.

The thumping was still happening, and he followed it, walking along the grassy strip that ran between the dirt road and the cliff's edge. Zev felt no fear at being close to the ravine. He never doubted his footing on his native Aeltan soil. Somehow he knew it wouldn't play him false.

His ears were leading him toward the sheer drop when the thumping suddenly stopped. Frowning, Zev strode forward, dropping to his knees to peer over the edge. He caught his breath at the sight that met his eyes. Barely out of his reach was a girl, clinging to the cliff face with what looked like her last ounce of energy. Her face, pale with terror, was framed by thick, dark hair which had come partially loose from a braid. The eyes that stared up at him were the deepest blue he'd ever seen, and currently showed nothing but blank shock at his sudden appearance.

Was this the girl who'd fallen from the bridge?

Instinctively, Zev reached his arm down toward her, but it was too far.

"Hold on!" he said, glancing back toward the cart, which was now some distance away. He was exasperated to see that Azai wasn't even watching him, distracted with the horse. He turned back to the girl. "I have a rope in the cart. I'll get it."

She opened her mouth, but only a croak came out. Panic flashed through her eyes, and Zev realized just how much her arms were shaking.

"Can you hold on while I get a rope?" he asked.

She shook her head frantically, and Zev's mind raced through his limited options. He cast his eyes around for something to use in place of a rope. On a sudden thought, he rocked back on his heels. He heard the girl's anguished croak as he disappeared from her view, but he wasn't abandoning her. He stripped his shirt off, buttons bursting loose as he worked too quickly for caution.

It was a good thing the morning had been cool and he'd worn long sleeves. He twisted the shirt into the longest stretch of fabric it could make, wrapping it around itself for strength. Then he leaned back over the edge, winding the end of one shirt sleeve around his fist and lowering the other toward her.

"Grab onto it," he said.

She stared uncertainly from the dangling shirt to his face.

"Go on," he urged, shaking the shirt so it wobbled. "It will hold long enough for me to get you up." His voice was strong and confident. "I won't let you fall. I promise."

The girl drew a deep breath, then shifted one hand from the rock and grabbed hold of the shirt.

"That's it," Zev coaxed. "Now the other hand. Hold on tightly."

The girl obeyed, her feet still braced against the rock but both fists now clutching the shirt.

"You can try to walk up the cliff if you want, but either way, I'll pull you up," Zev assured her. He started to pull the shirt hand over hand, his muscles taut with the effort. She was sensible enough to help with her feet, which he appreciated. He could feel the seams of the shirt straining, but she was almost within reach now.

As soon as she was close enough, he reached out, taking hold of her wrist with his hand and abandoning the shirt. She also let go of the garment, her other hand seeking until his clasped it firmly. With a final tug, he pulled her up and over the edge of the canyon.

He absorbed her impact as she slammed into him, taking a step back not from the force of the contact, but to put distance between them and the edge. The girl came with him, her breaths coming quickly and her eyes closed.

Slowly, she opened them, seeming to realize that one of her hands was still clasped in his, and the other was pressed against his chest. Her touch was cold and clammy on his skin. As awareness returned, she stepped back from him, her hands falling limply to her sides.

"Did you just...rescue me with your shirt?" she asked, her voice raspy and a little breathless.

Zev gave a low chuckle. "It seems I did."

"You should probably put it back on," she informed him.

Her voice, in addition to being croaky, was a little faint, no doubt from her ordeal.

"If you like," said Zev, amused by her fixation on this irrelevant detail when she'd just escaped a gruesome death by a hair. Or rather, by a shirt.

He strode past her, rescuing his shirt from where he'd dropped it near the edge of the cliff. He pulled it over his head, the sleeves comically stretched now from having the weight of a whole human suspended from them. He rolled up the cuffs half a dozen times on each side. He noticed in the process that one of his sleeves had blood on it. Frowning, he looked at the girl, his eyes searching her disheveled form until they found the source of the blood. Her hands were raw and bleeding.

"Are you all right?" he asked. He gestured to her hands.

"I'm fine," she said quickly. "It will heal." Her eyes were a little self-conscious as they met his. "Thank you, by the way. I forgot to say that, didn't I?"

"Your distraction can be forgiven," Zev assured her. "That was pretty close to disaster."

She nodded, her eyes sliding closed as she dropped to her knees. Zev watched in fascination as her fingers splayed into the dirt. It looked like more than just relief at being on solid ground. It was as though she was drawing something up from the soil. It was a curiously familiar gesture. He often felt as though the ground itself gave him strength. Sometimes he liked to sit and just...feel it.

"What in the world?"

The astounded exclamation announced Azai's arrival. Zev looked up, still exasperated that his brother had been of no help.

"Decided to look around you, did you?"

"What's going on?"

"I think I found the missing girl from the delegation that ran into trouble when crossing the bridge," said Zev mildly.

"Yes." She nodded, pushing herself clumsily to her feet. Her balance was off, and Zev realized that it was from more than just shock. She looked pretty bruised and scratched. "That's who I am. My name is Marieke."

"I'm Zev," he said. "And this is my brother, Azai."

"Why not tell her our life story?" Azai muttered sarcastically. He eyed Marieke. "You're from the delegation, you said. So you're Oleandan, are you?"

Zev gave him a long-suffering look, which Azai ignored.

"Yes, I am," said Marieke, thankfully seeming too distracted to notice Azai's tone. She pressed her fingers to her throat as she talked, her body relaxing a little more. "My voice is back."

That last mutter seemed meant for herself, but the brothers exchanged a curious glance.

"Your voice?" Zev asked.

She nodded. "It didn't work in the ravine. Or at least," she amended, "it didn't work after I hit the ground. It worked while I was falling, thankfully."

Zev couldn't help grinning. "Got a good scream out, did you?"

The look she sent him was unimpressed, and his smile broadened at this first sign of spirit from her.

"Not really, no. I didn't realize it was possible to be too scared to scream, but apparently it is."

"Hold on," said Azai, frowning. "If you really did fall, how did you survive?"

"I managed to slow my fall with the help of a rope and my song," said Marieke matter-of-factly.

The brothers exchanged another look.

"Your song?" Azai said flatly. "So you're Oleandan *and* a singer."

"Yes," said Marieke. She seemed to take in his demeanor at last, and those deep eyes passed shrewdly between the brothers. "Is that a problem?"

"Not at all," said Azai, his voice icy with politeness. "Well, since you're back on solid ground, we'll be on our way." He waved vaguely to the southwest. "If you're making for the capital, it's that way."

Marieke blinked, seeming unsure how to respond to this abrupt change in tone. "Thank you?"

"Don't be ridiculous, Azai," sighed Zev. "She can't wander alone all the way to the capital in her state."

Azai angled his body to block Marieke out and lowered his voice to a mutter. "This isn't our problem, Zev."

Zev just shook his head, not willing to get into it with his brother then and there. "The capital is still half a day's travel away," he told Marieke, pushing his brother out of the way. "And I'm talking about by horse. On foot, in your state, it would probably take days. I don't think you should try to set out today. Regardless of how you traveled, you wouldn't arrive before dark."

"Thank you," said Marieke. "I do appreciate the concern, but I don't have much choice. I have nowhere else to go."

"Ah well, best of luck, then," Azai said brightly.

"Azai." Zev pinned his brother with a glare. "For once in your life, just keep your mouth shut."

He turned back to Marieke, speaking over his brother's splutters of protest. "You'd best come back to our home. It's not far."

Marieke looked uncertain. "Thank you. That's very kind, but..." Her eyes flicked between the two broad-shouldered men, one of whom was scowling openly at her. "I couldn't impose."

For a moment Zev was impatient with her protestations in circumstances that were clearly too desperate for niceties. Then the real cause of her hesitation broke on him, and he chastised himself for being so oblivious.

"We don't live there alone," he assured her. "I should properly have called it our parents' home. They run the farm."

"Oh." She brightened a little, the reaction giving weight to Zev's guess as to the likely reason for her initial refusal. "Are you sure they won't mind?"

"Yes, Zev," said Azai. "Are you sure our parents won't mind you bringing an Oleandan *singer* back to our home?"

"Of course they won't mind," said Zev. "Unless we're late for dinner, in which case we'll all catch it. Come on." He strode toward the cart, Marieke hurrying in his wake. "You don't mind sitting in the back of the cart, do you, Azai?" he threw over his shoulder.

Audibly muttering, Azai climbed into the back while Zev untied the reins from the tree branch where his brother had secured them. He sprang up onto the seat, then offered a hand to Marieke. She accepted, trying unsuccessfully to hide her wince as his fingers closed around her raw palm.

"Sorry," he said, releasing his grip as soon as she was up. "Is that from the rope you mentioned?"

She nodded, hesitating for a moment before settling back into the seat. It had seemed like she might be going to say more about her experiences in the ravine, but he didn't press her. Why would she confide in a stranger? And graceless as Azai was in his way of expressing himself, he wasn't wrong. The less Zev had to do with a singer, the better. Receiving her confidences wasn't the path to avoiding connection.

"My mother has a way with just about any injury," Zev told her. "I'm sure she'll have a salve or something that can help."

"I can probably heal it myself if needed," Marieke said. "Basic healing is covered at the Academy of Song back in

Ondford. I just need to regroup a little, let my energy build up again."

"I think you'd best give my mother's salve a chance first," said Zev firmly.

She fell silent, seeming to catch on that it was time to direct the conversation away from singing. "This is my first time in Aeltas," she said, looking about her.

"What's it like compared to Oleand?" Zev asked politely.

"So far, much the same," she said, smiling. "Except for the falling into a ravine part."

"The ravine is no more in Aeltas than it is in Oleand," interjected Azai defensively from the back. "In fact, if you look at the original border, more of it falls in Oleand."

"My brother has a passion for geography rarely found in farmers," Zev said mercilessly. "He's quite wasted tilling the land."

"You're very funny," said Azai acidly.

Marieke had fallen silent, no doubt responding to the tension. The rest of the journey passed without speech, and Zev felt a distinct sense of relief when he saw their familiar gate. He would be very glad to hand the girl off to his mother and back away from the whole situation. Of course he didn't regret going to her rescue. He couldn't have justified leaving her to fall to her death. But he hadn't bargained on becoming entangled with a singer.

And he felt faintly aggrieved, he realized. It had really seemed like he'd been led to her by that connection he sometimes felt with the land, only for him to find himself in trouble as a result.

"This is your home?" Marieke broke her silence as they turned in at the gate. Her eyes scanned the sprawling farmhouse with apparent appreciation. "It's beautiful."

"Not quite what you're used to in your capital, I imagine,"

Zev said. "If it's anything like the one in Tarandon, your academy is no doubt very different from this."

"Oh, I don't come from the city," said Marieke. "I grew up in a small coastal town. No one was more surprised than my parents when I discovered the singing ability." Her eyes roved around the yard, and Zev had to admit she seemed quite comfortable. "Our town is in a farming region, so many of my neighbors were farmers. Moving to the capital to attend the academy was something of a shock."

The door to the house swung open before Zev could respond, his father striding out. "There you are, boys. We'd just about given up waiting for..." His voice trailed off as he took in first the disheveled and bloodied state of his firstborn son's shirt, and then the even more bedraggled stranger sitting beside him. "Who...?"

"This is Maria, Father," said Azai, already leaping down from the back of the cart. "Zev picked her up along the way. She's Oleandan."

Marieke sighed at Azai's mispronunciation of her name—she was probably smart enough to realize, as Zev did, that it was intentional. But any protest was forestalled as Azai spoke again, his eyes hard as he met his father's gaze.

"And she's a singer."

## Marieke

The whole demeanor of the middle-aged man changed at his son's words, and Marieke felt all her unease return. It was clear that this family had no good opinion of singers. She shouldn't have come here with these strangers. She was alone and far from her group. At least she had her voice now, but the current atmosphere told her she should use songcraft only as a last resort.

Her eyes flicked sideways to Zev, to find him watching her thoughtfully. A measure of peace washed over her. Whatever he thought of her singing ability, she couldn't believe he intended to hurt her. Perhaps she was being too trusting, but she felt herself relax a little. She turned toward the man now standing with a hand on the horse's head.

"It's not Maria actually," she said politely. "It's Ma-REEK-a."

She was used to people saying her name incorrectly after reading it, but not after hearing it. Azai was probably doing it on purpose. Refusing to be either baited or intimidated, she kept her tone light and respectful as she spoke again to the older man.

"And I'm very sorry to intrude. I became separated from my traveling group when crossing the bridge from Oleand, and your sons were nothing short of heroic in rescuing me from falling to my death in the ravine."

"Zev rescued her," Azai corrected. "I had nothing to do with it."

The older man interrupted his shrewd scrutiny of Marieke's face to raise an eyebrow at his younger son. "No need to sound so proud of that fact, Azai. I would be grieved to think any son of mine failed to help a fellow being in distress."

Azai jumped down from the cart, not looking chastened. But then, there hadn't been any real heat in his father's words. Marieke found them all hard to read. She had the constant feeling that silent conversations were going on underneath the ones she could hear. Perhaps it was simply because they were family. Perhaps she and her parents would seem the same to strangers.

"Marieke, did you say?" The older man turned back to her after watching his son disappear into the house. "I'm Gideon. And I'm sorry to hear your arrival in our land was marked by such catastrophe." He glanced at Zev. "Even if it turns out you were in good hands." His smile wasn't quite convincing as he looked back at her. "I trust you'll join us for the evening meal."

"Thank you," said Marieke. "I would be very grateful to do so."

"Come on," said Zev, hopping down from the cart and holding out a hand to Marieke. "I'll take you inside to my mother."

She placed her hand in his. In spite of the contact once again stinging the place where the rope had rubbed her skin raw, there was something comforting in the pressure of his hand. He seemed like a very solid person. Someone who wouldn't easily be swayed or shaken.

As soon as she was clear of the cart, Gideon led the horse toward a small barn nearby. Zev nodded toward the house, indicating that she should precede him.

"Don't be put off by my father's or brother's manner," he said, the words too comfortable to carry an apology. "My family are a little wary of strangers." He paused, then, seeming to feel further explanation was needed, added, "Perhaps it comes from living so close to the border."

"Being wary of strangers is natural," Marieke said as she mounted the steps onto the broad wooden porch that wrapped all the way around the farmhouse. "It's the very reason I'm questioning my sanity in coming here with you."

Zev gave a low chuckle. "Well, you didn't have many other options, did you?"

The words should have been frightening, but they weren't. When Marieke had arrived in the capital, nervously excited to commence her training at the Academy of Song, she'd been as inexperienced as she was alone. Surrounded by others with more privilege and influence, she'd quickly learned that there were some whose strength made those around them feel strengthened themselves, and others whose strength made everyone else more vulnerable. Her cautious assessment was that Zev seemed to fit the former category.

Hopefully she could trust her instinct, since he was right that her options were limited. Her thoughts flew to the delegation. They probably wouldn't have arrived at the capital yet. Solomon was no doubt mourning her loss. He and Kaine were probably still in shock from witnessing her horrific death.

"Mother?" Zev's voice pulled her thoughts back to her surroundings.

The house they'd entered was spacious and clean, the whitewashed walls and large windows combining to give an overwhelming impression of light, in spite of the approach of evening. She followed Zev tentatively as he crossed the hall and entered a comfortably sized kitchen.

"Zev, there you are." A smiling woman looked up from the table where she'd just placed a steaming bowl of bread. Her slender frame was a contrast to the broad-shouldered strength of her husband. "You were gone longer than we expected. Was the market interesting?"

"Not really," said Zev, stepping to the side to better display Marieke. "We have a guest."

"Oh!" The older woman looked Marieke over with interest, her smile remaining friendly. "I'm sure you're very welcome, my dear."

"This is Marieke," Zev said. "Marieke, my mother, Narelle. Mother, she's got some injuries that need attention."

Marieke tried to protest, but the older woman had already caught sight of her hands. Clucking disapprovingly, she ushered Marieke into a chair. She sent her son to fetch a box out of a nearby drawer and set to work. With a forbearance that surprised Marieke, she asked no questions about the cause of the injury.

"Zev said your salve was legendary, and I see he was right," Marieke said, as the woman slathered a thick, yellowish solution over her now-cleaned palms, instantly providing a measure of soothing for the pain.

Narelle chuckled. "Nothing magical about it, my dear. Just a good old-fashioned family recipe."

"Our guest knows all about magic." The interjection caused Marieke to look behind her, to where Azai was leaning against the doorframe into the hallway. "She's a singer. From Oleand." His eyes flicked to his brother. "Zev forgot to mention that part."

Marieke braced herself for more suspicion, but Narelle surprised her.

"You two boys brought home an Oleandan singer?" The other woman chuckled. "Knowingly?"

"It was Zev's idea," muttered Azai.

"Well, it sounds like a tale that will be worth hearing," Narelle said, winding a bandage around Marieke's hand.

Hoping to salvage the situation, Marieke spoke quickly. "It's very kind of you to welcome me. I hate to impose on strangers."

"My father used to say that strangers are only friends we haven't met yet," Narelle said cheerfully as she packed up her box of supplies.

Azai strode across the room, grabbing an apple from a bowl on the countertop. "Actually," he said, "as I recall Grandfather's saying, it was 'strangers are friends or enemies we haven't met yet'. And he was no great lover of Oleandans."

"True." His mother slapped the apple unceremoniously from his hand and back into the bowl, with a strength that belied her lithe frame. "Do you not see the dinner I've cooked? And your grandfather's prejudices are neither here nor there." She gave her son a hard look. "Either grandfather."

Azai just rolled his eyes, his focus seeming to be more on the food than the conversation. At no more than a gesture from their mother, both young men set to work assisting in readying the table for their meal, Zev laying an extra plate for the unexpected guest. By the time Gideon came into the house, all was ready.

"So Marieke," Narelle said, as she served up some chicken onto Marieke's plate, "where were you headed, before your accident?"

"To the capital," Marieke said. "I need to get there to rejoin my group as soon as possible." She glanced out the window. It was far from dark, but the mellow light of late afternoon had replaced the bright sunshine of earlier.

Zev shook his head. "Too late to set out tonight. I think you'll have to go tomorrow."

"Can the cart be spared in the morning, Gideon?" Narelle asked.

"The cart?" The farmer looked blank, and his wife gave him an impatient look. "One of the boys will take our guest to Tarandon, I assume."

"Mother," Azai protested, pausing in the act of shoveling potato into his mouth.

"I'm not sure that's the best idea," Gideon said in more measured tones, his brow creasing as he glanced at his eldest son.

But in spite of his father's words, the surprise on Zev's face was already shifting to an expression of resignation. Clearly he'd realized, as Marieke had, which of the brothers was more likely to bend to their mother's request.

Flushing in embarrassment at being such an imposition, Marieke spoke up. "That's not necessary. I'm sure I'll manage just fine."

"No, Mother is right," said Zev, not quite managing to hide his reluctance. "I can take you to the capital in the morning."

"Then it's settled." Narelle spoke briskly, saving Marieke the necessity of further polite protests. "You can sleep in the spare room, Marieke, and I'm sure Zev will be ready to set out at first light."

"Certainly." Zev didn't sound enthusiastic, but his tone was pleasant enough to avoid rudeness. "I'll see you back to your friends by lunchtime."

"Therefore missing most of the day's labor for a second day in a row," Azai muttered.

But everyone ignored him. If it was obvious to Marieke that his objection wasn't his brother's absence so much as the decision to help the foreign singer, then it must be very clear to his own family. Apparently not satisfied with the lack of response, Azai spoke again.

"Are we sure we should let her sleep in the spare room? Maybe the barn would be better."

Marieke eyed him, only her precarious position as a guest among strangers stilling her tongue.

"Azai." His mother sounded more long-suffering than actually angry.

"Well, she is a singer!" he pointed out.

Narelle shook her head indulgently. "And we'll trust that she won't sing our deaths over us while we sleep."

"That's not how singers usually operate," Marieke said, unable to help defending herself a little. "We're not a murderous bunch."

Azai snorted, and although he was the only one to openly respond, a coolness descended on the whole table. "At any rate, you'll be perfectly comfortable in the spare room," Narelle said, with the air of one placating combatants.

"Thank you," said Marieke, a little stiffly. "You're very kind."

The rest of the meal passed largely in silence, and Marieke was grateful when her hostess ushered her out of the kitchen and toward the stairs. Darkness had fallen now, but the second story of the farmhouse was still as pleasant and open in feel as the entrance had been.

Her hands had begun to sting dully again, and her body ached from her various bruises. Not to mention she was succumbing to exhaustion from her misadventures. Even so, she mustered the energy as she sank into bed to summon a soft song. She hoped fervently that none of her hosts heard and were offended, but she couldn't bring herself to go to sleep completely undefended. It wasn't just because of Azai's open dislike of her. The experience of being attacked by Gorgon down in the ravine—the very discovery that there were people hiding in Sundering Canyon—had rattled her too much to allow her to blindly trust strangers.

The magic of Aeltas responded to her as readily as that of her native Oleand. Singing as quietly as possible, she pulled a slow trickle of power from beneath her and up into her person. As always, the magic sought for immediate release, wanting to merely use her as a channel. But with her training, it was no great challenge to hold on to it, forcing it to pool within her as she drew more up to join it.

When she had enough to fuel a simple hedging enchantment, she released it, her voice molding the magic to her chosen purpose. It wound around the perimeter of the room, forming an invisible barrier that would linger after her song ceased. It wouldn't keep anything out—it didn't have nearly enough power in it for that. But it should alert her if anyone crossed it while she was sleeping.

This meager protection in place, Marieke at last allowed herself to relax enough to succumb to her weariness.

When Marieke woke, it was to the chill dimness of pre-dawn. She rose quickly, not eager to linger in her borrowed bed. The sooner she rejoined the delegation, the better.

She was familiar enough with farm life to be unsurprised to discover that the household was already stirring. By the time she reached the kitchen, Narelle was elbow-deep in flour, kneading dough for the day's bread.

"Good morning," Narelle said briskly, her focus remaining on her task. "I trust you slept well? I'm afraid you've missed breakfast with the others, but there's plenty left."

"I slept very well, thank you," said Marieke, surveying the

remains of the meal on the table. "And I'm sorry to be late rising."

"Not at all." Narelle gestured with her head toward a clean bowl sitting beside a pot of porridge. "I thought it best to let you sleep after your ordeal yesterday."

Marieke surmised from this comment that Zev had filled his mother in on more details of the previous day's events, but she didn't get into it. She just said another word of thanks as she ladled porridge into her bowl.

"I hope I haven't held Zev up," she said a few minutes later.

"Oh no, I'm sure you haven't," Narelle said vaguely. "He went out to do some chores with his brother, but I imagine he'll be ready to leave soon." She glanced over her shoulder. "If you're finished, you can go find him if you like. They went toward the barn, I believe. The main one."

"Thank you," said Marieke again, rising. She was eager to be off, but also a little curious to see more of the farm. It was unlikely to be very different from an Oleandan farm, but it was still an interesting opportunity to witness life in the other country outside the capital. After all, part of her assignment in coming to Aeltas was to discover if it was true that the land continued to be as fertile as Oleand used to be.

She made her way out of the farmhouse, breathing in the fresh air. It felt good to be in the countryside. She'd expected her visit to Aeltas to be limited to the city. And glad as she'd been to pursue a future in her own capital rather than in her parents' coastal community, the countryside always carried a definite feel of home.

Chickens scurried across the yard in the wake of the unfamiliar human, and a loud haw from out of sight announced the presence of a donkey. Marieke directed her steps toward a large barn, behind which she could see a glimpse of a field thick with half-grown wheat crops. Nothing wrong with the land's yield on this farm, anyway.

She entered the barn to the doleful honk of a goose, which fled toward the door at her arrival.

"Not supposed to be in here, hey?" she asked the fowl in amusement as it waddled past.

"No, they just don't like singers."

Marieke looked up to see Azai watching her from across the barn, paused in the act of pitching hay into a stall. She'd uncharacteristically held her tongue until now, conscious that she was in the family's debt. But no one else seemed to be around, and she didn't feel much obligation to be polite to the unfriendly son.

"Why are you so determined to hate singers?" she demanded. "What did we ever do to you?"

But apparently Azai wasn't in the mood to give her the satisfaction of an explanation. He just gave a laugh that had a nasty edge to it, returning to his task.

"Seriously," Marieke demanded, taking a step forward. "You can think you're better than me all you like, but you're the one made to look ridiculous by your prejudice."

Azai snorted. "I thought a fully-fledged singer would have graduated from an academy or something."

"I have," Marieke said, nonplussed.

Azai's glance was withering. "You're very ignorant for someone so educated."

Marieke frowned, too bewildered to be properly offended. Before she could ask any further questions, however, Azai dismissed her.

"If you're looking for my gullible big brother, he's not here." He jerked his head over his shoulder, indicating the opposite direction from the field Marieke had seen. "Through the copse."

For a moment, Marieke continued to frown at him. But it

didn't take her long to conclude that there wasn't much point in trying to press him for more answers. In her experience, those with prejudice as deeply rooted as Azai's couldn't give a logical explanation for it.

She strode back out of the barn, pausing only to toss over her shoulder, "Well, you have to at least admit that I didn't—what was the phrase? *Sing your death over you while you slept.*"

There was a hint of amusement in Azai's voice now. "Not this time, anyway."

Shaking her head, Marieke left the barn, wending her way around its outside in the direction indicated. As Azai had said, there was a little copse there that had been hidden behind the house before. She walked cautiously through it, hardly knowing what treachery or trap she suspected, just that she was reluctant to trust Azai's directions. The last time she'd followed someone's lead, they'd turned on her and tried to throw her off a cliff.

Well, not quite the last time, she thought fairly. So far, it seemed that she hadn't erred in following Zev back to his home.

A little track, not defined enough to be called a path, led her between the tree trunks. The copse was larger than she'd thought, and clearly hadn't been planted with any specific intention. Most likely it had been there before the farmhouse had. She'd been walking for some minutes before she saw the trees thinning ahead. When she emerged, she gave a gasp of delight.

She'd expected more wheat fields, but instead she was confronted with a beautifully laid out orchard. It was no recent project, either. The trees were old, their gnarled branches reaching across what had no doubt once been neat rows between them. Splashes of red showed that some of the fruit was already ripening. The apple Azai had tried to spoil his dinner with the night before had probably come from these very trees.

Momentarily forgetting her mission, Marieke wandered into the orchard, enchanted by the peaceful beauty of it. Not many of the farmers in her home region kept orchards. Most focused on crops and livestock. A feeling of contentment settled over her as she brushed her fingers against an apple dangling at head height.

"Marieke. You found my orchard."

She turned quickly, to catch a glimpse of Zev, two rows over. He was kneeling on the ground, his hands in the dirt as he cleared some grass from around the base of one of the trees. He finished his task in an unhurried way as Marieke wended her way between trunks to reach him.

She watched him silently, surmising from the dirt on his clothes and the way he wiped his forehead with his sleeve that he'd been at work for some time already. His sleeves were rolled up to his elbows, and she couldn't stop her eyes being drawn to the taut muscles of his forearms. To her own embarrassment, her memory flashed to the day before, when he'd removed his shirt to use it as a rope. She'd been much too distracted by the risk of imminent death to get a good look at him when he was pulling her up, and much too overwhelmed by the relief of being alive to think about his physique when she'd found herself briefly pressed against him. But now, she found that her mind was perfectly able to reconstruct in memory the firmness of his muscles and the general impression of strength she'd received as he yanked her from the treacherous cliff and against his form.

All in all, she'd better not tell her friends from the academy that she'd been rescued by a shirtless farmer, or she'd never live it down. They all loved to tease her for being a farm girl, although her parents didn't actually run a farm. They would find it hysterical that she'd traveled all the way to Aeltas only to get sidetracked from the capital and immediately fall in with a handsome farmer.

She winced at her own thoughts, but didn't really try to argue with herself. It would be senseless to pretend Zev wasn't handsome. He was muscled without being stocky, and even tousled from work, his tawny hair was swept back from his brow in a very appealing way. And unlike his brother, his face was usually settled in a relaxed expression which did nothing to mar his strong, straight features.

Yes, she thought mutinously, he was a handsome farmer. But in defense of her curiosity about him, he wasn't much like the many farmers she knew. Alongside the strength required to work the land, there was a confidence and sophistication that set him apart. His whole family had a strangely polished feel to them. Perhaps Aeltan farmers were simply more cultured than their Oleandan counterparts.

Glancing up, Zev caught her scrutiny. Mercifully, he seemed to assume she was engrossed by his activity rather than his person.

"It's better for the grass not to grow right up against the trunks," he explained. "Helps keep some of the pests away."

He straightened with the words, brushing his hands together then rubbing the remaining dirt off on his trousers. "What do you think of my orchard?"

"It's beautiful," Marieke said, looking around her again. "More than beautiful. It feels...magical."

She'd spoken without thinking, but although Zev's voice was dry, he showed none of the anger Azai surely would have.

"Don't describe it that way to the rest of my family. They won't appreciate it."

"Sorry," Marieke said absently, her eyes still on the branches above her. "I forgot you're all afraid of magic."

"We're not afraid of it," Zev corrected, sounding displeased. "We just don't have much use for it out here on a farm."

The answer was an unconvincing explanation for the family's prejudice, and he must have known it. Marieke didn't bother calling him out on it, just smiling ruefully.

"I'm more familiar with this debate than you can imagine. Half my community think I should return home now I've graduated and use my magic to help bolster the farms. The other half think magic has no place in farming." She cast her eyes back toward the out-of-sight fields. "I'm not surprised your family fall in the latter camp, given that your farm is clearly thriving without any magical aid. If that was the case for everyone back home, they'd probably all be glad not to have singers meddling with their time-honored ways."

She realized as soon as the words were out that she probably shouldn't have betrayed the fact that Oleand's farmland was suffering where Aeltas's apparently wasn't. But Zev surprised her by focusing on a different aspect of her tale altogether.

"And what do you want to do?" he asked. "Now that you've graduated. Do you want to take your skills back to your community?"

It took Marieke a moment to answer, not having expected him to be interested in her own plans. But she saw no reason not to be honest.

"I don't want to move back. If I'd grown up on a farm, I might feel differently. But I don't have a farm to help with my songcraft. My father is a horse doctor, and sometimes a farrier when needed. And using magic in the care of animals is very complex and risky. I would have to do specialized study, and since my parents aren't pushing me to do it, I'm not particularly eager. They agree that there are more opportunities for me in the city."

"It's nice that they're so open about your future," Zev commented, starting to lead her from the orchard.

"It is," Marieke agreed. She hesitated. "Are your parents not?"

Zev gave a low chuckle, sending an amused glance over his shoulder at her. "I'm under no one's control but my own, Marieke."

That she could certainly believe, she thought, eyeing his broad shoulders and confident stride as he reached the edge of the trees. She paused for a moment, wanting to linger under the branches.

"Something wrong?" Zev asked, realizing she'd stopped.

"Quite the opposite," she said, running a hand over a low-hanging branch.

If she'd been in less magic-despising company, she would have sent a soft song to mingle with the stately energy of the place. She would like to see what the magic of this patch of land felt like. Country power always felt cleaner than city power as it passed through her. She would warrant a guess that the power seeping from this orchard would feel as crisp and sweet as a bite of one of the ripe, red apples.

"You're quite taken with my orchard." Zev's words weren't a question, and he sounded pleased. "I'm very fond of it myself. I test my family's patience with how much of my time I devote to this part of the farm. It's not just the apple trees—we have several orchards." With a comfortable glance back at the thriving trees, he continued out of the orchard. "I prefer overseeing them to working the fields."

"Were you perhaps being hypocritical yesterday when you said your brother was wasted tilling the land?" Marieke asked, feeling bold to tease him.

Her words surprised a laugh out of her companion, who was now leading her through the copse.

"I don't think anyone's effort and strength can be wasted working for a good honest living, especially when that work feeds their community as well as their family," he said mildly. "But I confess that I don't find great satisfaction in the annual planting and reaping of the crops. It's important, but it's all so temporary. Only the cycle continues. The plants themselves are here and gone, leaving nothing behind. In the orchards, though…"

He trailed off, and Marieke finished for him. "The trees have been there long before us and will remain long after. I know what you mean. I think that's what makes it such a peaceful place."

Zev said nothing, but the glance he threw at her suggested she'd once again surprised him. Well, he was continuing to surprise her. Or at least, to reinforce her earlier reflections that there was a depth to his connection with the land that went beyond that of the other farmers she knew.

Half-ashamed though she was to think it, Marieke couldn't help feeling regretful that she wouldn't have the time to figure him out.

# Zev

Zev led Marieke through the trees in silence, mulling over the things she'd said. It had been very strange to hear this Oleandan stranger—a singer, no less—voicing his own thoughts about his orchard.

"We'd best get on the road," he said, when they at last emerged from the copse. "If your father works with horses, I'm guessing you can ride?"

Marieke nodded.

"That will be faster than taking the cart," Zev said, not mentioning that it would also save him the necessity of making potentially fraught conversation with her all the way to the capital. "And I can lead both horses back."

He glanced at the girl's hands, which were still wrapped in the bandages his mother had applied.

"Are you well enough to ride?"

"Of course," Marieke said quickly. "I'm fine."

Her gait changed as she sped up, but Zev wasn't deceived by this attempt to hide a slight limp. He'd already noted it. He had the impression she was pretty bruised and battered from the previous day's accidents.

Zev didn't press the issue, however. It wasn't for him to tell her what she was capable of, and in any event, he needed to get her safely to the capital and away from his farm. They had no real reason to fear visitors, but he still understood his family's tension.

Local visitors were one thing. An Oleandan who was not only a singer but was in Aeltas as part of an official delegation was something else entirely. He felt a little guilty for bringing her home, but what else could he have done? He couldn't have left her dangling from that cliff, and to abandon her injured and alone by the roadside would have been little better. Even Azai wouldn't actually have done that.

Probably.

"I'll get Azai to saddle the horses for us while I grab some things," he told Marieke as they crossed the yard. "Is there anything you need to get?"

She shook her head. "When I fell from the carriage into Sundering Canyon, I didn't have the foresight to take my pack with me."

Zev gave a perfunctory smile, already halfway to the barn.

"Azai!" he called through the doorway. "Can you saddle up the two mares, please?"

He didn't stay to listen to his brother's grumbling. The sooner Zev heard the end of Azai's complaints about him rescuing Marieke, the better. Anyone would think the girl ran the Aeltan Council of Singers herself, the way Azai seemed to believe she should bear responsibility for all the crimes of her kind. She wasn't even from their country.

*But she is a singer*, an inner voice reminded him. *She's a proud graduate of her own country's academy, and fully convinced of their way of thinking.*

He'd do well to remember it.

It took him very little time to gather a few supplies and tell his mother they were leaving. To his irritation, though, he realized that one of the items he sought wasn't in his room where it should be.

Resigning himself to Marieke's inevitable observation, he left the farmhouse. As expected, Marieke was waiting for him, and followed cheerfully as he crossed the yard toward the smaller barn where the cart was kept. He could sense her curiosity as he rounded the structure.

"What's this?" Marieke asked as the yard behind came into sight. Her deep blue eyes passed over the low fence and the small, wooden storage house. "It looks like a smaller version of the training yard at the academy."

"That's probably because it is a training yard," Zev said evenly, cursing his own carelessness in leaving his weapon locked in the storage house instead of in his room. He'd carried it on the previous day's journey, of course, but he and Azai had engaged in a bout after Marieke had gone to bed the night before, and he'd obviously been distracted when cleaning up. He glanced at her, hoping she wouldn't dwell on it. "Were you trained in combat at your academy?"

Marieke shook her head, watching with interest as he unlocked the storage house and removed his sword. He felt as self-conscious as a young boy as he strapped it on under her observation.

"No, the training yard isn't actually part of the academy. But the Academy of Song and the Council of Singers are all part of the same complex. The official guard of the council has its buildings there as well."

Zev just grunted. Having seen the Aeltan equivalent, he had a fair idea of what complex the Oleandan buildings were on.

"Do you always wear a sword?" Marieke asked, clearly fascinated.

"Not always," said Zev. "But I wouldn't go on a journey without it."

"That's unusual for a farmer," Marieke observed. "At least in my area." Her gaze traveled slowly around her, much too shrewd for Zev's taste. "I've certainly never seen a farm with a training yard before."

If she was this struck by the training yard, Zev could only be thankful she hadn't had time to explore the house and see the library. Or perhaps his mother had possessed enough fore-thought to lock it.

"Travel can be treacherous under the best of circum-stances," Zev said lightly. "And we do live close to Sundering Canyon, which everyone knows can be a volatile area."

The look Marieke shot him was unexpectedly piercing. "Volatile as in the land itself, or as in there's danger of attack?" she asked. "Are there...are there people living in the ravine?"

Her question wasn't as casual as she tried to make it appear. Zev, his task complete and his sword now at his side, paused to look her over. "Why do you ask that?" He narrowed his eyes. "Did you see something down there?"

Marieke twisted her hands behind her in a gesture so blatantly suspicious it was almost endearing. She took a moment to consider him before answering. "I was just wondering about your choice of words, that was all."

Zev frowned slightly. She clearly wasn't giving him a straight answer, but he didn't really blame her for not confiding in him. Was it possible she'd actually seen the band of outlaws who lived in the canyon?

His eyes lingered on the way she was favoring one leg, and he remembered the wounds he'd seen on her hands. Seen the outlaws, or run afoul of them?

Zev felt his face harden. He knew the rumors of the community living in the canyon, defying those in power and calling themselves monarchists. Everyone in the area knew about them. Azai might like the idea of someone willing to openly oppose the Council of Singers, but Zev had never warmed to the tales. Whatever the justice or otherwise of their views, he didn't like the idea of the outlaws using violence as a way to express their grievances. Seeing an example of it before his eyes made him angrier than he would have expected.

"Come on," he said gruffly. "Azai should have the horses ready by now."

His prediction proved correct, as did his unspoken guess that his brother wouldn't be able to resist a few more snide comments and dark looks as the pair mounted up. Zev ignored them, and Marieke seemed to have the sense to do so as well.

His father was out in the fields, but his mother came out to bid them safe travels. She was polite but not warm as she said her farewells to their unexpected visitor. To his own surprise, Zev felt sad at the necessity—and the prejudices—that made his family so half-hearted in welcoming a stranger in need. He was sure that had circumstances been different, his mother would have been effusive in her hospitality.

But circumstances weren't different, and hadn't been in the whole course of his life. So he'd get the inquisitive singer away from their property as quickly as politeness allowed, see her back to her group, and then his family could be free to never think of her again.

The mares made short work of the familiar track that led off their farm and skirted the properties of their closest neighbors. For a while they rode single file, traveling up the steep ring of hills that surrounded the region where Zev's family farm was located, then navigating the extensive area of gentler slopes on its other side. Zev wondered what his companion made of the phenomenon—looking at it with fresh eyes reminded him how out of place the line of steep hills were in a region of otherwise flat farmland.

Defensible, his father called it. Likely Marieke wouldn't give the terrain a second thought.

By the time they reached the main road, Zev had been given ample opportunity to see that the Oleandan could indeed ride. She seemed very comfortable atop the easygoing mare, and clearly knew how to handle the creature. That was a relief.

The main road wasn't busy, but there was enough traffic to require them to slow their pace regularly as they traveled southward. On one of these occasions, Zev noted how closely Marieke was studying the farmland past which they were riding.

"Is Aeltas what you expected?" he asked, a little amused by her somber expression.

She looked up, self-conscious at finding herself scrutinized.

"More or less. The land is clearly very fertile," she commented. Her voice dropped a little. "Even here, close to the border." She transferred her clear gaze to his face. "Is most of the country this arable?"

Zev shrugged. "From what I know. Most of the farmland, that is. Further south the climate changes. We have a whole region of jungle, and then the tropical beaches of the southern coast."

Marieke nodded. "Yes, of course. I meant the farmland."

Her eyes passed back to the rows of crops waving idly in a light breeze, allowing Zev to study her face. She'd said nothing of her own country, but her question seemed to support the rumors that Oleand's landscape was deteriorating. He'd heard some describe it as barren, although that was likely an exaggeration.

Azai would probably be delighted with the confirmation, but Zev couldn't find much cause for celebration in the troubles of their northern neighbor. Not only was a weakened and struggling Oleand likely to create problems for Aeltas down the track, but the possible cause of the change was troubling in itself. If his father was right about why Aeltas wasn't struggling...well, the responsibility of preventing that from happening weighed heavily on Zev, even if Azai didn't seem to feel it.

As Zev had predicted, their progress on horseback was much faster than it would have been in the cart. Marieke rode confidently, and the hours slipped by without much conversation. They hadn't even stopped to eat the lunch Zev's mother had packed when the farmland began to give way to the various towns that flowed out from the walled city of Tarandon.

"Are we near the capital?" Marieke asked.

Zev nodded. "Just over this rise."

When they crested a small hill, the walls of Tarandon came into sight. The road beneath their horses' hooves ran straight to the city gate, and Zev could see the portal thrown wide. It didn't do much to make the thick stone walls seem inviting, though. Not for the first time, he wondered if Tarandon had felt like such a fortress in the days when a king ruled over Aeltas.

Probably.

As they joined the stream of people making their way through the gate, Zev glanced at Marieke. Her deep blue eyes were taking in every detail, from the stray dog digging through scraps down a nearby alley to the colorful pennants waving above the city wall. What did she make of his country's capital?

For his own part, Zev always felt an uncomfortable mix of emotions when he visited Tarandon. His father had made a point of taking him to the capital when he was a child, and encouraging him to visit regularly enough to be familiar with the place. But even at a young age, Zev had been astute enough to pick up his father's discomfort when they rode through the gates. The same conflict existed within him, some part of him wishing to feel a sense of belonging to the city, while other instincts tied the place inextricably to the sense of resentment Zev had been fighting since early memory.

"Do you know where exactly your group will be?" he asked Marieke, keeping his tumultuous thoughts inside.

"The delegation was to be accommodated by the Council," Marieke said. "I don't know where everyone is, but Solomon and I were going to stay at the Academy of Song."

Zev tilted his head inquiringly. "Solomon?"

"He's an assistant instructor from our Academy of Song," she explained.

"Another singer."

Zev's words weren't a question, but she nodded in confirmation anyway. "He and I are tasked with observing your academy and learning from any differences in approach compared to ours."

Zev gave a wry smile. "It's not my academy."

Marieke didn't respond, and the realization of how thoughtfully she was regarding him reminded Zev that he should watch his words. Azai had been more than blatant enough with his prejudices for both of them.

"I can lead you to the academy," he said, directing his mount up the main street. Most of those who'd entered the city with them were going the same way. Zev knew that the central market was straight ahead, but he turned off the main thoroughfare before that point, figuring they would make faster progress on a quieter route.

"Do you come to the capital often?" Marieke asked curiously.

Zev shrugged. "From time to time."

Marieke accepted this vague answer, but again he was

aware of her scrutiny. She'd obviously noted that he knew his way around, and he couldn't help wondering if she'd describe his familiarity with the city as being *unusual for a farmer*, as she'd said about his sword. Well, there was no help for it now.

They'd entered Tarandon from the north, and the elaborate complex of buildings that housed both the Council of Singers and the Academy of Song was situated closer to the southern end of the city. By the time they drew close, Zev was thinking they should have stopped to eat after all. But Marieke didn't complain.

"There it is." Zev slowed his mount, his eyes trained on the building ahead. His words were unnecessary, as his companion could hardly fail to recognize the council building, thanks to the large blue banner that hung down the whole front turret, emblazoned with the symbol of the council. Dispassionately, Zev studied the image of the budding tree, worked in bronze thread.

"It's a beautiful building," Marieke commented. "Amazing to think how long it's been there, isn't it?"

Zev just grunted. "Is it similar to the one in Ondford?"

"It is," said Marieke. "Not identical, but much the same feel."

Zev's eyes passed up the well-built stone walls, the conflicted emotions from the city gate washing over him with double the potency. Except any sense of homecoming he might feel at approaching the city had no place here. He'd never been inside the council building in his life, or the attached academy. He'd never so much as set foot on the grounds of the—but he'd be wise to guard even his thoughts. It wouldn't be good if the word *castle* slipped out. Everyone might know the building's origins, but no one referred to it by that name.

"Well," he said gruffly. "I suppose this is where I leave you."

"Oh." Marieke seemed taken aback, her blue eyes uncertain

as they traveled up the huge banner with the council symbol. "You're not coming in?"

"Do you need me to?"

Zev didn't really know what prompted the question. He should be staying firm, and leaving as soon as his obligation to return Marieke to safety was complete. But he couldn't seem to help responding to her obvious nerves, or the appeal in her voice. She was, after all, very young to be alone in a foreign country.

"I suppose not," she said, summoning a smile. "You've been very generous with your time and assistance, Zev. I'm very grateful to you, and your family." She shifted in the saddle, making to dismount from the borrowed horse.

"Hold on." Zev held back a sigh as he stopped her with a hand on her horse, more annoyed with himself than with her. "I'll see you to your delegation."

Marieke looked like she was about to politely protest, but she was cut off by one of the guards flanking the gate.

"Can I help the two of you?" the man asked, his tone communicating instead, *what are you doing loitering here?*

"Yes," said Marieke quickly, turning to face him. "My name is Marieke, and I'm part of the delegation who I assume arrived last night from Oleand. I'm supposed to be staying at the academy, but I got separated from the group."

The guard frowned, looking her over. "Are you claiming to be the girl who fell into the ravine?"

Marieke nodded. "That's me," she said, her light tone forced.

Zev wondered again just what she'd been through prior to him finding her clinging desperately to the cliff face.

"I thought you were dead." The guard's voice was faintly accusatory.

"I would be, if this man hadn't saved my life," Marieke informed him.

"Wait here," the guard said curtly. With a muttered word to his fellow, he turned and hurried into the grounds of the council building.

"I don't think my word is worth much in his eyes," Marieke commented to Zev with a touch of humor. She cast him a sideways glance. "He probably thinks about as highly of Oleandans as your brother does of singers."

Zev grunted, only the shadow of a grimace conveying his irritation over Azai's unguarded behavior.

The guard returned quickly and beckoned to them. "Please come through."

"Well," said Zev, sliding from his horse. "This really is where we part."

He held up his arms to assist Marieke to dismount. It wasn't really necessary. She could have handed him the reins of the borrowed horse while he was still mounted. But in spite of achieving his objective, he found himself curiously reluctant to relinquish all knowledge of Marieke's welfare.

"No." The guard shook his head. "You're to come, too."

"I see no reason for me to intrude," Zev said, irked by the stranger's authoritative tone. What right did he have to order Zev's time?

"You've been specifically requested," the guard informed him, as if the matter was closed.

Zev debated refusing outright, but feeling Marieke's eyes on him, he realized it would be foolish. Much as he'd hoped to avoid notice, making a point of defiance would only make it worse, given Marieke knew who he was and where he lived. She would surely tell those in charge about him. He would only become a more suspicious figure if he refused to appear before them as requested.

Reluctantly, he handed off his horse to another guard, watching as Marieke dismounted and did the same.

"Where can I collect my mounts afterward?" he asked.

"In the guard stables," the man said, gesturing in the direction the horses were already being led. "They'll be seen to in the meantime."

"They'll benefit from the rest before you ride home," Marieke pointed out.

Zev just sighed as he followed their guide toward the main entrance of what had once been the Aeltan royal castle. In spite of his annoyance about being forced into coming inside, he admitted privately to some curiosity.

He looked around thoughtfully as they passed under a grand archway and into a wide and airy entrance hall. No doubt it would be difficult to keep it warm in the winter, but the open space created an effect that was both pleasant and luxurious. Tapestries hung on the walls—not the building's original decorations, judging by how consistently they featured feats of songcraft—and two fires burned in grates at opposite ends of the large room.

"This way." The guard led them up a shallow flight of steps and came to a stop outside an open door. "If you wait here, they'll be with you in a minute."

He didn't follow them in, instead taking up a position outside the door as soon as they came to a stop next to the dark wooden table that dominated the small room.

"We're under guard," Zev said wryly.

Marieke's smile was a little strained. "I'm sure it's just a precaution until they make sure I am who I claim to be."

Zev examined the space, noting that even this small meeting room boasted costly decorations.

"It seems the Council of Singers doesn't want for

resources," he commented, nodding at a flat basin filled with flowers. It appeared to be made of solid gold.

"It must look ostentatious to someone who's not familiar with a council or academy building," said Marieke, without any trace of mockery. "But it's not purely for vanity. Gold is an excellent conductor of magic, and circular objects are ideal. That one's a talisman. Rare and valuable definitely, but not so much because of the gold."

A talisman? All the more reason to think it had come from the royal treasury, Zev reflected silently. All he said aloud was, "Are you sure?"

"That it's a talisman?" Marieke nodded. "I can sense the magic in it. But I'm not experienced enough to discern its purpose just from feeling it. My guess would be it's some kind of security measure. Like identifying weapons or something." Her gaze flicked to the sword still strapped to Zev's belt. "Well, probably not that, but something along those lines."

Zev frowned, not liking the idea that he was subject to unknown magic merely by being in the room. He hadn't anticipated the council building containing any such items, with latent magic stored in them in such a way that it didn't even require singing to activate it.

"I've heard of talismans, of course," he said. "But I thought no one knew how to make them."

"Yes, the knowledge has been lost," Marieke said. "No one's made a talisman in hundreds of years. Not since the monarchs were overthrown."

Zev said nothing, surprised to hear her speak so openly of the event. Most people seemed to avoid directly mentioning the coup that had wrested control of Aeltas and Oleand from their monarchs and given it to the two Councils of Singers.

"But there are still a fair few around from before," Marieke went on, her eyes on the golden basin. "All closely regulated by the council, of course. Or at least, that's how it is in Oleand."

Zev didn't respond. Swift footsteps were approaching, and they both turned to see three figures come through the doorway.

"Mari!"

The glad cry came from a man at the back of the group, younger than the other two newcomers by far. He was probably only ten years older than Zev, and his face was alight with relief.

"Solomon." Marieke's answering smile bordered on teary, and she moved forward to meet the speaker. "Yes, it's me."

"I'm so glad you're alive!" Solomon said, running a hand across his brow in a distracted motion. Zev noticed that his hands looked soft and polished, like he'd never done a day's work in his life. He was obviously the assistant instructor Marieke had mentioned.

"As am I." A middle-aged woman strode toward Marieke, relief lightening her somewhat severe features. "We thought you lost, child. You did very well to save yourself from a fall like that. Did you do so with songcraft?"

Marieke nodded. "Thank you, Councilor Isabel. I did use my voice to survive the descent. Along with a bit of luck. But I wouldn't have made it out of the ravine without Zev's help." She nodded toward him. "I'd made it most of the way up, but was stuck and at the end of my strength when he happened along and pulled me to safety."

The older woman studied Zev with interest, inclining her head in a nod. "Then as the leader of our delegation, I'm very indebted to you—even while I'm ashamed that your services were necessary. If I'd dreamed Marieke could have survived that fall, I wouldn't have left the area without her. But we had a decision to make if we were to have any hope of reaching the capital before nightfall.”

“I don't blame you,” said Marieke. “I thought I was sure to die as well.”

“It was horrible.” Solomon shuddered. “Absolutely horrible. I had nightmares about it last night.”

“How unpleasant for you.” Zev couldn't resist the dry comment.

“I'll send another messenger after the one we dispatched to tell your parents what happened,” the woman said. “With any luck the first one won't have left Aeltas yet. Accounts are that the bridge is still closed for repairs. He can return with your belongings.” Her eyes, uncomfortably shrewd, settled on Zev. “Zev, is it?”

“Yes, this is Zevadiah,” said Marieke quickly. “Zev, this is Councilor Isabel, and this is Solomon.”

Zev nodded calmly. “It's a pleasure to meet you. And I'm glad to have been of service to Marieke. It was fortunate I was passing at the time.”

“Very fortunate,” piped up the third of the strangers. This one was a gray-haired man, dressed in the official blue of the Aeltan Council of Singers. Not part of the delegation from Oleand, then. “We were all very distressed that the delegation's visit to our country should have begun with such catastrophe. I'm delighted things have been set right.”

Zev eyed him in silence. He'd never spoken in person to a member of his country's Council of Singers before. Much as he criticized Azai for being too open with his contempt, he found it hard to muster politeness for a man who represented everything Zev had been raised to hate.

“What region are you from, son?” the Aeltan councilor asked with a patronizing air that tried Zev's temper.

“I live on a farm about twelve leagues northeast of here,”

said Zev, again deploring the necessity of sharing the information. "No more than a few leagues south of Sundering Canyon."

"Ah." The interest in the councilor's voice told Zev that he knew the area, at least by reputation. "A most fertile region." He turned to the three Oleandans, his tone bordering on smug. "One of Aeltas's crowning jewels, in fact. It's serendipitous that this young member of your delegation had the opportunity to observe its bounty up close. Hopefully it can help inform your inquiries here."

The shadow of irritation that crossed the Oleandan delegation leader's face before she quickly banished it told Zev that they were as unimpressed by the councilor's boasting as he was. Although undoubtedly for very different reasons. It must be true that Oleand was suffering in some way. Marieke's delegation must have come to Aeltas to try to ascertain why the southern country was faring better.

Zev wasn't sure about serendipitous, but it was certainly a strange quirk of fate that Marieke had fallen right into his lap, given the purpose of her visit to Aeltas.

And the land itself had led him to her, he thought, feeling aggrieved all over again. And yet, as he surreptitiously studied Marieke's face, her disheveled gown matching the deep blue of her eyes, and her pale face framed by that dark braid, he couldn't quite bring himself to regret their meeting.

He was probably falling victim to a foolish preference for playing the hero, as Azai had accused him of the night before.

"I'd best be on my way," he said, directing the comment to Marieke. "I'm glad to see you safely returned to your group."

"How can I show my thanks for your intervention?" Isabel asked, before Marieke could answer. "On behalf of our delegation and our council, I wish to express our gratitude."

"No thanks are necessary," said Zev. "Marieke exaggerates my role."

"I don't," she contradicted, sounding affronted. "You saved my life!"

Zev fought down a smile. "In any event, I was glad to be able to help. I didn't do so for a reward."

"Showing true Aeltan spirit," the Aeltan councilor said in a satisfied tone. "Well done, young man."

It was all Zev could do to keep his tongue between his teeth. With the stiffest of bows toward the man, he turned to take his leave of Marieke.

"I'll walk you out," she said quickly. "Make sure the horses are ready for you." She glanced inquiringly back at the two members of the Oleandan delegation.

"We'll wait here for you, Mari," said Isabel. "Solomon can show you to your accommodations."

With a nod of thanks, Marieke turned to Zev, her deep eyes almost shy. Wondering yet again how exactly he'd gotten himself into whatever mess this all was, Zev turned and strode from the room, aware of her following close behind.

## Marieke

**M**arieke walked in silence behind Zev until they were clear of the building. To her own embarrassment, she found herself curiously reluctant to part from him. The appearance of Solomon and the councilor had been reassuring, but hadn't done as much as she'd expected to counteract the sense of being alone in a foreign land. Zev felt like a safe haven, an impression that she knew was as foolish as it was false.

"I didn't overstate your assistance," she said abruptly, as they neared the indicated stables. "I would be dead if you hadn't come to my aid."

Zev said nothing, but his expression softened slightly.

"Please thank your family for me again," Marieke added. "Especially your mother. It was very kind of her to house and feed a stranger."

Zev came to a stop outside the stables, his eyes hard to read as they rested on her face. "I'm afraid you didn't experience the true Aeltan hospitality we would have liked to show you, and I regret that." Perhaps he saw her confusion, because he added with a smile, "But I'll pass your thanks on to my mother."

Marieke nodded, wanting to say more, but not knowing what.

"They called you Mari," Zev said abruptly. "The ones from your group."

She nodded again. "It's what my friends usually call me." She searched Zev's eyes, wondering why he cared about the unimportant detail. "Are you sure you should leave straight way?" The words tumbled out of her as she shifted her gaze to the relative darkness of the stables. "The horses will be tired, and so must you be. I'm sure our delegation would welcome you to eat and lodge with us if you cared to stay for the evening meal and set off in the morning."

Zev looked surprised at the invitation, and it was a moment before he answered. "Thank you, that's kind. But I really must be going. I'm expected at home."

Marieke nodded, biting her lip and stepping slightly back. "Well, this is goodbye, then. Thank you, with all my heart. I was very fortunate to cross paths with you."

Zev took so long to respond this time, she began to feel embarrassed to be lingering. Should she turn and walk away? Surely he would at least say goodbye. Then, just as she was questioning this certainty, Zev raised his arms, his grip warm and unexpected as he seized her shoulders. His hands were strong with all the confidence of a life of honest labor, and Marieke's breath caught slightly in her throat as their splaying grip brought his fingertips into contact with the exposed skin over her collarbones.

"Well met, Marieke of Oleand," he said, his deep voice seeming to reverberate right through her. "May the land be firm beneath your feet and gentle under your touch."

As suddenly as they'd come, Zev's hands were gone. He stepped back from her, leaving Marieke dazed as she tried to identify the sensation that had swept over her with his strange words. She'd certainly felt something, and if she didn't know better, she'd almost have called it magical. But it wasn't magic, not really. It wasn't like the power that coursed from the ground into her when she sang. It was more like the peaceful security of the orchard on Zev's farm, where the air felt immortal and no troubles seemed too dire for time to overcome.

Or perhaps it was just butterflies in her stomach as her foolish mind succumbed to Zev's inconvenient attractiveness and the strength of his touch. For a moment, she'd felt as raw as the naive fifteen-year-old who'd arrived at the academy three years before.

"Goodbye."

The simple word from Zev brought her out of her trance, and she dipped her head in a quick nod of acknowledgment. Did he think she was so dim that he had to translate his earlier words as a farewell?

"Goodbye," she responded thickly.

The next moment, he'd disappeared into the stables, and Marieke found herself turning away and hurrying back toward the council building. When she neared the meeting room where she'd left the others, she slowed her pace, taking a moment to feel her heated cheeks. A few deep breaths restored her equilibrium, and she strode into the room feeling passably poised.

"Your escort has left, has he?" The indulgent voice belonged to the Aeltan councilor, whom Marieke was surprised to see still there. He appeared to be deep in conversation with Isabel and Solomon.

"Yes," she told him. "He needs to return to his farm."

"Well, well, our farms are our country's lifeblood," the councilor said unconvincingly.

Marieke had enough experience of the philosophy of her own Council of Singers to recognize his self-satisfied tone.

Singers all too often thought themselves superior to everyone else. He would no doubt consider the family who'd hosted her to be rustics.

But they were far from that, she thought with a frown. There was something about them that was very unlike any farmers she'd met before.

"So you stayed at their farm last night?" he asked her.

She nodded.

"What was it like?"

Marieke cleared her throat. "Very pleasant. It seemed to be thriving."

"I imagine so," he agreed. "They're likely very prosperous given the region they're in. The land really sings out there."

"The land sings?" Solomon repeated curiously. "What do you mean by that?"

"It's an expression we have," said the Aeltan airily. "Do you not say that in Oleand?" He gave a grating chuckle. "I suppose it might not be as relevant."

Marieke felt her own irritation radiating from the other two Oleandans. This Aeltan councilor was unbearably smug about the purpose of their visit. Were they all like this?

"The expression just means that the land is famous for its fertility," the man went on. "And not just in the crops it produces. What people plant seems to thrive out there, certainly. But it's also the natural environment. Entire groves— nearly forests—have sprung up in only a few generations, and even the land itself has risen. There's a whole ring of hills around the region that didn't exist in times gone by." He frowned. "Although I'm not sure that's such a benefit, really. It makes the area difficult to access, which isn't ideal when we'd like to study its success more closely."

"That does sound unusual," said Isabel. "I haven't heard of changes like that happening without prompting." She glanced at Marieke. "Do you think the inhabitants of the area might actually be singers, using their gifts to affect the land?"

Marieke shook her head. "Very unlikely, I think. The family I stayed with were quite clearly prejudiced against singers. I had the impression that our kind are very rare in the area. And probably not welcome."

"Provincial prejudice," scoffed the Aeltan councilor. "No amount of education will ever truly eradicate it." He rubbed his hands together, apparently pleased with the morning's efforts. "Well, well, we're glad you've arrived safely, uhh...Mary, is it?"

"Marieke," she said shortly.

"Yes, well, we're glad to welcome you, in one piece after all. I'll leave you to your companions, then."

And with the words he swept from the room.

"Are they all that insufferable?" Marieke asked Solomon, as soon as the Oleandans were alone.

"Most of them," he said gloomily.

"Our hosts are fulfilling the agreement we have with them," said Isabel, her tone dampening.

Solomon shot Marieke a look that told her they'd speak more freely when alone. "Come on," he said. "I'll show you the academy, where we're staying. I think your room will still be prepared. Obviously they didn't know about your accident until we arrived last night."

Isabel walked with them, her gaze piercing as she looked Marieke over. "Are you in need of medical attention, Mari?"

Marieke shook her head. "Zev's mother tended to my wounds, and I don't think there's any lasting damage."

"What exactly happened?" Solomon pressed.

Marieke described the process by which she'd managed to slow her fall, then hesitated. She wasn't entirely sure why, but she was reluctant to tell the full story of what had happened next.

They hadn't left the building, but the large corridor down which Solomon was leading them was hung with banners that proclaimed them to be in the Academy of Song. Back in Ondford, the council and academy were in separate buildings, although part of the same complex. It appeared that here, they were all in together. It was unfathomable that one family, however wealthy, had once owned and occupied this entire place. There could be little doubt that everything she'd been told about the selfish opulence of the royals of the past was true.

"How did you get out?" Solomon was pressing. "You surely can't have climbed all the way up. Did you use your songcraft again?"

Marieke shook her head. "Actually...my voice didn't work down in the canyon."

"What do you mean?" Isabel was frowning at her.

"I couldn't speak, and I certainly couldn't sing," Marieke explained. "At first I thought I was just winded from the fall, but after a while it became clear something else was at work."

"Something else?" Solomon pressed. "You mean some kind of magic?"

"Maybe." Marieke shrugged. "I couldn't sense any magic at work, but..."

"But what?" Isabel had come to a stop outside a closed door, and the other two did the same.

"But maybe I don't know everything there is to know about the magic of the region," Marieke said. "The land's magic is supposed to be at its most potent in the ravine, isn't it? Its most raw?"

"According to whom?" Isabel asked, her tone bordering on disdainful.

Surprised by her reaction, Marieke went on more tentatively. "Well, according to the man who attacked me down there."

"You were attacked?" Solomon asked, his eyes wide. "Down *in* the ravine?"

She nodded. "There was a whole group of people down there. I think they live there. They didn't all attack me, but one seemed to be rebelling against the others. He claimed that the land itself was against my songcraft, and honestly it felt that way. They called themselves monarchists, and they—"

"Enough," said Isabel sharply. Her earlier reaction had taken Marieke aback, but her clear anger now was even more unexpected. "I don't know what nonsense these people told you about that ravine, or about their own delusions, but no one knows the magic of the land like singers. No one knows the land *itself* like singers, given magic is merely an expression of the land."

"They didn't really tell me anything," said Marieke slowly. "Other than what I just said, and that they're clearly opposed to the Council of Singers."

"They actually called themselves monarchists?" Solomon asked incredulously.

"They did," Marieke confirmed. "I was astonished. I wouldn't have thought it was possible for anyone to still be holding loyalty to the despotic royals of the past after so many generations."

"It shouldn't be," said Isabel firmly. "These people are as foolish as they are delusional."

"Presumably they're Aeltan," said Solomon, still sounding shocked by the whole affair.

"One would assume," the older woman agreed.

"I assumed the same," Marieke said. She glanced around, making sure they were alone. "And I wondered if maybe things are different in Aeltas. If maybe the rule of the Council of

Singers is failing somehow. Is the country being poorly run compared to Oleand? That might explain why there's a group romanticizing the old ways."

Isabel looked like she wanted to say yes, but after a moment, she sighed. "I can't see any evidence of that." She also lowered her voice. "As we all know, the reason for our expedition is that Aeltas is thriving."

Solomon nodded slowly. "I know we haven't been here long, but from everything I've seen so far, there's no marked difference between the way the Aeltan and Oleandan councils are run."

"Well, then it's more bizarre than ever," Marieke said frankly. She looked at Isabel. "I suppose I should report the incident to the Aeltan Council of Singers. They might know the reasons behind the decision of a group of outcasts to live in Sundering Canyon. Do you think they'll want to question me about what I saw?"

The older woman frowned as she thought it over. "I think it would be best to leave it with me for now, Mari. For all we know, the Aeltans may claim that these ravine-dwellers are Oleandan and accuse us of foul play. I'll make discreet inquiries."

"All right," said Marieke.

Isabel's reasoning made sense. Aeltans were often suspicious of Oleandans—and the reverse, if Marieke was honest. But something about the delegation leader's manner still unnerved her. It wasn't the reaction she'd expected to the news. Solomon had seemed astonished, but the older woman had seemed more...wary.

Marieke just wished she could shake her suspicion that Isabel had another reason for wanting her to drop the matter. Perhaps she didn't want Marieke to find out more about the monarchists' cause. An Aeltan investigation might reveal that kind of information.

Enough, she told herself firmly. There was plenty of suspicion between the two countries as it was. No need to create it between Oleandans.

"I'll leave you to settle in, then," Isabel said, smiling wanly at her. "I'm very glad you're all right, Marieke."

"We're through here," Solomon added, opening the door outside which they were standing. Beyond was revealed a long hallway with many doors coming off it. "Not all the instructors live here at the academy, but those who do have rooms in this wing. And they've prepared guest suites for us."

"I've been elevated to instructor status, have I?" Marieke grinned. "That's a feather in my cap."

Solomon chuckled. "The suites are very nice. I think they're trying to impress us."

He led her down the hallway, past several closed doors. It was dim, with no external windows to illuminate the space. Presumably the suites themselves boasted access to the outside world.

"Did someone say my pack was sent back to Oleand?" Marieke asked.

"I'm afraid so," said Solomon. "But with any luck, it will be back here soon, if rumor is correct that the bridge is still not usable. This is me. I think you're next door." He glanced at her as he came to a stop outside one of the doors. "You've had quite the adventure, Mari."

"Misadventure, more like," she said ruefully. She ran a hand over her braid. She'd made it as neat as she could in the circumstances when she woke, but the half day in the saddle had pulled it loose. "I would love a wash and some clean clothes."

"I'll ask around," said Solomon. "I'm sure someone can lend you things until your own belongings arrive."

Nodding her gratitude, Marieke tried the door of the room he'd indicated. It was unlocked, and swung open to reveal an empty suite, clearly made ready for an occupant.

"Come in, if you like," she told the assistant instructor.

He followed her readily, looking around him at the spacious and pleasantly furnished receiving room, decorated in a pale blue. "It's just like mine," he commented, peering through the doorway at the sleeping area, complete with four poster bed, the bedspread of the same pale blue. "Except mine has green upholstery."

"It's very nice," Marieke said, glancing once out the window, where a pleasant garden could be seen, before sinking into an armchair.

Solomon sat in another one, apparently very ready to get out of whatever activity he'd been undertaking before her shock arrival. "It's very strange about these so-called monarchists in the ravine, isn't it?" he said.

"Very strange!" Marieke agreed, glad to receive a more natural reaction from someone. She sat up straighter. "Do you think Councilor Isabel's response was a little odd?"

Solomon frowned. "Odd? What do you mean?"

"Nothing," said Marieke quickly. "Never mind."

"No, really, you can tell me what you're thinking," Solomon said kindly.

"Can I?" Marieke could hear the dry note in her voice. "I won't wear you down with my endless questions?"

"Ah, of course." Solomon chuckled. "You were infamous for your questions at the academy, weren't you?"

Marieke bit her lip, her mind drawn back to the last conversation she'd had about her overly inquisitive personality. In the same way as Isabel had just now, the Head Instructor of her academy had surprised her in his reaction to her comments.

What had he said? *Discretion is important. No student would ever be expelled from the academy just for a simple question. But we must ask ourselves honestly what attitude is behind our questions.* What attitude had he thought he'd detected in her light comment about getting expelled for asking too many questions? And had Isabel likewise suspected her of some traitorous attitude in questioning whether the monarchists had reason for their rebellion?

"Infamous is a strong word," she said, leaning back wearily in her chair. "Did the instructors all talk about me?"

"Not maliciously," he assured her. "You were well liked, Marieke."

She didn't answer at once, not as heartened as she should be. "Yes, I didn't think I'd ever been in true trouble for asking questions," she said at last. "But when I made a joke about it to Instructor Rafael, he didn't seem to think it was funny to suggest I could have been expelled for asking questions."

"Well, I suppose expulsion isn't really a funny topic to a Head Instructor," Solomon said fairly. "If any student reaches the point of being expelled, it reflects poorly on the whole academy."

"Have you ever known anyone to be expelled during your time there?" Marieke asked.

Solomon shook his head. "No, not in my time as a student, or as an assistant instructor."

Marieke was just reflecting that the Head Instructor's sensitivity made little sense given the rarity of expulsions, when Solomon raised a hand.

"Hold on, there was one student. It was before my time, but recent enough to still be the source of gossip when I started my studies. I'd forgotten all about that old drama."

"What happened?" Marieke asked.

"I don't really know the details," Solomon replied comfortably. "But the general gist was that she was a promising student in terms of potential but extremely difficult when it came to attitude."

"The student was a girl, then?"

Solomon nodded. "What was her name? Janelle? Jasmine?" He snapped his fingers in satisfaction. "No, I have it. Jade. That sounds right."

"And what became of her?"

"I told you, she was expelled," Solomon said, surprised.

Marieke shook her head. "I mean after that."

"Oh. Who knows?" Solomon didn't seem especially interested. "What would you have done if you'd been expelled? I imagine she went home."

Marieke stared unseeingly out the window, wondering why this whole tale unsettled her so much.

"Yes, I would have gone home," she said. She directed a wan smile toward her companion. "In deep disgrace, of course."

He smiled in response. "What did your community think of you going to the academy?" he asked curiously. "I've never asked you about it before. You come from a farming region, don't you?"

"I do," Marieke said. She thought of the poor crop that had been causing their neighbors a great deal of stress the previous year. "Although not one where the land sings."

"That was fascinating, wasn't it?" Solomon said, resting his elbows on his knees with a scholar's light of learning in his eyes. "I've never heard the term before."

"Nor have I," Marieke agreed. "And to answer your earlier question, people back home were surprised when we discovered my songcraft, but on the whole I'd say proud. It conferred a bit of status on our little town."

"I only ask because of that Aeltan councilor's comment about provincial prejudice. I wondered if it was a general rule I wasn't aware of, that country folk think worse of singers than city-dwellers do."

"It's not the case in Oleand," said Marieke. "At least not in my experience. I was surprised by the prejudice of the family who hosted me last night. I'll be very interested to see if their attitude is common in Aeltas."

"Well, we might not get much chance to discover that, given we'll be based in the capital during our stay," Solomon pointed out. He rose. "I should give you some space to settle in. I suppose they'll be expecting me back in the lecture I was sitting in on, but to tell the truth, I was glad to escape. Theory of composition is as dull in Aeltas as it was in Oleand."

Marieke gave a distracted smile. "If you want another excuse to delay returning, I'd be enormously grateful if you could find me some food."

"Done," said Solomon quickly. "And I'll follow up about those spare clothes, too."

Marieke barely remembered to thank him as he took his leave. Her head was starting to pound, contributing to the uncomfortable sensation that it was full to bursting with the questions for which she was apparently infamous.

The whole purpose of this trip was to gather information, but the bewildering sequence of experiences she'd just undergone was something else entirely. She'd been in Aeltas less than two days, and already she'd been given enough to think about to last her a year.

# CHAPTER
# SEVEN

# Zev

Zev clucked his tongue to his horse, sensing that the creature was as relieved as he was to see the familiar gate. It had been a long day of riding. The sun would be setting soon.

The horse following behind on the lead picked up the pace a little as well, no doubt sensing home.

"You both deserve the day off tomorrow," Zev told the pair. "And an extra apple."

Naturally neither responded, although Zev's mount gave a faint whicker when he patted her flank.

He rode his mare straight to the barn, dismounting outside the door. A cheerful whistling told him that his brother was inside, likely mucking out the stables. As soon as Zev led the two horses in, Azai paused in his task and joined him.

"Smooth journey?" the younger man asked as he removed the saddle from the mare Marieke had ridden.

Zev nodded, grateful for both his brother's help and apparent good humor.

"Off-loaded the parasite cleanly?"

And there it was.

Zev hung up his own saddle with unnecessary force,

turning an irritated face to Azai. "Why do you have to be so venomous?" he asked. "Can't you let it rest for five minutes?"

Azai raised an eyebrow. "Have I offended you, Zev?"

Zev just glared at him, not really able to explain why his brother's snideness about Marieke bothered him so much. It didn't help that he was uncomfortably aware of how much of the return journey he'd spent thinking about the dark-haired Oleandan girl.

"You're not wise to be so unguarded. Don't think for a moment she didn't notice. You've made us seem more suspicious."

"You claim that *I've* made us suspicious?" said Azai incredulously. "When you're the one who insisted on riding with her all the way to the capital? Did you see her right into the castle?"

"It's not a castle anymore," said Zev shortly. He sighed as he set about rubbing his horse down. "But, yes, unfortunately I did."

Azai paused in his own efforts, staring at his brother. "You did? I was joking. Father won't like that."

Zev grimaced. "I didn't like it either, but it was unavoidable."

"Just like rescuing an Oleandan singer was apparently unavoidable?"

Azai didn't seem to actually expect a response to his challenge, and Zev didn't give one.

"What was it like?" Azai went on, after a moment's silence. "Was it grand inside?"

"Yes, it was grand," said Zev. "Opulent. But..." He cast his thoughts back to the council building. "But it felt soul-less. It's not a home. It's a place of business."

"A place of violence, more like," said Azai bitterly.

Zev gave a mirthless chuckle. "I don't think so, Azai. I think it's a dry and unexciting council building, with none of the intrigue and plotting you ascribe to it."

"Do you?" Azai raised an eyebrow. "Has one day with a graduate singer changed your beliefs so thoroughly?"

"Hardly," said Zev. "But you have to understand that the atrocities of the past are so long ago that even those you see as the perpetrators don't remember them. People like Marieke don't even know about them."

"I don't *have* to do anything," said Azai in a contrary way. "Not to please a bunch of singers, anyway."

They finished their task swiftly, and Azai left the rest of the stalls as they were in order to accompany Zev inside.

His parents greeted him gladly, a weight seeming to lift from his father's shoulders at the safe return of his firstborn son. Zev's mother, on the other hand, mainly seemed pleased that he hadn't delayed dinner.

As the family ate their meal, Zev relayed the events of the journey. Azai's prediction proved correct—their father wasn't pleased that Zev had entered the council building in his efforts to return the lost singer to her group.

"Did you tell them your name and region?" he demanded.

"There was no way to avoid doing so without being very suspicious, Father," Zev said calmly as he reached for the potatoes. "The councilor was more interested in the region than in me. I doubt he'll spare me a second thought."

"Let's hope so." His father still didn't look pleased. "Interested in the region, was he?"

Zev made a derisive noise in his throat. "Called it one of Aeltas's crowning jewels. Made a show of boasting to the Oleandans about the area's fertility, and how it's a good example to them of the way our country is thriving, unlike theirs."

His mother let out a crow of laughter that earned her disap-proving looks from her husband and youngest son.

"Well, don't you think it's funny?" she demanded. "I mean, he's perfectly right, isn't he? Our region is the best example the Oleandans will find of why our country is faring better than theirs."

"It's impudent, is what it is," said her husband. "Although I suppose we shouldn't be surprised that the council races to claim credit for the success of our region."

"No, we shouldn't," she agreed. She glanced around the table at her family. "You all need to lighten up. If I'd known the mood would be this somber, I'd have baked a cake to cheer us all up after the meal."

"It's not a laughing matter, Narelle," Zev's father said. He drummed his fingers on the table, his strategizing face on. "If getting to the root of the difference in the two countries' states is really the purpose of this delegation's visit, it could pose a real threat to us."

"I think you're overstating it," said his wife soothingly. "They won't think to look at us, or even consider any connec-tion between our area and the country's success as a whole."

"They likely wouldn't, had one of their number not stum-bled right into our midst," the older man said grimly. He looked between his sons. "I don't like the turn of events, is the honest truth. I think I'll call an assembly tomorrow."

"Good plan," said Azai brightly. "It's been too long since we've seen some of the others."

Gideon looked to Zev for his response.

He sighed, making a gesture of surrender. "I doubt it's necessary, Father, but I'm not against it. I'll also be glad to see everybody."

"Then it's settled." His father nodded decisively. "We'll gather after the midday meal tomorrow."

The following afternoon found Zev standing in the broad yard, welcoming the new arrivals with his brother. True to form, the clan had responded in force to the last-minute summons, and over the course of about an hour, some thirty people trickled onto the property. They all lived in the region, of course, so none had to travel far to attend the assembly.

"Zev!" One of his cousins greeted him with a clap to the shoulder that would have made a lesser man wince.

Zev just grinned. This cousin was descended from his father's youngest brother, and that whole family line was built like bears.

"Good to see you," he said. "How's that milkmaid?"

His cousin gave a guffaw. "She's not a milkmaid, impudent pup. She's sole daughter and heir to a wealthy dairy farmer." He flashed an even broader grin. "And she's agreed to marry me in the fall."

"Congratulations!" Zev told him. "You're a luckier dog than you deserve."

His cousin chuckled. "I know it, little cuz." He looked down at Zev from his superior height. "Speaking in terms of your youthful age, of course."

"Get in there," Zev said, shoving him good-naturedly toward the barn.

A few minutes later, Zev followed, satisfied that no one else was coming. The shutters of the barn had been thrown wide, letting the sunshine slant through in diagonal shafts filled with swirling dust. The familiar smell of hay met him, and one of the horses nickered softly at all the excitement.

All the members of Zev's extended family who'd come in response to his father's message were ranged throughout the space, sitting on hay bales or upturned buckets, the youngest of

Zev's cousins perched on the rungs of a ladder that led up into the loft. One uncle was absentmindedly mending a broken saddle-girth, and an aunt was scooping manure from an empty stall, apparently having been sidetracked while fetching a crate to sit on.

It wasn't the most comfortable or exalted of accommodations, but no one seemed to mind. They were all used to it, since the barn was the only space on the farm that offered the privacy of walls and a roof and was still large enough to host them all. The general mood was cheerful, although Zev noticed a few solemn faces. It was mainly the older members of the clan who looked wary—such as the two great-uncles who sat together on a large crate, watching Gideon with arms folded in identical postures. They were both younger brothers of Gideon's father—Zev's grandfather—who'd passed away in a farming accident some years prior. In spite of their advanced age, they looked to Gideon with expectant respect, as was usual. And they seemed to realize what their younger relatives didn't: that a last-minute assembly was just as likely the result of a crisis as of any cause for celebration.

"Thank you all for coming."

Gideon's voice brought an instant end to the general chatter. All eyes fixed on him as he rose to his feet toward the back of the barn.

"It's good to see you all. It's been too long."

"You should have come to the Spring Festival, Uncle Gideon!" called out the cousin sitting on the ladder. "There was lively enough music to get even your old bones dancing."

"Show some respect, pup," said one of the boy's uncles, cuffing him lightly on the back of the head.

Zev's father just smiled indulgently at the grinning scamp. "My clumsy dancing has nothing to do with my age. My wife will tell you I was no better in my youth."

"It's true," Zev's mother chimed in, appearing in the doorway. She came bearing a large basket from which steam rose promisingly in spirals.

"Narelle!" The cries of welcome were made more enthusiastic by the delicious smell that accompanied her.

With a general wave of greeting, Zev's mother passed the basket around, taking a seat beside her eldest son on a bale of hay. She then settled her gaze expectantly on her husband, prompting everyone else to do the same.

"Thank you, Narelle," Gideon acknowledged her before casting his gaze around the group. "As you would have guessed, I haven't called you merely for a social gathering. I thought everyone should be aware of some new developments we've learned about, regarding events in the capital. And I thought we should discuss what, if anything, to do about it."

His eyes lingered on Zev, who was listening in unmoving silence with his arms crossed.

"A delegation from Oleand arrived in Aeltas two days ago. The delegation was invited by the Council of Singers, and is being hosted by the council and the Academy of Song."

Murmurs passed around the room, the general tone derisive at this mention of the ruling group of their country. Gideon continued, unruffled.

"The only reason we're aware of it is that Zevadiah and Azai happened upon a curious situation. A member of the delegation—a young woman—fell from the bridge when the group was crossing Sundering Canyon. She was presumed dead by her party, which continued without her to Tarandon, but she actually survived. Zev and Azai rescued her from the cliff's edge when they happened to pass."

"Zev rescued her," Azai corrected. He was leaning back against the wall, hands behind his head. "For some reason I can't fathom." He must have seen the bewildered looks cast at him from all around, because he clarified, "She's a singer. Father forgot to mention that part."

"I didn't forget anything, Azai," their father scolded him. "You interrupted me."

"And as for my reason for preventing her gruesome death," Zev interjected, "I don't really think I need one. But if it would make you happier to have one, I was called to her aid."

Azai straightened, frowning. "What do you mean?"

"Well, you didn't hear her, did you?" Zev challenged. "Even when I drew your attention to it. She was banging on the cliff in a voiceless cry for help, and I felt the call through the land."

Azai's frown deepened at this new information. Some of those gathered looked impressed by this revelation, others skeptical. Zev knew he wasn't the only member of the family to have experienced the sensation that the land beneath his feet was almost sentient, and wishing to communicate with him. But others openly thought it mere sentiment. Zev wasn't troubled by their doubts. Everyone present loved Aeltas fiercely, and it made little difference what form their connection with the land took.

"Is that so?" His father studied him for a moment, then turned back to the group, his tone brisk. "In any event, they brought the girl here, and she spent the night. Yesterday, Zev returned her to her group in the capital." He nodded to his son. "Tell them what you learned."

Zev leaned forward, resting his elbows on his knees. "From what I can gather, the rumors of deteriorating farmland in Oleand are true. The purpose of the Oleandan delegation is to ascertain why our land isn't suffering similarly, and to see if there are any lessons they can apply to their own situation. The Aeltan Council of Singers is evidently eager to rub the delegation's faces in our success."

He felt his brow crease in irritation. "In fact, the councilor whom I met was quick to identify our region as an excellent example of the country's arable state."

Indignant mutters met this pronouncement, but one of the great-uncles fixated on a different point.

"You actually met a member of the Council of Singers in person?" he asked, alarmed. "Surely that was unwise."

"It was regrettable, but unavoidable," said Zev.

"So you claim."

Azai's mutter sent a flash of conscience over Zev. It was true that he couldn't easily have extricated himself after the guard had summoned him to accompany Marieke into the building. But he could have left prior to that. It was the silent plea in Marieke's eyes when he said he was leaving that had swayed him. *You're not coming in?* He could still hear her tentative voice.

And what had he replied? *Do you need me to?* It was the wrong response, at least as far as his obligation to his family was concerned. He should have simply told her he had to be on his way, wished her well, and left.

He didn't feel the need to confess his foolishness in that instance to all his gathered clan, however. Chastising himself in silence was enough. Even if it didn't seem to have succeeded in making him regret his actions.

"I went inside the council building," he added, seeing everyone was waiting for more.

"You set foot inside the castle?" The other great-uncle's eyes lit with interest. "I've never done as much in all my years."

"No need to sound so excited," his brother reminded him. "He entered as an unknown peasant, not the honored master he should have been."

"Peace, Uncle," said Gideon. He gave a faint smile. "We may be simple farmers to the likes of the council, but we're not exactly peasants. We're set for another excellent yield this year. Greater than the last, I expect."

"Aye, us too," chimed in a few voices from around the room.

"And Zev's orchard will bring in a plentiful crop," Narelle added, casting a fond look at her eldest son. "Times have never been better."

One of Gideon's brothers cast a look at his sister-in-law. "That may be true of your family line, Narelle, but it certainly isn't true of ours."

"Oh, calm down, Robin," said Narelle without heat. "Romanticizing the past won't brighten the future for any of us. Everyone in this room has a good life farming the land."

"At any rate, I was concerned by what Zev shared," Gideon interjected, before a squabble could arise. "It strikes me that it isn't in our interests for either the Oleandan visitors or the Aeltan council to investigate too deeply into why our land continues to thrive while our northern neighbors fall into decay. And it's especially unfortunate that the attention of the delegation has been brought to our own prosperous region."

"I think you're being overly cautious," piped up a cousin. "There's only risk to us if your theory about why Aeltas thrives is correct. And since it's based on speculation that even we don't know is true, it seems unlikely anyone else would make that connection."

"It's not just speculation," said one of the great-uncles, sounding affronted. "It's been borne out generation after generation. Never more powerfully than in our current times." His gaze passed to Zev. "If you want my opinion, it's because Zevadiah embraces the land so wholeheartedly. Rarely have I seen a love for Aeltas as deep as yours, Zevadiah, even in our line. You give both your heart and the work of your hands to the land and its people, and I applaud you for it."

Zev held the elderly man's gaze steadily, moved by the compliment but also feeling its weight. "Thank you, Uncle," he said, his deep voice reverberating around the quiet group. "But

I merely follow in the example set for me by those who've come before."

Both old men gave approving nods at this response. In the corner of his eye, Zev caught Azai's sigh. His brother had likely hoped to see Zev chastised for his intervention on Marieke's behalf. But Zev was convinced that in spite of her status as a singer, none of his relatives would actually have approved of him leaving her to her death.

"I add my approval without reservation," Gideon said, his gaze stern with pride as it rested on Zev. "Zevadiah does me credit, as does Azai. And Narelle is right that our family prospers as surely as does the land. I'm sure you all know that my purpose in calling the assembly was not to complain. But at the very least, we all should be on our guard. We need to be careful more than ever of what we say outside the family, particularly in relation to this Oleandan delegation. Hopefully we will avoid any further notice from them."

There were a few deep nods around the room, and one of the great-uncles spoke again.

"What do you think, Zevadiah? You're the one who spoke with the councilor and saw the delegation in person. Do you think there's cause for concern?"

"Yes," the other great-uncle said, nodding. "He's of age now." He directed his words to Gideon. "With your father gone and you our patriarch, Zevadiah is now heir to the stolen throne. He should be taking a more active role in these discussions, to build his leadership abilities."

An impish part of Zev found the man's solemn pronouncement humorous, perched as he was on a hay bale, surrounded by his farming family as they discussed the need for him to practice a leadership he would never be called upon to exercise. But he knew his lineage wasn't a matter to be dismissed as irrelevant, no matter how many generations had passed since his ancestors sat on the throne of Aeltas with full recognition of their royal status. He completely agreed with his father's assessment about the importance of their blood to the kingdom. Or rather, the country, he reminded himself.

"By all means," his father said, nodding to him. "I would be glad to give Zevadiah more authority."

"Thank you," Zev said, the words directed to both his father and the great-uncles who'd spoken up for him. "I agree with my father that we should be cautious. And I confess I do feel deeply concerned about the deteriorating state of Oleand. But the delegation doesn't seem to pose an imminent threat. While I did not intend either to share my name and home with a foreign singer or to make myself known to our own Council of Singers, I don't see what other course I could have taken in the circumstances that were presented to me. I did what needed to be done, and now there's nothing to do but await events and face whatever comes. As we've always done."

Again nods met his words, and one of his aunts leaned forward.

"Why do you feel so concerned about Oleand's plight? I don't see that it affects us."

"We share this land with them," Zev said simply. "And a complex history of connections between the countries, for better and for worse. However Aeltas currently thrives, I think we would be foolish to assume we can remain unaffected by Oleand's troubles."

"You speak with wisdom," said one of the great-uncles, and Zev leaned back, feeling his part was done for the moment.

"Thank you, Zev," his father said. "And thank you everyone. We are all as informed as we can be at present. Now, as Zev said, we will await events."

Conversation broke out again, everyone recognizing that the formal business was complete. Nearby, Azai and one of the cousins from the closest farm started making plans for a few bouts with their swords, to keep skills sharp.

"I'm getting bored of only having Zev for an opponent," Azai said, shooting his brother a smirk.

"Maybe I could join," said a younger sibling of the cousin enthusiastically. "Father's been training me in sword fighting, and—"

"You'll be studying," said his brother in a dampening tone. "You don't want to fail your history examination a second time, do you?"

The younger boy shot an embarrassed look between Zev and Azai, muttering angrily to his brother about sharing that information. Zev smiled kindly at him. "Don't worry. Azai failed his three times."

"Oi!" Azai aimed a punch at him, which he avoided. "It was only twice."

"Yes, he passed the third time," their mother said reminiscently. "It was a near thing, though."

"Thank you, Mother," said Azai in a long-suffering voice.

She just smiled at him before speaking to Zev in a lower tone. "You did well, Zev."

He looked at her in surprise. "I didn't do anything."

"You have a good head on your shoulders," she insisted, giving the object in question a pat that made him feel like a small boy again. "I'm proud of you, and so is your father. You've navigated many pitfalls with success. You don't realize it, but we do."

Zev was mystified by this praise, but he just smiled his thanks as his mother stood to go and chat with some of the aunts and uncles. Zev tuned out the proposal being discussed among the cousins—of reinstating the horseback archery tournament they'd indulged in a few years before. In spite of the company, he found his thoughts straying to his orchard. He might go for a walk there when everyone left, to clear his head. He just wished he could picture the familiar place without also seeing a dark braid dangling down against a deep blue gown, as an appealing face examined the branches above with eyes as blue as the fabric.

Where was Marieke now? Was he right that the delegation, her included, would likely spare no more thought for the family and their encounter? He knew it was the outcome he should hope for, but he found himself regretting it. She seemed to haunt his thoughts out of all proportion with their brief encounter, and it didn't bring him any joy to think the reverse might not be true.

Perhaps it was the same foolish sentimentality some accused him of in thinking the land spoke to him, but Zev couldn't deny the conviction that had been growing in him ever since he'd first set eyes on Marieke.

For better or worse, change was coming. And they could do nothing to stop it. All they could hope for—all they'd ever been able to hope for—was to shape its course in whatever way the waves of fate offered them.

# EIGHT

## Marieke

Marieke looked up at the huge stained-glass window, the varied colors of the image flooding her face.

"It's a beautiful room," she said politely.

"It is pretty nice," agreed Veronica, the final-year student who was showing her around. "We eat all our meals in here, and also have whole-academy gatherings. It's the largest room in the academy's part of the complex. I think the council buildings have an even bigger one."

Marieke nodded. "We have a similar space in our academy, but we don't have stained-glass windows like this. They're gorgeous." She squinted at the depictions. "What are they of?"

"Some old history," Veronica said dismissively. "From before. Battles, probably."

"It doesn't look like battles," Marieke commented. She studied the closest panel. "That one looks like some kind of festival. A harvest festival, maybe."

"I wouldn't know," said the Aeltan student. "I'm not from a farming region. But I doubt it. I'm pretty sure those types of festivals were introduced by the Council of Singers. I don't think they had anything that celebratory in the old days."

Marieke didn't respond. It seemed her reputation as a farm girl had followed her even here. But that comment didn't bother her. She was used to it, and not at all ashamed of her background. Her thoughts strayed to the family who had hosted her after her accident, and to Zev himself. From what she'd seen, Aeltan farmers had nothing to be ashamed of, either.

The other comment stuck in her mind more. For her part, Marieke found it hard to believe that the monarchs, however tyrannical, had succeeded in preventing any kind of celebrations or happy traditions. This stained-glass window suggested a different tale, but she wasn't surprised that Veronica was quick to discount it as evidence. The reaction matched the attitude back in Oleand. The only surprising thing was that the academy had chosen to leave the windows in place. Paintings and furnishings depicting a supposedly glorious past had all been destroyed in her own academy building. But she supposed stained glass was both more precious and harder to remove.

"So you have classes in the mornings and practical training in the afternoons?" she asked, following Veronica past one of the long, empty dining tables.

"Most days," the Aeltan confirmed. "But it changes in final year, when we get to choose electives. Everyone's schedules are different then."

"What electives are you doing?" Marieke asked curiously.

"Healing song and structural song at present," she answered.

"Structural song," Marieke commented. "I never did that. It's an important one."

The Aeltan student grinned. "Yes, everyone thinks of it as one you *should* do but no one actually wants to do, but I really enjoy it."

"That's great," said Marieke. "Everyone made fun of me for

doing agricultural song two years in a row, but I really enjoyed that as well. I guess it was just speaking my language."

"That makes sense." Her guide navigated around the end of the long table and led Marieke down the adjoining corridor. They walked in silence for a few minutes as they passed the open doors of classrooms, hearing catches of the lessons happening within.

"History," Veronica whispered, as they passed a class full of students with glazed eyes. "Everyone's most and least favorite class."

"Why most?" Marieke asked, once they were clear of the door and not at risk of disrupting the class. *Least* she understood without being told. Everyone at her own academy found history boring as well. They all understood the importance of knowing the tale of how the singers had redeemed the land from the despotic days of the past, but that didn't make sitting and listening to someone speak for hours any more enjoyable.

"Well, the fact that there's no practical aspect, while dull, means we get a free afternoon once a week," her guide explained.

"Ah." Marieke grinned. "That makes sense. At our academy, we didn't get that. We had choral class after history."

"Choral class?" The Aeltan looked at her curiously. "What's that?"

"Don't you do that?" Marieke asked, surprised. "Where you learn about pitch and rhythm, and all that? How to make your song actually sound good as well as making it magically effective?"

The other student looked fascinated as she shook her head. "That sounds great! I'd love to study that. They don't offer it here."

"Huh." Marieke smiled slightly as she thought of one of her instructors back home—a beloved but very...memorable woman. Perhaps the class had been introduced because of her. "It has more than one use. It's an excellent opportunity to practice control, because the whole exercise is channeling magic through song but trying *not* to form it into anything."

"That would be handy," Veronica said. She rolled her eyes. "So many students, especially the ones from really good families, are much too full of their own strength, and give far too little attention to their control."

"I know the type," Marieke assured her. "We have plenty of them in Oleand, too."

The other girl grinned. "Well, that's a relief. Since I've just remembered I'm supposed to be making us look good, not bad."

Marieke laughed aloud at that. "Our countries like to think we're different, but the greatest sign of how similar we are is our identical determination to convince each other that we're better."

The two of them chuckled as they exited the building through a set of double doors flung open. A few shallow steps led from the doorway into a huge courtyard, surrounded on all sides by wings of the building. Marieke recognized it immediately as a large training yard. It made her think again of Zev—something she was doing with alarming frequency—and the strange phenomenon of a farm having a proper training yard.

"I assume this is used by those studying combat song?" she said.

Her guide nodded. "It's also used by the council guard. They combine training to learn from each other and develop coordinated strategies."

"That's smart," said Marieke. "I'm not aware of them doing that in Ondford. Although I never studied combat song, so I might be wrong."

Really, she reflected, it was a shame that there was such

prideful rivalry between the two countries. Exchanges like this should have been happening for years. It would surely benefit both the Oleandan and Aeltan academies.

"What haven't you seen yet?" Veronica asked. "Would you like a tour of the library?"

"Definitely," said Marieke. She followed her guide back into the building, moving in the opposite direction from the classrooms. "Are students allowed free access anytime, or is it restricted?"

"We're allowed to access it anytime during opening hours," Veronica said. "I think there might be some restricted records only accessible to those studying the relevant specialties, but I've never needed any of those, so I'm not sure."

Marieke nodded. It was similar at the Oleandan academy. When they entered the room, she looked around with interest. It was much smaller than the dining and assembly hall, but had a similarly grand feel. It boasted the same high ceiling, and while there was no stained glass, the oriel windows were just as appealing.

And the rows of wooden shelves, packed with books and scrolls, gave the place a quiet dignity nowhere but a library could achieve.

"Good morning, ladies."

The cheerful voice drew Marieke's attention to an older man sitting behind a desk in the corner of the room. His friendliness was a contrast to the librarian in her own academy, who was rather severe. The Aeltan librarian peered at them over the top of the small pile of books he seemed to be repairing.

"Veronica." He nodded to the Aeltan student before transferring his smile to Marieke. "You don't look familiar. Are you a new student?"

Marieke shook her head, moving forward to better greet

him. "I'm part of the delegation from Oleand. I'm a recent graduate of our academy. My name is Marieke."

"Ah, I see!" He leaned back, looking perfectly at ease. "In that case, welcome. We'd be glad for you to examine any records that catch your interest. If there's anything I can assist with, let me know."

"Marieke specialized in agricultural song," said Veronica helpfully. "She's from a farming region, like you."

"It was only one of my elective subjects," Marieke said quickly. "I didn't undertake advanced study in the area."

"Ah." The librarian's eyes lit with interest as he studied her. "Not from the city, eh? I'm the same, and it's made me something of an oddity among my colleagues. Most who chose a life in academics are from established city-based singing families."

"The same is true in Ondford," Marieke assured him. She hesitated then decided to pursue what seemed a good opportunity to get information. "Although I wouldn't say that country folk in Oleand have any particular dislike for singers. I understand it might be a little different here?"

"No." The librarian looked surprised, and Marieke deemed his lack of offense to mean he was genuine in his reaction. "I wouldn't say that at all. Singers are well regarded in the area I come from, anyway."

"I've never had that impression, either," Veronica commented. "What made you think that?"

"Oh." Marieke tried to sound casual. "I must have misunderstood. My mistake."

Inside, her mind was going back over all her interactions with Zev and his family. If the councilor's dismissal of their attitude as provincial prejudice was inaccurate, it made their position all the more marked. Why did they hate singers so much?

"How are you finding our academy so far?" the librarian asked, drawing Marieke's mind back to the conversation.

"It's an impressive institution," she said politely. Her smile became more natural. "Honestly, it's very similar to ours."

He chuckled. "I figured as much. I'd still be curious to visit Ondford one day, though. Perhaps these exchanges can become more frequent."

"That would be great," Marieke agreed. Privately, she was thinking that the Oleandans were less likely to welcome a similar delegation than their southern neighbors had been. They had nothing to be ashamed of in the state of their academy. But the increasingly barren landscape wasn't something they would be eager to invite the other country to observe more closely.

"Well, feel free to look around." The librarian waved generally toward all the books.

"Thanks, but I want to show her the student accommodation wing," said Veronica. She smiled at Marieke. "You can always come back to the library later."

"I might do that," Marieke agreed.

"Well, I'll bid you farewell, then," the librarian said. "Or safe journeys, or whatever parting words are politest in your culture. I would have read up on Oleandan customs if I'd known I was to have a foreign visitor."

Marieke laughed. "Goodbye is perfectly acceptable," she said. A thought occurred to her, and she added, "Although I think I do know the customary greeting in Aeltas. What is it? *May the land be firm beneath your feet and gentle under your touch.*"

As she repeated Zev's parting benediction, she could almost feel the phantom sensation of his callused fingers warm on the skin of her collarbones.

"That's not Aeltan," objected Veronica. "I've never heard that before."

"Really?" Marieke looked from her to the librarian. "I thought…it seems I misunderstood again."

"No, hold on." The older man looked thoughtful. "It does sound vaguely familiar. Give me a minute." He heaved himself from his chair, bustling across the room to a tightly packed shelf next to one of the oriel windows. The two girls followed more slowly.

"Here it is," said the librarian, after a few minutes of silent searching. "The talk of foreign customs triggered my memory. This is a book written by an Oleandan visiting Aeltas almost two centuries ago. They recorded some of our customs of the time, and that phrase seemed familiar. It's right here."

He pointed to the page, and Marieke leaned forward to read the account.

*They greet strangers with great intention in both city and countryside. Farewells are usually accompanied by a word of blessing for the journey, however short. In the capital, these greetings and farewells are accompanied with more formality than in the rural areas. Unlike in Oleand, even those with status and wealth are in the habit of acknowledging the dangers that could befall one another before next meeting. The highest and most substantial of farewells is used primarily by the wealthy and influential. It is an invocation for the land to be solid beneath the other's feet but yielding under their hands.*

"There." The librarian sounded pleased. "That's quite similar to what you said, isn't it?"

"I suppose so." Veronica was clearly unconvinced.

"No, it is," said Marieke. "Very similar." Zev's words had indeed felt like an invocation, as the record said. But he wasn't from the city, nor did he hold a wealthy or influential position. He was a farmer, with no reason to use fancy, formal greetings from a bygone time.

"In any event, if it was a traditional blessing, it's a very old-fashioned one, out of use for a long time," the librarian said, returning the book to its place. "We're less formal in our greetings and farewells now, I'm afraid."

"As are we," Marieke agreed distractedly.

More than ever, she was unable to banish Zev from her mind. There was something very unquantifiable about him. And yet, nothing she'd experienced or learned lessened her conviction that he was just as solid and dependable and unshakable as he seemed. She'd never before met someone who managed to be so uncomplicated yet also so steeped in questions. It shouldn't have been possible.

She was aware of giving less than her full attention to the rest of the tour. She just couldn't pull her mind from the young farmer, who had all the strength and confidence of a man raised to work hard for his family and bread, but who spoke like an educated man, carried a costly sword, and conversed with a member of the Council of Singers without the slightest sign of awe or intimidation.

And who had a poor opinion of people like her, she reminded herself disconsolately.

Although he at least had been kind in spite of that prejudice. Most intriguing of all was that her inquiries didn't support the idea that the curious details about Zev and his family were simply a difference between Aeltan and Oleandan farmers. It seemed they were an anomaly even in their own country.

The next few days were spent in a similar fashion. Marieke

explored the academy, rifled through records in the library, sat in on a couple of classes, and observed the practical exercises through which the student singers were trained to harness their songcraft. She tried to be attentive in spite of her divided focus, but other than small variances in style and emphasis, she couldn't observe anything strikingly different from the way Oleandan singers were trained.

Solomon often joined her in her observations, although at other times he shadowed instructors rather than students. Each evening they discussed the day's observations, and they were in agreement. They'd seen nothing that would provide an explanation for why the land of these singers thrived so much more than their own land. The Aeltan singers were learning the same magical theory, being exhorted to exercise the same control and care, and being prepared for similar types of service as their Oleandan counterparts. It was hard to imagine that the general exercise of magic across Aeltas was wildly different from their northern neighbor.

And yet, in her ride from Zev's farm to the capital, Marieke had seen indisputable evidence that the land was as fertile as Oleand had once been, if not more so. Meanwhile the Oleandan countryside she'd traversed on her way to Sundering Canyon was failing quickly.

Why would the border between countries be such a stark divider? It didn't seem natural.

But then, nothing about Sundering Canyon seemed natural, she reminded herself. A shudder went over her as she remembered Gorgon and his attempt to throw her from the cliff path. Where was he now? Had he been chastised by that intimidating woman in charge? Or did they all just think she'd escaped, with none the wiser about his role in her disappearance?

Marieke had been in Aeltas for less than a week when Isabel sought her and Solomon out during the midday meal. They were eating with some of the senior students in the large dining room, the table decorated with beautiful patches of color from the light coming through the stained-glass windows.

"I'm afraid I have some sobering news," the councilor said, joining them at the table. "It seems we'll have to cut our visit short."

"Return to Ondford?" Marieke asked, disappointed. "Already?"

"It's unfortunate," the older woman agreed. "But given the report I just received, I don't think we have much choice."

"What report?" Solomon pressed.

"The team of structural singers have finished repairs on the bridge," Isabel said. "And although they've cleared it for crossing, they've officially registered their concern with the council. They don't have confidence in the stability of the structure once the initial reconstructive power wears off."

"What does that mean?" Solomon asked, aghast. "Are you saying they might close the bridge altogether?"

"They might be forced to," she said. "Neither Oleand nor Aeltas will wish to risk travelers plummeting to their deaths every time they cross the bridge." She looked between them. "As you can imagine, there's a significant number of travelers hurrying to cross now, many of whom have been waiting days to be allowed to continue their interrupted journeys. If there are structural concerns, the wear on the bridge will be accelerated by so much passage."

"So we need to go now or risk being stuck here," Marieke said slowly.

"That's it in brief, yes."

Marieke felt a sinking disappointment that she knew was foolish. Much as she'd been enjoying her time at the Aeltan academy, there was nothing to keep her there. She'd expected weeks not days, but she'd already observed enough to draw what little conclusions she could.

She had a shameful suspicion that her disappointment at leaving Aeltas immediately, and likely forever, had more to do with the fact that it would end any chance of another encounter with a certain well-built, unflappable farmer. But that was absurd. Staying in Tarandon wouldn't bring her across his path again anyway.

"What will they do if the bridge is no longer usable?" asked Veronica, who was sitting nearby. She and Marieke had become friendly. "How will we trade and pass information between our countries?"

"The loss of the bridge will certainly provide challenges," said Isabel, in a non-response typical of the council's diplomatic ways.

"Perhaps we'll have to start sailing again," said Veronica. "Maybe they'll reopen Port Taran."

"The port city northwest of here?" Solomon asked. "I thought Aeltas abandoned that city after we ceased contact with the continent to the west."

"We did," Veronica confirmed. "But that was because when we were only trading between our two countries, we could do so more effectively by land. But Sundering Canyon has gotten much bigger since then, and now the bridge may no longer be usable…" She trailed off with a shrug.

"I see you do your history instructor credit," said Isabel with a smile that didn't quite reach her eyes. Marieke could tell she was concerned about the developments. "But we will have to leave these matters for later solutions." Her eyes passed back to Marieke and Solomon. "For the moment, we need to focus on the immediate future."

They both nodded. "We'll be ready to leave whenever you need us to be," the assistant instructor said obligingly.

"We'll depart the city first thing in the morning," the councilor said. "So use this afternoon for any further inquiries or farewells."

It didn't take long to pack—thankfully Marieke's belongings had actually made it back to her, a bit pointlessly since they were now to turn around and head once again for the border. Saying their farewells was a simple task as well. This time, Marieke refrained from attempting to impress anyone with her knowledge of customary partings. And no one at the academy or council copied Zev in sending them off with an invocation for their journey.

The ride to the bridge was a very different experience from Marieke's journey with Zev. The only similarity was the early morning departure. She was once again in a carriage with Solomon, only the guards riding mounts. And there was no winding through dirt tracks or traversing unexpected hilly areas. A broad and well-kept main road led from the capital to the bridge, and there was no need to deviate from it during the hours of their journey. They stopped once at a posting house for rest and refreshment, but otherwise maintained a quick pace. Clearly Isabel was eager to see her charges safely back into Oleand as efficiently as possible.

Of course Marieke could see less from her carriage than she had on horseback, but that wasn't the only reason the journey felt so different. The direct route didn't take them through much farmland. It was more populated than the area where Zev lived, with towns scattered regularly all the way along the main road. Marieke realized that she was probably the only member of the delegation who'd had the chance to really observe how much more arable Aeltas was than Oleand.

And that didn't help anyone much, because she had no idea what to make of it.

They reached the bridge not long after noon, and as expected, they joined a long line of parties waiting to cross.

"Apparently it was much worse yesterday."

The cheerful pronouncement came from Kaine. On arrival at the bridge, he'd emerged from whatever vehicle he'd been in before, insisting on traveling across with them. Supposedly he intended to prevent catastrophe.

Beyond a dark look, he wasn't even deterred by Solomon pointing out that his presence hadn't prevented Marieke from plunging into the canyon last time.

"No one's plunging anywhere today," said Marieke firmly, ready to drop the topic. Her stomach had begun to twist in uncomfortable knots from the moment she caught sight of the bridge through the carriage window.

They weren't in the carriage now, instead standing with their packs behind the other travelers waiting to cross the bridge. Part of the reason there was a delay was that no one was crossing in vehicles. Their empty carriages were to be led across by one coachman per vehicle, and the rest of the party would cross on foot. It seemed that the singers who'd repaired the bridge felt that it would be safest to distribute weight more gradually. It was more tedious, but would make the power of the reconstructive enchantments last longer.

Marieke hadn't been thrilled with this information. She'd planned to stay in the vehicle this time, rather than going to the canyon's edge for a closer look. She felt she'd seen more than enough of the ravine to last a lifetime.

But she didn't complain. She just clutched her pack tightly, trying not to let her eyes stray to the terrifying drop past the edge of the canyon ahead. She could feel the sensation of falling much too clearly, and remember the terror of those first instants when she'd been certain she would die.

Regretting the food she'd just eaten, she shifted so her back was to the canyon. Solomon was chatting to Kaine, both of them seeming oblivious to her discomfort, which was probably for the best.

In spite of her misgivings, when they eventually reached the front of the line, the bridge held firm beneath their feet. They crossed over it at a brisk pace that wasn't much slower than the carriages had taken them, everyone's spirits lifting as their own country came into reach. Struggling it might be, but Oleand was still home, after all.

When they reached the central point of the bridge, where the arc peaked and began to once again descend, Marieke couldn't stop herself from glancing into the canyon.

"It's a long way down, isn't it?" Solomon said beside her. He and Kaine had kindly flanked her so she wasn't near the edge.

She just nodded, directing her eyes forward again. It was hard to believe she'd survived that fall only a week ago. Was Gorgon down there, still angry about her escape? One of his fellow monarchists had accused him of being obsessed with watching the bridge. Was he watching their passage now?

In spite of being able to feel the reconstructive enchantments coating the structure, Marieke didn't breathe naturally until they stepped off the other side of the bridge. They'd made it. They were back in Oleand.

She and the others moved off the road, standing in a clump to one side as they watched the rest of their delegation cross. Other travelers continued on, some to where vehicles were waiting. Last of their group was Isabel, who'd insisted on seeing everyone else in the group cross before doing so herself. She was flanked by two guards, both of whom looked as tense as Marieke felt. But they traversed the structure without incident, stepping off onto Oleandan soil to join the rest of the delegation, now standing some distance from the bridge. The delegation leader gave a nod of approval as she came to a stop next to Solomon. They'd escaped disaster this time.

The thought had barely occurred to Marieke when a rumbling sound reached her ears. Everyone still on the bridge —which included no one from their group—froze, looking around in fear. But as Marieke swiveled her own head around, she realized that the noise wasn't coming from the bridge. It was coming from the edge of the canyon nearest their own position, the accompanying vibrations spreading to the ground immediately beneath her feet.

"What's that?" Solomon gasped. "Do you feel it?"

Trying to master her panic, Marieke focused her extra sense, realizing what he meant at once. It didn't feel like the last time, when power had rushed up from the canyon toward her in a concentrated beam. It was more like the magic in the ground at their feet was unsettled, rebelling against the bounds of the earth. She turned slowly, wondering how she'd managed to maneuver herself to be the closest to the canyon. Not that she was especially near the ravine's edge.

The guards who'd been flanking Isabel sprang into action, ushering the group further from Sundering Canyon. Marieke had barely taken a step, however, when the rumbling intensified, and a crack made her glance behind her. To her horror, she saw a fissure opening in the ground itself, rushing from the ravine's edge toward her. Before she could move, the soil she was standing on rose and fell like a wave, sending her to her knees.

A cry beside her suggested that Solomon had also been affected, but she had no aid to give him or anyone. She was too busy trying to scramble to her feet, a task that proved impossible as the ground continued to pitch beneath her.

Fear clawing at her, she gave up trying to stand, and just clung to the rolling ground. Casting her eyes around for help, she saw with dismay that Kaine on her other side was in even worse straits, his legs dangling into a chasm in the earth that hadn't been there a minute before. As she watched, another guard, lying flat across the pitching ground, reached out a hand and tugged him back onto solid footing. On Marieke's other side, Isabel and Solomon were stranded on a miniature island of rock, the gap between them and the next stable ground too far to jump. As Marieke watched, the delegation head let out a terse, controlled song, and a large exposed root stretched itself out into a tenuous pathway which she and Solomon dashed across in turn, received by the guards awaiting them further away from the canyon's edge.

Marieke was chastened by the older woman's example. She'd been on edge since they'd neared the bridge, and she'd let her panic distract her from addressing the crisis through her songcraft. She'd been better trained than that. Still on her knees, she stretched her fingers out into the dirt, seeking the power she knew lingered beneath the surface of the land. But just as she was marshaling her thoughts to craft a song, she felt the bucking ground start to settle. The rumbling died down, and within moments, all was still.

Marieke raised her head, staring in awe around her. The bridge and its immediate surrounds appeared to be unaffected. But the same couldn't be said for the patch of ground where the delegation had chosen to congregate. The rest of the group now stood huddled at the new edge of the canyon, a significant distance from where the ravine had begun before. Only one spit of land, the one on which Marieke was perched, jutted precariously halfway out to the canyon's former edge. The fissure that had seemed to be racing toward her had obviously branched off in a different direction.

Not wanting to take chances, Marieke scrambled to her feet

and hurried toward the firmer ground where the rest of the group awaited her.

"Are you all right?" Solomon's pale face loomed into her vision.

She nodded, coughing as dust swirled around them. "I seem to have dodged it. Or it dodged me. You?"

"I'm fine," he said. "It was close for a moment there, though." His eyes were unnaturally wide as he peered down toward the ravine's edge. "What was that?"

"I've heard rumors that Sundering Canyon has been expanding," one of the guards said, sounding shocked. "But I had no idea it was happening so dramatically."

"It's not," Isabel said grimly. "Or at least, it hasn't before now. Not that I've ever heard."

Marieke squinted as she tried to make out the far side of the ravine. It didn't look as though the edge had moved there at all. Or on any other section of the Oleandan side. Just their own little patch.

"The sooner this blasted crossing is behind us forever, the better," Solomon said fervently.

"I agree." Isabel spoke crisply, signaling to the guards further back who were watching the horses and vehicles. "Dealing with the change in the land here is not our role. My priority is getting us all safely back to the capital."

No one made any complaints as they were ushered into the carriages and began the long onward journey to Ondford. Kaine rode with them again, and he and Solomon talked animatedly about the scare they'd just received, speculating about what force of nature or magic was accelerating the growth of the canyon.

Marieke, far from her usual talkative self, took no part in the conversation. She just sat back against the carriage wall, holding her pack tightly to her. Even miles down the road, her heart was still pounding. Although she'd escaped a fall this time, when she closed her eyes, she still felt the sensation of plummeting into nothingness.

She should be glad that the bridge was intact, given how many people had been crossing it at the time. But she was unnerved that only their group had been affected by whatever had just happened. Surely it was too strange a coincidence that both of their crossings had been attended by such catastrophes.

As for her, she knew she'd been lucky. Somehow she'd been the only one of those standing close to the new ravine's edge to not have the ground actually fall away beneath her. The others had needed to be rescued, either by the guards or their own songcraft. She'd just had to wait it out.

Staring unseeingly out the window, feeling again in memory the way the shaking earth had felt under her splayed fingers, all she could think of was a strong grip on her shoulders and an invocation spoken in a low, confident voice.

*May the land be firm beneath your feet and gentle under your touch.*

# Zev

Zev walked along the row, inspecting the growing stalks. His father was right. This year's yield was likely to be even better than last year's. Provided no disaster overtook them.

Not that Zev was one to anticipate disaster. He didn't see the benefit in borrowing troubles from tomorrow. Or in pulling them from yesterday to taint today's sunshine, he reflected ruefully, his eyes lingering on his brother's figure at the far end of the field.

Azai had been in a disgruntled temper ever since hearing Zev's news from the capital. He seemed to be most affronted by the fact that the Council of Singers was congratulating itself on the country's prosperity. Zev was irked by it as well, but he was able to move past it in a way that seemed beyond his brother. Even after a week, Azai regularly brought it up.

"Zev! Azai!"

The faint voice carried from the direction of the yard, and Zev shouldered his hoe. His weeding task was sufficiently completed for the day, anyway. There was nothing causing concern in this field. It was early for dinner, though. What had made his mother call them? Curious, he made his way down the row, his eyes straying in the direction of his orchards. He'd hoped to have an hour to spare for them before the evening meal.

Azai was waiting for him at the edge of the field, and the two brothers walked toward the house together.

"Look," Azai said, gesturing with his head toward the horse tied to a fencepost in the yard. "Someone must have called in."

In light of this information, the two men took a moment to wash up in the trough near the side door before entering the house. Sure enough, they found both their parents seated at the scrubbed dining table, their mother pouring cold cider into a glass for a tall man with a fiery beard.

"Afternoon, Leonard," said Zev, recognizing one of their neighbors.

"Afternoon, boys. Thank you kindly, Narelle." He sat back, receiving the cider from Zev's mother. "Trust I find you all well?"

"I'm not sure I like this plan, Leonard," said Zev's father, disregarding the pleasantries. "If the bridge is on the way out, is it really the sensible time to invest in building relationship with the Oleandan farmers' collective?"

"Oleandan?" Azai repeated, predictably unimpressed by the suggestion of cooperation with the northern country. "What are you talking about?"

Leonard took a draft of the cider before responding. "You remember. There was talk at our last meeting about the idea of sending assistance to the Oleandan collective."

"We weren't at the last meeting," Zev reminded him. He took a seat across from the older man, who served as a representative of their local farmers' collective. "One of our mares was foaling."

"Ah, that's right. I forgot." He nodded. "Well, we've all been hearing the rumors that times are hard for farmers in Oleand. One of our members has links to an Oleandan collective in the southern part of their country, because his daughter married across the border. Their region seems to be suffering more than most. A whole generation of seed was spoiled. They're desperately in need of fresh seed, and some other supplies, or they'll be setting up for yet another terrible year."

"Let their own country take care of them," said Azai indignantly. "We don't want to strengthen ties with Oleand. The Council of Singers is doing more than enough of that nonsense."

"That's precisely the point, lad," Leonard said calmly. "Many at our collective see the benefit in forging our own ties, independent of the council or the high and mighty from the city. Not with the Oleandan elite, but with those like us. We don't want to be dependent on the Council of Singers to speak for us to our neighbors. Not when they don't know the first thing about what we do or how we live."

"There's something in that," mused Gideon. "But what if the bridge is already closed by the time the group gets there?"

Leonard sighed. "Then they'll turn back, I suppose. Word is they're going to start a ferry service over at the old port city, for another way into Oleand. That's probably how the group would have to come back, I suppose."

"What's happening with the bridge?" Zev asked, pouring himself some cider.

"There was another incident," Leonard said. "Strangely enough, it was when the delegation from Oleand was crossing back over."

"What do you mean?" Zev's voice was sharp as he sat up straighter. "Were they injured?"

"No injuries, I believe," said Leonard, raising an eyebrow at his tone. "It wasn't actually even the bridge that was damaged.

It was the land, on the other side. Apparently a whole section of the ravine has widened."

Azai gave a low whistle. "So those rumors are true as well, are they? Sundering Canyon is extending further northward. Oleand really is in trouble, isn't it?"

"Which makes it a strategic time to show goodwill, if you ask me," Leonard said. "They won't forget a good turn when they're in need. And when they rally, as I'm sure they will, bonds will be all the stronger."

"An admirable attitude," Gideon said, his tone not giving much away. "And we can certainly spare some seed. Zev and Azai will bring some around tomorrow. But personally I wouldn't advise going on the expedition. These are uncertain times in Oleand, from all we hear."

"Thank you, Gideon." Leonard chuckled. "And I'm not joining the group, don't you worry. They are looking for more able-bodied volunteers, but they don't want old folk like me. They want young, strong things, like these two." He nodded his head toward the brothers.

"Not likely," Azai muttered.

Zev, on the other hand, considered his neighbor thoughtfully. "They're looking for volunteers to join the trip into Oleand, are they?"

"Zev." He heard the warning note in his father's voice, but chose to ignore it.

"When do they leave?"

"In a few days. Word is the bridge may not be open much longer, so we need to act quickly." Leonard looked him over with interest. "Should I tell them you're interested?"

Zev considered for only a moment before giving a curt nod. "Yes, I'll go."

"Zev!" It was Azai who protested this time.

Leonard chuckled at the younger man's shocked face. "The

invitation is open to you too, Azai." He turned to Zev. "I'll have my boy come past tomorrow with the details. He's going, too, and fair excited about it. You young people have more energy for adventure than we do."

With the words, Leonard drained his cider and took his leave. Azai barely waited for him to exit the dwelling before turning on his brother.

"Zev, what are you thinking?"

Zev shrugged. "That I'd like to go. It will be an interesting experience, and I agree that it's worth forming ties with our Oleandan counterparts, separate from any formal council agreements." He looked at his parents. "Everything is in hand here. It's not as though harvest is near—it's good timing."

"We can manage here," his father said slowly. "That's not my concern. Zev, I don't know if it's wise for you to leave Aeltas."

"It's not a question of wisdom," said Azai hotly. "It's a question of loyalty."

"Azai, that's enough." The sharp voice belonged to their mother. "Questioning Zevadiah's loyalty is taking it too far."

"Is it?" Azai gave his brother a challenging look. "Or am I right in thinking your sudden interest in going to Oleand relates to a certain starry-eyed Oleandan girl who, in case you forgot, is a *singer*?"

"Don't be absurd," said Zev, annoyed with his brother for the accusation and even more annoyed with himself for being rattled by it. Even his mother had cast a quick look at him on Azai's words.

"It didn't escape my notice that you offered to join the expedition only after learning that her group had returned to Oleand," Azai said, his eyes narrowed.

"Marieke would have no connection to a farming collective in Oleand's south," Zev said impatiently. "Her family home is in the northern part of the country, and I'm fairly sure she lives in the capital, anyway. She has nothing to do with this."

"So you claim." Azai still didn't sound convinced, but Zev was out of patience with his brother.

"If we're not needed in here any longer, I'll go see to the orchard. If I'm going away for a while, it'll need extra attention." He cast a look at his brother. "I can't imagine you're going to keep it in order while I'm gone."

"No," Azai retorted. "I'll have my hands full doing your share of the work around the rest of the farm."

Zev ignored him, abandoning his cider and striding from the building. He was unmoved by his brother's complaints. His parents could easily afford to hire extra help in his absence if needed. Just like when Zev had taken the day to see Marieke safely to the capital, Azai's issue wasn't really with Zev getting out of work so much as with his decision to help the singer.

A decision Zev would never regret, regardless of how much his brother complained. As his steps took him toward the orchard, his mind was full of thoughts of Marieke. He'd found it uncomfortably difficult to put her from his mind in the days since he'd seen her safely to Tarandon. And whatever he told his brother, the unspoken possibility of encountering her had played a role in his decision to travel to Oleand.

It wasn't likely, he knew. It was perfectly true, what he'd said to Azai about the lack of connection between the life of the newly graduated singer and the farming collective he was to visit. But he nevertheless found himself, for the first time in his life, drawn by curiosity to explore outside his own country. He'd never imagined leaving Aeltas, and he felt a stirring of excitement at the prospect.

And if fate once again brought him and Marieke together, the way the land itself seemed to have led him to her last time, who was he to fight it?

Zev stepped off the bridge, leading his horse behind him. So this was Oleand.

It wasn't the best first impression, he noted, as an Oleandan border guard chivvied him along, face tense as he turned to the next arrival. But to be fair, the Aeltan guards on the other side of the bridge had shared the same anxious demeanor. Zev was inclined to think that Leonard was right, and they would have missed their opportunity to cross if they'd delayed much longer. The bridge seemed to be in fine shape for the moment, but if its structure couldn't be trusted, it wouldn't be able to remain in use.

He glanced sideways, taking in the jagged edge of ravine that jutted considerably further northward in one section than along the rest of Sundering Canyon. So that was where the Oleandan delegation had nearly been swallowed up, at least according to the tale going around. Had Marieke been affected? Looking at the edge of the canyon, he could almost see her pale face, deep blue eyes wide, and dark hair disheveled as she clung to the rock.

But that had been a different day, a different side of the ravine. His side, he reminded himself grimly. For all Azai's smug attitude to Oleand's troubles, there was plenty of reason to think Aeltas would be affected in time as well.

Zev's life, at least, had already been affected.

Once the whole group had crossed the bridge, they remounted and reassembled. Ramsey, Leonard's son, positioned his horse beside Zev's.

"Well, we made it across," he said cheerfully. "It was a bit boring, actually. I was expecting something more dramatic."

Zev smiled. "I think we should be grateful this part was

boring. We'll have to look for excitement elsewhere on the trip."

"If not excitement, at least some variety," Ramsey said, bouncing in his saddle. "This is fantastic, Zev. No farm chores for days, possibly weeks!"

Zev held in a chuckle. Ramsey was a few years younger than him, and it showed. He was close to Azai's age actually, but his undimmable enthusiasm didn't bear much resemblance to Zev's brother.

"Rumor is that Oleandan girls are prettier than Aeltan ones, too," Ramsey said, his voice lowered conspiratorially. "Might have to keep our eyes open."

"Really?" Zev raised an eyebrow. "Who told you that?"

"Azai said something along those lines," Ramsey told him, as the group started to move along the road. His forehead creased in confusion. "The tone wasn't quite as complimentary as the words. But it's often that way with Azai."

Zev sighed. "Do me a favor, Ramsey, and forget everything Azai said to you about this trip."

"All right," Ramsey said compliantly. "I suppose he's just sour that he didn't get to come."

"Sure," said Zev. "Let's go with that."

The group continued along the main road, their pace steady but not quick due to the two carts of supplies they were bringing with them. It gave Zev ample time to observe the landscape around him. It was startling how sudden was the change as soon as they crossed the border. It wasn't as though Oleand was a barren wasteland. But everywhere Zev looked, he could see the signs of a much harder season than his own region had enjoyed. No wonder the Oleandan collective was seeking aid.

They traveled northward for most of the day before turning to the east and stopping at an inn just off the road. Apparently the town they were making for, from which the collective was based, was only a few hours' ride east of the junction.

They spent the night in the inn, Zev sharing a room with a heavily snoring Ramsey, and started again bright and early. They were all farmers, and all up before the sun. Breakfast conversation consisted mainly of how strange it was to wake with no task awaiting them.

By mid-morning, they'd reached the town, and received a much warmer welcome than the guards at the border had extended. Ramsey positioned himself beside Zev when they unloaded the cart, his eyes full of unashamed interest as he examined the town square.

"I'm not surprised they're asking for help. Look at that—even their decorative trees look stunted."

Zev nodded as he lifted a barrel of seed onto one shoulder. "It's quite a different picture from our region, isn't it?"

Ramsey seized a sack of feed, following Zev to where they were piling the supplies under a makeshift shelter.

"It's not as though the weather is inclement, is it?"

"No," Zev agreed shortly. "It's not the weather."

"Thanks boys," said a burly local man. "We've got some food for you in the hall over there once you're done unloading."

Ramsey's eyes lit up, and he redoubled his efforts with the contents of their cart. Zev followed more slowly, his eyes on the middle-aged man with whom the speaker was now conversing. The man had been waiting with the locals when they arrived, but he didn't look like a farmer. He had more the appearance of a city-dweller, and he was carrying a notebook in the crook of one arm.

When the cart was empty, Zev moved toward the indicated hall, noting that the man was still there.

"He's a singer from the capital, apparently," one of the other Aeltans told Zev, seeing the direction of his gaze.

"Someone told me they're sending them out to all the farming collectives to take reports on the problems with the crops."

"Ooh, a singer." Ramsey perked up. "I wonder if he'll do some songcraft for us." He shot a sideways look at Zev, as if remembering something. "Oh, sorry, Zev. Your family is a bit funny about singers, aren't you?"

A pained expression crossed Zev's face. "Can I extend my earlier request? Can you just forget everything Azai has ever said to you?"

Ramsey chuckled, slapping Zev good-naturedly on the shoulder as he loped into the hall, sniffing hopefully at the air.

Zev paused under the veranda. He was glad Ramsey wasn't one to dig too deeply, but Azai's lack of discretion was still troubling. He really needed to speak to his brother about being more circumspect regarding his views on singers.

Not that Azai was entirely to blame, Zev reflected. Their father might be more guarded in his way of expressing himself, but there was no denying he'd raised his sons the same way he'd been raised—to see singers as a dangerous enemy, not to be trusted. When he'd met the oily councilor in Tarandon, Zev had felt in full agreement with this assessment. But that man was part of the country's ruling body, a representation of everything that had been done to Zev's ancestors. Azai's hatred seemed to extend to every singer, even someone like Marieke... Zev found that harder to agree with.

His mind flitted to a couple of days before, when he'd taken leave of his family for this journey. He'd been surprised when his father walked him all the way to the barn and watched while he saddled the mare.

"There's something I need to say to you, Zevadiah," the older man had said. "I don't know if your brother is right that your decision to leave Aeltas for the first time and venture into Oleand is connected in some way with the girl you brought here. And I'm not going to ask you to explain yourself," he'd added, to the great relief of Zev, who'd had no quick answer ready. "But you need to be careful over there, especially around any singers. We can't trust them—we can't forget what they've done."

Zev's father had placed his closed fist on his son's chest, right over Zev's heart. "Remember, Zev. The only song you need is right here."

"I know, Father." Zev could hear his own low voice in memory. Part of him wished he'd said more, perhaps challenged his father on the full ramifications of his prejudice. But it would likely have led nowhere, and Zev wasn't even sure he disagreed with his family. Somehow, since Marieke's brief and dramatic appearance in their lives, he found himself conflicted in a way he'd never known before.

Sighing, Zev began to turn, ready to follow Ramsey into the building for some food. But as he cast his gaze around the town one more time, something caught his eye.

The singer from the city was standing near their now-empty cart. He was chatting with a pair of the locals who'd helped unload the supplies. What drew Zev's notice, however, wasn't the people. It was the tree beneath which they were standing. It was an old chestnut tree with broadly spreading branches. Its foliage looked a little sad, but the tree itself had clearly been around and thriving long before the recent hard times that had hit Oleand. To Zev's eye, it wasn't scraggly, or dying.

That was why it was so surprising to see an apparently healthy branch starting to list, as if about to break off.

Zev had taken several steps toward the trio when a crack split the air and he sprang into motion. The three men were looking around, clearly confused as to the source of the noise, not realizing the danger was above them.

Zev knew what had made the sound, but he didn't waste time looking up at the precarious branch. He'd already launched himself forward, and he collided bodily with the singer a second later. Zev felt the branch connect with his arm with an unsettling crunch, but for the moment his body was swirling with too much energy to feel the pain.

He and the stranger both hit the ground hard, the other man crushed momentarily beneath Zev's form before Zev rolled away, onto his uninjured arm.

"What are you—?"

The singer's angry protest died as he pushed himself to a sitting position and caught sight of the enormous, spiky branch now resting right where he'd been standing. The beam was almost as thick as his torso. His eyes passed to Zev, who was supporting his scratched and bleeding arm with the other hand.

"Did you...you just..." The singer seemed at a loss for words. Ironic, Zev reflected, given his voice was his main asset. "You may well have just saved my life. I don't know what to say except thank you."

Zev grunted, shuffling so that his back could rest against the tree trunk. He leaned his head back onto it and closed his eyes. His head was spinning a little from the pain in his arm, but he didn't think it was anything lasting.

"No thanks necessary."

"We'll have to agree to disagree on that." The singer adopted a business-like tone. "Let me look at your arm." Cool fingers took hold of Zev's injured limb, their light, uncalloused touch very much that of someone unaccustomed to labor. "I can do something about that, at any rate."

The grip on his arm disappeared, and Zev opened his eyes to find the singer looking seriously at him.

"Are you comfortable for me to attempt a healing song on your arm?"

Zev hesitated for a moment. He was surprised by the man's deferential manner. He hadn't really expected to be asked his permission.

What would his family think of him allowing a singer to work on his own body? But the pain in his arm was increasing rapidly, and he figured he'd already catch it from Azai for saving a singer's life for a second time in the span of about three weeks. He may as well go the whole distance.

"All right," he said, not as graciously as he probably should have. "If you're sure you know what you're doing."

"I don't specialize in healing song, but I've studied it more than the average singer," the man said reassuringly. "I won't do anything I'm not confident will work."

Zev nodded, bracing himself in preparation. But before the man could act, one of the locals spoke up.

"We'd best move first, I think."

He sounded worried, and following his gaze, Zev understood why. The cracked stump of the limb still attached to the tree was green and fresh inside, with no sign of the age or decay that would explain a branch dropping. And the branch itself, lying on the ground at Zev's feet, looked healthy, covered in green leaves.

If he hadn't been there and seen with his own eyes that no one had been in the tree, Zev would have suspected someone had hacked the branch off.

And it had fallen straight for the singer.

"Yes, good idea," the stranger said. "What if more branches are in the same state?" He stood up, offering to help Zev stand. He didn't seem to grasp the reason for everyone else's unease— perhaps he knew very little about trees.

Zev pushed himself to his feet without assistance, moving

well away from the chestnut tree and into open space. At the direction of one of the locals, he sat on an upturned crate, still holding his injured arm under the elbow.

The singer approached, once again taking hold of Zev's arm.

"Now, don't be alarmed that I'm going to tell the magic what to do in so many words," the singer told him. "I know that's not as sophisticated as what a specialized healing singer would do. But it will help a relatively inexperienced one like me direct the power with precision." He smiled in a friendly way. "And have the benefit of explaining what I'm doing to you as I go. When I've been to see a healing singer, I've always preferred to have the process explained to me. And many experienced healers don't think to do that."

Zev just grunted. The man had clearly overestimated his subject's knowledge of singing—Zev had understood very little of the explanation. But he had enough pride to wish not to advertise his ignorance.

The man positioned his hands around the part of Zev's arm that had been hit by the branch. He cleared his throat meaningfully, then began to hum. The sound was wordless, the man's mouth not even open yet, but Zev had the sense it was doing its job. Perhaps it was his fancy as he imagined the power pouring from the ground and into the man's body, but the singer seemed to swell as he hummed. Looking again at the man's face, Zev realized that the stranger was singing now, although the song was wordless. He had a deep voice which was pleasant to the ear, traitorous as Zev felt to find anything to admire in songcraft.

In spite of himself, he listened in fascination as the man's song changed, his pitch staying low but a definite melody appearing. His voice wove around the words, and Zev was surprised to realize he was addressing himself to Zev's arm. The words of the song worked their way through the hidden layers of Zev's body, telling his bone to hold strong and solid, instructing his muscles to knit themselves together. His nerves, his veins, his skin...all received attention. And as the song grew, Zev could feel his body respond. The pain receded. It didn't disappear altogether—it wasn't a numbing sensation. Rather, it settled to the dull ache of a healing wound. The abrasions on his skin were still there, but the bleeding had stopped. It was as though the healing process had been advanced by weeks.

At last, the man let his voice drop, not all of a sudden, but in a gradual descent that was strangely soothing to the ears. All was silent for a moment as Zev regarded his much-improved injury.

Zev was the first to speak. "I thought you would speak to the magic, not to me."

The man gave a distracted smile as he looked his handiwork over. "I could have done so. But I find it easier to speak with the voice of the magic, if you know what I mean."

"I don't," Zev said bluntly.

The stranger lowered Zev's arm carefully, looking up again at last. He was visibly more tired than before, as though the effort of the healing song had cost him a great deal of energy.

"It looks good to me. It will take some time to heal all the way, but I think it will be fine. And what I mean about my choice of words is that I like to phrase it as if I *am* the magic, vocalizing whatever task I want the magic to do. It's as though the magic is telling your body to heal."

He seemed to catch Zev's expression, because he frowned. "Is everything all right?"

"With my arm?" Zev said. "Yes, it feels much better now. Thank you. With the rest of it..." He flexed the fist of his newly healed arm slowly, watching his own movements with furrowed brow. "I'm not quite sure how I feel about my body obeying commands from a magical force, without my mind even having a say."

The singer gave a smile. "Well, that's the beautiful, dangerous power of magic, isn't it? It's strong, whether used for good or evil. That's why those of us with the ability to channel it have such a solemn responsibility to learn to control it wisely and reliably." He stood, picking up his notebook from where he'd laid it on the ground. "That's also why I asked for your consent before commencing the healing. It's a core teaching of the Academy of Song not to use magic on another human being without that person's approval. Did I err in proceeding?"

"No," said Zev, acknowledging to himself the justice of this point. "No, you didn't err. I'm very grateful to you. I'd be a lot less use to the community here with an arm in a sling."

"Your attitude is to be commended," the singer said warmly. "But I haven't even asked your name!"

"Zevadiah," Zev said.

Somewhat to his unease, the singer wrote it down in his notebook. "Thank you again, Zevadiah. I'll be sure to give an account of your heroic conduct to the council."

"I'd really rather you didn't," Zev said firmly. "There's no need whatsoever to make a fuss."

"Actually, I think some fuss might be necessary," said one of the locals. His eyes were fixed on the branch lying under the tree. "Not regarding Zevadiah's involvement, if he doesn't wish it. But I'm not convinced that limb was shed naturally. That's a healthy tree." His voice turned dry. "We've got enough dying plants around here to know how to recognize one that's actually thriving."

"What are you saying?" The singer frowned. "You suspect sabotage? But no one was in the tree. And if by not natural you mean magical, well..." He shrugged. "I can sense the release of magic, you know. I didn't feel any."

"Well, I don't know anything about that," shrugged the local man. "But I do know about trees, and that chestnut has stood outside my family's house for longer than your life and mine combined. All I feel qualified to say is that I think the incident bears further investigation."

The singer looked very thoughtful. Zev wished he could edge away and remove himself from the conversation, but he couldn't see a natural way to do so. It was a strange circumstance. It was the second time in only a few weeks that he found himself regretting, not his decision to save someone's life, but the potential for that decision to bring him to the notice of the Council of Singers. A different country's council, in this case.

"Very well," said the singer slowly.

He also glanced at the leafy, splintery limb on the ground, then up at the tree. Was he reflecting, like Zev was, that the branch had seemed almost targeted in how exactly it had fallen onto his position?

"If you think it's worth investigation, I'll make a report to the council," the man went on. "Someone more qualified than either of us can decide whether anything was suspicious about it."

The local man nodded, seeming satisfied, and Zev took the opportunity to stand. He would likely be called upon to share his account of the incident, which was unfortunate. But he comforted himself with the reflection that however grateful this singer might be for Zev's intervention, the council was unlikely to be impressed by the simple action he'd taken.

If anyone from the capital so much as remembered his name an hour from when the report was taken, he'd own himself surprised.

CHAPTER

# TEN

*Marieke*

Marieke leaned into the carriage window, trying to get a good look at the city looming up before them. The journey from Sundering Canyon to Ondford had felt endless, especially when they'd been held up for over an hour only that morning by a road closure no one had bothered to explain, at least to their carriage.

But they were here at last. They passed under the city wall and continued straight on up the slight rise that was the main street. The complex of beautiful stone structures that housed both the council and the academy sat right in the center of the city, atop the low hill on which Ondford had been built. As the familiar building finally came into view, Marieke flopped back in her seat, beyond relieved to be at the end of the journey.

"What's that?" Solomon's sharp voice brought her sitting upright again.

She peered out the window. "What's what?"

"The flag." Solomon shifted in his seat to better look up at the council building as the carriage pulled to a stop, far back in the line. "It's lowered."

Marieke said nothing, a sick feeling racing over her as she

regarded the flag that displayed the symbol of the council. Solomon was right about its position, and that never meant good news. The last time she'd seen the flag flying that low had been when the former Head Instructor had passed away. He'd been years into retirement at the time of his death, but he'd still been honored in accordance with his former position.

As soon as the vehicle was no longer in motion, she swung the door open, tumbling out with Solomon not far behind her. It was only the two of them, Kaine having ridden with some of his fellows for the final leg of the journey. As she stretched her cramped limbs, Marieke scanned the mounted guards, wondering if they had more information.

She caught sight of Kaine, swinging down from his horse, and hurried toward him. He was more likely to answer her questions than the others.

"Did you see the flag?" she asked quickly.

He nodded. "I see it. I think..." He hesitated, then glanced around him. "I think it might have to do with that roadblock this morning."

"Really?" Marieke frowned. "Why? What was it about?"

"Some kind of accident that had just happened," he explained. "We were told when passing by that some people had died. I've only just heard the rumor that those people were from the council."

"What?" Marieke's mouth fell open. "You mean singers?"

"I don't know if my information is accurate," the guard told her. Someone called his name, and he stepped away. "I have to go."

Marieke moved back, biting her lip as she watched him jog to his commanding officer for instructions. The next thing she knew, she was being ushered inside the building by another guard, Solomon and Isabel along with her. The rest of the group followed, but more slowly.

"Why are we being hurried ahead of the others?" she asked Solomon.

He just shrugged, looking as anxious as he had during the latest incident at the canyon. Marieke wished she could return to her comfortable conviction of moments before, that their journey—and its attendant dangers and discomforts—was over.

"I'll find out what's going on," Isabel said reassuringly. "The two of you are free to return to your rooms to rest and unpack." She nodded encouragingly to Marieke. "Mari, we sent word ahead about our early return. They'll have the same room you stayed in prior to the journey ready for you. I'm sure you're eager to return home to your family, but you'll be wanted on site until we've all made full reports on the time in Aeltas."

"Of course," said Marieke quickly.

She felt a little guilty for the thought, but returning home to her family was the last thing she wanted to do. She wanted to stay in the capital until she knew what was going on. She'd returned to Ondford after graduating with the express purpose of finding a role or position in the city, after all.

Of course, now that she was back in Oleand, she was once again at the bottom of the chain of information. She didn't see Isabel for the rest of the day, and it was only by seeking Solomon out at the dinner hour that she finally got her answers.

"Yes, it's true," he told her heavily, as they both ate in the dining hall with the students of the academy. "There was a particularly bad accident on the main road south. A carriage overturned into a small ravine, and its three occupants were thrown out." He shook his head sadly. "All three died."

"And they were from the council?" Marieke pressed.

Solomon nodded. "During our absence, the council decided to send out representatives to all the farming collectives to assess the state of the land. These singers were three of those representatives. They were all going to different collectives, but were traveling part of the way together, before their paths split."

"How awful," said Marieke, her food forgotten as she cupped her face with both hands. "Three of them! And killed while on official business, too. No wonder they've lowered the flags. What a terrible tragedy."

"Yes," Solomon agreed. "From what I hear they were very unlucky, too. It was a bad crash, but should have been survivable. For all three to land in such a way..." He trailed off, obviously not wanting to elaborate on the gruesome details.

For a few minutes the pair ate in silence, their demeanor in keeping with the somber mood of the dining hall at large.

"So I guess the council is acknowledging the deteriorating state of the land more publicly," Marieke said at last. "They must be, if they're sending singers out to meet with the farming collectives about it."

"I suppose so," Solomon agreed. "I think everyone knew we couldn't keep ignoring it forever. It's not like the rest of the country hadn't noticed."

Marieke didn't answer, lowering her spoon as she watched someone enter the room. The student was a stranger to her, but he carried the unmistakable air of someone with news. She watched him make his way to the group nearest the door, discussing something with them in hushed tones. The new information quickly made it around the room, a younger student pausing to impart it to the assistant instructor and the graduate.

"The survivor from the accident just arrived in Ondford," she said. "Apparently the council is interviewing him now."

"The survivor?" Solomon frowned. "I thought all three of them died."

The student nodded. "The three singers all died. But there was also another passenger, a member of the Smiths' Guild, hitching a ride in the same direction on other official business. He was thrown out of the carriage as well, but sustained only minor injuries."

"Minor injuries?" Marieke repeated. "And all three of the others died on impact?"

The student's face was solemn as she nodded again.

"Is he under any suspicion?" Solomon asked.

"I don't think so." She shrugged. "But I suppose the council will determine that for certain after interviewing him."

She moved on to carry the news to the next table, leaving Marieke frowning in thought.

"That's very strange, isn't it?" she said.

Solomon grunted in agreement.

"Do you think...does it make you think of what happened at the canyon?" she pressed.

"What do you mean?"

"Well..." Marieke's frown deepened. "When the ravine widened all of a sudden like that, the ground only fell away beneath you, me, Councilor Isabel, and Kaine."

"We were all standing together, weren't we?" Solomon pointed out.

"Yes, but...we're all singers," said Marieke. "The *only* singers in the whole group."

Solomon put his spoon down. "What are you saying? You think there's a connection between the two incidents because the victims were singers both times? I thought the widening of the canyon was a problem we'd been aware of for ages. Besides," he added, "the ground didn't fall away beneath you, did it? It just shook. And you're a singer."

"That's true," Marieke acknowledged.

She thought again of Zev's parting blessing, but didn't

mention it. She wasn't sure she wanted to share that information with anyone. And how could it have had any impact on the situation? Zev wasn't a singer, and there was no way he was wielding one of the few remaining talismans. It was impossible for any words of his to have conveyed some kind of magical protection.

Solomon was probably right that she was stretching to draw a connection between the ravine's deterioration and the tragic carriage accident. But the thought troubled her, making it impossible to simply return to her meal.

The thought of Zev contributed to her unrest as much as anything else. He was still on her mind as she made her way to her bed soon after the meal. What was it about him—about his whole family—that felt so strange for farmers? And why did it bother her so much to know he thought poorly of singers? They were near strangers—she shouldn't care so much about his opinion. She thought she would have found it easier not to care if the prejudice had been widespread among his countrymen, or even those in his class or region. But it seemed to be more pointed than that.

And, whether logical or not, that made it feel more personal to her.

In spite of her troubled thoughts, Marieke was exhausted enough after the journey to sink straight into a deep sleep. She didn't stir until morning, and only fleeting images at the edge of her awareness suggested that she'd spent at least some of her sleeping hours far from Oleand. Perhaps in the regal tranquility of an apple orchard.

Marieke was pleasantly surprised to receive a summons from the Council of Singers as she was finishing her breakfast. She'd thought she might have to wait days to give her report on the trip into Aeltas, given her unimportance and the tragic events of the day before. But she would be glad to have the task over with.

She followed the messenger into the council's chambers, a large, circular room with high windows that curved cleverly around the upper walls. Light flooded into the space, and rich tapestries lent some color and softness to the stone walls. A soft hum greeted Marieke's ears as she walked through the doorway, telling her that at least one of the guards flanking it was a singer. He was likely releasing some kind of security song, perhaps designed to detect any hidden objects or something along those lines.

There were more people in the room than Marieke had expected. The two rows of straight benches set against one of the rounded walls were almost full. It seemed much of the council had gathered to hear the delegation's report. It was heartening to know they were taking so seriously their responsibility to find a solution to Oleand's deteriorating state. But it was also intimidating.

Marieke's nerves calmed a little as she was ushered to a small row of seats in the middle of the room, and realized she wasn't to make her report alone. Solomon was already there, as were a number of others from the delegation. Isabel sat with the other council members rather than with the delegation, but her presence was also reassuring simply by its familiarity.

"Solomon."

Identifying the speaker, Marieke recognized another familiar face. She should have realized the academy's Head Instructor would be present—his role gave him an automatic position on the Council of Singers.

"What are your reflections on the Aeltan Academy of Song?" the Head Instructor was prompting.

Solomon cleared his throat. "I formed a good impression of the academy," he said. "It was honestly very similar to ours." He went on to recount the reflections he and Marieke had discussed at length. She was just starting to think that she might not be called upon to say anything, when the council member who seemed to be chairing the meeting turned to her.

"You are Marieke, recent graduate of our academy?"

"That's right, Councilor," she said, rising to her feet and inclining her head as she tried to project confidence.

"Do you agree with the impressions formed by Solomon?"

"Yes, Councilor, I do," said Marieke. "I couldn't see any difference in Aeltan teaching or method that would explain the more arable state of their land." She paused, then added, "And I had more opportunity to observe the countryside than the others, as I was separated from the delegation by an accident. It can't be denied that it's noticeably more fertile than Oleand's current state."

"Yes." The councilor's face was stern, but that might just be his usual manner, for all Marieke knew. "We heard of your accident. I'm sure I speak for the whole council when I express how pleased I am at your incredible survival." His voice became even heavier. "Our community has suffered enough tragic loss of life in recent days."

Murmurs of agreement went around the room, and Marieke bowed her head in respectful acknowledgment of the three deceased singers.

"I understand that your fall was not the only trial endured while in Sundering Canyon." The change in the councilor's tone made Marieke stand up straighter. She had the sense he was choosing his words very carefully, which made her think she should do the same.

"Yes, Councilor," she said slowly. "I was amazed to encounter a group of people living down in the ravine."

Mutters passed over the council again. It seemed this information was new to some of them.

"And from Councilor Isabel's account, I gather that these people were hostile?" the councilor pressed.

Marieke hesitated for a moment. Only the young one, Gorgon, had offered her violence. But then, the others hadn't exactly been warm. The leader had almost certainly been planning to lock Marieke up.

"Yes," she said. "I'm afraid they were."

The councilor made a tutting noise with his tongue. "It seems that Aeltas has problems of its own, whatever the state of its land."

Not for the first time, it occurred to Marieke that while they'd all chosen to assume the monarchists were Aeltan, there was no real reason they couldn't be Oleandan. The canyon was, after all, right on the boundary of the two countries. She refrained from voicing this thought aloud, however. It hadn't escaped her that if Isabel had indeed told the tale to this other councilor, he must know about the canyon-dwellers' claim to be monarchists. But he hadn't mentioned that in front of all these people, and she had the sense she would be wisest not to do so either. Especially when the councilor's eyes seemed hawklike in their focus on Marieke's face.

"Thank you, Marieke," the councilor said, releasing her to resume her seat. She did so as the man turned to Isabel.

"Do you wish to add anything beyond what you've already told us regarding the Aeltan Council of Singers?"

"No," said Isabel. "Other than to reiterate that, as Solomon and Marieke have said about the academy, my main observation of the council is that it is run very similarly to ours. The structure is nearly identical—its thirty members are singers, elected by the country's singers, with the exception of one singer member who is elected by the non-singing population, and two non-singer members elected by the non-singing population as their particular representatives."

"An excellent system, as we can attest," said the officiating councilor with a smile. "And unsurprising that it closely mirrors our own, given that the model was developed in cooperation between the singers of both countries at the time they joined together to liberate both Oleand and Aeltas from the despots who once ruled them."

Another councilor nodded sagely. "I think we can conclude that the foundation of our council, as with the Aeltan one, is above reproach. Aeltas's fertile soil only reinforces our conclusion that there's no reason to think the magic of our land is rebelling and causing deterioration as a result of the structure of our leadership."

"Above reproach?" The words slipped out before Marieke could stop them.

"I beg your pardon?" The tone of the councilor chairing the meeting was icy, and nerves rushed over Marieke as every eye turned to her.

But she told herself to be bold. Her family was loyal to Oleand and its Council of Singers, but this was an area of frustration she'd often heard them express. When would she have another chance to say so in front of most of the council?

"I didn't mean to speak out of turn," she said, lowering her head deferentially. "I agree that there is no reason to think that the land's magic would rebel against our system of government, which clearly operates at least as effectively as the Aeltan one."

The councilor nodded in stern acceptance of this correction. His eyes began to flick away, but Marieke wasn't finished. Her rural community would be unlikely to get another chance to have an advocate before the council itself—which was precisely her point.

"But while the structure both we and the Aeltans use is

surely above reproach from the perspective of the magic of the land, it is open to reproach from the land's people."

"Marieke," Solomon muttered beside her.

"I mean no disrespect," Marieke insisted. "But surely it is in the council's interests to recognize that some among the population may feel frustration that singers are so overrepresented, both in their votes and in the actual councilors."

She saw one man shift in his seat, leaning forward slightly. His expression was more open than most of the councilors, and she realized that his robes were lined in a different color. He was one of the non-singing representatives, then.

"If you have a problem with those chosen by nature to bear the solemn responsibility of songcraft, I suggest you take it up with the magic of the land itself." The face and voice of the chairing councilor were anything but open. "Our system is unbiased for the simple reason that we cannot choose who is and is not born with song. Some of our own children are not singers, and they do not complain about the structure of our council."

Rebuttals burned on Marieke's lips, but she was sensible enough to know they would serve no purpose. Isabel's eyes beamed caution, and Instructor Rafael looked angry. It would only be inflammatory to point out that non-singers privileged enough to enjoy all the status and wealth that came from having a parent on the council had little cause to complain. Or to reflect aloud that it wasn't entirely true that there was no way to control who was born with songcraft. She'd long since learned that in the city, it was common practice for singers from established and powerful families to couple with singers from other such families, to dramatically increase the chances of their children being born with the gift of song.

Satisfied she wouldn't speak, the chairing councilor said no more to her. Instead he turned to the academy's Head Instructor, a hint of acid still in his voice.

"It seems your teaching may not be entirely above reproach, Instructor. I thought your academy was fully committed to *not* graduating seditious singers."

Marieke winced at the mortification she saw hidden under the Head Instructor's lowered brows. *Seditious* seemed unduly harsh, but she'd probably been very out of line to speak up in this company. She hadn't intended to reflect badly on the academy. But she had loyalty to her original—very non-magical—community as well as to the community that had welcomed her when she'd shown signs of songcraft.

"We are, Councilor," said Instructor Rafael stiffly. "As you're well aware."

Marieke looked between the two councilors, realizing that they were speaking of something specific with their veiled words. And she had a suspicion she knew what. Solomon had said that the expelled student, Jade, had displayed an extremely difficult attitude. Had her crime been to question too harshly the way in which their country was run? How grievously could she have made her point for it to justify expulsion, though?

"Thank you for your reports," Isabel said to Marieke and Solomon, her gaze encompassing the other members of the delegation who were seated with them. "You're dismissed."

Still drowning in her own discomfort, Marieke stood and followed Solomon out of the freezing atmosphere of the room.

CHAPTER

# ELEVEN

*Marieke*

Marieke expected to be scolded for the incident in the council chamber, but other than a quiet word from Isabel, she heard no more about it. The councilor's words reflected those of the Head Instructor in his office on that day that felt a lifetime ago.

*Questions are encouraged,* Isabel had told her. *Opinions are welcome.* But her manner hadn't matched the words, especially as she hastened to remind Marieke that discretion should be exercised in how and when those questions were voiced. *We must be honest with ourselves about the attitude behind our objections,* she'd said, with an air of openness that didn't sit right with Marieke.

In fact, the exhortation left Marieke more unsettled than ever. Not because she felt she'd erred as obviously as Isabel seemed to think. But because she was coming to increasingly suspect that all the fancy words that followed were actually a way of changing the meaning of *questions are encouraged* to be *questions should be avoided.*

She knew she'd often irritated her instructors with too many questions when she'd been a student, but she didn't

151

remember it being like this. Had she just not noticed it, or had something changed? Why had the mood of the council meeting been so tense, even before she'd challenged the use of the phrase *above reproach*?

Marieke couldn't shake the memory of the councilor's snide comment to the Head Instructor, and Instructor Rafael's obvious embarrassment in responding. If she was right that the veiled reference related to the expulsion Solomon had mentioned, then whatever had happened with Jade had caused distress not just at the academy but at the council as well.

The councilor had used the word seditious. Just how bad had Jade been?

All this swirled through Marieke's mind as she ate breakfast in the students' dining hall. Solomon wasn't with her this time. Perhaps avoiding her controversial presence after the display at the council meeting, she thought wryly. Marieke didn't regret eating alone, however. She'd learned in her time as a student that for those without the connections to get information directly, the dining hall was the best place to keep up to date with the latest gossip. And the morning's meal was no exception.

Marieke was still mulling on the unknown story of the student, Jade, when the mood of the dining hall changed. She could feel the whisper of new information passing around the assembled diners almost as surely as her extra sense could detect when magic was released. This time no one brought the tale past her table, but by sliding along to the nearest group, she was able to listen in on the gossip.

"Another accident?" a student was saying in dismay. "And it was another one of the representatives sent to the farming collectives?"

A different student nodded eagerly. "A tree branch fell, and apparently the singer has requested an investigation into the incident, so he must be suspicious that there's more to it."

"He's requested it?" a third student piped up. "So he survived?"

"He wasn't even hurt," the first student clarified. "Rumor is that he was saved by an Aeltan farmer."

A strange thrill went over Marieke at the words. A singer, saved from disaster by an Aeltan farmer? Of course it had nothing to do with her own experience. She was being absurd to draw any connection. The words had just been so familiar.

"Aeltan?" The speaker didn't sound too impressed.

"A group traveled across the bridge before it was closed, bringing seeds or something," the first student said dismissively. "I don't know the details."

Marieke bit her lip. An Aeltan group bringing aid to Oleandan farmers? Why couldn't she shake the idea that Zev would be the type to be involved in that? Another foolish thought—his family likely wouldn't let him.

"So are they going to send a group to investigate?" Marieke asked. "Where did this happen?"

The students looked at her, apparently just noticing the presence of a non-student in their midst.

"I assume so," the first student said. "As for where, I think it was pretty far south."

Marieke nodded, her thoughts far away as the others finished their breakfasts and hurried away for classes. Soon she was almost the last in the dining hall. Of course she had no classes, and no formal role to keep her at the academy. Now that she'd given her report to the council, she supposed she was probably expected to leave the complex. It was disheartening, since she'd so hoped that her inclusion in the delegation to Aeltas might create opportunities for a more permanent role.

Picturing the expression on the face of the chairing councilor when she'd questioned his words, she realized she'd probably blown that chance.

When the kitchen staff began to wheel away the tray on which the students had all deposited their dirty bowls, Marieke stood abruptly. If she was soon to lose her excuse for being at the academy, she'd be wise not to waste whatever time she had left. The question of the expelled student simply refused to be banished from her mind, and she couldn't think of anywhere but the academy that she might find answers.

Emboldened by her experience in the Aeltan academy, Marieke made her way to the library where she'd spent many studious hours during her training. As usual, the librarian was to be found striding down the rows of shelves with her clipped gait, ensuring no one was making noise or putting volumes away incorrectly.

Marieke did a circuit of the library before approaching her, hoping vainly that she might find what she was looking for without assistance. When she gave up on that foolish idea, she gathered her courage and made her way to the desk where the librarian had paused her own patrol.

"Marieke." The older woman raised an eyebrow. "I'd heard you were back at the academy. Never done learning, eh?"

"That's right." Marieke smiled, trying to make her voice natural. "I was invited to be part of the delegation to Aeltas, which was an excellent learning experience in itself."

The librarian nodded. "Did you observe their academy? I've heard their library is extensive."

"No more than ours," Marieke said, hoping her attempts to put the older woman in a good mood weren't too obvious. "It was similar in size, at least. I didn't have time to explore too deeply."

Glancing around, she refrained from commenting that their own library was dark and enclosed compared to the Aeltan one, even the layout of the shelves making it feel less open and approachable.

The librarian nodded. "I heard your trip was cut short. I'm glad you all made it back before the bridge was closed."

"Yes, so am I." Marieke realized her hands were fidgeting, and folded them behind her back. "So, I was wondering if you might be able to help me find some information."

"That is my job." In spite of the words, the librarian's tone wasn't what she'd call encouraging.

"Does the academy keep student records?" Marieke asked, aware that her casual tone sounded forced.

"Of course," the librarian said, raising an eyebrow. "But they're not in the library. That would hardly be consistent with maintaining the necessary confidentiality. The Head Instructor is responsible for their maintenance. I can, however, provide you with the appropriate application form if you wish to access yours." She pinned Marieke with a searching look. "Are you concerned about what might be recorded there?"

"Oh, no," said Marieke quickly. "I don't wish to access my records. I was actually wondering about a different student."

The librarian had opened a drawer, presumably to fetch the application form, but she closed it with a snap. "In that case, I can't help you. It would require extraordinary circumstances for someone to be able to access another student's records. Would you wish others to be able to access yours?"

"No, I suppose not," Marieke admitted.

She hesitated, wondering if she should give up on her inquiries altogether. The librarian was unlikely to take well to her next question. But if she was to depart the academy soon, she might not have another opportunity to pursue the mystery of Jade.

"I was wondering about expulsion records, actually," she said boldly. "I heard that there was a student—Jade, I think her name was—who was expelled some years ago. I wondered if the circumstances were a matter of public record."

The librarian leaned back against a pillar, her arms folded as she studied Marieke's face. "Now why would you wish to know that? You're a graduate, Marieke. You're not in danger of expulsion."

"I know." Marieke smiled faintly. "I just wanted to understand the circumstances."

"Well." The librarian pushed herself upright briskly, stepping forward and resuming her seat. "I recall Jade—a bright but recalcitrant student—and I recall her expulsion. My opinion at the time was that it was well-deserved."

Her gaze was still uncomfortably shrewd as she held Marieke's gaze.

"In any event, I can't help you. Expulsions are not conducted secretly, much as it's not something the academy would wish to advertise widely. But nor are they an exception to the rules regarding confidentiality of student records. I don't have any records of the incident in my library."

"I see." Marieke bit her lip. She was tempted to inquire further—clearly the librarian remembered more details than she'd shared. But the body language of the older woman, who was now drawing a stack of parchments toward herself with purpose, wasn't encouraging. "Thank you for your time."

The librarian nodded without taking her eyes off her task, and Marieke withdrew. She wished she had a task of her own to throw herself into, but she was at a loose end. She found herself wondering disconsolately whether the friend who'd hosted her prior to the trip to Aeltas would take her in again. But she didn't want to impose, especially not for an indefinite period. Unless she found a more concrete avenue to pursue for a role with the council, she would probably need to return to her own home.

Marieke was about to pass through the library's doorway when a group approached from the corridor. She stepped back, allowing them to enter. With a smile of greeting, she recognized her former history instructor. The instructor returned her smile pleasantly, although her companions seemed less cheerful. Marieke chuckled internally, remembering Veronica's words in Aeltas. History was no one's favorite subject.

She realized as she watched the students file past that they must be a brand new class. They all looked so young and fresh. Had she really been that young when she arrived in Ondford?

The group congregated in a huddle just inside the library, while the history instructor explained the room to them. The librarian stood, considering the new students from behind her desk with an experienced eye. Marieke hid a smile. She'd probably perfected the skill of spotting troublemakers from their first day.

"Most of what we'll be covering during history classes this term is contained in records in this section," said the history instructor jovially, pointing to a row of shelves. "So if you feel inspired, you can spend your evenings reading up for extra points."

A few nervous titters issued from the group.

"Now, let's see who's done their assigned reading before class," the history instructor went on. Her eyes scanned the group quickly, settling on a boy who, unlike most of his fellows, wasn't trying to avoid her eye. "You. Can you summarize how the Sovereign Realms came to be?"

He straightened, nodding. "Yes, Instructor. Once, Oleand and Aeltas were ruled by monarchies, just like the kingdoms on the continent of Providore, across the westward sea. In those days, singers worked under the monarchs, serving the kingdoms with their songcraft and causing the land to prosper. The monarchs had no magic of their own, and they grew jealous of the singers. In spite of having no claim to power, like the singers were born with, they were despotic with their rule, demanding heavy taxes and indenturing their people to serve them."

He drew a breath, whether nervous or pleased with the attention, Marieke couldn't tell.

"The land and people suffered under the rule of the monarchs until the singers banded together to rescue both kingdoms. Singers from Oleand and Aeltas formed an alliance, and used their combined songcraft to depose the monarchs. The former royals, with their families and supporters, abandoned these lands rather than treating with the singers. They sailed west to Providore for sanctuary, taking false tales with them. As a result, the countries of Providore cut off our Sovereign Lands and ceased trade and communication with us."

"But we've prospered nevertheless," piped up another student. "While as far as we know, the countries of Providore all continue to suffer under monarchies."

"Very good, both of you." The history instructor smiled. "That was an excellent summary, and over the coming weeks and months we will delve into the details of everything you just mentioned."

"What about Sundering Canyon?" The question came from another student, and all eyes turned to her.

"What about it?" the history instructor asked.

"That wasn't mentioned in the summary, but didn't the canyon appear around the same time as the monarchs were overthrown?"

"Yes, that's right." The instructor nodded encouragingly. "And as I said, we will study the details further as we go. Now if you'll follow me through here, I'll show you where you can find the records regarding the structure of the Council of Singers. We'll be covering that in our course as well."

The class moved forward, and Marieke at last slipped through the door, her thoughts heavy. She remembered learning the same details of the history that these students were to learn, and it had made her proud to have been blessed by nature with the gift of songcraft. It had made her feel like she was part of a group who had rescued their people from an oppressive reign and caused their land to prosper.

Except Oleand was no longer prospering. She didn't know whether the rule of the Council of Singers was failing, or whether there was some other cause. But she no longer felt buoyed by the comfortable assurance that their ancestors had undoubtedly chosen the right path because all was as it should be.

Not to mention the accidents now befalling singers from the council. Marieke couldn't shake the fear that they weren't random accidents at all, but connected incidents targeting singers. Marieke's mind strayed again to the tale she'd heard at breakfast, about the singer saved from a falling branch by an Aeltan farmer.

She knew it was absurd to even imagine that farmer could be Zev. He'd been fully settled at his farm such a short time ago, with no indication of wanting to leave Aeltas. And yet, between that errant thought and her suspicions about the series of accidents, she found herself desperately wishing to join the group heading south to investigate.

With that desire in mind, when she received a message that afternoon calling her to once again attend the Head Instructor's office, she dared to hope she might be invited to join the group. After all, the last time she'd been to see Instructor Rafael, he'd offered her a place in the delegation to Aeltas.

Hoping against hope, Marieke hurried through the

academy building toward the wing where all the instructors had their offices. The Head Instructor's office was naturally the largest, consisting of a receiving room that led to his actual office. The door to the receiving room was open, and Marieke went straight in. It was only as she was crossing to the second door that she caught the angry voice issuing from the Head's office and drew up, her stomach dropping. That didn't sound like someone about to extend her a flattering invitation. She should have known it after the incident at the council meeting.

Heart heavy, Marieke walked more slowly, raising her hand to knock on the door, which was only open the tiniest crack. But Instructor Rafael's words made her pause.

"I thought you assured me Marieke wasn't going to be a second Jade."

"She's not."

The responding voice was familiar as well. Marieke was too distracted by the overt comparison of her to Jade to wonder why Isabel was there.

"Marieke is a good girl," Isabel went on. "Honestly, Rafael, I think you're overreacting."

"You heard her in the council meeting. And now I'm told she's been asking about Jade's expulsion?"

"So she's heard the rumors. It's a widely known story," Isabel insisted. "She probably went looking because of what was said about seditious students in the council meeting."

"I hardly need remind you," the Head Instructor's voice was acid, "that ill-advised comment didn't come from me. And the librarian said she asked after Jade by name. She didn't hear that at the council meeting."

"Rafael, you're overreacting," Isabel insisted. "She's not a second Jade. She got curious about a sensational story of an expulsion. It's not like she's asking about heartsong."

*Heartsong?* Marieke frowned over the unfamiliar word. The

guilt she felt at her eavesdropping was well and truly subsumed by her curiosity now. And the Head Instructor's reply, issued in a sharp tone, only increased it.

"Careful what words you bandy about, Isabel." The creaking of a chair made Marieke think that Instructor Rafael had stood up. "You told me yourself Marieke spent time with a group of self-proclaimed *monarchists*. Who knows what stories they filled her head with? In light of that, how can you possibly promise me she won't be a second Jade?"

"I can't promise anything," Isabel said calmly. "But I think you underestimate Marieke's good sense and good intentions. She's not looking to hurt anyone or make trouble. She just needs a little guidance."

Marieke drew a shaky breath, the reality of her own conduct catching up with her. Isabel's affirmation shamed her, given she was listening at the door like a thief. She edged backward all the way to the outer door before striding across the room with as much bustle as she could. The voices in the office fell silent in time for her knock to ring out clearly.

"Enter." The Head Instructor's voice was tight, but when Marieke walked in, Isabel gave her a bracing smile.

"You called for me, Instructor?" Marieke asked, trying to sound like she hadn't just been listening to the exact reason he was upset with her. Not that it had made a great deal of sense.

"Yes, I did." Instructor Rafael pinned her with a hard look. "I thought, Marieke, that Councilor Isabel had explained to you why your little outburst at the council meeting was not appropriate."

A flicker of defiance rose in Marieke. She was still unconvinced that anything she'd said had truly been inappropriate. But she knew what he meant, and this wasn't the moment to quibble.

"She did, Sir."

He didn't look mollified. "Then why do I hear that you've been continuing to make unfounded accusations?"

"Accusations?" The hint of a laugh in Isabel's words sounded forced to Marieke. "I'm not sure how you conclude that, Instructor Rafael."

"I'm not aware of having made accusations," Marieke said cautiously.

"I was led to believe that you were harassing our librarian," Instructor Rafael said sternly. "It seems I need to remind you, Marieke, that you're no longer a student of the academy. We do not employ a librarian in order to answer your every stray question."

"Yes, Sir," said Marieke.

Her voice was steady, but underneath she was a tangle of defiance and mortification. It seemed that, for her at least, questions were no longer encouraged. She thought she under-stood the change now, at least in part. It was clear from what she'd overheard that her exposure to the monarchists in Sundering Canyon had marked her as a threat to the Head Instructor for some reason. It was quite possible that the chairing councilor had reacted so warily to her for the same reason. He'd questioned her about her fall, so he'd obviously heard the story as well.

It all made her feel tainted.

"She understands." Isabel again intervened on her behalf, her voice soothing as she addressed Instructor Rafael. "I'm sure you need say no more. Are we finished here? I'd like to farewell the group heading south for that investigation, and I gather they'll be leaving any time now."

The casual comment seemed like a mockery of Marieke's earlier hope, although of course Isabel knew nothing of it. For her part, Marieke couldn't believe she'd been fool enough to think she was being summoned to be offered another position.

The Head Instructor's next words made it clear that matters were quite the reverse.

"Yes, and I imagine Marieke will wish to be packing to leave as well," he said. "Given she's made her report to the council."

"Yes, Sir."

Marieke's words were clipped this time. Once, as a fresh student, she would have been cowed by these strictures. But now, as an adult free of the academy's oversight, she found that the more unreasonable the Head Instructor seemed, the more she rebelled against his authority. If he was worried about seditious students, she thought irritably, he should stop creating them.

She left the office in a mood of rebellion that would have shocked even her a few short weeks ago. But perhaps Instructor Rafael was right that her experiences in the ravine had changed her. And not just the monarchists—Zev and his family, the prosperity of Aeltas, the disdain of the council when she'd made a very reasonable comment on the structure of their government.

Far from being brought into line by the reprimand, she was starting to feel like her mistake up until now had been not asking *enough* questions. Because there was clearly plenty she didn't understand about the world of singers that she'd been thrown into, and she had a sinking feeling she wasn't going to like what she found when she peeled back the layers.

Which was exactly what she was determined to do.

And the question she found most burning—perhaps because it had become personal across the dramatic incidents at the border crossing—was why were singers falling victim to terrible accidents?

A recklessness seized Marieke as she hurried back to her temporary room. The Head Instructor had told her to pack and prepare for departure, and she intended to do so with a vengeance. It was the work of a moment to shove her belongings into her pack and sling it over her shoulder. The next minute found her hurrying through the hallways, hoping she wasn't too late. Isabel had said the group was to leave any time.

Marieke's heart did a lurch that was half excitement and half nerves when she emerged into the courtyard out the front of the building and saw three carriages assembled there. And best of all, Isabel wasn't present.

To Marieke's delight, she recognized one of the guards in the group mounted at the back. Kaine!

She jogged up to him, summoning a friendly smile. "Phew, looks like I just made it! I was running so late, I thought the group might have left without me."

"Oh, you're coming on this delegation too, are you?" Kaine asked brightly.

Marieke matched this tone, only the slightest jolt of guilt niggling at her. "That's the plan."

"Well, you'd best hop in, then." He dipped his head toward the nearest carriage. "We're about to leave."

Marieke didn't wait for further invitation. Aware that Isabel might appear at any minute, she scrambled into the carriage, relieved that with only two occupants inside, there was plenty of room for her.

"Who are you?" asked one of them, wearing a tunic with the official emblem of the council emblazoned on it.

"I'm Marieke," she told him, dipping her head respectfully. "I'm a singer."

He eyed her lack of uniform. "Are you a council representative? I don't think we've met before, have we?"

She shook her head. "No, I'm not employed by the council. But I'm a recent graduate of the academy, and I've taken a particular interest in this incident."

He leaned back with a sigh, apparently ready to accept it. "I don't know how many singers they think we need to investigate a tree branch falling, but all right."

As he spoke, the carriage lurched into motion, the gray stone of the council building rolling past their window.

Marieke leaned back as well, both impressed and unnerved by her own daring. There would probably be a price to pay when she made it back to Ondford, but for the moment, she didn't care. She was in the group now, and no Head Instructor or disapproving council stood on the road ahead between her and the answers she was determined to find.

The accidents befalling the singers were just the start. There was also the question of what exactly the council was afraid a group of renegade monarchists might have told her, and what Jade had done to get herself expelled. Not to mention what Isabel had meant by heartsong.

And, if it was anything worth knowing, the identity of the heroic farmer who might be waiting for her down the road to the south.

# TWELVE

# Zev

"Zev!"

Zev turned at the shout to see Ramsey beckoning to him. With a grunt, he lowered the sack of seeds he'd just hefted into his arms, mildly irritated by the interruption. They'd been in the Oleandan town for a few days now, and there was plenty to do. The group was only staying a couple more days, and he could already tell that they wouldn't be able to do all they'd hoped to in that time. The locals would have to take over processing their donations once they'd left.

"What is it?" he asked, once he'd exited the storehouse and joined Ramsey in the dubious shade of a scraggly tree.

"A group's just arrived from Ondford," Ramsey told him, looking far too enthusiastic. "Apparently they're here to investigate what happened with that branch, and they want to hear your account. Time for that hero's applause you've been waiting for."

The last comment was accompanied by a cheeky grin. Ramsey was well aware of Zev's feelings on the overblown praise he'd already received for his unremarkable act. Most irritatingly of all, the singer who'd been underneath the branch had developed an annoying habit of hovering near Zev, as if hoping for a chance to repay the favor he felt he owed Zev.

For his part, Zev would really rather just avoid attracting attention.

Right on cue, the singer appeared behind Ramsey, beckoning to Zev with a smile. "Are you free, Zevadiah? The group we requested from the council are here to speak with us."

Zev sighed, dusting his hands off on his pants as he strode across the dusty ground, Ramsey trailing curiously behind him. The singer made it sound like Zev had been the one to encourage investigation of the incident. He had no interest in anyone the Oleandan Council of Singers might send to speak with him.

Or at least, so he'd thought. When he rounded a corner and saw the dark-haired young woman waiting amongst the small group of strangers in uniforms, he performed a rapid recalculation. Suddenly the whole encounter had become considerably more interesting.

"Mari?" The name slipped out before he thought it through.

Her eyes flew to him, and she looked as startled as he felt. So she hadn't known he was there, then. She hadn't come all the way from the capital especially to seek him out.

Of course she hadn't. What a foolish thought to even occur to him. And why had he called her by the nickname she'd told him her friends used? He was only humiliating himself.

"Zev! You're part of the Aeltan group."

The obvious statement didn't seem to require a response, and Zev just stood there.

"You two know each other?" One of the other newcomers looked between Zev and Marieke, whom he noticed was looking flushed.

"Not well," she said, a little too quickly. "We met during the recent delegation to Aeltas."

"You were on that delegation as well?" the man asked. His tunic bore the insignia of the Council of Singers, so he must have been someone official. "They didn't give you much rest before sending you out again, did they?"

Marieke said nothing, her expression suddenly veiled. Zev cleared his throat, deciding it was time to stop his impression of a senseless scarecrow.

"I didn't expect to see you," he said. "Are you here to investigate the incident with the branch?"

"Yes." Marieke's tone turned businesslike, and she turned to one of the others, who smoothly took control of the conversation.

"We are indeed. I understand that you were directly involved?"

Zev shrugged. "I happened to be present at the time."

"And very lucky for me that he was," chimed in the singer who'd almost been crushed by the branch. "I'm ashamed to say I hadn't even noticed anything amiss before he came flying at me and pushed me out of the way. Sustained a nasty injury to his arm in the process."

Zev noticed that Marieke's eyes flew quickly to him at this comment, her gaze raking over his form as if concerned for his welfare.

"You are to be commended," said one of the other singers. "I trust your injury isn't lasting?"

"He healed it at the time," said Zev. "It will be fine."

"You let him heal it with magic?" Marieke's raised eyebrow made Zev wince a little. Her memory was sharp.

"Please tell us what you saw," the first singer encouraged.

Keeping his words succinct, Zev described how he'd noticed the branch looking loose even before hearing the final crack. There wasn't much to his tale, and as he'd hoped, the investigating group soon redirected their interest to the singer who'd been under the branch.

All except one.

"What's your opinion?" Marieke's question caused everyone's eyes to flick to her, then, following her gaze, back to Zev.

She had an inconvenient habit of bringing attention onto him, Zev reflected.

"My opinion on what?"

"On the branch falling," she said. "Do you think it was an accident caused by natural processes, or something more sinister?"

"I can't speak to that," Zev said noncommittally. "All I can recount is what I witnessed."

The others were already turning away again, but Marieke persisted.

"That's not true. You can also give your opinion. And I'd be curious to know what it is."

Zev gave her a look that likely showed his impatience too clearly. But answering her question was probably the fastest way to shift the focus off himself.

"If by *sinister*, you mean whether it was caused by magic, I really don't have an opinion. Not being a singer, I'd have no way to assess that."

"But?" she prompted.

"But," he said, his lips quirking a little at how well she seemed to read him, "I was very surprised by the incident, as were the locals who witnessed it, I think. The tree seemed healthy, and the branch was strong and alive. Even after the branch fell, and its interior was exposed, there was no sign of decay that would explain its deterioration."

"Hm." One of the other investigators frowned, his eyes thoughtful as they traveled from Zev to the almost-victim. "But you say you noticed nothing before this young man rushed toward you?"

"That's right." The singer nodded. "I heard the crack just as the branch was falling, but I sensed no magic before or after the noise. Nothing that would suggest the damage wasn't naturally occurring."

"If it was caused by magic, that doesn't mean it wasn't naturally occurring," Marieke pointed out. Her expression was thoughtful and her tone not quite normal, as if she was quoting something to herself rather than trying to convince others with her own words. "Magic comes from the ground itself, doesn't it? Magic is part of nature."

"True," one of the investigators said slowly. "But he didn't sense any magic."

"Yes." Marieke seemed even more troubled than the others. "Which means whatever caused the branch to drop, it likely wasn't an enchantment released by a singer in the way we know it."

A few of the investigators shot her bewildered looks before the main spokesperson regained control again.

"Let's have a look at the location, shall we?"

The singer whom Zev had saved nodded briskly, beckoning for the group to follow him. Zev hovered, unsure whether he was expected to follow or could now slip away. To his surprise, Marieke also made no move to join the group. She stayed in place, neither saying a word until they stood alone in the patch of yellow grass that had probably once been a pleasant village square.

"I wondered," Marieke said, her voice abrupt. "When I heard that an Aeltan farmer had rescued a singer from a near-fatal accident. I knew the chances weren't high, but I wondered if it was you."

Zev took a moment to process this information. Had she...

was it possible she had come all the way from the capital to seek him out after all?

"You've made quite a habit of that particular type of heroics, haven't you?" she prodded, a smile lifting her full lips and further softening her already cheerful face.

Zev grunted. "The rumors of heroics are vastly exaggerated. I was barely involved."

"That's what you said about your actions when you pulled me from the edge of a cliff," Marieke said flatly. "And in that case, I happen to know that your role was *not* exaggerated in the slightest." She eyed him. "What will your family think of you saving yet another singer?"

"I'm sure my family, like any decent people, would wish me to do all I could for a fellow human being in danger," said Zev mildly.

"A non-answer," she muttered. She looked him over, her eyes lingering on the bandage still wrapped around his arm. The rough fabric of it just poked out from under his rolled-up sleeve. "So is that really all you did? Just pushed him out of the way?"

"Of course," said Zev, surprised. "What else would I have done?"

"I don't know," she said slowly. "But I am curious as to how you knew something was wrong before he did. How did you sense it if a singer couldn't?"

"I didn't sense anything," Zev protested. "I used my eyes—handy tools for those not blessed with songcraft."

"No need to be snide," Marieke said, although she sounded more amused than offended. "You make it sound like the singer had his eyes closed and ears blocked."

"He did fail to notice that a branch was dangling over his head," Zev pointed out. "Something I could see from halfway across the square."

This time, Marieke's smile turned into a chuckle. It was a light sound that made Zev's lips curl in response.

"Fair point." She let out a breath. "So that's all there was to it, then."

"What more would there be?" Zev asked, nonplussed.

"Nothing at all," she said, her words too airy. "I'm sure there wasn't anything else you could have done. Not being a singer, you have no way to sense or access magic, isn't that right?"

"Indeed," Zev said steadily, wondering what was behind her cautious tone and searching questions. Even the way she pursed her lips at his reply seemed to hint at unspoken thoughts behind her words. Did she suspect him of hiding secret songcraft? That was a laughable thought.

*Remember, Zev. The only song you need is right here.*

His father's words floated unbidden through his mind, and he felt again the pressure of the older man's fist on his chest, right over his heart. Perhaps it wasn't completely laughable for Marieke to wonder if he had access to some kind of power. But surely she couldn't be *that* perceptive, could she? As far as he was aware, no one had suspected him or his family for decades. Centuries, even.

He understood why his father felt uneasy at the lines of inquiry being pursued by the two councils as they compared the varying states of their lands. Still, Zev couldn't believe that Marieke knew anything about heartsong. Where would she have learned of it? It certainly wasn't taught at either country's academy, of that much he was confident. He wouldn't be surprised if even the instructors knew nothing of it. The singers who'd overthrown the monarchs certainly hadn't. If they had, everything might have unfolded differently.

But that was useless to speculate about.

"Well," it was again Marieke who broke the silence, "I'm glad to run into you again, anyway."

"So am I," said Zev, responding involuntarily to the warmth of her smile.

"I understand that the group from Aeltas came to offer aid to the local farmers' collective," Marieke said. "That was kind of you." Her smile became a little more shy, the sight making Zev's heart pound harder for some reason. "It's actually another reason I suspected you might be involved somehow."

He swallowed, thrown by the compliment. He decided not to try responding to it. "My neighbor organized the trip," he said instead. "A friend of his has a daughter who married an Oleandan—someone in this collective. They requested some assistance."

"And how do you find the land?" Marieke asked.

Zev raised an eyebrow. "Is that an official question from the council?"

To his surprise, a grin broke out across Marieke's face. "Far from it. To tell you the truth, the council didn't send me. I sort of snuck into the group because I wanted to conduct my own investigations. I suspect I'll be in for a scold when we return to Ondford."

"Really?" Again, Zev found an answering smile tugging at his lips. "I didn't guess you were such a rebel." He considered her shrewdly. "Why did you want to conduct your own investigations?"

Marieke sighed. "Because I'm as concerned as everyone else is." She met his eye unflinchingly. "We both know why your group is here, just as we both know why my delegation came to Aeltas. Our land is failing—we may as well speak openly. After all, I've seen the state of your farmland with my own eyes, and you've now seen the state of mine."

Zev nodded slowly, appreciating her honesty. "The state of

the land here is worse than I expected," he said. He leaned back against a cart, folding his arms. "Ramsey and some of the others wouldn't agree. They think it's not as bad as we'd been led to expect. And I understand why—rumors in Aeltas whispered that Oleand had turned into a barren wasteland, and that's clearly not the case."

"Not yet," Marieke interjected soberly.

Zev considered her. "Yes. Not yet." He cast his eyes southward, toward his own distant country. "In an obvious sense, it's not as bad as we thought it might be. But there are more subtle signs that seem worse to me."

"Like what?" Marieke asked, frowning.

"Like the fact that we're hearing consistent rumors of problems with water sources on local farms," Zev said. "It's all perfectly natural things," he added. "An animal drowning in a dam and the carcass going unnoticed for long enough to contaminate the water, a dry spell causing levels in reservoirs to dip too low for them to sustain both the stock and the irrigation of the plants, that kind of thing."

His gaze followed a local man as he carried a crate of produce across the town square, his brow furrowed with the look of tension worn by every townsperson Zev had met.

"There are other stories as well. Everyone celebrating when they finally get a good rainfall, only to discover there was a leak in the roof of the main storehouse, and whole barrels of seed are now affected by rot. Scarecrows blown over by gusty winds just as a flock of particularly destructive birds comes through the town."

"Do you suspect sabotage?" Marieke asked quickly.

Zev shrugged. "Not really. Not as widespread as these types of problems seem to be. Most of what we've heard doesn't seem deliberate—many of the incidents *couldn't* be caused intentionally, I wouldn't think."

"Just like the seemingly healthy branch that suddenly fell," Marieke murmured, looking more troubled than ever.

"Yes." Zev nodded. "It seems less like sabotage and more like a lot of bad luck with the land combining all at once. And that's a more widespread problem than I'd anticipated, not to mention harder to address." He jerked his head toward another wagon. It belonged to his group, and had stood empty for a few days under the fateful chestnut tree. "A few loads of donated seed won't help much."

He brought his gaze back to Marieke's face, surprised by her reaction. She'd bitten her lip—the gesture more distracting than it should have been—and her general demeanor was uneasy.

"That doesn't sound good," she said, curling the end of her braid around one finger absently. "All that bad luck combining at once, in many farms across Oleand. With nothing like that happening in Aeltas. Not seeming like sabotage, but not entirely natural either. It's what I was afraid of, really."

"What are you thinking?" Zev asked, fascinated by the focus of her dark blue eyes. Once again, he was almost overpowered by the desire to know what thought she wasn't speaking.

"It's a foolish idea, probably," she hedged.

Zev just waited, his arms still folded and his posture expectant. After only a brief moment, Marieke caved.

"I can't shake this fear that all our troubles are connected," she said. "And I know it sounds very arrogant, but sometimes I'm afraid that they're connected to *me*."

"To you?" Zev uncrossed his arms, taken aback. "What connection would your country's troubles have to you?"

"Well, the deteriorating state of the farmland couldn't relate to me, logically," Marieke acknowledged. "But the accidents that are befalling singers..."

"You mean the tree branch?" Zev asked skeptically.

"It's not just that," she told him. "Three singers died in a carriage accident just recently. While the only non-singer in the carriage sustained only minor injuries." She wrapped her hands around her middle, uncomfortable. "The first such accident I heard of was the bridge collapse that sent me plummeting into the canyon. And it seems they've continued steadily since then, including when we crossed the border back. And given the reaction of the council to my experiences down there in the canyon, I can't help but feel that I'm...tainted somehow. As if I'm somehow causing problems. Like I brought a scourge back into Oleand with me."

"Hold on." Zev held up a hand. "There's a lot I didn't understand there. What happened on your crossing back into Oleand?"

"The canyon suddenly expanded northward," Marieke said. "The ground began to violently shake, but only under the singers in the group. It fell away completely, although we all managed to escape unscathed." For some reason she wasn't meeting his eye anymore.

"Only the singers?" Zev mused aloud. He pictured the scene he'd witnessed under the chestnut tree. "That is...marked."

Marieke nodded, her demeanor more natural as she lowered her arms. "The only carriage to run into trouble on our first crossing was mine, as well. Three of the group's four singers were in it."

"What did you mean about your experiences down in the canyon?" Zev pressed. "What did your council take issue with?"

Marieke hesitated, once again curling a finger around the end of her braid.

Zev met her gaze. "You'll have to decide to either trust me or not trust me," he told her simply. "I can't convince you with words, and I'm not going to try."

She let out a breath. "I didn't tell you the full story when you pulled me up," she said. "Falling into the ravine wasn't my only...misadventure."

Zev just waited, and after a moment she continued.

"There were people down there. They called themselves monarchists."

"Did they hurt you?" Zev realized the muscles in his arms had tensed, and he forced his body to relax.

"Most of them didn't seem inclined to," she said. "Although I'm pretty sure the leader was going to lock me up if I hadn't escaped. But there was one, a young man named Gorgon, who attacked me. He would have killed me if he could. I'd just escaped from him up a pathway when you found me. The path was blocked near the top, and I had to climb the rest of the way, and..." She trailed off with a shrug. "Well, you saw how that ended."

"Yes." Zev's voice was tight. "I remember." His hand had curled into a fist somewhere during her story, and he tapped his knuckles against his leg. "Did you learn much about these people?"

Marieke eyed him. "You don't seem surprised to learn that there were people at all."

"I've heard rumors," he grunted. "Everyone in my area has. They've been down there for a long time."

"Interesting." Marieke looked away from him as she thought this over. "Well, as for what I learned about them, the main thing was that they called themselves monarchists."

Zev's muscles were tensing again, and he tried to look natural as he leaned back against the wagon. "Did they?"

Marieke's eyes were back on him, and a little too shrewd. "They did, and I think that's why my council reacted so strongly to the whole situation."

"You told the authorities that they called themselves monarchists?" Zev asked.

Marieke seemed surprised by his question, and he realized he should be more cautious. Most people probably didn't refer to the Council of Singers as *the authorities.*

"Yes, I told them," she said slowly. "I didn't tell the Council of Singers in Aeltas about it. Our delegation head encouraged me not to, which I thought strange at the time."

Zev gave a grim smile. "Don't let the oversight trouble you. I'm pretty sure our Council of Singers knows about them. Although you were probably wise not to tell the council that you'd had contact. I don't think they care much about the renegade canyon-dwellers as long as they're keeping to themselves and not influencing anyone else."

Marieke frowned as she thought this over, and Zev wondered if he'd said too much. But if she'd encountered the monarchists herself, there was surely no need to pretend ignorance about them.

"If they'd known you spoke with the monarchists, they might have subjected you to much closer questioning," he explained. "Something which I assume you wouldn't welcome."

"Not especially," she confirmed. "In fact, I think I would have been hesitant to tell my own council if I'd known it would change how they'd respond to me." She sounded disgruntled, thinking over some conversation or incident she didn't choose to share. "They seemed to be very reactive and suspicious after I told them. They weren't like that toward me before."

So the Oleandan Council of Singers was as wary of the tales the monarchists might tell as the Aeltans, were they? Zev would expect no less. The two bodies had much the same history and therefore much the same weaknesses. He watched in silence for a moment as Marieke pursued her train of thought.

Then she came out of her reverie, giving him a wan smile. "Perhaps they were right to be wary of me. Something the violent monarchist, Gorgon, said to me has stuck in my mind more than I care to admit." She gave Zev an inquiring look. "I think I told you when we met that my voice hadn't been working in the canyon?"

Zev nodded.

"Well, Gorgon knew I was a singer. He heard me singing to save myself when I was falling. And it was enough to make him want to eliminate me. He claimed that the magic of the land is at its strongest and least corrupted in the canyon, and that it was the magic that had taken my voice away. He said that was proof that the land itself is against me and others like me." She pinned Zev with a hard look. "One could say he was like a violent version of your brother."

Zev grimaced. "Azai's a bit of an idiot, but that seems a harsh comparison."

"Why does he hate singers so much?" Marieke insisted.

Zev brushed the question off. It wasn't as though he had any other option.

"Just one of his quirks. Why has the comment by this Gorgon stuck with you so much, Marieke?"

He hardly knew what to make of his own reaction to the information. A frisson had gone through him at her words—Marieke didn't realize it, but what the monarchist had told her was much more revealing than Zev would have liked a singer to hear. It was also uncomfortably aligned with the views of Zev's own family—uncomfortable because it came from a would-be murderer.

But none of that was what had Zev feeling unsettled. He was more thrown by the fact that his own reaction to Marieke's account had been defensive, not on behalf of the land or his ancestors, but on her behalf. He'd felt much too keenly the injustice of her being called a blight deserving of death merely because she'd been born with a gift she couldn't control.

Maybe Azai was right. Maybe this unexpected connection with Marieke was more dangerous to Zev's foundational principles than he'd imagined.

"It stuck with me because of what's come since," Marieke said, reminding him that he'd asked her a question. "He spoke as though the land was against me, and the pure magic of the ravine had marked me as evil. The council also seemed to think that my contact with Sundering Canyon made me dangerous. And I can't help but notice that the string of unexplainable accidents befalling singers has come after my return to Oleand. And they've all basically happened along the route from the border, either in the wake of my group, or just ahead of it."

She nodded at Zev. "Or in the wake of your group. It's like a malignant presence has followed me from the canyon back into my country—after all, I've heard no rumors of mysterious accidents in Aeltas." A shudder went over her. "I can't shake the feeling that Oleand is cursed. The land has been slowly deteriorating, after all. And now the curse seems to be targeting singers. And I'm the one who unleashed it."

For a moment, Zev didn't know how to respond. She thought the land was cursed? With a curse that affected Oleand but not Aeltas? He was fairly certain she had most of the details wrong, but there was no denying that she was much more perceptive than he'd given her credit for.

Which made her dangerous, and yet he couldn't seem to bring himself to see her as a threat.

"What are you thinking?" Marieke's tone was self-conscious. "Probably that I've lost my mind."

Zev gave her a crooked smile. "I'm trying to decide whether to deplore your vanity in thinking yourself so central to a situation so far outside your control, or to commend you for caring so much, and reassure you that you don't have to carry so much on your shoulders."

Her response wasn't what he'd expected. He'd hoped she would laugh at his strictures—taking a gamble with the possibility that she might instead be offended—but she just studied him with an expression closer to fascination.

"You know, you don't speak like a farmer," she told him.

Zev shifted, unease washing over him yet again. He was becoming as incautious as Azai. At least with Marieke. She seemed to bring down his walls, and the worst of it was he could tell that she wasn't even trying to. If she ever did that, he would really be in trouble.

"I'm in no position to prove that the land isn't cursed," he said, ignoring her comment. "But I feel very confident in saying that if it is, the curse doesn't originate with you. I doubt these accidents, whether magical in nature or not, have anything to do with your unplanned visit to the depths of Sundering Canyon. You certainly don't bear any blame for them."

Marieke smiled weakly. "So my logic tells me. But I confess, I feel heavy over it all."

"A natural reaction to tragic deaths," Zev said. "At least, from anyone with any compassion."

He studied her, the truth of his own words sinking deep into his mind. Whatever Azai might think of singers, Marieke truly bore no blame for any of it. Not for the distant past, not for whatever was causing the more recent problems. It was absurd for anyone—including her—to think that she could.

"So that's why you snuck onto this trip, as you put it?" he asked. "To see if this incident supported your theory that a curse of some kind had followed your group from the border into Oleand?"

She shrugged. "In part. I came because I have a number of questions, and I had exhausted my avenues of inquiry in the capital for the time being. I thought there might be more I could learn with the investigating team." A mischievous twinkle leaped suddenly into her eyes. "Probably foolhardy of me to venture out, though, if some malignant magic is targeting teams of singers from the council. I'll have to stay close to our favorite Aeltan rescuer to ensure my safety."

Zev gave a grunt that was half scoff, hoping the sound covered the heat tingling up his ears. He found himself not at all averse to the idea of Marieke sticking close to him. He certainly didn't intend to let her be harmed while in his company.

"You're talking even more nonsense," he informed her brutally. His forehead creased. "So the deaths you mentioned, the carriage accident—they were an official team from the council?"

Marieke nodded, sobering. "The three singers were each sent to meet with a separate farming collective—just like the singer you rescued from the tree branch. They were en route to a central point where their paths would split." She looked over his shoulder, her expression changing. "Oh, they're beckoning to me. They don't know I'm not supposed to be on the delegation, so they'll be expecting me to take full part in the investigation. I'd better go."

Zev trailed after her, frowning as he thought over her words. He had no more idea than Marieke of the cause of this spate of accidents. But if official groups from the Council of Singers were being targeted...well, Marieke had attached herself to just such a group.

And all banter about his supposed heroics aside, for as long as she was within his reach, he'd prefer not to stray too far from her side.

CHAPTER

# THIRTEEN

*Marieke*

The next two days passed too quickly for Marieke's liking. The investigation process was so dull that she was tempted to confess to her fellow travelers that she wasn't part of the delegation at all, and bow out of the tedious process of interviewing every villager who might have seen or heard something out of the ordinary around the time of the accident. But she couldn't quite bring herself to confess her deception to anyone but Zev. She'd felt no hesitation telling him. Somehow she'd been confident he wouldn't turn her in.

For such a simple incident, there was an amazing amount of paperwork involved. And none of it yielded anything of great interest. The only notable discrepancy was when a local who'd been crossing the square at the time the branch broke claimed that one of the Aeltan visitors—someone other than Zev—had also seen it happen, from the far side of the square. But all of the Aeltans were accounted for at the time. With the exception of Zev, they'd all been eating in the nearby hall. And yet, it was unlikely that the local man would have failed to accurately identify someone from the community, given it wasn't a large town.

183

The possibility of a stranger's presence in the area at the time generated some interest from the investigators, but they were soon forced to conclude that they could do little other than record the account. No one else had seen or heard any sign of a stranger, and after all, the man had been well back from the chestnut tree, and the would-be victim had sensed no songcraft in use. There was no obvious way the unidentified man could have been involved in the accident.

And all the while Marieke was stuck in fruitless investigative meetings, Zev was nearby but just out of reach. She often spotted him through the window, always hard at work with the other farmers, both local and Aeltan. Sometimes she caught him glancing her way, and she couldn't help wondering if he felt the same pull she did to continue their conversation from when she'd arrived. She knew he hadn't come to this random farming town with the faint hope of meeting again, as she had. But, singer though she was, he didn't seem averse to her company. On the contrary, he usually sought her out at mealtimes, not saying much as he ate beside her or across the table, but always solidly nearby.

At the end of their second day in the village, a messenger rode into the town. They witnessed his arrival through the window as they ate their evening meal. He wore a simple tunic with the council's crest emblazoned in miniature just over his heart. Not a singer, then, but a non-magical employee of the council.

The man dismounted, then passed from their view, reappearing shortly in the doorway. Marieke knew a moment of anxiety as he approached the leader of the group of investigators, a note in his hand. Had Isabel or someone else discovered that she'd inserted herself into this trip without authorization and sent someone to deal with her? Was she about to face some kind of punishment?

But the ashen expression on the face of the group leader as he scanned the page told Marieke that whatever news the letter contained was much more serious than a new graduate's misdemeanors.

"What is it?" asked another member of the group, voicing the question that had them all frozen in their seats. Even Zev had swiveled from his position back-to-back with her at the next table over, his eyes fixed on the group leader.

"We're to return to Ondford immediately," the man said.

"Why?" Marieke asked sharply.

He met her eyes, his own expression heavy. "More accidents. Two more dead, and as many near misses. All singers on official business for the council. They're recalling all teams to the capital as a precaution."

"So...so they think these accidents aren't accidents at all?" another team member asked. "They think they're intentional? Like sabotage?"

"The letter didn't say that, and neither did I," the leader said shortly. "It said they're recalling all teams as a precaution. And that includes us. We'll leave first thing in the morning. We've gathered enough information for a report on the incident."

Everyone turned back to their meals, conversation continuing in hushed tones. Marieke could read on the faces of the other team members that they were eager to be gone. And she didn't blame them—she'd suspected from the start that the accidents were targeted in some way. Now that the council seemed to have formed the same impression, it made sense no one would want to be part of an official team stationed far from the safety of the capital. After all, no accidents had befallen singers in Ondford, only out on the road.

But for her part, Marieke found herself reluctant to leave. She agreed with the team leader that they'd fulfilled their investigative role well enough to justify returning to Ondford. But the incident with the branch had only ever been of token interest to her. It was the broader picture she wanted to understand, and she still had so many questions. Not to mention she might be in for a great deal of trouble when she returned to the capital and the council realized she hadn't gone home as she'd intended them to assume when she left.

Zev's presence in the rural town had nothing to do with her reluctance to leave. Naturally not.

"I suppose you'll be glad to pursue this latest avenue."

The deep voice, more familiar than it had any right to be, made Marieke turn. She hadn't even noticed how many of her fellow diners had trickled out of the room while she'd been lost in thought. Zev had swiveled on his bench to face her, his feet now planted in the space between their two tables. There was no one immediately nearby but the two of them.

"Returning to the capital will help you with your own investigations, won't it?" Zev tried again. "Since there are more incidents to consider now."

Marieke sighed. "I doubt it," she said. "I don't think I'll be allowed access to the investigation again, considering I basically stole it this time." She shrugged. "I doubt there will be any surprises, though. I strongly suspect the deaths and near-misses will be the result of seeming accidents that no one can quite explain."

Zev tilted his head toward her, considering her. "You're not eager to return to Ondford?"

She shook her head slowly. "Not especially. But I don't know what else I would do."

"You could travel with us."

The words were abrupt, and Marieke looked at Zev in surprise. "With...with you?"

"We'll also be leaving soon," he said. "To travel back to Aeltas."

Marieke didn't know how to respond. "But I thought the bridge was closed," she said, stalling for time to answer the real question.

"We're not taking the bridge," Zev said. "We're going to travel by land to the western coast of Oleand, and take a short voyage around the canyon to reach Aeltas by sea. We'll sail to Port Taran. From there we can travel by land again back to our homes."

Marieke's interest perked up at the mention of the abandoned trading city. She never thought she'd have the opportunity to visit Port Taran. Historically speaking, it was one of the few remaining links to the continent of Providore, with which the Sovereign Realms had once been closely connected. Its existence was a fascinating glimpse into the past.

But it was a distraction from the questions she'd promised herself she would find answers to.

"I don't have any reason to return to Aeltas," she said reluctantly. "Although I do appreciate the offer to travel with your group."

"I wasn't suggesting you spend time deeper in Aeltas," said Zev. "It's Port Taran I thought you might be interested in."

Marieke considered him. Could he read thoughts? "Why did you think that?"

"Because you said you wonder sometimes if the land is cursed," Zev said steadily. He paused, his eyes flicking around to check no one was near. It was a movement so subtle, Marieke almost missed it, but it certainly caught her interest. "I think you're asking the right questions," he went on. "But I don't think you'll find the answers in your capital." He gave a wry smile. "Or in mine. As you've already found, you can't search very freely in the council's backyard."

"What does that mean?" Marieke sat up straighter, intrigued by the air that surrounded him. She had the sense he was walking some line between recklessness and caution. "Zev, what do you know that I don't?"

He gave a genuine chuckle at that. "A great many things, city-dweller."

"Oi." She leaned forward to give him a playful shove. "I'm a farm girl, remember?"

"So you claim." He crossed his arms, leaning back comfortably against the table behind him. "There are tales to be told in these lands of ours, Marieke. Some you were told at your academy, but not all. You learned for yourself that Sundering Canyon has its own stories to tell. I suspect Port Taran might as well."

"You're being very cryptic," Marieke complained. "Why can't you just tell me what's in your mind? If you know something about all this, can't you share it?"

There was less humor in Zev's chuckle this time. "I'm telling you much more than I should, believe me." His storm-cloud eyes were sharp as they searched her face. "But I have to trust my own judgment."

"And what *is* your judgment?" Marieke asked, as fascinated as a mouse in the grip of a falcon's stare.

"That you're a smart girl, Marieke," Zev said simply. "And rightly or wrongly, I trust that you're not my enemy."

"I don't want to be anyone's enemy," Marieke said, taken aback both by the praise and by the confidence. If such veiled comments could be called confidences.

Zev's smile was grim. "That sentiment sounds admirable, but don't be too hasty with your generosity. Some people should be your enemies—some people won't hesitate to make you theirs."

"Well, I hope you're not one of those people, anyway,"

Marieke said briskly. "I'm intrigued by your suggestion." She threw him an unimpressed look. "As I'm sure you knew I would be, speaking in riddles like that. But even if I came with your group to Port Taran, I'd have no way to get back. I confess I am curious about the abandoned city, but not enough to wish to settle there forever."

Zev smiled. "I could see you safely back into Oleand," he said. "My group can travel on without me, and I can catch up. Assuming you have the resources to travel from the coast back to the capital, or your home, or wherever you're going."

Marieke stared at him, once again feeling tongue-tied. When did he become so determined for her company? Was she out of her mind to read into it? Likely she wouldn't know the real reason for his attitude until she understood what information he thought she'd find in Port Taran.

"I think I have enough coins," she said. "But...can you do that? Surely you're expected home with the rest of the group."

Zev put his hands on his knees, pushing himself to his feet with the easy confidence that characterized him. "I think I told you once before, Marieke, I'm under no one's control but my own." In a gesture much more casual than anything Marieke could have achieved in her current state, he touched a hand to her shoulder. "You can sleep on the offer. Let me know what you think in the morning. I'll be there when your group leaves, to say goodbye if you're going, or help with arrangements if you decide to stay."

And with the words, he strode from the room, leaving Marieke staring after him, her shoulder tingling from the memory of his touch.

She made her own way to bed quickly, only to toss and turn for a long time before sleeping. She wasn't wrestling with her decision, though. That was a foregone conclusion. Nothing whatsoever awaited her back in Ondford, except for closed doors and possible censure. But she was honest enough with herself to acknowledge that wasn't the key factor in her decision.

Since they'd reconnected, Zev had given her no reason to think he had any kind of magic that would explain what had happened to her—or rather hadn't happened to her—at the second border crossing. And yet, he must have a different type of power, because she couldn't deny that she was under his spell. In spite of him never giving the slightest sign of pushing her, there was just something about him, something she didn't even think he was conscious of.

If he wanted her to come with him, she was following.

And something told her that in doing so, she just might find answers to questions she wouldn't be able to ask in Ondford. Answers to questions she didn't even know she needed to ask.

True to his word, Zev was waiting unobtrusively nearby when Marieke joined the investigators early the following morning. As she'd anticipated, the leader was stunned and skeptical when she announced she wasn't going to travel back to the capital with the group. He seemed inclined to forbid her to stay, citing her youth and his own responsibility. Marieke considered confessing that she'd come on the expedition out of her own curiosity rather than been assigned as an official council representative. But she feared that would only make him more insistent that she accompany them back to the capital to let the council decide how to respond to her imposture.

She'd wondered if Zev might help by reiterating to the group leader his offer for her to travel with the Aeltan group when they departed the village. But he hung back, showing his usual reluctance to draw any attention to himself—a trait she found incongruous with his general air of confidence and capability. He only stepped forward to join her after she'd finally convinced the group leader that she was determined to stay, and short of using force, he wouldn't be able to change her mind.

The investigating singers left promptly once the matter was settled, no one else showing any inclination to linger. Marieke, her pack slung over her shoulder, watched the carriages trundle out of the dusty yard.

"Questioning your decision?"

She turned to find Zev's eyes fixed on her, and shook her head.

"No. Just trying to guess what the council's response will be to learning that I stayed behind, and what the group's response will be to learning that I was never supposed to be here in the first place." She gave him a smile. "None of which is my problem, at least not at present. I'm certainly not important enough for anyone to be sent after me. If I return to the capital, then I might face some repercussions, I suppose."

Zev gave no reply, and her eyes strayed to the carriages, now disappearing from sight around a bend in the road.

"I hope they make it back safely," she said. "Without any tragic *accidents*."

"Yes." Zev's voice was heavy. "I hope so too." His eyes held a hint of mischief when she glanced over at him. "And I hope the curse on your kind doesn't follow my group when we leave, since you're burdening us with your company."

"You're the one who invited me," Marieke protested. But she couldn't maintain true annoyance as he let out a deep chuckle. She just shook her head. "You're on my turf now, Aeltan, so I'll thank you to leave the mocking of poor, lost foreigners to me this time."

"I'm neither poor nor lost, but you can certainly attempt to mock me if you like," he said amicably. "Just enjoy it while you can. I was notified first thing this morning—we're to leave tomorrow, and it'll take us two days to reach the coast. After that we have a short voyage around the border to Port Taran, and then you'll be back in my territory."

"You make that sound ominous," Marieke complained. "But I'm not afraid, either of you or of Aeltas."

Zev just chuckled again. "How our mighty empire has fallen."

He'd already turned toward the building where the Aeltan group was accommodated, but Marieke called after him nevertheless.

"Empire is a stretch. Even for the days of the despots."

Zev's stride checked for a moment, but then he continued on, only giving a vague wave of his hand in acknowledgment of her words.

Much of the day was spent in a flurry of activity as the Aeltans prepared for departure and tried to assist their Oleandan beneficiaries as much as possible before leaving. Never much inclined to sit idle, Marieke pitched in wherever she thought she'd be useful, readily using her songcraft as requested by the locals to speed up otherwise tedious processes. More than once, she noticed Zev watching from a distance while she did this, but he never approached close enough to listen. In fact, she saw very little of him until the following morning, when the group gathered to leave the town.

Zev approached her, leading two horses by the reins.

"Good morning," he said. "I wondered if you'd like to ride?"

"I'd love to," said Marieke, who'd been eyeing a lumbering, empty wagon with gloomy resignation. "But I assumed I wouldn't have the option. I can't pay to hire a horse and still have enough to get myself home from the coast after I part ways with the group."

"No hire necessary," Zev said. "It's not a local horse. I asked around, and one of our farmers is willing to ride in the wagon and lend you his mount for a while."

"That's very generous," said Marieke, brightening. "Please point him out to me so I can thank him."

In minutes, she was mounted beside Zev, feeling much more optimistic about the two-day journey. Another Aeltan farmer, noticeably the youngest in the group, drew up on her other side. Marieke had met him in passing during her time in the town, and she greeted him with a friendly smile.

"Ramsey."

"It's great you're joining us," Ramsey said enthusiastically. "I for one don't object to some younger company than this lot," he jerked his head toward a trio of middle-aged men mounting up nearby, "and extra bonus that you're a singer! Maybe you can show us some tricks while we're on the road."

Marieke laughed. "I don't think I know any tricks, as such, but I'm happy to sing when it's helpful."

She was unsurprised by Ramsey's eagerness. Unlike Zev, he'd approached close any time he heard her singing the day before, listening with the avid fascination her own experiences had led her to expect from country folk when she'd first arrived in Aeltas.

Before she met Zev's family, that was.

"She's not a performing bear, Ramsey," Zev said mildly.

"Of course she's not." Ramsey winked at her. "She's much prettier. Speaking of which," he raised his eyebrows at Zev, "we'll have to tell Azai he was right, won't we?" He smiled at Marieke, adding for her benefit, "Azai is Zev's brother."

"Yes, I know," said Marieke warily. "What was he right about?"

"That Oleandan girls are the prettiest," Ramsey said, grinning.

"Azai said that?" Marieke was skeptical, to say the least.

"Well, he said that Zev thinks they are, or something along those lines," Ramsey amended. His grin encompassed them both now. "And as I said, we'll have to tell him he was right."

Marieke felt her face coloring, and even the normally stoic Zev looked discomposed by Ramsey's banter.

"Marieke's met Azai," he said, throwing Ramsey a look of annoyance. "So she already knows he's an idiot."

"Oh." Ramsey looked between them in surprise, obviously not having heard the full story of their acquaintance. "I see I'm missing some information. Does that mean you'll be accompanying Zev all the way back to our region, then?" There was still mischief in his eyes as he threw another glance at Zev. "Azai will be able to draw his own conclusions."

"Thankfully not," Zev said flatly. He seemed to catch Marieke's discomfort, because he looked at her quickly, his smile turning self-deprecating. "Apologies. That came out rude. What I meant was, it's probably a good thing you don't plan to travel all the way with us, because then none of us will be subjected to Azai drawing his own conclusions. It's a process that rarely ends well."

Marieke smiled weakly, still embarrassed by the whole topic. "You don't need to worry about my feelings. Azai's opinion of me isn't really in any doubt."

"If he's wary of you, it's probably a compliment to your charms," Ramsey assured her, taking a bite of the apple he'd just pulled from his saddle bags.

The group had started to move out of the yard, but even in the kerfuffle, the cheerful young farmer must have caught her disbelieving expression.

"Because he thinks you might be a danger," Ramsey clarified. "To himself or to Zevadiah here." He pursed his lips, spitting out an apple seed with an expert maneuver, so that it flew past Marieke's face and pinged off Zev's shoulder. "We all know how picky Gideon and Narelle are for their boys. It's a bit of a running joke in our region. They won't be allowed to marry just anyone, you know. They have very high expectations, and Zev and Azai have always been very standoffish with the ladies as a result. That's probably why Azai seemed cold to you."

Marieke looked from Ramsey to Zev, noting that the latter once again seemed both annoyed and uncomfortable at his friend's jesting words.

"What, are your parents going to arrange a marriage for you?" she asked with dry humor. "That seems excessive. A little high and mighty for farmers, isn't it?"

"Of course not," said Zev shortly. "No one's arranging anyone's marriage."

"But Oleandans and singers are both low on the list, right?" Ramsey was enjoying his friend's discomfiture far too much, and Marieke wasn't surprised when Zev reached his limit.

"Drop it, Ramsey. No need to make a fool of yourself."

The other young man took this rebuke with grinning good humor, and mercifully the conversation moved on. But Marieke felt she'd been given plenty to think about. Not that she'd really needed further evidence that Zev wasn't a typical farmer.

The two-day ride west to the coast passed smoothly. Marieke was very grateful to the farmer who'd loaned her his horse, as he seemed content to ride in the wagon alongside another man who was apparently a neighbor and friend. She rode alongside Zev and Ramsey, most of the journey filled with the cheerful chatter of the younger man. Much of what he said was cheeky, but she couldn't help warming to him.

He certainly provided a contrast to Zev's naturally serious demeanor. She noticed that Zev was particularly watchful, and it occurred to her that he may not have been entirely joking when he expressed the hope that no mysterious accidents would trail their group because of Marieke's inclusion in it. But thankfully, no disasters befell them as they traveled.

When the group neared the coast, Marieke felt her spirits lift. Although her own home was on the very opposite side of the country, the sea still felt like a familiar friend. The smell of the air calmed her, giving her the first sense of normalcy she'd had in a long time.

"You seem happy," Zev commented, no doubt noticing how she'd sat up straighter in the saddle.

"I love the coast," she said. "There's nothing like the sound of the waves crashing against the cliffs. The absence of it was one thing I could never quite get used to in Ondford."

"Doesn't Ondford sit beside a huge river, though?" Ramsey chimed in.

Marieke gave him a pitying look. "If you think that's the same thing, you've clearly never seen the ocean."

"I haven't," he admitted unashamedly. "I'm looking forward to it."

For the final stretch of their ride to the coast, the path took them right alongside Sundering Canyon. Once again, Marieke felt an unpleasant crawling sensation creep over her as she remembered what it had been like to fall into nothingness. She noticed that Zev, his movements subtle enough not to attract Ramsey's attention, maneuvered his mount so that he rode between her and the edge. It was a gesture she appreciated, although it was unnecessary. The path was set far enough back that it would take quite a catastrophe for anyone to be in danger of falling over the edge.

The third time Marieke cast a glance into the ravine, Zev commented.

"Don't be uneasy. Look at the path. It's sound." His voice was low and steady, and although Ramsey rode nearby, the moment felt intimate.

"I know," Marieke assured him. "I'm not worried. Just curious. The magic of this area really does feel different from elsewhere."

"Different how?" Zev asked, his gray eyes pinning her with their usual focus.

"It's chaotic." Marieke shrugged. "Unpredictable, maybe? I can usually assess the level of magic in the ground without thinking about it. It's part of my training, learning to be prepared at all times to draw magic into myself as needed. Some areas give off more magic than others, whether because the magic is naturally stronger, or less accessed by other singers, or whatever the reason. But here, it's different. It's strong, definitely. But it's in a constant state of flux. It's not necessarily accessible to me." She frowned. "Remember what I told you about when I was down there? In spite of the volume of magic, I couldn't access it. I couldn't even use my voice at all."

"I remember." Something in Zev's tone told her he remembered more than just that detail. "I also remember that you thought it meant the land here rejected your craft altogether."

Marieke shifted uncomfortably in her saddle. "Well, that's what Gorgon told me. I don't know if I believe it or not."

"What's that?" Ramsey pulled his horse closer alongside hers, inserting himself cheerfully into the conversation. "Who's Gorgon?"

"No one," said Marieke quickly. "It's nothing important."

In another moment, the slight rise they were traveling sloped away again beneath their horses' hooves, and the sea came into sight. Marieke leaned forward, her spirits lifting once again as a gull swooped overhead. A smile danced around her lips as Ramsey let out a low whistle.

"It's quite a sight, isn't it?" he said. "Does it just...go forever?"

"Well, the continent of Providore is out there somewhere," Marieke reminded him. "Beyond that…I guess we'll never know." She nodded at a small vessel anchored out to sea a little way. "Is that waiting for us?"

"It is," Zev confirmed.

"It doesn't look big enough for us all," Ramsey commented.

"It will have to make multiple trips," agreed Zev. "But that won't be too much of a hardship, given how short the distance. We just have to get around Sundering Canyon. The real challenge will be fitting the wagons."

Marieke followed the line of the canyon with her eyes, noting that it did indeed continue all the way to the water's edge.

"It's hard to believe that Sundering Canyon didn't exist in the time of the monarchs," she commented. She caught the swift look Zev threw her, but kept her eyes on the point where the ravine met the water. "It's such an enormous feature of the land to have appeared over a relatively short amount of time."

"Not relatively short," Ramsey corrected. "It appeared suddenly, when the monarchs were overthrown."

She frowned at him. "It can't have been that sudden."

"It was," he assured her. "My people have farmed the land in our region for more generations than our histories go back. We're only a stone's throw from the border, you know. The appearance of Sundering Canyon is a tale handed down in our local stories. It was so dramatic, everyone heard the splintering crack of its formation from our ancestors' farms."

"What?" Marieke looked between the two young men. "That's not what I've been taught. I thought the ravine started small, and grew over time. Just as it's been growing now."

"Growing northward," Ramsey said. "It hasn't expanded southward in living memory, you know. Not so much as an inch."

"Truly?" Again Marieke looked to Zev for confirmation. "Is that actually the case, or is it just Aeltan pride claiming that?"

He smiled faintly at her plain speaking. "That's my understanding as well. Our road runs right along the canyon, and hasn't shifted in my parents' or grandparents' lifetimes."

"And the other part?" Marieke demanded. "Did your ancestors pass down stories of hearing the border split into a canyon in one sudden incident?"

Zev took a moment before answering this time. "My people have farmed the land for a long time, but not as long as Ramsey's family. I don't know of any ancestors of mine who lived in the region back when the monarchs were overthrown. My people lived in the capital. They do tell tales of their own from that time, but they don't relate to what they could or couldn't hear on the farms."

Marieke studied his face, intrigued by the many things he clearly wasn't saying.

"I'd be very interested to hear the tales they passed down from the capital," she said.

Zev's answering smile was twisted, the expression unfamiliar on his face, and not at all flattering. "Would you? I doubt it. As with the canyon's formation, our tales are likely not what you've been taught."

"Well, I haven't been taught much at all about Tarandon's history," Marieke said fairly. "My own history lessons related primarily to Oleand, and our own capital." She frowned as she looked forward, toward the small quay at the end of which a rowboat was tied. "And I don't know why you think I wouldn't want to hear other stories. I'm traveling with you to Port Taran specifically because I want to learn history that I *won't* find in my own capital."

"Is that why?" Ramsey asked jovially. "And here I thought it was because you wanted more of the company of a certain handsome young farmer." He pulled his horse close enough to nudge her with his elbow. "Speaking of myself, of course."

"Of course," said Marieke dryly.

The front of the group had reached the quay now, and their little conversation gave way to the general bustle of figuring out how best to organize the short sea voyage. Marieke took no part in the process, assuming she would fall at the end of the queue, given she wasn't really part of their group.

She spent the time examining the canyon, going closer to the edge than she'd dared further along. The ridge did slope down toward the water, making the fall less death-defying than at the bridge to the east. But still enough that it could be fatal, and certainly enough to make it impassable for horses or vehicles. A skilled climber might be able to cross it on foot, but the risk would be considerable. And although the ocean pooled into the ravine in a lagoon of sorts, the water didn't look deep enough that she would trust it to save her if she jumped down.

"Marieke."

Zev's quiet call made her turn, raising an inquisitive eyebrow.

"Are you ready to board?" he asked, holding out a hand.

She stared from it to the rowboat, surprised. "Already?"

"We're going with the first group," he told her. "Our horses will follow later. This way we'll have time to look around Port Taran before the sun sets. Since visiting the abandoned city is your main purpose in joining us."

"Oh." Marieke supposed she shouldn't be surprised that, in his usual indefinable way, Zev had managed to take the lead and achieve his desired outcome without any sign of pushing for it. "Thank you."

She swung her leg over her horse, ready to slide down. Her breath caught a little as Zev's hands found her waist, guiding her safely off her mount. His grip was strong without being directive, in keeping with his usual manner, and the warmth of his hands seemed to reach through the fabric of her gown more fully than was natural.

When her feet touched the ground, she paused for a moment, her awareness of Zev's proximity behind her heightened. She swiveled slowly, finding that he hadn't stepped back, and his hands still rested loosely on her sides. For an endless second, he just looked down into her eyes, his own expression unreadable. Then he shifted away, gesturing for her to precede him down the short wharf to the rowboat bobbing on the waves.

# FOURTEEN

## Marieke

Marieke collected her pack from the saddlebags with clumsy movements, annoyed at herself for her breathlessness, and the flush of color she could feel on her cheeks. Anyone would think she'd never stood close to a man before.

The truth was she'd had plenty of exposure to strong-willed, confident—often overly confident—young men during her time at the Academy of Song. As a green newcomer from a rural area, she'd been a target for the displays of the influential, eager to make sure she knew their place at the top of the hierarchy, and by extension, her own near the bottom. Some had tried to intimidate, others had tried to charm—she liked to think she'd learned fairly swiftly to see through both forms of bravado.

But none of them had ever affected her like Zev did, unassuming farmer though he was. He gave no air of trying to prove his superiority or demonstrate his strength. He never demanded attention or deference. And yet, he received both. She'd seen during her short time with the Aeltan group that people followed him naturally, even unknowingly, including those older and more experienced than him.

And as for her...well, when he moved, she seemed drawn to follow with a magnetic pull no domineering son of wealth or influence had ever created in her. And when she knew herself to have his full attention, she had to fight hard not to let it go to her head.

*Enough*, she told herself firmly, as she walked along the wharf, both Zev and Ramsey close behind her. She wasn't a naive fifteen-year-old visiting the city for the first time. She was a capable, trained singer with plenty to offer and no need to win Zev's approval. And Ramsey's jokes aside, she wasn't with the group to endear herself to Zev. She was there to discover what exactly he thought she would find in Port Taran, and why he believed it was something she'd want to know.

"I'm not too sure about this," Ramsey commented uneasily as he stepped into the rowboat behind Marieke. "This doesn't feel stable at all."

"It's safe," Marieke assured him. "On a calm day like this, there's nothing to fear from a short rowboat trip."

"This is calm?" Ramsey demanded, as a swell caused him to lose his balance and fall onto the bench seat in an undignified heap.

Marieke couldn't help laughing. "Yes, Ramsey. This is very calm."

Several others clambered into the vessel with them, and the man who'd been waiting for the group at the wharf began to row. Ramsey stared avidly out at the larger ship toward which they were headed, and the ocean beyond, but Marieke noticed Zev studying the shoreline they'd just left, his gaze too intent for idle curiosity.

"Is everything all right?" she asked him.

He looked over quickly, with the air of being caught in the act of something.

"Yes, I'm sure it is," he said.

"What is it?" Marieke demanded, frowning. "I've had too many traveling misadventures lately to want to be kept in blissful ignorance. Don't lie to me."

"I'm not lying." Zev seemed surprised, but not offended. For a moment he seemed to debate whether to go on, then he said, "I felt uneasy all the way along the canyon. Something was off. If you want the truth, I'm glad to be leaving Oleandan soil."

"What kind of something?" Marieke demanded.

Zev just shrugged. "Hard to say. Probably nothing."

Her frown deepened. "You can't sense magic, though, right?"

"No, I can't." Zev's eyebrows lifted in amusement. "You know that. Why do you seem to keep wanting me to confirm it?"

She ignored the question. "So if you sensed something strange, it was natural, not magical. Do you mean the feeling of being watched, or followed?"

"Something like that," Zev admitted. "But it could well have been nothing more than my fancy."

Marieke gripped her pack more tightly in her lap, not convinced by the airy assurance that Zev clearly didn't fully believe himself. She'd been relieved that no disaster had befallen her during their ride, as had happened to far too many singers on the road lately. But perhaps she'd been in danger after all.

"No, I don't like this at all." Ramsey's decisive words brought Marieke's attention to his face, which looked queasy as they rose and fell with the swells, and salt water from the oars splashed in on them. "Will the bigger boat be even worse?"

Marieke smiled. "No, it will be more stable. And the voyage is very short, isn't it?"

"Less than an hour, the captain tells me," Zev confirmed.

"I still don't know why we have to risk the open ocean,"

said Ramsey, gripping the edges of the boat with white knuckles. He cast Marieke an aggrieved look. "Aren't you supposed to be a singer? Couldn't you just sing us a bridge or something?"

She laughed outright at that. "No, I'm afraid I'm not so skilled."

"Why is it a stupid suggestion?" Ramsey asked, wounded. "Isn't that what they did with the main bridge?"

"No, it's not," Marieke said, trying to curb her amusement to spare his feelings. "It's a real bridge, built of stone. It's just reinforced with magic. Or it was, before the supports failed. Songcraft isn't unlimited in what it can do, Ramsey. Even if the magic of the ground was plentiful—and cooperative—enough, I couldn't just create a solid bridge with my voice."

"What's the use of you, then?" Ramsey complained.

Marieke deemed it allowable to laugh at that. "Compared to a singer trained in structural song, I'm no use at all. But even those who are trained in that area don't make materials appear out of nowhere. Their songs can assist in more swiftly and more accurately carving out the desired building materials, and positioning them into their places to form something like a bridge. They can also coat the structure with power afterward."

"They can make the blocks fly through the air into position?" Ramsey sounded impressed. "That would be fun to watch."

Marieke nodded. "That part is fairly straightforward. Most singers are trained in how to use raw power to move things without touching them. But that's still usually limited to what the singer could do with their hands if circumstances allowed." She nodded toward the receding shoreline. "For example, I couldn't use magic to lift that wagon, because it's so much heavier than I could lift with my actual body. Really strong singers can increase their capacity as they learn to harness magic, and shift things that are beyond their physical strength.

But there's still a limit. Most of our training focuses more on finesse than showy displays of strength. For example, when I was falling into the canyon, I directed a rope to tie itself into a bush to help stop my fall. It was a knot that I could easily have done with my hands, but doing it with raw power required more precision than volume of magic."

"Structural singers could carve out rocks with their hands?" Zev asked skeptically, as the rowboat reached the larger vessel at last.

Marieke smiled in acknowledgment of her simplification, pausing the explanation to clamber up the rope ladder that had been thrown down to them.

"No, of course they can't," she admitted, once they were all on deck. "But they could wield the relevant tools with their hands. A preliminary step in learning to mine materials for building would be learning to direct the tools to do it without touching them. With time and practice, the singers could then learn to direct power to serve the function of the tool, skipping the middleman, so to speak. Trying to do it without learning the intermediate step would likely result in damaged materials and unreliable structure. But I don't know much about it, given I never focused on structural song."

"Well, what did you learn?" Ramsey asked, leaning on the railing and looking much more comfortable than he had on the rowboat. "Give us a demonstration."

Marieke grinned. "Given your background, you'll either be pleased or offended to learn that one of my areas of focus was agricultural song."

"Why would I be offended?" Ramsey asked, bewildered.

Marieke waved a hand in the vague direction of her home, to the northeast. "In my local farmland, at least, opinion is divided on whether magic-use should meddle in farming affairs. Some are eager, others consider it a sacrilegious interference with generations of tried and tested practices."

"There isn't much magic intermingled with our farming practices," Ramsey acknowledged. "But our crops and farms seem to thrive nonetheless."

"Better than ours, lately," sighed Marieke. She glanced south along the coastline, to the land beyond the canyon's edge. "It didn't take me long on my visit to see that Aeltas is prosperous and well-run." She smiled ruefully at her two companions. "I thought Oleand was as well, but recent events have cast some doubt on that."

"Our country is the better one," Ramsey said cheekily. "As everyone knows."

Marieke opened her mouth to join in the banter, but Zev's voice cut across hers, his tone nothing like Ramsey's jovial one.

"Do you really think Aeltas has no problems?"

"Oi, Zev," Ramsey complained. "Keep a united front before the enemy."

Zev ignored him, his storm-cloud eyes still fixed on Marieke. "I'm asking seriously. You were in our country for what, a week? On what basis did you conclude that all of Aeltas is prosperous, and that the country is well-run?"

"Well..." Marieke faltered under his intense scrutiny, taken aback that he seemed to be criticizing rather than defending his own country. "Your farm certainly prospers. As does all the farmland I saw when we rode to the capital. And the city itself seemed clean and orderly."

"What part of the city?" Zev raised an eyebrow. "We rode straight from the gate to the council building, and unless I'm mistaken, you spent the rest of your visit in the Academy of Song."

"Yes, that's true," Marieke said slowly. "I wasn't in control of my own schedule, you know. I would have liked to have seen more of the country."

He nodded. "I'm not criticizing you, Marieke. I'm just pointing out that you formed your conclusion as to Aeltas's prosperity and the success of its government based on your observations of the wealthiest and most fertile of its farming regions, and on your interactions with the most privileged elite within our society—the council-sanctioned singers." His eyes bored into hers with unspoken meaning. "There are plenty of others in the country, not all of whom would agree with your assessment."

Marieke closed her mouth, no reply coming to her lips. He was right, and she understood his veiled reference as well. The monarchists in Sundering Canyon most certainly wouldn't agree with her description of Aeltas's state. And while they might be an extreme example, there were likely plenty of people who landed somewhere in the middle. Hadn't she gotten herself into trouble just recently for pointing out exactly that to her own council, regarding Oleand? She'd just said that she'd always considered Oleand well-run until the recent problems emerged, but that was an oversimplification, given the frustrations of people like her parents regarding the very structure of the council.

"This is getting too heavy," Ramsey complained. "I want to hear what sort of magic you learn in agricultural song."

Marieke gave herself a little shake, coming out of her reverie. "Lots of things. There are ways to use magic to identify weaknesses in crops, or areas of danger in farming conditions." She deflated a little. "Lots of that's been going on in recent years, without anything being identified as to what's causing the poor harvests. But there are other things, too. Just as a structural singer can enhance the normal processes of building, an agricultural singer can sort of boost what a farmer would normally be doing."

She leaned into the wind, closing her eyes. "I think agricultural song is one of the easier types, myself, because it has so much to do with the natural elements. Nature is easier to affect with power than manmade structures, because magic comes from the ground, and is part of nature itself. For example, it's not all that complex to direct the wind using power, even though that's something your hands couldn't do without magic. It's just a case of remolding natural power from one form into another. Doing it with discretion is another matter, however. That's a big part of what we learn in agricultural song training—how not to mess up the natural weather patterns with incautious magical interference."

"What about people?" She didn't need to open her eyes to see the impudent grin on Ramsey's face. She could hear it. "Are they harder or easier to control than rocks or structures?"

"People," she told him firmly, opening her eyes at last and giving him a haughty look, "can't be controlled by magic. At least not directly. We all have control over our own bodies and movements."

"So there's no way to make a pretty girl fall in love with me, for example," Ramsey pressed.

"There is," Marieke told him, her tone and expression perfectly straight in face of his flirtation. "It's called charm, and it's nothing to do with magic. You either have it..." her eyes met his with calm impassivity, "or you don't."

"Oof." Ramsey mimed taking a blade to the heart. "You are savage, lady singer."

Marieke let out a chuckle, her eyes straying in spite of herself to Zev. He wasn't looking at her or Ramsey, his focus almost pointedly remaining on the ocean through which the boat was now making steady progress.

"What did you mean that singers can coat the structure with power?" he asked abruptly. "When you were talking about structural song, you said they can speed up the process of the building, but afterward they can also coat the structure with power."

"You're no fun, Zev," Ramsey sighed.

But Marieke wasn't averse to redirecting the conversation to her craft. It was much less personal than trying to draw Zev into jokes about charm and attraction.

"It's advanced training," she said. "Moving things with magic is one of the first skills we learn. Molding magic into enchantments that linger—directing the power to undertake a broader task even after the song is finished—is something we build up to. When I crossed the bridge over Sundering Canyon, I could feel the enchantments that coated it, lending strength to the points most likely to weaken with time and weather, and generally increasing the stability of the structure. But even doing that successfully, without accidentally causing structural problems, requires the right training." She shrugged. "Which I don't have, in this particular area."

Zev nodded slowly, still seeming reluctant to meet her eye or fully commit to the conversation. After a moment, he pushed himself upright. "I'm going to consult with the captain," he said. "See how long until we reach Port Taran."

Marieke watched him go in consternation.

"Is it something I said?" she asked Ramsey, trying to speak humorously.

"Everything you said, probably," he told her, the brutal words softened by a grin. "Zev's whole family are a bit funny about singers and songcraft."

"Yes, I noticed that," Marieke said, her eyes still on Zev's upright figure.

"Personally, I found it fascinating," Ramsey assured her. He leaned on the railing such that he was slanting into her personal space, one eyebrow raised suggestively. "And *my* family aren't at all restrictive when it comes to romance."

Marieke swatted at him, her heart not in the banter. Turning his jokes aside with some of her own seemed the best way to keep the tone light. But truthfully, she had no interest in flirting with Ramsey. Poor Ramsey. She doubted many girls would have much interest in flirting with him when Zev was nearby.

The voyage was as brief as Zev had said. They watched the mouth of Sundering Canyon sail by, and soon enough, their destination came into view. Port Taran was no rural launching point like the one they'd departed from in Oleand. The stone wharf stretched far out into the deeper water, where full-sized ocean-going vessels had once dropped anchor, laden with wares from the now-inaccessible continent of Providore.

But as they drew closer, Marieke saw that the wharf wasn't intact. There were whole sections where the stone had crumbled away, and some of the pylons leaned against the structure haphazardly. Their vessel made for a point perhaps a third of the way along the wharf, where a section jutted out perpendicular to the main gangway. The water was deep enough for the smaller boat, and soon the crew had successfully moored the vessel at the end of the section of wharf.

Zev, who'd been aloof since their earlier conversation, appeared at Marieke's side, as if ready to assist her to disembark should she need help. She didn't, of course, having grown up around boats, and when she climbed nimbly from the vessel, he made no attempt to push his assistance on her. He just followed smoothly, Ramsey close behind.

"And just like that, we're back in Aeltas," Ramsey said, even more cheerful now that his feet were once again on solid ground.

"Yes." Marieke's eyes strayed ahead to the point where the wharf met the land. Even in this shorter stretch, some sections looked deteriorated. They would have to walk with care. "My second time in your country. That's twice more than I ever expected."

Ramsey strode forward, apparently eager to get further from the water, but neither of the other two made any move.

Marieke glanced at Zev, to find him also studying what they could see of the abandoned port city. From the wharf to the buildings, the overwhelming impression was one of crumbling stone.

"So you've spent some time in Port Taran before?" she asked.

"Me?" Zev seemed surprised. "No, I've never been here before."

"What?" she demanded. "I thought you hinted that I'd find answers here."

"Did I?" Zev asked, maddeningly obtuse.

Marieke scowled at him. "You know you did. Why would you imply that if you've never seen yourself whatever this place has to offer?"

"Like I said, Marieke," Zev's voice was serious as he started to walk down the wharf, "you're not the only one who's heard stories of the past. And there are some occasions—some places—where the tales I've been told coincide with the ones you've been taught. This might just be one of those places."

"You're being cryptic again," Marieke complained. But she followed him nonetheless, picking her way over dubious patches of stone.

When she reached the end of the wharf at last, she glanced back. The rest of their fellow travelers had disembarked, and the boat was a bustle of activity, the crew already casting off to return for the next group.

"Should we look around while we wait for the others?"

Zev's words were inviting, but his demeanor was somber enough to dampen any excitement of exploration. Marieke didn't blame him. There was certainly a heavy air about the place. The decay and ruin were sobering, but the city didn't just feel abandoned. It felt...destroyed. She followed Zev down the nearest street, noting that he skirted around where Ramsey was standing with a few of the others from the boat. She didn't object—she would also prefer to look around the city without the cheerful chatter and flirtation of the young farmer.

"What did you mean that our different stories might coincide here?" she asked Zev, her gaze moving from a pile of rubble up to the second story of the building, where the window box from which the stone had fallen was still partially intact.

"Well, let's find out," said Zev evenly. "Where does Port Taran come into your stories?"

"It was a trading city," she said, feeling like she was back in class. "A huge and prosperous one. It was the key point of contact between Providore and the Sovereign Realms." She paused. "Not that we were called that back then, I suppose."

Zev nodded. "That much is the same in my stories. Go on."

"Well, it was also a place of significant contention in the growing conflict between the singers and the monarchs," said Marieke. "Although it's in Aeltas, it was used as a trading point by both countries. The Aeltans charged a levy for Oleandans to use it, which was fine up to a point. But the monarchs became greedy."

"Which monarchs?" Zev asked.

"Both," said Marieke. "The Aeltan ones, while giving the Oleandan royals and nobility increasingly favorable treatment, taxed the common Oleandans more and more heavily. And the Oleandan monarch, instead of advocating for his people, started charging his own levy on their imports as well, a questionable process to which his Aeltan counterpart turned a blind eye. It became almost impossible for any but the very wealthy to trade with Providore. And even those not directly involved in the trade suffered, because further levies on imported goods were charged when they were sold in regular markets further into each of the kingdoms. Any attempts to bypass these levies were met with harsh penalties, sometimes even executions." She paused, glancing at Zev. "Those are some of many examples of the tyrannical way the monarchs ruled, at least in the history I was taught. Have our tales diverged?"

There was a long moment of silence before Zev responded, his voice heavy. "No. So far they are aligned. Or at least," he glanced down a side street that was almost fully overgrown by foliage, "they're similar enough. You speak as though that was the least of the monarchs' sins. I understand that point to be the height of their increasing failures. It was immediately after that stage that they were overthrown, was it not?"

"Yes," Marieke acknowledged. "That's true. And that's where Port Taran plays another part in the history. When the singers took a stand against the monarchs, and it became clear that they had the strength to overthrow them, both monarchs fled here. The cooperative of singers had strategically combined forces and coordinated their moves, knowing that otherwise the monarchs would turn to one another for assistance. As it was, both had their hands full with their own affairs."

"But both fled here, you said," Zev prompted, when she paused.

Marieke nodded. "They met here, along with much of their courts, escorted by singers to ensure they didn't offer violence to anyone along the way. From here they sailed west, to exile in Providore. And whatever tales they carried with them made the kingdoms of Providore decide to cut all contact and refuse to trade or communicate with us any longer."

"And now," Zev said, coming to a stop, "we've reached the point where our stories well and truly part ways."

Marieke frowned at him. "What do you mean?"

"I mean that's not the tale I was told," Zev said evenly.

"It seems I should have sat in on more history lessons during my brief time in Tarandon," said Marieke. "Is the Aeltan account so different from ours?"

Zev shook his head. "I suspect the history taught in the Academy of Song in Tarandon is much the same as the one you just recounted. But I'm not a singer, remember? I didn't attend the Academy of Song."

"And your local village school taught a substantially different version of your country's history?" Marieke asked, skeptical.

There wasn't much humor in Zev's chuckle. "I didn't attend the local village school. It's not required, and most in my area don't."

Marieke stopped walking, turning fully to face him with a frown on her lips. "If you expect me to believe you have no formal education, think again. I grew up mostly surrounded by people who didn't bother with book learning, and then was catapulted into the world of people who absolutely live and die by book learning. Everything about you contradicts the idea that you belong in the former category. The way you speak, the way you think...the way you *carry yourself*."

This time Zev looked inclined to actually be amused. "I don't know what you mean by that, but I suppose it's a compliment? So thank you?"

"I know you don't get what I mean." Marieke shook her head. "But it's obvious to everyone else. Even Ramsey speaks to and about you differently from how he is with the rest of the group. You're not a typical farmer, Zev."

He sighed and started walking again, Marieke hurrying to

match his stride. "I am what I am, Marieke. And I am a farmer." He glanced at her. "My parents are intelligent people, educated after their own fashion. They taught my brother and me how to read and write, and many other things."

"Including a different version of history from what your academy teaches," Marieke said.

He didn't confirm it, but neither did he deny her words. With a jerk of the head, he invited her to follow him down another overgrown side street. The plants underfoot muffled their steps, but the empty silence of the place still echoed eerily in Marieke's mind. From what she remembered from history class, the port city had been gradually abandoned over the years after the coup, because the end of all trade with Providore made it obsolete. But the city didn't feel like somewhere that had dwindled away and been forgotten. It felt like something that had been destroyed. Something the ghost of which still lingered fretfully.

She was being fanciful, she knew. But Port Taran felt like nowhere she'd ever been before, and she was surprised by how much it unnerved her.

"So if our stories have diverged, what does your version of history say?" she asked, feeling the need to dispel the crushing silence.

Zev didn't answer her question. Of course he didn't.

"I think the main square is through here," he said instead. "I caught a glimpse of it when we left the rest of the group near the wharf."

His sense of direction proved accurate. They emerged from the side street into a large open space. Or at least, it had obviously once been open. A few trees had now grown up from the ruins of what had once been a central fountain, if Marieke's guess was correct. Maneuvering around it, she could see that the main street of the town cut straight from the square to the water's edge. Overgrown and uneven as the paving now was, they still had a clear view of the start of the long wharf.

"So according to what you were taught," Zev said, "the monarchs at the time of the coup retreated here, to this city, and sailed west from that wharf to the continent of Providore."

"Yes, that's right," Marieke said, unable to keep her tone from being slightly defensive. "And they maligned our countries to the kingdoms of Providore, forcing us to become fully self-sufficient, without any of the benefits trade used to bring. A last act of malice against the people they'd mistreated, one could say."

"Could one?" Zev repeated. His tone was mild, but again, Marieke felt defensiveness rising up in her.

"If you have something to say, Zevadiah, say it."

"Very well, Mari." Zev's use of her nickname to match her use of his full name was more effective than it had any right to be. Marieke found herself fidgeting under his steady stare. "Look around this place," Zev instructed her. "What do you see?"

"An abandoned city," she said promptly.

"Is that how it feels to you?"

Zev's question made her fidget more. It touched much too accurately on her earlier thoughts about the heaviness that hung about Port Taran.

"And why was the city abandoned?" Zev pressed, when she didn't answer.

"Because trade with Providore stopped," Marieke said.

"True." Zev directed his eyes toward the deteriorated wharf, giving Marieke relief from his piercing gaze. "But that doesn't seem enough to justify the level of decay to me. I could understand if the decline of the export industry made the city shrink gradually over generations. But to be suddenly deserted, within mere years of the trade stopping? That seems extreme to me. It was supposedly a bustling, prosperous city. I would have thought the population large enough to sustain a comfortable life even without the trade to make it thrive."

"Yes," Marieke acknowledged reluctantly. "That's a reasonable point."

"I'm also struggling to find an explanation for that in the tale of gradual dwindling you've told me."

Zev was pointing at the remains of the fountain, and following his arm, Marieke saw something she hadn't noticed before. The stone structure hadn't just crumbled. The hole that lanced right through it didn't make sense for a gradual collapse over time. It was more like it had been blasted away.

"What would cause that?" Marieke felt her forehead crease as she leaned in for a closer look. "I don't know what weapon would do that to stone."

"No weapon I've ever wielded," Zev said lightly. "Perhaps one that you have."

"What?" Marieke said distractedly, still studying the damage to the fountain. "I don't have much experience in weapons. I didn't study combat song, remember?" She frowned as she suddenly caught his meaning. "Wait, is that what you're suggesting? That the *weapon* which caused this destruction was magic?"

As usual, Zev didn't give her a straight answer. "Whatever it was, its mark is all over this place."

Looking around, Marieke realized Zev was right. Where other parts of the city had shown only decay and crumbling stone, the main square seemed to have suffered extensive damage that called to mind the brief discussion of military history included in Marieke's training at the academy. It was as though a series of catapults had attacked the city.

"What is it you're implying?" she asked Zev, pausing her study of the ruined square to examine his face instead. "When and why would this city have sustained a magical attack? Why won't you tell me what your version of the story says?"

Zev surprised her with his response. She'd expected another overconfident, cryptic remark, but instead he sighed, running a hand through his hair.

"Because I was taught certain things under an oath of secrecy," he said frankly. "I've already said more than I'm supposed to, but I haven't said nearly enough."

And he was back to cryptic. There was the Zev she'd come to know.

"Have you seen the start of the canyon?" Zev asked.

"Yes, and so have you," said Marieke. "We saw it when we rode alongside the ridge up to the coast, back in Oleand."

Zev didn't look convinced. "I think that lagoon is another example of the canyon's northward expansion. From what I understand, Sundering Canyon begins here, in Port Taran."

"What?" Marieke looked around. "Clearly that's not the case."

"Well, I can't confirm it," said Zev reasonably. "Like I said, I've never been here before. But since we're here, I'd like to find out if it's true."

# FIFTEEN

## Marieke

With that, Zev strode off eastward away from the wharf, where the main street continued in the opposite direction. Marieke kept pace with him, her mind swirling with questions. What was it Zev was trying to tell her? And was she sure she even wanted to know?

But the answer to that was never really in debate. Even before she'd somehow managed to fall quite suddenly from the favor of those in charge at the council and the academy, she'd been known for her irritatingly curious nature. She'd always asked a lot of questions, and she'd never asked a question to which she didn't want the answer.

For several minutes, they walked in silence. Zev's stride was even and his expression calm, but Marieke could sense his tension. This place affected him as much as it did her, although she couldn't be sure it was for the same reasons. She couldn't be sure of anything much when it came to guessing what was in Zev's head.

When the main street suddenly disappeared up ahead, Marieke let out a gasp. Zev had obviously seen it too, because he slowed his pace, coming to a stop at the edge of a sudden precipice. Once again, the destruction before them was much too dramatic to be explained as the natural decay of time. The ground fell away instantly, this ravine not running across the path, but starting from a seemingly random point and widening into a crevasse that stretched out in a straight line in front of them before bending a little northward up ahead. Marieke could see that surrounding roads were still intact, only the main street having suffered this drastic fate. Presumably the group was to continue out of Port Taran on one of the other roads.

"I believe," Zev said quietly, "we're looking at the birthplace of Sundering Canyon."

Marieke studied the area, the questions that had risen to her lips dying as her senses picked up more than she'd expected. She hadn't specifically intended to scan the area for power—it was just second nature, a standard part of taking in a new situation.

"I sense magic." The words came out sharply, her every nerve on high alert.

"The magic of the canyon?" Zev asked. "Didn't you say it feels different from elsewhere? Chaotic, I think you called it."

Marieke shook her head. "I did, but this is something different. I can feel the magic in the ground, of course, but what I'm talking about is an enchantment. Something put in place by a singer."

"What?" Zev looked around quickly, his tension increasing. "Someone is singing nearby? Using magic on us?"

"I don't think so." By contrast, Marieke relaxed a little as she tested the air and got a better sense for what she was identifying. "I'm not feeling the movement of magic. Just some lingering in place somewhere. It's very faint."

She turned away from the crack that opened in front of her feet, following the invisible signature of power. She didn't have to go far. Only a few feet from the origin of the ravine, there was a large boulder. Unlike many of the chunks of rock around it, it didn't appear to be part of a ruined building that had fallen. It stuck out of the ground almost to the height of her shoulders, a monolith that she suspected hadn't been placed there by human hands. A faded marking up high suggested that it was a mile marker, perhaps indicating that travelers down the now-sundered road had entered Port Taran proper.

Some rubble lay in front of the boulder, with a few scraggly bits of greenery reaching from the rocks to the mile marker. Still following the faint tug of the magic, Marieke pulled at the foliage with her hands before kicking the broken stone away with one sturdy boot.

Zev had followed her, and she felt him go still beside her as a message was revealed on the boulder. This one wasn't etched into the stone like the original distance marker. It looked like it had been painted on, and although it was weathered, the message—covering the whole bottom half of the boulder—was still quite clear.

*You can wash away the blood that was spilled here, but you cannot hide the curse on the land. The ground beneath your feet bears testimony.*

*- J*

Marieke felt her mouth fall open as she read the words. Cold seemed to rush over her, some foundation deep within her cracking ever so slightly. A glance at Zev showed him trans-fixed, his gray eyes unreadable as they passed over the words again and again.

Obviously he knew things she didn't, but Marieke had the

impression that her companion was as surprised as she was to find this sinister message.

"It seems I'm not the only one who's wondered if the land was cursed," she murmured. But a frown marred her forehead with the words. Her suspicions had related to Oleand, in light of its general deterioration. But they stood in Aeltas now, and this message presumably related to the southern country.

"It seems so." Zev's low voice was calm, but there was an energy behind the words that betrayed his tension. "Who do you think left this message? Who is J?"

Marieke didn't answer, although a strange premonition crept over her at the question.

"I mean, they didn't have to sign the message at all, did they?" Zev pressed. "It seems they wanted someone to find it— someone who might know who they were. Someone they thought wouldn't want this message out there." He ran his fingers over the painted words. "Perhaps no one but us has ever found it, though. I don't think it would be left here if they had."

"I'm not sure it can be removed." Marieke's voice sounded hushed in her own ears, as if she was attending a deathbed. "The only reason I found it is because I sensed the magic on it. I suspect it's some kind of protection enchantment, preventing the words from being rubbed off. It must have been strong when it was placed, in order to still be functioning."

"Could it have been here for hundreds of years?" Zev asked, raising an eyebrow, although his gaze remained on the boulder.

Marieke shook her head. "No way, not that long. But ten years, twenty years..." She trailed off with a shrug. "I think it's possible. I'm no expert." She studied his profile, half afraid to continue. "You're not asking the obvious question, which tells me you already know the answer," she said.

Zev turned at last, meeting her eyes unblinkingly. "What's the obvious question?"

"Whose blood was spilled here?" Marieke said. "What exactly is it that the ground bears testimony to?"

Zev didn't answer, his expression somber.

"Zev?" Marieke pressed. "This is what you've been hinting about, isn't it? This is the story you were told, that's so different from mine."

Still he said nothing.

Marieke stepped forward, seized by a strange desperation. She couldn't bear to have those she'd trusted proven liars, but even less could she stand the idea of wondering without knowing for sure. Barely aware of her own movements, she grabbed Zev's shirt in her two fists, anchoring him to her, as if by doing so she could prevent him from yet again maneuvering his way out of answering her questions.

"The monarchs were sent into exile in Providore," she insisted. "Along with all those in their court who refused to give up their corrupt titles, relinquish their ill-gotten lands, and swear allegiance to the emerging councils."

She didn't phrase it as a question, and Zev didn't offer an answer.

"Zev," she said, still gripping onto him with childish determination. "They were exiled. Weren't they?"

"I'm twenty-one years old, Marieke," Zev said. "What reason do you have to believe my word on things that happened hundreds of years ago? If I thought I could—or should—convince you of anything, I wouldn't have brought you here to draw your own conclusions. There's no use asking me questions. The ground beneath your feet bears testimony."

The words painted so ominously on the stone, repeated in Zev's low, steady voice, sent a shiver through Marieke that was deeper than fear. It had the ring of raw truth, more terrifying than any unanswered questions.

More world-shattering, harder to escape.

But more real and tangible as well.

The intensity of the moment was increased by Zev's nearness. He'd made no move to detach her hands, or to back away, although she'd pulled herself almost against him with her grip on his tunic. His eyes were deep and unyielding as she stared up into them, and the moment felt intimate in a way no discussion of historical discrepancies had any right to be. She felt exposed, but she also felt as if Zev was hiding himself from her less than he ever had before.

Her breath coming a little fast, Marieke released his clothes, resisting the urge to smooth the crumpled fabric before she stepped back. When there was a more breathable amount of distance between them, she dared to meet his eyes again.

"Are you saying the monarchs and their supporters were killed?" she asked. "Are you claiming the singers slaughtered them?"

"I claim nothing."

There was a new edge to Zev's words now, but Marieke was too caught up in her own revelations to examine the nuances in his reactions. She barely noticed as he started walking, although she found herself following him back toward the main square.

"You think the damage in the square up ahead was caused by magic," she went on. "You think that magic was used against the monarchs and their supporters. But why would any of that have happened in Port Taran? The only reason the monarchs came here was to embark from the port, so they could sail westward and leave the Sovereign Realms. Why would the singers kill them if they were leaving?"

Zev shook his head, his lip curling in a way Marieke didn't appreciate.

"What?" she demanded.

"You're struggling to think of a reason why a group of

people who'd just orchestrated a coordinated and violent coup against the rulers of their two countries might attack those rulers," he said shortly. "Only someone who'd been taught—and fully swallowed—an extremely rose-colored account of the uprising and its perpetrators could possibly find the idea confusing."

"If you think I'm going to be rattled by you insulting my intelligence, you underestimate me," Marieke said, a surge of anger giving fire to her words. "I know that I don't just blindly believe what I'm told, and I have no need to prove it to you."

Zev ran a hand down the back of his neck, surprising her by looking chastened. "You're right," he said. "I spoke arrogantly. I know you're smart enough to ask questions—to actually ask the right questions, which is even more rare. It's why I haven't been able to..." He trailed off, his steps slowing as they re-entered the ruined main square.

*Been able to what?* Marieke wanted to press. To keep his secrets fully hidden? To treat her as the enemy his family clearly thought her? Dare she wonder it...to stop thinking about her?

But those weren't the questions that mattered right now, and she didn't want to be unworthy of the compliment that she was smart enough to ask the right questions.

"You called the uprising violent, but it wasn't," she said. "It was a bloodless coup. That was the whole ethos behind the formation of the Councils of Singers. That those with power—like the artificial power of the monarchy or the actual, meaningful power of songcraft—shouldn't abuse it or use it as justification to oppress others."

"Isn't the very occurrence of the coup—a historical incident no one disputes—evidence that the singers saw their songcraft as justification for seizing power?" Zev countered.

"Seizing power isn't the same as abusing it," Marieke insisted. "I know a little of your life, Zev, and I know you've had hardly any exposure to your own council. But I've lived and trained alongside both the Council of Singers and the Academy of Song in Oleand. I've personally witnessed the way the council uses its power to govern the country to the best of its ability, promoting order, regulating the markets, helping those who struggle. And I've read with my own eyes reliable texts recounting the ways the monarchs abused power. And not just texts written by singers—even some of the last king's own court criticized his despotic ways."

She reached out, grabbing Zev's arm and causing him to stop walking and face her.

"Give me a straight answer for once. Do you deny either of those things?"

He drew in a long breath and let it out, his eyes more open and vulnerable than she'd seen them before.

"No, I don't. I'm not claiming either council to be made up of fully corrupt tyrants. I'm certainly not painting the monarchs of the past as saints, either. But things are rarely so black and white, Marieke."

"That we can agree on," she said quietly. She started to release his arm, but to her surprise, his hand suddenly appeared over hers, its grip strong and insistent, his gray eyes almost pleading.

"Everyone deserves the truth, Marieke. Even when the truth is far from black and white. That's all I'm arguing."

"And yet you took an oath of secrecy around the tales you were taught," she challenged.

Zev dropped his hand from hers, looking conflicted.

"That's not black and white, either."

She didn't respond, releasing his arm and moving forward again. She felt shaken and adrift. Part of her wanted to deny all of it, and retreat into the comfortable convictions she'd carried before she met Zev. But looking around the main square again, she had to admit she could think of nothing but magic that would cause the kind of damage she saw. And Zev was right that these signs threw into question the story of a non-violent uprising. If the singers had not only overthrown the monarchies by use of their magic, but had then pursued the fleeing rulers to the port city and attacked and slaughtered them rather than letting them leave the continent, it certainly cast the singers of the past in a different light.

And what did that mean for the singers of the present, such as herself?

She was inclined to agree with Zev that the people of Oleand and Aeltas deserved the truth. On one level, the singers' actions in institutionalizing a false version of their own conduct were more offensive even than the initial violence.

"Even if your version of history is right," she said, a sudden thought occurring to her, "some of them must have sailed west. Some of the monarchs' supporters reached Providore, because someone spread the tale there that caused the two continents to cease communication."

"Yes," Zev agreed steadily, walking alongside her as they left the square and followed the now-uneven main street back toward the wharf. "Probably many of the monarchs' supporters escaped."

"Maybe the monarchs were even among them."

He paused. "Maybe."

He didn't sound convinced, and Marieke didn't press the point. Neither of them could know for sure, after all. It had all happened so long ago.

When they reached the wharf, it was to find that the boat was arriving with its second load of passengers. Those who'd come on the first vessel with them had set up a mini camp to wait just before the start of the wharf.

The youngest member of the waiting clump turned as they

approached, his features relaxing when he caught sight of them.

"There you are," said Ramsey brightly. He flashed a grin toward Zev. "You were gone so long, I was getting worried. I thought I might have to come after you, to protect Marieke's reputation."

Zev didn't reward this joke with a reply, and even Marieke felt more irked than usual by the young farmer's banter. She hadn't for a moment been afraid for her reputation—or for herself—during her time alone with Zev. But she did feel as though her innocence had been shattered, and it was no joking matter for her.

Recognizing that she would only be in the way, Marieke hung back while Zev and Ramsey assisted in the unloading of the boat. She felt ill-at-ease, the city feeling even more sinister in presence than it had when she'd first arrived. The sun was close to setting, and she wondered if she would have to spend the night here before she could return to Oleand. It wasn't an appealing prospect.

And what about traveling back to Oleand with Zev—how appealing or otherwise was that prospect? She couldn't help asking herself the question. He'd promised to see her back over the border. Presumably they could sail back after the last boat-load was delivered. Would he really accompany her, or would seeing her onto the boat be enough in his mind?

She didn't deny to herself that she wanted him to come with her. The discomfort caused by the day's revelations didn't reduce Zev's fascination at all. On the contrary, she found herself more eager than ever to unravel his secrets.

She also found herself more drawn to him with every minute they spent together. When she'd grabbed his shirt, shamelessly forcing him to stay where he was and engage with her, she'd been able to feel the steady beat of his heart under her fist, strong and even and unflappable. It was a rhythm that had steadied her, even in that moment of inner tumult. With that memory came another, of his hand closing around hers on his arm, silently entreating her not to let their difference of opinion turn her against him.

Why he should care what she thought of him, she couldn't say. But it warmed her to think that he did. More than warmed her. The sensation that shot up her body when she remembered the earnest look in his eyes could better be described as heat.

But she'd be wise not to get carried away with thoughts of Zev's strength or appeal. She was starting to get a sense of why his family had reacted to her the way they did. They believed a version of history which painted her kind as not only murderers but liars. And whatever conflict he might feel when face to face with her, Zev was a product of that same teaching, that same loyalty. For all she knew, he was as much a monarchist at heart as Gorgon, who'd tried to kill her merely for the crime of being a singer.

As she wrestled with these reflections, Marieke wandered along the water's edge, not straying far from the start of the wharf. It took her a moment to realize that her meandering wasn't aimless. She was once again following a trail her senses had identified without her mind trying to.

Magic.

Marieke's breath caught in her throat as she recognized the same type of faint mark she'd felt at the start of the canyon. She stumbled a little as she hurried to the edge of the stone walkway that rose up from the water's edge, and from which the wharf extended. The magic came from below, and it didn't take Marieke long to find a mostly ruined staircase that led down to the water level. After navigating down it, she followed the magic back toward the start of the wharf, coming to a stop a few feet from the point where the stone walkway stretched out above her head.

Just as at the main square, she had to shift some rubble to find the source of the magic. It seemed that someone, unable to remove the words, had at least made a token effort to cover them up.

Because words there were, written in the same unnaturally preserved paint.

*Here they were betrayed, as your deception has betrayed us all. A wound to the back is never by an honorable hand. Your lies have been exposed, and I will not forget.*

*-J*

Marieke swallowed hard, her throat dry as she stared at this second cryptic inscription. Here they were betrayed? Did this relate again to the monarchs? Had the singers prevented them from boarding the boats that would have saved them? A wound to the back...that certainly sounded like the singers had hunted fleeing quarry.

"J," Marieke muttered. She wrapped one arm around herself, the same suspicion she'd felt at the last message hardening within her. She could still hear the anger and fear in the Head Instructor's voice when she'd eavesdropped on his conversation with Isabel.

*I thought you assured me Marieke wasn't going to be a second Jade.*

And Isabel's reassurances hadn't seemed to soothe his concerns. He'd remained fixated on her encounter with the group down in the ravine. Just like the councilor who ran the meeting where the delegation gave its report, the Head

Instructor seemed to consider Marieke's brush with the monarchists dangerous. He'd openly said as much to Isabel.

*Who knows what stories they filled her head with? In light of that, how can you possibly promise me she won't be a second Jade?"*

Marieke had no proof that *J* was Jade, but she didn't need it in order to be convinced. It was clear that she wasn't the first student to learn that not everyone agreed with the version of history taught by the academies. She supposed she should count herself lucky that she'd learned this information after graduating, or she might have been expelled for the discovery just as Jade had been.

Of course, it seemed that Jade had gone looking for answers—and apparently aggressively—whereas Marieke had stumbled accidentally upon them when she plunged into the ravine. But she'd been considered just as tainted, she reflected, an ember of anger growing inside her.

Her anger cooled a little as she realized she wasn't being entirely honest about her own role in her change in circumstances. Encountering the monarchists had only been the beginning. She hadn't just let the matter rest. She'd wanted to understand more—she'd even begun to suspect a connection between what she'd witnessed and the deteriorating state of the land.

All in all, she thought she'd been wise to sneak into the group of investigators rather than advertising her search for answers. It seemed that unlike Zev, the council didn't consider asking the right questions to be a trait worthy of praise. Even though they claimed to be trying honestly to find the cause of Oleand's problems.

Marieke climbed back up to the level of the wharf with a heavy heart. She was past the point of trying to convince herself to deny Zev's claims about inaccurate history. The cryptic messages themselves might not have been enough. But they became more compelling in light of her suspicion that the mysterious "J" was the student whose memory had caused such consternation from the Head Instructor and the council. The very student whose trail she'd been trying to follow. Not to mention the fact that in putting together what was happening in her country and what she'd witnessed in the ravine, Marieke had independently begun to wonder whether the land was cursed. And now she found that this precise conclusion might be what had caused Jade to fall from favor.

Marieke couldn't yet see clearly how it all fit together, but there were too many lines of connection for her to just dismiss it.

When she reached the end of the wharf, Zev was stepping off it, his eyes scanning the area as if looking for something. She barely noticed the way he relaxed when he caught sight of her, too consumed by her own thoughts. Zev had suggested she might find answers in Port Taran, but every so-called answer only uncovered more questions.

"Why now, though?" she blurted, not very comprehensibly, when Zev came to a stop in front of her. "That's what doesn't add up to me."

"Why now what?" he asked.

Marieke folded her arms, frowning at him. "If it's true that the first councils slaughtered the fleeing monarchs and their supporters, and that this unleashed some kind of curse on the land that caused Sundering Canyon to appear, why is Oleand only deteriorating now? It's been generations."

Zev raised his eyebrows. "You seem to have traveled a long way in my absence."

Marieke narrowed her eyes at him, wishing she felt less petulant. "I didn't say I'm convinced of anything." She drew in a deep breath and released it before adding, her voice low, "I found another one. Another message from J. Under the wharf."

Zev's eyes widened slightly as his gaze flicked to the wharf behind him.

"I'll have to check it out." He ran a hand over his chin, which Marieke noticed had become a little scruffy during their travels. "I have to say, I didn't expect these messages. Who's been following this trail before you? And why haven't I heard anything of it?"

"I'm not sure why you would hear," Marieke said in a dampening tone. "You're not exactly the hub of information in the Sovereign Realms. As for who it is, I'm pretty sure I know."

"You do?" Zev's eyes shot to hers, startled. "Who is it?"

Marieke lifted her chin slightly, deciding to abandon dignity and lean into petulance. "I don't think you need to know that information. See how you like getting half-answers and cryptic challenges."

Zev's lips twitched. "Fair is fair, I suppose." He glanced again toward the underside of the wharf. "If it helps, I'm not hiding any information about your last question. I have no idea why Oleand is deteriorating only in recent years. If something's changed, I don't know what it is."

"That makes two of us," sighed Marieke.

She felt more disheartened than ever. As much as she wanted to know the truth about the long-past history of the coup, her more immediate concern was figuring out what was causing her country to falter. And, by extension, what was causing the land to rise up in violence against singers, herself included. The two phenomena must be connected.

And she was determined to get to the bottom of the mystery. Which meant not getting distracted, no matter how intriguing both Zevadiah and his secrets might be.

# SIXTEEN

# Zev

"That's the last of it."

Zev nodded in acknowledgment of the older man's words, relieved to see the other farmer was right. The night was well advanced, and he'd long been ready to be done with the unloading from the final boat trip. But they'd all arrived now, even the horses.

He led his own mare carefully down the uneven wharf, murmuring soothingly to her as he went. She clearly hadn't enjoyed the short sea voyage, and he felt guilty for abandoning her to brave it without his presence.

He'd chosen instead to stay with Marieke. And it had certainly been an illuminating exploration. Much as he'd hoped Port Taran might make Marieke question the tales she'd been told about the supposedly bloodless coup, even he had never imagined just how much they would find. Such as the mysterious messages. Who was J? Who, before Marieke, had come to this site of history asking the right questions? And what had become of them as a result? It wasn't as though they'd advertised their suspicions far and wide, was it?

Zev wondered what his family would make of this new

information, but he tried not to dwell on the question. Because that would mean thinking about how they'd react to the rest of his situation, and he had a feeling he would be in for some censure when he recounted his movements. He doubted it would be much use to assure them that he hadn't sought Marieke out, or expected her to appear in the random farming town to which their group had gone. Azai certainly wouldn't believe it. Zev could only be glad none of them had witnessed the moment near the canyon's beginning, when Marieke had grabbed his shirt and clung to him as if he was her only point of stability in a world turned upside down.

And thankfully, no one, not his family, not Marieke, had any way to know how her touch had made his heart throb, or how much the earnestness in her eyes had gone to his head.

The object of his thoughts appeared before his gaze as he reached the end of the wharf. Half the group had settled hours ago for an uneasy sleep among the ruins of the port city, but Marieke wasn't among them. She knew that if she wanted to catch a ride back to Oleand on the small ship, she'd need to be ready when the vessel sailed back for a final time. It was unfortunate that the transfer of their party had taken so much longer than anticipated, and she would now be arriving on the other side of the canyon in the middle of the night.

"Are they ready for me?" Marieke's soft voice was barely audible over the lapping of the waves against the stone wall from which the wharf jutted out.

"Yes, they're ready for us."

She didn't miss Zev's correction, frowning at him. "You don't have to come, Zev. It's the middle of the night, and you must be exhausted. You should sleep, along with the rest of your group."

"I said I'd see you safely back to Oleand," Zev said, no compromise in his voice.

She shook her head at him. "But how will you get back? The ship isn't sailing here again."

"I'll climb across the canyon where it's shallowest, near the water," Zev said. "It won't be hard on my own, without a horse or gear."

"In the dark?" Marieke protested.

"Stop wasting time," said Zev. "Do you want them to sail without you?"

She didn't look convinced, but she moved forward, her form sagging with the same weariness he felt as she passed him. Zev hurried to hand his horse over to Ramsey with instructions to look after her until Zev caught up with the group, or all the way back to his farm if necessary. He was worried Marieke would convince the crew of the vessel to embark without him if he dallied.

But the ship was still there when he returned, the sailors looking eager to set off. With a word of thanks, Zev boarded, taking nothing but his pack.

The ship cut silently through the waves, no one much inclined for conversation. Marieke leaned against the railing, staring out at the water. Her dark braid was draped over her shoulder, and the moonlight gave her slim figure an air of mystery. How had this girl upended his life so completely, when she'd clearly had no thought of doing it?

"How will you travel home?" Zev moved up alongside her, his voice low to match the hushed mood of the ship.

She turned to him, her eyes taking a moment to focus on his face as she came out of whatever reverie had kept her so engrossed.

"I'll walk to the closest town," she said. "The one we passed not too long before the wharf. Then I'll pay for a ride on a public coach. I might have to wait a day or two for the next one, but it shouldn't be too difficult."

"And it will take you to the capital?"

She didn't answer at once. "I'm not sure if I'm going to the capital," she said. "I mean, I'll have to pass through there, but I don't think I'll linger. I might be wise to make myself scarce for a while, in case the council is inclined to be angry about me sneaking onto that investigative team."

Zev could hear the heaviness in her voice as she expressed this doubt in the council she'd been so loyal to when they first met. His heart ached a little for her disillusionment, even though he knew it was necessary.

"So you'll go all the way to your parents' home?" he pressed.

"I suppose so." She didn't sound eager. "It will be interesting to learn whether things have gotten worse in the region. I just hope I won't be too far removed from the action to hear about any more accidents befalling singers. It will be hard to figure out what's going on if I don't have the latest information."

"It's not your job to fix whatever is ailing your country," Zev pointed out. "You don't have to take it all on your shoulders."

Her lips were set in a thin line that made her view of this attitude clear. Zev held back a smile. He knew her well enough by now to guess that she wouldn't be inclined to sit back and let others solve the crisis. He just hoped her determination didn't come from some lingering superstition that she'd somehow brought a curse back into Oleand with her because of her misadventure in Sundering Canyon.

The voyage passed slowly, the lateness of the hour making everything seem sluggish. When they finally docked at the tiny wharf on the Oleandan side, the crew dispersed, obviously having made arrangements ahead of time for the end of their task. It wasn't part of the deal with the Aeltan group for them to assist Marieke to find accommodation for the night. Zev didn't blame them, but he did feel uneasy. The same prickling sense of being watched that had followed them all the way to the coast had returned, almost as soon as they made landfall.

The town Marieke intended to walk to was much too far away for her to traverse at this hour alone. Even together, he wouldn't want to make the journey in the middle of the night.

"It's very dark," he said decisively. "And I'm weary. I don't think I'll try to climb across the ravine tonight after all. I'll find a place to camp and try it in the morning."

"Are you sure?" Was it his imagination that Marieke's voice seemed tinged with relief? "Won't the group get too far ahead of you?"

"They'll be sleeping anyway," Zev pointed out. He strode along the water's edge, toward the lip of the canyon. Marieke followed behind him, and soon they were both looking down into the lagoon. "I think there's a decent chance of finding a sheltered cave in the side of the ravine," he said. He raised a challenging eyebrow. "Are you up for it, city girl?"

Marieke didn't rise to the bait. "You're out of your depth here, farm boy. The coast is my domain. This isn't the first time I've clambered over seaside cliffs in the dark."

As if to prove the words, she pushed past him, her footing sure as she seized an overhanging rock and swung herself down the side of the canyon. Zev had to restrain the impulse to reach out and grab her arm, or tell her to be careful. Although the ravine was much lower here, a fall could still be dangerous.

He followed her down, pleased to find his prediction proved right. It took very little time for Marieke to locate a small cave in the side of the cliff.

"It's not much," she said brightly, as he climbed in after her. "But it's dry, and out of the wind. And the dirt in here is a bonus. I expected hard rock." She frowned. "I don't think I'll be able to make a fire with what I've got on me, though."

"It's mild enough I don't think we need to," Zev said. "I'm not worried about any predators up here, and I don't think there can be more than a few hours before dawn."

Marieke nodded, already busy pulling a couple of spare gowns out of her pack. "Pillow," she explained, when she saw him watching her. "It won't be very comfortable, but I'm exhausted enough I think I'll sleep anyway."

"Go ahead," Zev said. "I'll do a quick scout of the area, and then I'll join you."

She gave him a suspicious look. "You're not going to stay awake and keep watch while I sleep, are you? Just to be some kind of martyr?"

He smiled. "I'm as exhausted as you are. If I can sleep, I will."

Satisfied, she nodded. "All right, then. Scout away, if you really think it's necessary."

Zev wasn't at all sure he did think it necessary, but he didn't say so. He just edged out of the cave, feeling his way down the now-navigable drop in the moonlight. The truth he preferred not to admit was that he didn't know how to be natural in a small space with Marieke while they settled for sleep. He thought it would be less embarrassing for both of them if she was already out by the time he returned.

She obviously hadn't exaggerated her own weariness, because that was exactly what he found. When he'd satisfied himself that no humans or other creatures lingered close by, and that their cave—halfway up the cliff face—wasn't in danger of being flooded by the lagoon, he climbed silently back into the little sanctuary to be met with the deep, even breathing of slumber.

Feeling both foolish and a little guilty, he paused to study her features. She looked very peaceful in sleep, her dark hair framing a face that gave an impression of pleasant roundness in spite of the high cheekbones and straight nose. She had a warm face, he decided. It suited her.

Marieke had settled at the back of the small cave, and Zev laid himself across the entrance. He didn't think they'd be disturbed while they slept, but just in case, he'd make sure anyone wanting to do them a mischief would have to come through him first. He faced outward, his eyes on the starry sky above as he felt sleep creeping toward him. It made him uncomfortable to picture Marieke sleeping in here alone. He couldn't believe he'd been planning to dump her at the wharf in the middle of the night and return immediately to Aeltas.

But no real guilt attached to the thought. Because he knew deep down, as he drifted into unconsciousness, that there had never been any possibility of him doing that.

When Zev woke, the light on his face told him at once that he'd slept longer than he intended. He rolled over, his muscles protesting at the hard ground, to be confronted with an empty cave.

He was surprised by the anxiety that lanced through him. Marieke wasn't his responsibility, he reminded himself. And she certainly wasn't defenseless.

Nevertheless, he lost no time in climbing the short distance down the cliff to the rocky ground below in search of her. He made his way along the shaley surface, sticking close to the cliff wall as he reached the area where water pooled into the ravine from the ocean.

The cliff veered away northward as he went, opening up into the lagoon he'd seen when they passed the end of Sundering Canyon the previous day. To his relief, he spotted Marieke some distance ahead, kneeling at the water's edge with her hands immersed in the salty water. He heard her voice a moment after he caught sight of her. From his distance, her song was only a soft, melodic hum. The water swirled gently under her hands, the magic serving no purpose he could see other than being beautiful. Zev came to a stop, guilt creeping over him for more than one reason as he watched her.

After a moment, he forced himself to turn away. She probably wanted privacy if she was freshening up, and he shouldn't be eavesdropping on her singing. He couldn't seem to help himself being drawn to Marieke, but nor could he silence the voice in his mind that chided him for his fascination—a voice that sounded irritatingly like Azai's.

Worst of all, he wasn't just fascinated with Marieke herself. It was also her songcraft. He'd been enthralled by her explanation to Ramsey and himself on the boat the day before. He'd been extensively educated on the privacy of his family's land, in all kinds of areas most farmers would never have cause to study, but songcraft was one topic that had never been addressed. The family rarely spoke of it at all, and it would certainly have been discouraged for him to seek out knowledge of the mechanics of the magic.

But when Marieke had described how it worked, he'd been captivated. It didn't sound evil or out of control when she spoke of it. It sounded like a powerful and positive tool, one the country would be mad not to use. His own reaction had created such conflicted feelings within him, he'd distanced himself from both the conversation and Marieke.

It was an approach that wasn't going to be very practical if he intended to see her safely all the way to her destination.

A quiet splash and the sudden absence of Marieke's song were the only tangible things that announced something had changed. But Zev felt it on a different level. The unease that had trailed him on their journey to the coast came rushing back in a torrent, and he spun around.

There was no sign of Marieke, and it took him a moment to realize that the water where she'd been kneeling was rippling strangely. He took two strides forward then stopped, telling himself not to overreact. If she'd slipped in, she would soon pull herself back out, and might prefer not to have an audience for her embarrassing escapade.

But the seconds passed, and there was no sign of Marieke emerging. Zev propelled himself back into motion, his strides turning quickly into a run as the surface of the water remained unbroken.

He threw himself down where Marieke had been kneeling, fear washing over him as he was finally able to see her form. The water was deeper than he'd realized, and she was not only fully submerged, but thrashing wildly without any part of her able to reach the surface.

Zev didn't stop to think. He just threw himself into the lagoon, filling his lungs with air in the moment before he hit the water. At once, he was sucked down with shocking force, the movement of the current not at all what he'd expected from the seemingly peaceful scene above. He reached out his arms blindly, trying to grasp Marieke—or anything solid—but his hands found only swirling water. He was a confident swimmer, having learned in the dam on his family's property. But he'd never swum in water like this. His body seemed to have lost all buoyancy, the current trying to suck him ever downward. He felt his feet collide with the bottom, and the next thing he knew, pain slashed across his leg.

He forced his eyes open against the stinging of the salt, trying to make sense of what was happening. A trickle of blood met his eyes, and following it, he saw that his leg had scraped along a jagged root that stuck up from the lagoon's muddy floor at a vicious angle. It had torn right through his leggings and ripped into his skin.

But he didn't have time to think about that now. The water wasn't what he'd call clear, thanks to the mud being stirred up by the current, and his own blood now joining the mix, yet his frantically questing gaze found Marieke. Her brilliant eyes were wide open and locked on to him. He'd thought she might have also run afoul of a root, perhaps gotten tangled, but he couldn't see any sign of that. She seemed to just be pulled downward by a vortex of water too strong for her to fight. She wasn't far from the submerged bank, however, and with a huge effort Zev kicked out against the flow with his uninjured leg, one grasping hand grabbing a root that protruded from the muddy side of the lagoon.

Anchored in place, he reached for her with his other hand through the chaotic swirl of water. Marieke reached out too, grasping his arm with her hand, allowing him to complete the hold by locking his fingers around her arm as well. His lungs were screaming for air now, but he didn't falter. Muscles straining, he heaved her toward him, fighting the current with everything he had. To his immense relief, his efforts were rewarded as her form glided through the water toward him. A moment later, she'd grabbed hold of the bank as well, and wasted no time in pulling herself up.

Zev let go of her arm as she reached for the rocky edge above them, instead grabbing at her leg and helping to push her upward. When she disappeared above him, he tried to follow, but his injured leg crumpled as he tried to use it to push himself upward off the wall. The water tugged at him mercilessly, and he could feel his strength leaking from him. His head was spinning from lack of air and from the pain in his leg, and the muddy roots were slippery under his fingers. He fought panic as his hold on the bank loosened, the current trying relentlessly to pull him back into the lagoon.

Then, all of a sudden, the water changed. The sucking vortex turned momentarily to pure, directionless chaos, then the current surged underneath him, pushing him up toward the surface. His head broke into the sweet, life-giving air, and he drew in a ragged gasp. Not intending to give the current the chance to drag him back under, he reached at once for the bank, his arms shaking with exhaustion as he pulled himself upward. It took a moment for him to catch the steady, almost stern voice swelling in song around him. His eyes found Marieke, her dark braid and thick gown dripping as she once again knelt on the bank. Her eyes were fixed, not on him, but on the water, as she sang words he mainly couldn't catch. Something about seasons, which made little sense to him, although the mention of tides seemed more relevant.

As he stared at her, his mind finally comprehending that her intervention was what had saved him from the savage current, her focus shifted. Her eyes locked on his, and for a moment he thought she was going to sing him right out of the water. But he should have known better—hadn't the singer who'd healed his arm told him they didn't use magic on other humans without their permission?

Instead, Marieke reached out an arm, sliding it under one of his armpits and tugging with all her might. Zev assisted with his other arm, and under their combined efforts, he emerged fully from the water.

Marieke fell backward from their momentum, Zev unable to catch himself as he followed. He landed practically on top of her, and for an endless heartbeat, they just stared at each other, both breathing hard as water dripped from his hair onto her face.

Then he got his arms underneath him, placing his hands on

either side of her head and lifting his weight so as not to crush her. But he didn't immediately sit up, his eyes searching her features with an urgency he knew he had little right to feel. She looked pale and waterlogged, but otherwise no worse for wear. Yet the relief of this discovery was short-lived. Instead of being glad, Zev found himself filled with an anger stronger than he'd felt in a long time.

He'd had no time to think it through while he was fighting the current, but now he was out of the water, the conclusion was inescapable. That had been no natural tide. Someone or something had attacked Marieke—in an attack as targeted as the one against the singer in the farming town, an attack designed to incapacitate her best weapon. And had the attack succeeded, the outcome would certainly have been her death.

Zev hardly knew how to process the intensity of his reaction. Coming back to himself enough to regain control of his limbs, he pushed himself up to a sitting position, energy coursing through the arms that had been shaking and weak a moment before. Marieke followed as soon as he was clear, hastening to sit. But she didn't scramble up and away from him. Instead, she grabbed his arms with the same insistence she'd shown when she seized his tunic in the ruins of Port Taran. Her slim fingers clasped his arms tightly as she pulled herself in a little, her eyes searching his features.

"Are you all right?" she asked breathlessly. "Are you hurt?"

Zev's mouth opened, but no words came out. She was worried about him? It was the last thing he'd expected her to be concerned about after what she'd just experienced. His eyes met her brilliant blue ones, her magnetic pull stronger than ever before.

He hadn't answered her question, but he wasn't interested in words. He found himself leaning forward, his arms coming up to mirror her posture. But he didn't grab her with the intensity she'd shown. Instead he placed his hands gently just below her shoulders, his fingers hesitant as they spread across the wet fabric of her gown.

He was so wrapped up in his own emotions that it took him a moment to realize that she was leaning forward as well—he surely wasn't imagining it. His eyes darted down to her lips, and he thought he saw her own eyes start to flicker shut.

Zev pulled back with a ragged breath, releasing his hold on her and pulling himself together. What was he doing? What was wrong with him? He was too old and too sensible to let himself be caught up in the emotion of a near miss, throwing out everything he'd been raised on in the process.

It didn't matter if he wanted more with Marieke. The reasons he shouldn't—couldn't—have more with her were many and insurmountable. He needed to keep himself in check, and stop losing his head like a green youth.

Marieke scrambled to her feet as soon as he pulled back, her cheeks burning with heat that made Zev feel guilty. He was the one who should feel embarrassment, not her. He stood more slowly, avoiding her eyes as she attempted to wring out her gown. It seemed they were both going to pretend that hadn't just happened, and he could only be grateful.

Because although he thought his family—who would surely tell him to back off completely from Marieke—were wrong not to give the young singer a chance to prove she wasn't corrupted, there was a limit. There were lines he couldn't cross.

No matter how much his racing pulse and pounding heart forced him to admit that he wanted to.

CHAPTER

# SEVENTEEN

*Marieke*

Marieke's heartbeat thudded in her ears, her mind struggling to catch up with the series of abrupt changes in her interaction with Zev. How much had she just humiliated herself? Had it all been in her head? But surely he'd been the one to lean in first, the one whose ragged breaths had made her heart falter for a moment.

"Looks like I need to thank you again," she said, trying to make her voice light. "That's the second time you've saved my life."

"If I saved your life just now, we can call it even." Zev's voice was gruff, guttural. "You saved mine right back. I don't think I could have fought my way out through that current without your intervention." He met her eyes, his own serious. "Marieke, that wasn't a natural current."

"I know," she said heavily, scanning his form for reassurance. He hadn't acknowledged any hurt, but he didn't seem quite his usual unflappable self. "Not that I needed extra proof that water shouldn't behave that way, but I'm pretty sure I actually felt magic when—"

248

She broke off abruptly, her eyes finding the jagged gash on his leg, and the blood seeping steadily from it.

"Zev, you're hurt!"

He followed her gaze, flicking his shoulder as if getting rid of an irritating fly. "I'm all right. It's nothing."

"It's not nothing," she contradicted sternly. "Look how much blood you're losing! You can't walk around on that."

"I have some bandages in my pack, back in the cave," he said. "I'll wrap it up, it will be fine."

Marieke glared at him, glad to have a safer focus for her tumultuous emotions. "Don't be ridiculous." She made an imperative gesture. "Sit down. You're not bandaging anything. I may not have specialized in healing song, but I learned the basics, same as every other student at the academy. You're not taking another step until I've attended to that injury."

She expected Zev to protest, but to her surprise, he sat as instructed, with only an incoherent mumble to show his disapproval. Anxiously, she reflected that if he was acquiescing so readily, he was probably in a great deal of pain. In spite of her confident words, she felt a trickle of nerves. She hadn't attempted a healing song since her graduation, and if she made a mistake, she might cause further damage, or inflict greater pain.

But as she examined the wound, trying her utmost to keep her touch gentle, she relaxed a little. It wasn't a complicated injury. The gash was deep, and it probably hurt a great deal. But the muscle didn't seem to be torn, and there was no sign that an artery had been severed, or anything alarming like that. It should be within her basic skill level.

Mindful of the core teaching regarding consent, she raised her eyes to Zev's.

"May I attempt a healing song on you?"

Zev's storm-gray eyes were unreadable as he met her gaze.

The moment stretched out so long, she wondered if he was going to refuse.

"Yes," he said at last.

With a nod, Marieke refocused her attention on the injury to Zev's leg. It was bleeding quite a lot, and she wondered if she'd been too hasty to reject the bandages from Zev's pack. There was no sense in wasting energy to do with songcraft what she could as efficiently do with her hands. But knowing how strange Zev was about singing, she was concerned that if she didn't act on his permission now, he might change his mind and refuse to let her heal him.

With a businesslike gesture, she flipped back her wet skirts, noting with some amusement Zev's startled expression as he followed with his eyes. But Marieke's dress was plenty long enough for her action not to be scandalous as she ripped a length of fabric off the underlayer of the gown.

She fashioned a clumsy tourniquet on Zev's leg, aware of his eyes boring into the back of her head as she bent over him. But he said nothing, just letting her work. When the bleeding had slowed, and she'd washed the wound as best she could with water from the lagoon, Marieke cleared her throat. She felt nervous, as if she was sitting an examination back at the academy.

She started humming to herself, testing the power in the ground. So near to Sundering Canyon, the magic of the area was intense and less ordered than she was used to. But at least there was plenty of it. Drawing power into herself, she let her hum turn into a song, using one of the formulaic melodies they taught at the academy for when molding the magic required too much focus to allow the singer to come up with a tune.

It was a solemn melody, rising and falling with gentle undulation. For some reason, it made Marieke think of the hills surrounding Zev's home, where the mounds rose and fell softly, and the long grass rippled in the breeze. It wasn't the dramatic, chaotic song of rapids, or the soothing, steady repetition of a flat ocean. It was somewhere in between, and it suited Zev, somehow. It felt like the right fit for coaxing his reluctant mind to relax into the song and let the magic do its work in his body.

So much for the melody. Now for the words. Marieke felt buoyant from the volume of power swelling inside her, and she was only too ready to let it out. She would probably be wise to keep it simple, given her rudimentary training in healing song, but she didn't feel the need to take the beginner's approach. The raw intensity of the magic, and the comfortable fit of the melody, made her feel empowered, capable.

She sang simple words about the steady passage of time, calling to mind her training about the human body, and using it to picture the ways in which Zev's body would naturally heal the wound if left to its own timeline. Still using only vague words, she wove her song and its power around that process, not trying to interfere with or redirect it. Not trying to take away any agency from Zev's body. After all, he was, in his own words, under no one's control but his own. Unconscious as the body's natural healing process might be, she had a feeling the magic would be more effective if working with his body rather than trying to overpower its approach with a different strategy.

To her satisfaction, she could feel the power responding to her direction. She'd been afraid that it wouldn't work—as she'd explained to Zev and Ramsey, the easiest way to use magic was to direct it to do more strongly or more efficiently what your hands could do without it. And removing magic from the equation, she certainly didn't have the ability to speed up time.

But it seemed her understanding was sound, both of the natural healing process of the human body and of what Zev would respond most effectively to. It wasn't advanced healing songcraft she needed here—the wound wasn't complex. It was advanced understanding of the nuanced relationship between the particular magic she'd pulled into herself and the chosen subject of her power. And for that, her studies in agricultural song were useful—focusing as they had on the different forms magic took in different types of terrain—and the time she'd spent trying to figure Zev out was even more useful.

Her song grew in volume and confidence as the power latched on to the healing that had already begun—though there was little measurable evidence yet—and enhanced it. She could feel the magic accelerating the process far beyond what could otherwise be possible. She sang of the timelessness of the land around them, picturing in her mind how it had been there before Zev was injured, and would be there long after his wound healed of its own accord.

When she felt her own loss of energy reaching a problematic stage, she let her song begin to drop. The only downside of using advanced magic in a more general field, instead of the specialized song a healing singer could have used, was that it took a great deal more energy. And it wasn't until she actually stopped singing that she realized how drained she felt. She'd probably pushed it further than was wise, and it would slow down her onward travel.

No matter. As she examined Zev's leg and saw that the wound had fully closed over, only a scar remaining where the deep, jagged gash had been, she felt pleased. It was worth adding perhaps half a day to her journey to restore Zev's strength. Not to mention giving him a positive experience of the craft of which he was so inclined to be wary.

"There," she said, her voice soft and weary as she smiled at her handiwork.

"How did you do that?" Zev's hushed question brought her gaze up to his.

"What do you mean?"

"How did you heal it so completely like that?"

She stared at him blankly. "With...magic?" The answer, which was surely superfluous, came out like a question. "I used songcraft, obviously."

"Yes, I know." Zev's smile was self-deprecating rather than mocking. "I mean, how did you do it without even mentioning the wound, or the healing process? The singer who almost got crushed by that branch healed my arm then, and he was much more obvious with his words. And yet, the healing wasn't as impressive."

"Well." Marieke found herself flushing with pleasure at the compliment to her songcraft. "I'm no expert, but I did graduate from the Academy of Song, you know."

"So did he," Zev pointed out.

She couldn't help that her smile crept toward a smirk. "Yes, I suppose he did."

Zev's eyes were intent on her face, and something in his expression shifted as she held his gaze.

"Your voice is much more beautiful, as well," he said, his own voice low and throaty.

Marieke said nothing. She couldn't think of a single response, her lips suddenly too dry for speaking. Zev was watching her with a look she'd never seen on his face before.

"I haven't heard much song in my life," he admitted. "When you sing, it sounds nothing like I expected. No one can make magic sound the way you do. I almost...feel it. Not the magic, the music. In my bones."

Marieke tried to lighten the moment with a smile. "Thankfully the wound hadn't affected your bones, or it would likely have been beyond my skill."

Zev refused to be deterred. "You know that's not what I meant. I've always thought of magic as dangerous and wily. How do you make it sound so...pure? So...well, beautiful?"

"I don't know," said Marieke honestly. "I just sing the only way I know how. Every singer's voice sounds different, I suppose. They do train us a little in the actual music of song at the academy. Teach us how to make our voices more pleasant to the ear, that sort of thing. But I don't know that my singing voice changed much through that process. From the first time I felt the urge to sing, and discovered I had the ability, the music has felt joyful as it comes out. I'm not sure how else to put it."

She couldn't read his expression as his eyes roved over her face, and she wondered if he could tell how her cheeks were heating.

"What?" she asked, when she could take the scrutiny in silence no longer. "What are you thinking?"

He pulled his eyes away, smiling a private smile to himself as he tested his healed leg with one strong hand. "You're just not at all what I expected, that's all. And when you're the one wielding it, magic isn't what I expected, either."

Marieke couldn't help smiling, pleased at the success of her secret hope to wear away Zev's prejudice toward songcraft.

"Well, it's done its job this time, anyway. That leg looks good to me. I would think it should be fine to walk on straight away, but you'll need to be careful when navigating that canyon. It's not ideal to attempt a treacherous climb so soon after a healing."

"The canyon?" Zev repeated, coming fully out of whatever pensive mood had gripped him. "I'm not climbing the canyon. At least not anytime soon."

Marieke frowned. "I thought you said you were going to climb across the canyon where it's shallowest."

"That's obviously changed now," Zev said. He was looking at her like she'd lost her mind. "Marieke, do you not realize that you just almost died?"

"Yes, I'm fairly aware, thank you," she said, hoping her tart tone hid the warmth spreading through her at his concern.

"I don't know how it happened," Zev went on, "but it was clearly targeted at you. There's no way I'm leaving you to travel on alone. I'm going to see you home."

"That's not necessary," Marieke said. "I appreciate the impulse, but that's asking way too much of you. Besides," she added, "I'm not going home. I'm going to change course and head for the capital. If I get in trouble for my stunt with the investigation team, so be it. This is too serious now for me to just keep it to myself."

Zev eyed her. "You mean whatever just happened to you?"

She nodded. "I already suspected it, but now I'm sure that the accidents befalling singers aren't natural. I started to say it before—I think I felt magic that time. Active magic. As the water pulled me under."

"Active magic?" repeated Zev.

"Magic that was being directed somehow," Marieke clarified. "Magic that wasn't coming from the ground."

"You think there was a singer nearby?" Zev pressed.

She shook her head slowly. "I don't know. It wasn't really like any song I've felt before. Of course, it all happened very quickly, and I wasn't really focused on investigating what I felt when I was trying desperately to reach the surface and not drown." She gave her head a little shake. "Either way, I need to report this to the council. If they haven't acknowledged that these accidents aren't accidents, then they need to. They can't bury their heads in the sand anymore, not if they genuinely want to get to the bottom of whatever's happening."

"All right." Zev didn't sound enthusiastic, but he certainly seemed resigned. "You've dragged me along to my capital. No reason not to drag me along to yours as well, I suppose."

"No one's dragging you anywhere," Marieke said, amused

by his stoic air. "It's kind of you to want to accompany me, but it's not necessary."

"It's necessary to me," said Zev shortly. "So don't waste time and breath arguing with me." His storm-cloud eyes were serious as they met hers. "Besides, I want answers too. This isn't the first *accident* I've been caught up in, you know."

Well, that was true. Marieke couldn't dispute it as her gaze traveled down Zev's form to the torn and bloodied legging which still bore testimony to the wound she'd healed. But she still felt compelled to offer one more protest.

"I don't want to be an imposition," she said. "I know you're expected home, and your family—"

"This isn't my family's affair," he interrupted, his eyes serious as he held her gaze. The concentrated effect of his full attention was almost overpowering. "This is between you and me, Marieke."

"All right."

Marieke didn't quite know when she'd decided to yield, but she couldn't deny the combined effect of his determination and her own desire for him to stay with her. A flicker of amusement lightened his spell when she saw that one of his hands had strayed to the hilt of his sword.

"I admit I'd be glad of the company," she told him. "But like I said, I'm going to the capital. It's the most secure place in the country. There's no need to act like we're heading into battle."

"The fact that you're going to the capital, to put yourself in the hands of the council itself, is half the reason I feel compelled to think about your safety," he told her sternly. "Since you don't seem determined enough to do it yourself."

Marieke raised an eyebrow, not entirely pleased with this lofty pronouncement.

Perhaps Zev caught her thoughts, because he smiled, the expression softening the somber lines of his face. "Like you said, I've been involved in saving your life twice now. I'm starting to feel a certain level of investment in your survival."

Marieke gave a reluctant chuckle. "Fair enough." She gestured at his tense posture. "But if we're traveling together, you're going to have to relax whatever this is. Because you're acting like a hired bodyguard. I know you're skeptical of singers, but I'm not. I don't need protection from the council. I know I said I might be in hot water for sneaking into that last group, but for all the council's faults, it's not in the habit of literally silencing dissenters."

She'd intended the words to be an overt exaggeration of his fears, for effect. But to her surprise, she saw that Zev was once again stony-faced.

"As far as you're aware," he said, the words curt. "I for one would be interested to know where *J* is."

Marieke shut her mouth with a snap, unease washing over her. It was a question worth asking. If Jade had been determined to challenge the council's conduct—which the Port Taran messages suggested she had—why had Marieke never heard of her until recently? Why had she and her criticisms never surfaced publicly?

She still thought Zev was being too harsh, but she was honest enough to admit to herself that he had a point. She would be wise to be careful, including in her dealings with the council.

If she could have her way, her preference would be not to make her report to the council at all until after she could discover what exactly Jade had found in her frowned-upon inquiries, and why her activities had caused such a stir. Not to mention what had become of her.

Marieke didn't feel the need to share all these thoughts with Zev, at least not yet. But she would take his cautions to heart. If at all possible, before answering the council's questions, she would try to find some answers to questions of her own.

And it seemed to her that a good starting point would be to ask the question the Head Instructor had seemed most afraid she, like Jade, might pursue. What was the mysterious magic he called heartsong?

# EIGHTEEN

## Marieke

"Just a meal, sir?" The man in the inn's serving room eyed the travelers with a hopeful eye. "Or a room for you and your lovely wife?"

Marieke felt her cheeks heat, and even Zev's serious demeanor flickered as a muscle jumped in his jaw.

"Rooms, please," he said. "Two of them." His eyes scanned the serving room, taking in the borderline rowdy banter of a nearby table of patrons. "Adjacent, if possible."

Marieke held back a sigh. Zev had been like this at the last two inns as well—overprotective and not afraid to demonstrate to anyone watching that Marieke wasn't on her own. She didn't know whether to be embarrassed or grateful.

The man clucked his tongue. "Not possible, I'm afraid. We have many staying here on their way to the seasonal market that starts in the capital tomorrow. I can give you two rooms, but," he squinted down at the ledger in front of him, "the best I can do is opposite ends of the same floor."

Zev grunted, clearly not liking it, but Marieke jumped in before he could make more of a scene.

"We'll take them, thank you," she said. She reached for the

pouch tucked into her gown's pocket, but her hand was intercepted by Zev's, the grip of his fingers warm and strong.

"Let me."

Marieke wanted to protest, but she knew it would do no good. She watched, bemused, as Zev paid for both of their rooms. She'd been surprised by his resources all the way from the coast. Not only had he paid for their accommodation on the three nights they'd spent on the road, but he'd also paid for both of their places on a public coach that had considerably shortened their journey.

Aeltan farms were certainly prospering.

If she'd been paying the travel expenses of two all this way, Marieke would probably have wanted to push straight on into Ondford that evening, avoiding the need for another night on the road. But Zev showed no eagerness to reach their journey's end. He'd been the one to suggest that they stop for the day in this tiny town on the capital's doorstep, in spite of there being a few hours left of daylight.

And, weak creature that she was, Marieke had readily agreed. She was almost ashamed of how much she wanted to prolong their time together. It was foolish, probably. It wasn't as though their journey had been marked by warm conversation or intimate moments. There'd been no more sleeping in the same cave. Zev had insisted on securing them rooms—separate rooms—each night. And while he hadn't exactly been cold during the days, his manner had been cautious and reserved. The time on the public coach didn't allow for private conversation, and even during the stretches where they walked, he'd seemed more inclined toward silence. It had required serious discipline for Marieke to curb her natural tendency to chatter.

And yet the silence hadn't felt natural, even from Zev. She had a feeling he was holding himself consciously in check as well. The memory of the moment near the lagoon—when Marieke still believed he'd almost kissed her—seemed always to hang between them, filling the silence until it was louder than any casual conversation could have been.

There was one lonely stretch of road when she'd managed to draw him out. Well, that had been her intention, and she'd felt as though she succeeded, but looking back, she realized the reverse was closer to the truth. She'd been the one to ask him questions, but somehow it had been her who'd talked at length about herself, her childhood and family, the tale of how she'd discovered her songcraft. But he'd seemed interested, even fascinated, so she still counted it as a success.

Neither spoke as a servant showed them to their rooms. Zev took the key to his own room when it was offered, but instead of going in, he kept following to see where Marieke was placed. When the servant had given Marieke her key and trotted back toward the stairs, Zev sent a searching glance through the open door before turning to Marieke.

"Meet you downstairs for a meal shortly?"

"Yes, but you should come in first," Marieke said.

He looked at her warily, and she sighed.

"Don't be foolish, Zev. I won't suddenly change personality and—what was it?—*sing your death over you* if you dare to be alone in the room with me."

Zev's features softened slightly in amusement, although his tone was wry. "That's not my concern, actually. It's not you who needs to keep your conduct above reproach in order to earn trust that shouldn't be too freely given."

Marieke bit her lip, taken by surprise that he would say so overtly the true reason he stayed out of her room.

Well, overtly for Zev.

"It's not really up to you to decide when you've earned my trust, Zev," she pointed out. "And you have. So stop being unnecessarily difficult and come inside so that I can check your wound."

"My leg is fine," he said dismissively, although he was already backing down under her glare.

"Again, that's not for you to say," she informed him. "It was my healing song, and I have a professional interest. I'll keep checking it daily until the leg is fully healed."

And she wasn't above using the injury to give her an excuse once per day to actually touch him. The new reserve he'd adopted since their moment by the lagoon was more of a trial than it should have been. It wouldn't have been so bad if he hadn't first shown her how intoxicating his touch could be.

A little embarrassed by her own thoughts, Marieke tried to adopt a businesslike tone as she ushered him inside her room. She rolled her eyes when Zev pointedly left the door open, but didn't really object. Once he'd taken a seat, with every sign of reluctance, she knelt before him, carefully feeling the injured leg.

"Any pain?" she asked, glancing up.

She found him already looking down at her, his eyes instantly locking on to hers with an intensity no amount of his careful reserve seemed able to fully banish.

"No."

"Do you feel as strong as you used to?" she pressed. "Before, I mean?"

This time Zev took a moment to respond. "Yes," he said, his voice slightly gruff, and the muscle jumping under Marieke's touch seeming to belie the words.

"May I magically assess the wound?" she asked punctiliously.

He sighed. "Yes."

Marieke let out a soft song, sending a gentle current of

magic to encompass Zev's leg, with instructions for it to cling to any weak points or imperfections. It found none.

"Well, it seems to be doing excellently," she said brightly, standing up.

Zev hastened to copy the movement. "As I said."

But the irritation in his voice was unconvincing. It wasn't the first time Marieke had suspected he found the excuse for contact relieving as well. It somehow released the tension of keeping one another at arm's length all day.

By the time they were served a hearty stew in the inn's serving room, the space was full of guests and noise. Neither of them attempted much conversation. They'd become practiced at silence, and the one time it felt companionable rather than forced was when they were eating together. Marieke was weary enough to be ready for bed as soon as the meal was complete, and Zev insisted on walking her to her door before returning to the serving room, presumably for an ale and to garner what information he could.

Zev hovered in the doorway of her room while she released a quick song, putting simple protections in place. She was pleased to see him give an approving nod to no one in partic-ular—the campaign to soften him toward magic was proceeding swimmingly.

If she was completely honest with herself, however, she was even more pleased when lying awake an hour and a half later, to hear him stop by her room on his way past. And, unless she was mistaken, he was responsible for the firm tread that woke her twice more through the night hours. Certainly none of these approaches activated the enchantment she'd placed on the door and window to detect danger.

After the third time, she let herself drift fully, surrendering herself to the deep sleep of safety.

"Well, here it is." In spite of her night of broken sleep, Marieke's voice was bright as she gazed up at the familiar building. "Our council and academy complex. Pretty nice, isn't it?"

Zev's answering smile was more polite than enthusiastic. "As you said, it's similar to the one in Tarandon."

Marieke gave him a sideways look, noting his choice of words. He didn't seem to like claiming the Aeltan council or academy.

They walked forward together, conversation once again petering out as they approached the gate of the complex that housed both the Academy of Song and the headquarters of the Council of Singers. Two huge banners hung down the wall on either side of the gate, purple where the Aeltan ones had been blue. They were emblazoned with identical silver images of a bird in flight, beak open in song. The symbol of the Oleandan Council of Singers.

The gate currently stood open, and the guards standing on either side of it didn't attempt to stop their progress. If they wanted to enter the council building itself, they would need to explain their business to the guards at that entrance. But the complex was open to the public. Marieke could see people strolling through the manicured gardens that separated the council and academy buildings.

"All right," she said briskly. "Your first stop is over that way." She pointed to an outbuilding attached to the council's headquarters. The sign over the door read *Healing Center*.

"What?" Zev seemed bemused. "Why would I need to go there?"

"Because that Healing Center is open to the public," Marieke told him. "And I want my handiwork checked by a singer properly trained in healing song."

"My leg is fine," Zev said impatiently. "I'm not wasting my gold on that."

"A simple check will be free," said Marieke, giving him a look. How typical of Zev to refuse to spend a single coin on songcraft when he'd been perfectly ready to waste gold on unnecessary luxuries like rooms at inns in weather plenty mild enough for camping.

Zev looked at her in surprise. "Really?"

"Yes, really." Marieke chivvied him with her hands. "You'll have to wait in line, but it shouldn't be too busy at this time of day. Your council in Tarandon has a similar clinic, you know."

"I didn't," Zev said, still looking faintly impressed. He hadn't budged, seeming oblivious to Marieke's attempts to push him toward the Healing Center. But a frown descended on his brow as he glanced down at her. "And what will you be doing while I'm supposedly getting my leg checked over for free?"

"I want to visit the academy before we approach the council," Marieke said, aware that her breezy tone sounded forced. "It shouldn't take long. I'll meet you at the Healing Center when I'm done."

"I'd prefer to stick together," Zev said, his gaze uneasy as it flicked around the courtyard.

Marieke found his wariness absurd. There were plenty of people coming and going about their business, the general atmosphere one of public bustle. It wasn't exactly an abandoned alleyway at midnight.

"No one is going to leap out from behind a building and attack me right in the council's complex," she told him sternly. "You're not my bodyguard, remember?"

"Who says it's *your* safety I'm worried about?" Zev muttered mutinously.

Marieke's lips twitched. She couldn't help it. The image of strong, stoic Zev being scared for his own safety was laughable.

"You'll be fine," she informed him mercilessly. "I'll see you soon." With one more shooing motion, she turned and hurried toward the academy, pausing once to glance back and make sure he was obeying. He looked reluctant, but he was moving toward the Healing Center. So that was something.

Marieke slowed her pace as she neared the huge double doors that led to the Academy of Song. The wood was beautiful, not as old as the stone around it, but old enough to feel weighty and important. Each of the doors was covered in intricate carvings depicting books and learning. Around the borders were carved birds, some nestled among branches and others taking wing—a nod to the symbol of the Oleandan Council of Singers.

Marieke had walked through these doors many times without thinking twice about it. Now, she felt almost as nervous as she had on her first day at the academy, when she'd been painfully aware of her own ignorance and afraid she would be terribly out of place.

There had been difficult moments, certainly, but on the whole she hadn't felt like an outcast. She'd felt like she belonged in the community of singers, and had taken pride in that fact.

Now, with her recent doubts regarding the origin of the council and the accuracy of the academy's teachings, she didn't know what to feel.

She did, however, know that she was older and more capable than the fifteen-year-old who'd arrived so nervously at the academy. She wasn't going to wait to be given answers at the discretion of the instructors. She was going to seek them out.

Whether she was right to do so alone, she wasn't sure. It was possible she'd been too cautious in deciding not to share her questions about heartsong with Zev. But given he was clearly reluctant to reveal all the things he knew and she didn't—and especially with how he'd been keeping himself at arm's length during their recent journey—she hadn't been convinced she wanted to include him in her investigation. After all, he was Aeltan, and inclined to be prejudiced against singers. If what she found incriminated her own council and academy, she might regret giving him the information.

One of the guards nodded to her as she entered the academy building, obviously recognizing her from her recent time as a student. There was no telling how long she would be left to her own devices before someone sought her out. She had to assume that the investigators from the official group had reported her desertion by now, and that her questionable conduct in pretending to be part of the delegation had been discovered. Someone, whether from the council or the academy, would probably want answers of their own. The question was how long it would take for someone relevant to get wind of her arrival.

She just had to hope she could find some answers before that happened. And she knew of only one place to look for them. Her steps carried her swiftly to the library, although she couldn't help pausing outside to steel herself. Remembering her last encounter with the librarian, Marieke would have preferred to ask a trusted friend for information first, someone like Solomon. But she had no idea where to find him, and asking around after him was probably more conspicuous than simply examining the records.

A pair of students bustled past her, intent on their own errand, and Marieke strolled into the room in their wake, hoping to avoid notice. Her eyes darted to the desk on the other side of the room, and her heart lifted a little. A younger library assistant seemed to be on duty rather than the head librarian. That was a good start.

Even so, Marieke didn't approach the younger woman with her question. Instead she made her way to a small, angled table set under one window, with an enormous book propped open on its surface. She couldn't see it past the student currently poring over the tome, but she knew from experience that a placard hung from the little table, reading *Library Index*.

Marieke joined the small line of students waiting to access the index, feeling conspicuous and impatient. When at last it was her turn, she flicked quickly through the alphabetized volume. The index was designed to point students to the section of the library in which they might find information on the topic of their interest. It likely wasn't comprehensive enough for her purposes, but she might as well try.

Her hand stilled as she reached the letter H. She turned a few pages back and forward to confirm, disappointed but not really surprised to see that there was no entry for *heartsong*.

Whatever it was, it didn't seem to be a topic taught at the academy. Unless it was entered as a sub-category under another topic, but without further information, she had no way to ascertain that. The index was enormous, and would take hours to trawl through page by page. Marieke stepped aside to let the next student access the index, her own eyes straying to the library assistant. Given her area of expertise, the other woman probably knew some record-keeping song capable of identifying the word in the tome if it was there. But it didn't help Marieke. If she felt free to ask about the concept of heart-song, she could just ask what it was outright. But she'd already decided she needed to be more cautious than that.

Disheartened, she made her way to the section of the library that the closest records in the index had referenced. She pulled a few books down, flipping through them with swift fingers. She was feeling increasingly like she was acting on borrowed time. It was possible that there were answers in these volumes, but she wouldn't find them without taking the time to properly read through them all.

She grabbed the four most promising books, making her way to the desk where the library assistant was still sitting.

"Borrowing those?" the girl asked, her friendly smile telling Marieke that she either didn't recognize Marieke or she wasn't privy to Marieke's last interaction with the head librarian.

"Yes, please," said Marieke. She gave her student number as requested, grateful that graduates were permitted to borrow books for two years after finishing at the academy. And that she apparently hadn't been put on some prohibited list.

The library assistant, blissfully unaware of Marieke's seditious tendencies, entered her selections faithfully in the ledger and handed the books over.

"There you go," she said, her attention already back on her interrupted task.

Marieke thanked her and turned for the door, clutching the books against her chest. If she found nothing in these, perhaps she'd have time to come back for a few more.

But this optimism was dashed as she neared the doorway. To her dismay, she was still inside the library when a familiar figure stalked into it, looking as stern and aloof as always.

Ignoring the childish temptation to try to hide behind the shelves, Marieke straightened her back, arranging her features into a pleasant smile.

It wasn't reciprocated by the head librarian. The older woman's brow lowered as she caught sight of Marieke, and she came to a stop.

"Marieke. What are you doing here?"

"I'm actually just passing through the capital," Marieke said brightly. "And I thought I'd stop by the academy."

The librarian was unimpressed by her light manner. "Does the Head Instructor know you're back?"

"I...don't know," Marieke said, trying to sound bemused by the question.

"I heard that you joined an official team of investigators without authorization," the librarian told her. "Instructor Rafael has been wishing to see you. I will inform him at once of your return."

"Yes, all right," said Marieke, deflating. "I was intending to speak with him before leaving."

The librarian didn't look convinced, but Marieke didn't care what she thought. She was telling the truth after all. She'd come to the capital to make a report to the council, and the Head Instructor was a member of that council.

The older woman looked like she wasn't sure whether to insist Marieke stay where she was until the Head Instructor could be fetched, and Marieke decided she should make the most of her freedom while she had it. With a nod to the older woman, she strode forward again, the books still gripped against her chest. She saw the librarian's eyes flick to the volumes, but she didn't say anything. The next moment, the librarian had turned as well, striding to the desk.

"What books did that former student borrow?"

Marieke caught the question from the hallway, which she'd just entered. She winced as the library assistant answered, sounding surprised at her superior's tone.

"Uh, let me check. They all related to heart magic, I think."

Marieke didn't stay to give the librarian the chance to chase her. She hurried down the corridor, heading for the side door that would open onto the manicured public gardens. She knew for certain now that she didn't have much time before she would have to speak formally to the council, or at least the Head Instructor. And for all she knew, she might be thrown from the complex after that, with no more opportunity to seek answers.

Perhaps that knowledge was what made her skin crawl with the sensation of being watched as she hurried through the gardens. She kept glancing over her shoulder, but from what she could see, the only thing following her was her own sense of impending crisis.

Disregarding the few strollers she passed, she found a bench to settle on and pulled out the first book.

*An Exploration of Heart Magic: History and Theory.*

It took only a few pages for Marieke to be convinced it was as dry a tome as the title promised. And there was no new information of interest. She'd learned about heart magic in her foundational classes. Any graduate of the academy would understand the concept. It wasn't a different type of magic so much as a deep source of the same magic they all knew and felt in the ground everywhere. But it required a connection to the land in question—a connection in either blood or heart, or both—which gave the singer access to a new level of responsiveness from the magic. It tended to be more relevant in defined regions, like forests, or mountain ranges. Sometimes Marieke had noted, on visits home during breaks, that the magic of her own area seemed easier to manipulate than that in Ondford. But in her spread-out coastal farming region, that was probably the extent of the presence of any heart magic in her songcraft.

And although she, like every other student, had learned the basic theory of heart magic that was in this volume, she'd never heard anyone refer to it as heartsong. And there was certainly nothing in the concept of heart magic that would provoke the uneasy reaction she'd overheard from the Head Instructor.

Putting aside the theory book, she pulled out another volume that seemed to have more of a focus on heart magic in practice. Maybe that one would be more likely to have information she didn't already know. After all, with so many students at the academy hailing from the capital, there hadn't been much opportunity to actually practice heart magic in lessons. Heavily populated cities didn't tend to carry the right type of connection to create heart magic. And those students from regional areas were studying far from the lands they were connected to.

Marieke had only just opened the book when she was startled by a voice.

"Marieke? I didn't expect to find you here."

She looked up to see Isabel, pausing mid-stride as she hurried past.

"When did you arrive back in Ondford?"

"Just this morning," said Marieke, laying the book aside and observing the other woman's face with concern. Something beyond her own misdemeanors was clearly wrong to have Isabel looking so drawn.

"Well, I'd like to say I'm glad to see you, but to speak frankly, you'll find yourself in some strife with Instructor Rafael. He's none too pleased about your stunt with the investigation team. And since he's the one who recommended you for our delegation, he's taken it a bit more personally than—but never mind that." Her eyes strayed back to the path she'd been taking. "I'd like a few words with you myself, Marieke—I thought you were more sensible than that. But it will have to wait. There are bigger issues to deal with now."

"What issues?" Marieke asked, putting the chiding to one side in her concern over the usually calm councilor's demeanor. "What's wrong? Was there another attack on a council singer?"

Isabel ran a hand over her hair, smoothing the tight bun it was pulled back into. "Yes. Another death, I'm afraid." Her eyes darted to Marieke's, coming suddenly into focus. "Hold on. You said attack, not accident."

Marieke nodded, her throat dry. "That's why I'm in the capital—to report an incident to the council. After I left the investigation team, I experienced another so-called accident myself. And I'm not convinced that they're accidental at all."

Isabel looked her over in alarm. "If that's so, I'm very glad you're all right. You did well to survive unharmed." She let out a breath as she gave Marieke another once over. "I may as well tell you—the gossip is all over the city. Even I heard it first through unofficial channels. Your instinct about these *accidents* is sound. The recent incident was targeted at two singers. One was regrettably killed, but the other survived. He reports feeling magic racing at them before it happened. And more than that, he was actually successful in intercepting two strangers trying to flee the scene after the magic was unleashed. They've been caught and brought in for inter-rogation."

Marieke found herself on her feet, her books forgotten behind her. "They caught actual people carrying out the attacks?" she demanded.

She'd known something unnatural was at work, but even she hadn't realized it was so concrete. A group of people were orchestrating the accidents? So much for the land rising up as the result of a curse.

"Whether they really were behind the attacks remains to be seen," Isabel corrected. "But you can be sure the council will do everything possible to get answers." Her eyes strayed ahead again. "And I'm sure you can understand why I don't have time to stop and talk to you right now. I want to speak to you further before you leave the capital, though."

"Of course," said Marieke.

Isabel barely stayed to hear her reply. Marieke watched her hurry off, stunned. The councilor didn't need to worry about her running away anytime soon. This new development would keep her in Ondford if possible. Like everyone else, she wanted to know what the interrogation of the two captives would uncover.

The councilor had barely disappeared from view when a sudden movement from a nearby shrub ripped Marieke from her reverie. She watched in astonishment as a man she'd seen once before emerged, stepping straight out of the bush into her secluded reading nook. For a moment, Marieke could only stare stupidly, unable to comprehend how her would-be murderer from the depths of Sundering Canyon could be here, right in the heart of Ondford.

"Well," Gorgon said, his eyes hard and narrowed as they rested on her. "That changes things."

# CHAPTER
# NINETEEN

## *Marieke*

"Gorgon?" The name escaped Marieke as a gasp.

He raised an eyebrow. "Remember my name, do you? That's more than I expected." His eyes roamed over her, their expression faintly contemptuous as he took a small step forward. "Strange to hear you speaking. I'd hoped that, in its wisdom, the magic of the canyon might have taken your voice permanently."

The words, as well as the subtle forward movement Marieke almost missed, propelled her into action. This man had twice tried to murder her in cold blood. Why was she standing there staring at him instead of preparing to defend herself?

Using the only weapon with which she was proficient, she raised her voice, drawing magic into herself from the ground below her feet.

She hadn't judged Gorgon's intentions too harshly. He was already diving toward her by the time the wall of raw power hit him. There'd been no time for Marieke to shape it to anything sophisticated—it was nothing but an invisible force, not unlike an enhanced wind. Gorgon was bowled over, and Marieke didn't stay to unleash anything else. She leaped forward, giving him a wide berth as she sprinted away from the bench, trying to escape into the rest of the garden.

She wasn't quick enough. Gorgon recovered more nimbly than she'd expected, his hand shooting out to grab at her ankle. She came crashing down, barely bringing her hands up in time to break her fall as she connected with the paving stones. Before she could push herself to her feet, Gorgon was on her, his grip rough as he threw one arm around her head, muffling her mouth, and ripped one of her arms out from under her with the other hand.

Marieke tried to cry out in pain, but he had her mouth effectively blocked. She scrabbled desperately with her free hand, but Gorgon had her other arm twisted around at such an angle that she couldn't get purchase. She bit down hard on the arm that was across her mouth, desperation giving her fresh energy.

It did no good. Gorgon had come prepared, and acknowledging her bite with only a muted grunt of pain, he made swift use of her open mouth. Before she well knew what he was about, he'd yanked a length of fabric from his sleeve and pulled it across her mouth, securing it so quickly she suspected he'd been practicing. The next thing she knew, both of his hands had grabbed her wrists and twisted them behind her, and his knee was pressed into her back. Marieke could only let out a silent scream of anger and frustration as he bound her hands with rough twine that cut into her skin.

"Finally." He must have leaned down because his breath was hot against her ear, the sensation horrible and panic-inducing. "I've been trying to kill you since the canyon marked you as unworthy, and I'm embarrassed how long it's taken me. In my defense, that annoying farmer has barely let you out of his sight since you left the bigger group."

He yanked her up and shoved her toward the bench, pushing her over it so that her face collided painfully with the stone. Marieke struggled violently as one of Gorgon's hands disappeared from her bound wrists, and she caught a flash of silver. But it was due to no movement of her own that Gorgon suddenly paused, his dagger grasped loosely in his hand.

"What's this?"

Marieke twisted around, confusion lancing through her terror and desperation. Gorgon was looking at the books on the bench beside where he was holding Marieke down.

"Heart magic?" Gorgon pushed one book off the top of the small stack with his dagger, sending it to the ground in a crumpled heap that would give the librarian a conniption. "And more of the same."

Gorgon directed a thoughtful look at Marieke, who was continuing to struggle to no avail.

"Why are you reading about heart magic all of a sudden?" Perhaps he caught the way Marieke's bewildered eyes flicked from the books to him, because he gave a harsh laugh. "Yes, I can read. I know you were told none of us monarchists can, but I know a lot of things my narrow-minded leaders have no concept of. Never mind that, though." His eyes were piercing as they studied her frantic features. "Are you...is it possible you're trying to find out about heartsong?"

Marieke stilled, astonishment briefly eclipsing her fear. If she had her voice, she would have demanded what he knew about heartsong, but of course she couldn't speak around the gag.

"Is that why you went to Port Taran?" Gorgon asked, the question giving chilling proof that he really had been following her. "Are you trying to follow Jade's trail?"

This time Marieke twisted so violently, she succeeded in catching a glimpse of his face. He knew about Jade? *What* did he know about Jade? And how? He was from a group of hermits in Sundering Canyon, far from Ondford and the academy Jade had been expelled from.

But as she met his eye, Gorgon's arrested expression melted back into the hateful derision he'd shown a moment before.

"Do you think yourself a hero, singer? Trying to follow Jade's trail? And are *you* willing to pay the price?" He snorted. "I doubt it."

He tightened his grip on her bound wrists, forcing her face back down against the bench.

"You're no hero. You're a singer, and the magic of the canyon marked you as the enemy you are. Don't think I've forgotten. You're wasting your time anyway. Do you hope to harness heartsong? As a mere, pathetic singer, your understanding of magic is too basic to even comprehend the power that tied the royals to their land, let alone wield it. Your kind disdained that ancient magic, and so doomed our lands. Do you think they want to advertise that? You won't find anything in your precious academy books about heartsong."

Desperately curious as she was about his words, Marieke hadn't given up trying to get free. As he spoke, she shifted her feet slowly, trying to get her balance and center her weight.

"I don't think so."

Abruptly, Gorgon's knee pressed once more into her back, his hand gripping her hair instead and wrenching her head up. When he spoke, his voice was again close to her ear, his anger poorly contained.

"The land needs to be rid of your kind, and one day it will be. I failed when I made that bridge collapse under you, and I failed when I extended the ravine. The water would have succeeded had your farmer sweetheart not gotten in the way. I would prefer to find another subtle way, but I'm out of time. I don't know how my men got sloppy enough to get caught, but they've forced my hand. I know they won't talk—they're too committed to the cause for that. But you've been into the canyon—you'll recognize them as some of my people. And I can't have you identifying where they come from."

In grabbing her hair, Gorgon had released her hands, which were after all still bound. All the while he spoke, Marieke was working the bindings on her wrists. Her skin was rubbed raw, the cord slicing into her like a knife, but she didn't feel the pain. She could sense the death he wanted to mete out crawling inexorably toward her, and it gave her the strength of desperation.

But her desperation wasn't enough to save her. She'd just started to feel the cord loosening on one of her hands when Gorgon raised his blade, the sharp edge glittering in the morning light.

"So this is where we part ways, singer," he said, malice in his voice as the blade came flashing down.

CHAPTER

# TWENTY

# Zev

Zev strode out of the Healing Center, his steps agitated. He'd known the exercise would be a complete waste of time—as he'd expected, his leg had been declared perfectly healed—but he hadn't realized just how much time. If he had, he never would have agreed to pacify Marieke. He'd had to wait for what felt like an eternity for his turn to be seen, and in all that time, he didn't know where Marieke was.

The sense of being watched that had been with him most of their journey together was gone, but that didn't make him feel better. It was just a reminder that she was gone as well, outside his range of vision and therefore protection.

And his anxiety wasn't lessened by the gossip that had spread like a locust swarm through the waiting patients just as he was finally called up for his turn. Two more singers had been targeted, one of them now dead. And if rumor was to be believed, this time there was concrete reason to think the disaster wasn't accidental.

He needed to find Marieke.

There was no sign of her outside the Healing Center, and Zev didn't even consider waiting for her there as she'd

280

instructed. She'd said she was going to the Academy of Song. He would head that way.

He'd barely started across the courtyard, however, when he was surprised to hear his name.

"Zevadiah?"

He turned to see a middle-aged woman with a straight nose and rather severe mouth whom he'd met once before. He'd forgotten her name, but she was from the delegation that had come to Aeltas. She'd been there when he'd returned Marieke to her group.

She crossed the courtyard with a no-nonsense gait, her brow wrinkled in surprise.

"It is Zevadiah, isn't it?"

"Yes," he said, dipping his head slightly. "I believe we met in Tarandon, didn't we?"

"We did," she confirmed. "You're the young man who helped Mari get out of Sundering Canyon."

He nodded in acknowledgment, irked to see one corner of her lips twitch up as if in amusement.

"Don't tell me you've followed her all the way here? I know she's very pretty, but—"

"Marieke and I met again by chance when I was in the south of Oleand on behalf of my farming collective," Zev cut her off flatly. "I agreed to travel with her to Ondford for reasons unrelated to our initial meeting."

"Ah, so you're here with her, are you?" The woman nodded, her flicker of humor long gone. Now that Zev looked at her, she seemed very stressed, a contrast to the collected poise he remembered from their other meeting.

"I am, but I've lost track of her," he said. "I don't suppose you know where she is?"

"As a matter of fact, I just saw her," the woman said. She gestured behind her. "She's in the public garden, not far that way." She held out a hand as Zev stepped eagerly forward. "But you might want to wait a few minutes before seeking her out."

Zev stared at her. "Why would I do that?"

"Because," she said with a grimace, "you're not the only one looking for her. I just passed the Head Instructor from our academy, and sent him in the right direction as well. He wants a word with her, and I'm not sure she'd thank me for inviting you or anyone else to witness it."

"Thank you for the warning," said Zev woodenly.

"Well then, well met, Zevadiah."

To Zev's relief, the Oleandan just nodded before striding off, clearly too preoccupied with her own affairs to check whether he followed her advice.

Of course he didn't. If anything, his sense of urgency was increased by the information that the Head Instructor—a member of the Council of Singers, from what Zev understood—was seeking Marieke out for a private interaction. Marieke might think the council above directly removing any threats to their credibility, but Zev didn't share her generous nature.

He hurried in the direction indicated, soon reaching the start of the garden the other woman had mentioned. It seemed to be something of a maze, and after a few minutes he began to fear he wouldn't find the pair. But just as he was wondering if he should retrace his steps, he caught sight of a portly figure hovering behind a large shrub, dressed in the same purple robes as the woman who'd just given Zev directions.

A member of Oleand's Council of Singers. Zev relaxed slightly, slowing his steps. This, presumably, was the Head Instructor who'd gone looking for Marieke. And if he was here, standing alone in the garden, then he wasn't with Marieke, haranguing her or worse.

Zev hadn't been trying to sneak up on the older man, and he was surprised when the stranger didn't turn. Slowing his steps cautiously, Zev noted that the man was stiff with tension, every line of his frame frozen, as if he was receiving news he couldn't quite believe.

Frowning, Zev came to a stop completely, several paces back from the man. Once he was still, he realized he could hear a low, angry voice issuing from the other side of the scrub. It was undoubtedly what held the Head Instructor so spellbound.

"You're no hero," the voice of the obscured man was saying. "You're a singer, and the magic of the canyon marked you as the enemy you are."

Marked by the magic of the canyon? Zev frowned as he crept a tiny bit closer. Was the stranger speaking of Marieke? A chill went over him as the man ranted on. Was he speaking *to* Marieke?

Zev was about to push past the Head Instructor—who still seemed oblivious to his presence—when the angry stranger's next words stopped him in his tracks.

"...your understanding of magic is too basic to even comprehend the power that tied the royals to their land, let alone wield it. Your kind disdained that ancient magic, and so doomed our lands. Do you think they want to advertise that? You won't find anything in your precious academy books about heartsong."

*Heartsong.*

Had he said heartsong? Zev suddenly found himself as frozen in place as his fellow eavesdropper, trying to comprehend the significance of what he was hearing. Was he wrong that the unseen man was speaking to Marieke? Or was it possible that Marieke was much further down her trail of questions than he'd realized? Could she actually know about heartsong? And if so, what had he done, exposing himself and his family to her attention? How deeply had he betrayed his own in failing to sever the bond that he'd let grow between them against everything he'd been taught?

He was still caught in this turmoil of thought when the invisible man's voice changed abruptly, the new words an ugly growl.

"I don't think so."

Zev listened in mounting horror as the stranger confessed to his attempts to kill whomever he was speaking to. The details left no room for doubt. It was Marieke on the other side of that scrub, Marieke being threatened by this unknown man. The same Marieke whose discoveries might endanger every member of Zev's family, and everything they'd built over generations.

Zev's eyes strayed to the Head Instructor, still listening silently. Surely he would intervene now. He couldn't fail to understand what was being said, what this man would do if not stopped. It should be a matter of ease for an experienced singer like him, acting with the advantage of surprise, to conjure up a song to incapacitate the man still spewing threats.

But the other eavesdropper showed no sign of action. And in spite of everything Zev had to lose if Marieke really had discovered the secret of heartsong, he didn't hesitate when he heard the unseen man's voice change again, the sudden calm more terrifying than the anger had been.

"So this is where we part ways, singer."

Zev propelled himself past the immobile councilor, over-taking him well before the sentence was finished, and charging around the scrub in time to see a lithe young man, younger than Zev, standing over Marieke. He seemed to have shoved her face-first onto a bench. Zev let out a cry of fury as the man swung his arm upward, a blade glinting in his fist.

The stranger spun wildly at the sound, but Zev had already lunged. He tackled the other man, noting as he did so that

Marieke was struggling upright, her face bruised and her arms bloodied.

Zev didn't have time to examine her more closely. He had his hands full fending off the frantic stabs of the stranger he'd just prevented from murdering Marieke. In his haste, Zev hadn't even pulled his own blade before charging at the man, and he had only his hands to use in defense. He had them clasped around his adversary's wrists, holding the man back by sheer strength, but some of the jabs of that lethal dagger were coming dangerously close to his face.

Without loosening his hold on the other man's wrists, Zev maneuvered his foot, hooking it around the stranger's ankle. For a moment he relaxed his body, letting his opponent think he was losing strength. Then, as the man's eyes glinted in triumph, Zev sprang back into motion, thrusting his hip upward into the stranger at the same time as he rolled to the side as hard as he could. His adversary, ankle still pinned in place, couldn't prevent himself being dragged along and was soon pinned under Zev, their positions reversed.

The stranger let out a cry of rage as Zev tightened his grip, trying to wrest the dagger from his hand. He was putting up a good fight, and the outcome was far from certain when both men were distracted by a voice swelling suddenly into song behind them.

Zev spared the flicker of a glance from his adversary, to see that Marieke had rid herself of her bonds and ripped the gag from her mouth. Her voice, filled with an icy rage that Zev had never heard or imagined from her, was somehow even more beautiful than before. And with the sound came a wind that whipped around the small patch of garden, sweeping any loose stones or sticks up in its path, and flinging them into the other man's face.

Zev felt the man's arms slacken as he gave a stifled shout,

and it was the work of a moment to yank the blade from his hand. Zev pushed himself to his knees, clutching the dagger firmly as his breath came in pants. The other man looked just as winded, his gray garments filthy from their tussle in the dirt, and his eyes glinting furiously.

"You'll answer for everything you've done, Gorgon." Marieke's voice quivered with anger as she stepped toward them. She came to a stop at Zev's side as he rose to his feet. "I'll make sure the whole council knows exactly what—"

Her words cut off into a gasp of shock as the young man—Gorgon—sprang lithely into motion. He was quick—even Zev, standing so close to him, hadn't suspected his intention until he was already in movement. To his horror, he saw the stranger pull another dagger from behind him, his eyes fixed on Marieke as he leaped forward.

There was no time to think, and certainly no time to hesitate. Zev intercepted Gorgon's motion, one hand raising the man's confiscated dagger in defense as he moved in front of Marieke, while the other hand shoved the attacker's blade arm to the side. The motion of the stranger's lunge carried him straight into his own initial dagger, a horrible gurgle escaping his lips as the blade plunged into him.

He dropped to the ground, Zev releasing the dagger so it fell with him. For a moment, both he and Marieke could only stare down at the other man in shock, watching as the life drained rapidly from his eyes.

There were no final words, no oaths or promises of vengeance. Gorgon, whoever he'd been, was simply gone.

Zev turned away from the man's body, his blood still pounding as his eyes fell on Marieke. She brought her gaze slowly up to him, her eyes haunted and her breath coming quickly. A powerful tangle of emotions rose up in Zev as he took in the bruise blossoming on her cheek, and the blood dripping from what looked like rope burn on her wrists. He remembered how he'd hesitated when listening behind the scrub, distracted from the urgency of the situation by the possibility that Marieke had uncovered his family's greatest secret and the foolish fear that she might be a threat to them.

He saw again in his mind's eye Gorgon's upraised blade, and all at once it broke upon him just how close he'd come to losing Marieke forever, and all through his own cowardly hesitation. The thought was unbearable. He felt like everything inside him was screaming for her, demanding that he pull her close and protect her from the world.

None of this could he have put into words if his life had depended on it. But he couldn't seem to drop her gaze—those brilliant blue eyes holding him as surely as if she'd bound him to her with rope.

"Mari," was all he managed to choke out.

Then his arms reached out of their own accord, and he tugged her against him with more force than finesse. She melted into his form as his lips crashed down on hers. Zev felt her arms snaking behind him, gripping the back of his tunic so tightly they shook as she pushed herself up onto her toes and responded to his kiss with all the passion that was currently coursing through his own veins.

# TWENTY-ONE

## Marieke

Energy raced through Marieke, stronger and more intoxicating than any magic she'd ever pulled from the ground. Zev's lips moving against hers was like fire in her veins, and she'd never felt more secure than she did pressed against his unyielding chest. The pure bliss of it washed away all the terror of the attack she'd just endured, making her heart sing as joyfully as her voice had ever done.

And then, far too soon, Zev pulled away from her. The movement was so abrupt, Marieke opened her eyes in confusion, her gaze darting around for new threats.

Instead, she was met with the embarrassing sight of Instructor Rafael bustling into their corner of the garden, his eyes wide with horror as they rested on Gorgon's body.

Gorgon's body. A shudder went over Marieke as she looked down at the deceased monarchist. Somehow she'd forgotten for a moment. But it all came rushing back, only Zev's solid presence beside her keeping her from stumbling blindly away.

"Sun and shade, what happened here?" the Head Instructor demanded, his gaze swiftly shifting from the grisly sight before him to pass between Marieke and Zev.

"He tried to kill me," Marieke said, her voice not coming out as steady as she'd like. "But Zev got here in time."

She was half afraid that Instructor Rafael would doubt her account, and accuse Zev of unmerited violence. But he didn't seem inclined to come to the dead man's defense.

"Thank goodness for that," he said instead, his eyes flicking to Zev then quickly away.

Marieke felt Zev stiffen beside her, and she looked up at him to see that his expression was stonier than she'd ever seen it as he stared back at the Head Instructor. She couldn't read what was in his eyes, or make sense of his demeanor. It was certainly a far cry from the passion he'd shown mere moments before, when he'd crushed her in his arms and kissed her as if the world was ending.

A different kind of shiver passed over her at that memory, and heat crept up her cheeks as she noted that Zev, while still looking coldly at Instructor Rafael, was hovering very close to her. After all, it was only reasonable that the arrival of the Head Instructor would change the atmosphere drastically. In a surreptitious movement, she slipped her hand into Zev's and squeezed reassuringly.

He started at the contact, and his gaze passed quickly to her face. His eyes softening, he returned the pressure of her hand with fingers that were comfortingly warm and strong.

"But who is this man?" Instructor Rafael asked, apparently oblivious to their moment. "Or rather," he grimaced delicately, "who was he?"

"His name was Gorgon, and he's the one behind the attacks on singers," Marieke said. "The attacks that were made to look like accidents. He said as much to me before Zev arrived. He actually admitted to trying to kill me because I'm a singer, from the bridge collapse when I first crossed into Aeltas, to a recent incident where I almost drowned. And he referred to the suspects who've been brought in for questioning as 'his men'. I think he was the ringleader, the one giving the orders to attack singers and make it look like accidents."

"Song preserve us," muttered Instructor Rafael. His eyes fixed searchingly on Marieke's face. "But why was he trying to kill you here, now? Merely because you're a singer?"

Marieke bit her lip. "That was his original motivation. But as for why he risked coming into the open to attack me directly, he said that he didn't want me to identify the men who've been captured. He thought I would recognize them as part of the group who live in Sundering Canyon." She met the Head Instructor's eye. "I told the council about them, remember? This man, Gorgon, was there when I fell into the ravine. He attacked me on that occasion as well. But I managed to escape him, and I think he's had something of a vendetta against me ever since."

Instructor Rafael made a tutting noise with his tongue. "So it was personal, then. This Aeltan was an evil person, it seems."

"What makes you think he was Aeltan?" Zev spoke up for the first time since the Head Instructor had joined them. "Sundering Canyon straddles the two countries, and none of us know much about the group living down there. They could be from Oleand just as easily as from Aeltas."

The councilor glanced at him, but didn't respond. "In any event, there's clearly more to this tale, Marieke, and it's a report for the whole council. Come along, child, we must have those injuries seen to. I will arrange a room for you at the academy, and convene the council as soon as possible, likely tomorrow. You can give us a full report." He held out an arm in a gesture inviting her to precede him from the garden.

"Yes," said Marieke unenthusiastically. "Of course."

But she didn't move forward. Obviously she knew she'd need to report the matter to the council, but she didn't see what the hurry was if the council wouldn't be ready for her until the next day. What she longed for most of all was a moment alone with Zev, to address all that had just happened, both with Gorgon and between them. His expression was still stony, and she had no idea what was going through his mind. But the Head Instructor was hovering pointedly, apparently determined to see her safely to the academy building.

Marieke half turned to Zev, who pulled his eyes from the councilor to meet hers.

"Come along, Marieke," said Instructor Rafael imperiously. "I need to send someone to deal with…" He trailed off, his gaze shifting quickly to Gorgon's body then away. "Anyway, we shouldn't dally here."

Marieke took a step forward, relieved when Zev moved at her side. He seemed tense, and it was rubbing off on her. She didn't really think she was in any danger now Gorgon was gone, but she would be glad to reach the safety of a private room nonetheless.

"Do you have somewhere to stay, young man?" the Head Instructor asked Zev as they made it out of the garden.

"No, he doesn't," Marieke interjected, before Zev could reject all offers of help as he would no doubt like to do. "We stayed at an inn outside the city last night, and settled our bill there when we left this morning." With any luck, Zev would be given a room near hers in the academy building.

"Well, I'm sure we can accommodate you at the council building," Instructor Rafael said, dashing that hope. "I imagine the council will wish to hear your account as well."

"I will be there," said Zev coolly.

Marieke snuck a look at him, hoping for some kind of reassurance, but he didn't meet her eye this time.

"Very good." The Head Instructor's tone was businesslike as they reached a side door into the academy.

He flagged down a passing servant and handed Marieke over to her with instructions about preparing a room. Marieke hovered, again hoping for a moment alone with Zev, but the Head Instructor chivvied her toward the waiting servant.

"It's no time to hang about, Marieke. I'll need to speak to the head guard about what happened here, and settle your Aeltan friend into a room of his own. You'll be contacted with the time of the council meeting."

Marieke was tempted to refuse to cooperate—if Zev had shown any sign of doing so, she would have joined him readily. But he didn't. He just stood silently, not even meeting her eye. Reluctantly, Marieke submitted, following the servant down the corridor. She glanced back as they reached a corner, disheartened by the sight of Zev motionless right where she'd left him, his stony-faced demeanor making it hard to hold on to the fire and certainty she'd felt when he'd taken her in his arms.

He might be everything she wanted, but he was still Zev. She'd been foolish to believe for a moment that he was *her* Zev. Those gray eyes and that silent mouth still held far too many secrets—secrets he clearly had no intention of letting her into.

# TWENTY-TWO

## Zev

Zev slept little that night. His logic told him that Marieke would be safe, in a proper room at the academy, with the council officially expecting her report the following day. But every time he closed his eyes, he saw Gorgon's raised blade, Marieke crumpled below it.

And any time he managed to banish the vision, his peace was shattered in an entirely different way as he remembered what had come next. When he'd pulled Marieke into his arms, he hadn't been thinking about the future, or anything resembling common sense. He'd acted on pure instinct, fueled by a heady mixture of fear and relief.

Not that he'd acted against his own inclination. There was no denying he wanted Marieke. Every impulse longed to stay close to her. But his feelings didn't change the reality of who he was as the carrier of his ancestors' royal line, and what she represented as an academy-trained, council-sanctioned singer. And that was even without the fact that she was apparently closing in on the theory of heartsong, unknowingly threatening the exposure of his family, and in turn their very existence.

Perhaps he would have been wiser to do as Azai said, and

distance himself much earlier. But none of these unarguable realities made it any easier to stop dwelling on the feel of her lips on his, the eagerness of her touch, the way she'd fit so perfectly in his arms.

He was in trouble, there was no doubt about it. A kind of trouble he'd never been in before. The only way to extricate himself was to return to his home, far from Marieke's world. But that went against the almost overpowering urge he felt to protect her from the threats she was surrounding herself with.

It was an impasse that kept him awake most of the night. He was already awake and up when a simple breakfast was brought to his room with the information that the council was to convene in half an hour.

Zev acknowledged the servant's message with a grim nod. The Head Instructor, at least, was wily enough to be cautious. He'd gone to some lengths to prevent Marieke and Zev from having private speech between Gorgon's attack and the report to the council. It frustrated Zev, who longed to warn Marieke about a number of dangers she may not fully have grasped. But then again, how effectively could he have done so, if he wasn't willing to speak freely to her?

And he wasn't. There was so much he couldn't tell her, not just for his own sake, but for the sake of all his family. He couldn't even speak freely about the Head Instructor's actions in failing to intervene—not without revealing that he also had been standing unseen, listening to all that passed between Gorgon and Marieke.

In spite of all the restrictions on their communication, his tension lifted when he arrived at the door to which he'd been directed, and found Marieke waiting for him outside it.

"Are you all right?" he asked her softly.

She nodded, relief lightening her features as well as she looked him over. "I didn't sleep much."

"Neither did I," Zev admitted. His eyes passed between her face and her wrists. The bruise on her cheek was still there, but the bandages half-covering her hands were clean, and she moved naturally as she tucked a strand of dark hair behind her ear. Hopefully she'd been seen by a healing singer and wasn't in any pain.

The door before them opened, and a servant beckoned them in. "They're ready for you."

Marieke nodded, straightening her back as she passed the guards on either side of the doorway and stepped into a high-windowed, circular room. Zev followed, his thoughts wry as he took in the many robed councilors seated expectantly in two rows of straight benches on the far side of the room. He'd managed to lie low and avoid notice all his life—as had his family for generations. And now, thanks to Marieke's dramatic entrance into his world, he'd escalated rapidly from speaking to a member of the Aeltan council, to being noted by name by an official Oleandan group, and now appearing formally to testify before what looked like the entire Oleandan Council of Singers.

There was no help for it, so he'd better just get on with it.

He and Marieke were directed by the servant into seats in the center of the room. The second row of council members sat on elevated chairs, to enable everyone to see one another. It meant that he and Marieke were looking up at half the councilors, but otherwise, the set up wasn't as interrogative as Zev had expected.

"Marieke." A man he didn't recognize stood up in the middle of the front row of councilors. "You're back before us again. And with an even more somber report this time, I understand."

"Yes, Councilor," said Marieke, standing.

The man's eyes shifted to Zev. "And your companion, of

course. Will you identify yourself formally for the council, please?"

Zev stood, the movement unhurried. "I am Zevadiah of Aeltas."

The man nodded, and Zev realized that someone at the end of the row was scratching away on parchment, taking notes of the meeting. It was to be expected, but he still didn't like it.

"Marieke, please give your testimony to the council regarding what happened in the public gardens yesterday," the chairing councilor said.

Zev sat back down as Marieke cleared her throat. "Certainly," she said, her voice confident. "But to do so fully, I'll need to go back further." She glanced along the row. "Last time I stood before this council, I told you about how I'd fallen into Sundering Canyon and encountered a group of people living there. The man who attacked me yesterday was one of those people. In fact, he attacked me on that occasion as well."

There was some general shifting among the councilors, but no one interrupted, every eye trained on Marieke in full attention. Scanning their faces, Zev thought their interest seemed genuine. Except for one face. The Head Instructor sat partway down the front row, his expression of concerned consternation unconvincing in Zev's eyes.

Zev listened as Marieke described her run in with the monarchists in the canyon. She gave more detail about the interaction than she had to him—detail which made his blood boil on her behalf—but he noticed she never used the word monarchist. She made it sound as if it was a group who simply hated singers for some undisclosed reason.

Under the council's questions, she went on to describe the incident when the ground fell away beneath her and the other delegation singers on their way back into Oleand. She expressed the view that Gorgon had been behind that incident, and had been loosely following the group from that point on. When she recounted traveling to the coast with Zev's group she made a notable omission, not mentioning that she'd actually crossed back into Aeltas and visited Port Taran. Instead, she spoke of the incident at the lagoon, again laying the attack at Gorgon's door.

"But you say that you felt magic," one of the councilors said, frowning as she leaned forward. "How, if this Gorgon wasn't a singer, did he harness magic to make the water pull you under?"

Marieke shook her head slowly, her words sounding measured and cautious to Zev. "That I can't answer. I may have been mistaken about feeling magic, however. The magic of the canyon itself is potent and chaotic. I may simply have been feeling that. Perhaps Gorgon lured me through means I didn't witness into a naturally dangerous part of the water. In any event, he himself admitted that he'd attempted to kill me at the lagoon, so although I don't know how he did it, I'm confident in saying that he was behind it."

Zev refrained from raising an eyebrow. Naturally dangerous? There had been nothing natural about that vortex, and Marieke knew it as well as he did.

The councilor who'd asked the question nodded, leaning back in her seat with a thoughtful expression. Zev saw a few others exchange looks, but no one said anything.

"Which brings us to yesterday's incident?" prompted Isabel, the councilor who'd told Zev where to find Marieke in the gardens.

Marieke nodded. "Which brings us to yesterday's incident." She drew a breath and recounted the details of Gorgon's attack. Or at least, some of the details. Having overheard part of Gorgon's words to her, Zev had excellent reason to know that she wasn't being entirely forthcoming. She made no mention of heartsong, for example, which came as a great relief to him. She gave the council the same reasons she'd given the Head Instructor the day before as to why Gorgon had been trying to kill her. And why he'd been targeting singers in general. Anyone listening would have no hint that she was questioning the version of history she'd been taught regarding the singers' coup.

But Zev had come to know her well enough to recognize how carefully she was speaking, and how intentional was her light tone.

"Well," said the councilor who seemed to be chairing the meeting, when Marieke was finished. "With this Gorgon gone, two of his men captured, and the truth of these accidents exposed, it seems unlikely they will risk staging more disasters. But it seems the group in the ravine is a threat we would be foolish to ignore." He glanced at some of his fellow councilors. "We should convene with the Aeltan Council of Singers to discuss how to deal with this issue."

"If I may, Councilor." Marieke's interjection was the epitome of politeness, and everyone turned again to her. "I am fairly confident that Gorgon, although the leader of the group attacking singers, was a rogue in terms of the community in the canyon. When he attacked me after I fell into the ravine, he was chastised for it, and no one else offered me violence. I would be very surprised to learn that those in charge of that community were even aware of his activities up here, let alone approving of them."

"Thank you, Marieke," said Isabel. "We will certainly take note of your observations when deciding how to respond to the threat."

Marieke nodded and sat again.

"In any event," the chairing councilor took control of the conversation again, "you are both to be commended. Especially you, Zevadiah. Your selfless efforts in putting your own safety at risk to overpower this Gorgon and neutralize the threat he represented leave us in your debt. And you, Marieke. Without your testimony, the plot Gorgon perpetrated may not have been so fully exposed. We can all be glad that he can no longer hurt any of our people."

The man inclined his head to Zev, but Zev ignored him. He wasn't interested in this stranger's praise. He'd acted to save Marieke's life, certainly not to please the Oleandan Council of Singers. Instead, he directed his attention to the Head Instructor. The older man was looking at the chairing councilor, giving every appearance of sage agreement with the man's commendation of Zev's heroics in rushing in to stop Gorgon from killing Marieke. But under Zev's sustained stare, his eyes were eventually drawn—almost unwillingly, it seemed—to meet the Aeltan's.

For a long moment, Zev held the Head Instructor's gaze. He wasn't going to call the man out. He didn't have any faith in this council to back the case of justice if he did so. And if they thought he was threatening any kind of exposure to one of their own, it might put a target on Marieke's back as well as Zev's.

For now, it was enough that the Head Instructor knew that Zev saw through his polite front. They both knew that the councilor had been given full opportunity to come to Marieke's aid, and had chosen not to do so. Chosen with the expectation that neither his presence nor his failure to intervene would ever be known.

Studying the portly man's discomfort, Zev didn't think that the Head Instructor would ever do something as direct and uncivilized as kill Marieke himself, or even order her death. But it was clear, to Zev at least, that in the moment he wouldn't have objected to someone else—someone barbaric, like Gorgon —getting rid of the inconveniently perceptive graduate.

He must have heard what Zev heard. He must know that Gorgon had told Marieke something of heartsong. And his reaction was enough to convince Zev that whoever else was ignorant of it, the Head Instructor had at least some awareness of that ancient magic. An awareness he didn't wish Marieke or others like her to share.

The Head Instructor had the potential to be a dangerous man where Marieke was concerned. Worse, it was the kind of danger that made Zev most uneasy, because it was the kind that lurked in the shadows, never declaring itself, perhaps never fully taking shape at all if the circumstances didn't align.

Zev wasn't concerned for his own safety. He didn't care if the Head Instructor formed any intentions against him. He would rather the man knew that Zev had seen him there behind the shrub, and knew that his deceptions might not be as hidden as he thought. Perhaps he would think twice before acting against Marieke if further opportunity offered.

Marieke, apparently oblivious to the silent standoff between Zev and the Head Instructor, said all the appropriate things in response to the council's commendation. Zev barely heard them.

"Do you have anything else to add to your report, or any questions for us?" Isabel asked Marieke kindly.

The Head Instructor pulled his eyes from Zev to stare fixedly at Marieke. Zev could see his tension as he waited to see whether she would reveal any other knowledge. It must be eating him up inside not to know exactly what or how much Marieke had discovered.

"No questions," Marieke said, bowing her head to the council at large. "As you said, I'm relieved that the threat is over and Gorgon and his followers can't hurt anyone else." She gave a self-deprecating smile, adding with passable tranquility, "I'm also relieved to have the answer to all the accidents. I imagine the council is aware that I took it on myself to join an investigation team without authorization. I know I overstepped, but I was truly concerned about the unexplained danger to us all. Now I can stop worrying that the land was somehow turning against singers, and can stop looking for a magical explanation of what turned out to be a very human plot."

Nods of approval passed around the council, a few of them too eager to be entirely natural. Zev saw Isabel give the Head Instructor a meaningful look that seemed to say, *what did I tell you?* The Head Instructor didn't look entirely convinced, but he certainly didn't challenge Marieke's words.

For his part, Zev felt a heaviness descend on him. He didn't buy for a moment that Marieke really thought there were no more questions to be asked regarding all the incidents that had befallen singers. And while he wholeheartedly applauded Marieke's discretion, he also felt a flicker of grief at her disillusionment. When he'd first met her, she'd never have thought to hide her true reaction like that. The things she'd seen and experienced were changing her, as surely as the passage of time.

"Well said," the chairing councilor said with a nod. "And now I'm sure you'll both be glad to be released to whatever errands Gorgon's shocking attack interrupted." He nodded to them both. "You are released, with our thanks and commendation."

And without further fanfare, Marieke turned and walked from the room, Zev following close behind her.

# TWENTY-THREE

## *Marieke*

Marieke drew in a deep breath as the door to the council chamber closed behind her. She felt as though a weight had been lifted, but conversely, a new heaviness had settled on her. Things had changed since the last time she'd been inside that room. Or at least, if the reality around her hadn't changed, her perception of it had. The very fact that she'd intentionally misled the council with her report spoke volumes. She had a feeling she'd never be able to go back to how she was before she'd joined the delegation to Aeltas.

She cast a sideways glance at Zev, walking silently beside her as they left the council building.

In spite of everything she'd lost, she didn't want to go back to how she was before.

When they emerged into the morning light, she hoped Zev would say something. This time they had no Head Instructor hovering, preventing private speech. But her companion remained silent, and Marieke found herself directing their path, without any clear idea of where she was going.

Following the impulse of the moment, she led the way out of the council and academy complex. She thought she felt Zev's tension lift slightly when they were back on the public street, and she cast him another curious glance. As was so often the case, she would give a great deal to know what he was thinking. But she didn't bother asking.

The silence between them—a contrast to the growing bustle of the city through which they were walking—remained unbroken until they reached a nearby market square. The stalls were in full swing, and amid the chaos and noise, Zev finally seemed to feel free to speak.

"What will you do now?" he asked, the question abrupt as he turned to her.

Marieke let her eyes travel over the market, letting out a long breath before responding. "I think I'll go home to my parents' place, on the coast." She looked up at him. "I think I'd be wise to lie low for a while. I'm not afraid of the journey—I don't think my life is in any immediate danger now that Gorgon is gone. He clearly had it in for me since the moment I fell into his ravine."

Zev nodded slowly, not meeting her eyes. She longed for the courage to ask him to come with her to her home, but it was hard to be brave when his body language gave so little away.

"Thank you, by the way," she said instead, her voice soft amid the noise of the market. "For saving my life yet again. I neglected to say it yesterday."

Well, to say it with her words, at least. She felt she'd said it pretty clearly with her lips in other ways. The memory of their kiss crashed over her, making the awkward restraint of the current moment almost unbearable.

And still, Zev didn't respond.

Marieke cleared her throat, determined to draw him out. "In spite of the immediate danger from Gorgon being gone, I'm not convinced that the threat is over," she told him. "What I said to the council was true—I don't think Gorgon acted on behalf of the monarchists in the ravine. I got the sense when I was down there that he was a hotheaded young rebel, causing frustration to his leaders with his fiery vendettas."

She frowned, her eyes shifting from Zev to stare unseeingly at the crowd.

"But I'm not sure he acted alone, either. I don't see how he could have. He definitely knew things a hermit from Sundering Canyon had no business knowing. He knew about Jade—the student who was expelled for asking the wrong questions before my time. She's the one who I'm pretty sure is J from the messages in Port Taran."

She looked hopefully at Zev, but although his brow was furrowed in concentration, showing he was listening with interest to her words, he still didn't speak.

"He also knew about...heartsong," Marieke said, deciding in a burst of determination to be open where Zev was apparently determined to be aloof. "He mentioned it to me."

There was a long moment of silence, the stillness between them somehow more charged than before. Marieke would have given a great deal to read Zev's mind in that moment. His face was giving nothing whatsoever away.

"Heartsong?" he repeated at last.

She nodded. "I don't exactly know what it is, but it's some deep or dangerous form of magic, the history and function of which has been obscured. Perhaps intentionally."

Again, Zev wasn't quick to answer. "And Gorgon mentioned it?"

"He did," Marieke confirmed. "And I've heard it mentioned before, in a conversation between Councilor Isabel and the Head Instructor. A conversation I wasn't supposed to hear. It seems that the student, Jade, was trying to research it. I think that's what got her expelled."

"And that cautionary tale doesn't make you reluctant to

continue her investigation?" The hint of humor in Zev's question was a little off somehow.

"I've already graduated," Marieke reminded him. "I'm not in danger of expulsion." She smiled grimly. "Plus, I'm not so easily deterred."

"Because," Zev supplied, "unlike what you told the council, you have more questions."

"A great deal more," Marieke agreed.

Zev's exhaled breath was almost a sigh. His eyes passed thoughtfully to her face. "What do you mean when you say you don't think Gorgon acted alone?"

"I don't exactly know," Marieke admitted. "Only that I don't see how he could have. The council glossed over it in front of us, but I'm sure they're discussing it fiercely behind closed doors—some of the so-called accidents can't easily be explained as attacks without magic involved. I really don't think Gorgon or his conspirators were singers. He reviled singers. But they somehow harnessed magic to fuel their attacks. I wasn't entirely frank with the council. I don't think I might have imagined magic at the lagoon—I'm very sure that I felt something come toward me. And I felt something when the bridge collapsed on my crossing into Aeltas, too. Plus Councilor Isabel told me that the singer who survived the most recent attack felt magic."

"What are you saying?" Zev asked, seeming genuinely lost. "What exactly do you suspect Gorgon achieved?"

"I don't know." Marieke raised her hands helplessly, frustrated with how often she was saying the phrase. "But some kind of magic was at work. It must have been. It's not just the attacks, either. The failing crops, the general deterioration of our land." She met Zev's eyes in a silent appeal, desperate to get all her thoughts and fears off her chest. "I think all of it is connected somehow to the absence of the monarchs who once ruled Oleand."

Zev's eyes searched hers with the intensity that always turned her head a little. "Why do you say that?"

"Because of Jade's messages, and something Gorgon said about the past," Marieke answered. "And because there must be a reason the council's tried so hard to suppress the truth of the coup." She shook her head slowly. "Whatever heartsong magic is, I think we lost it when we killed our monarch." She took a tiny step closer to him, hardly aware of doing it. "Zev, I think I was right before, in a way. I think the land *is* cursed. And I think the attacks, the barren fields...all of it is connected to what happened back then."

Something flickered in Zev's eyes, and for a moment Marieke was afraid he'd laugh at her, or tell her she'd lost her mind. To her relief, when he spoke, it was in his usual, serious tones.

"Even if the land was cursed," Zev said, "how would Gorgon harness that to attack someone?"

Marieke shrugged. "That's one of the questions I'm still determined to answer. Maybe that's what heartsong is. Maybe they were able to somehow use heartsong magic, in spite of not being singers."

"I really don't think that's the case," said Zev, his voice flat.

"Probably not," Marieke acknowledged with a sigh. "But I intend to find out."

She glanced up at Zev to see that he looked worried, his brow furrowed as he considered her.

"I know," she said quickly. "But I'll be careful. I know I *need* to be careful." She twisted the end of her braid around her fingers in a distracted gesture. "I meant it when I said I'm not easily deterred, but I do intend to learn from Jade's story."

"Learn what?" Zev asked, his frown deepening.

Marieke let her braid drop. "Well, I think whatever trail she was following revealed the truth regarding the slaughter of the monarchs and their supporters. The messages in Port Taran make that pretty clear. And judging by the tone of those messages, I think she either confronted the council with that information or intended to."

"And?" Zev pressed, perhaps noting the shudder that went over her.

"I suspect that was a mistake," Marieke said, her voice small. "One I'm not inclined to repeat." She bit her lip as she looked up into his storm-cloud gray eyes and lowered brow. "Something Gorgon said has been playing on my mind since yesterday—about Jade, and paying the price. Zev, I think…" She swallowed. "I think she might have been killed, just like the monarchs were, for her questions."

Zev's eyes were troubled as they searched hers, but he offered no reply. What was there to say, after all? Neither of them had these particular answers.

"All of which is to say," Marieke forced her tone to become more businesslike, "I understand that I need to be cautious. That's why I misled the council into thinking that I was satisfied with Gorgon's vendetta as the explanation for all the attacks, and that I had no more questions. But I'm not really done looking for answers."

Zev was still looking down at her, concern clear on his face, and something else she couldn't read. Feeling emboldened by the fact that he was at least no longer being cold and aloof, Marieke took a bigger step forward. He didn't retreat, and she found herself standing almost flush against him, looking up into his face.

"Perhaps," she said, swallowing around a suddenly dry throat, "perhaps we can try to unravel it all together."

Still Zev said nothing, his eyes intense and conflicted as he held her gaze. Gathering her courage, Marieke tilted her head back, shifting her weight onto the balls of her feet as she prepared to raise her face to his. She was dimly aware that they were in a public place, but no one knew them here, or cared what they were doing. No one would pay much attention if Zev pulled her all the way against him and kissed her like he had in the gardens the day before.

These intoxicating fantasies crashed down around her as Zev shifted back, his hands gentle but firm as he placed them on her shoulders and created a more respectable distance between them.

"Marieke, I can't get involved. Whatever magic or cursed land or human plots are plaguing Oleand, it isn't my fight. My place is in Aeltas, and I've already been away too long."

"Yes," Marieke said stupidly, blinking quickly and trying to pretend her heart wasn't shattering at these reasonable yet brutal words. If Zev was determined to pretend yesterday's moment hadn't happened, she wouldn't gain much by confronting him with it. "Yes, I know you have. I understand."

"I'm sorry to leave you here on your own," Zev added quickly, the attempt to soften his words entirely insufficient. "I agree that your life is probably not in imminent danger with Gorgon gone. But I'm glad you're planning to go home and stay out of sight for a while. And I think you're wise to be guarded and not to trust the council completely." A frown marred his high brow. "Especially the Head Instructor."

Marieke raised an eyebrow, confused by the cloud that descended over Zev's face with the words. Why the Head Instructor specifically?

But before she could ask for more information, Zev stepped suddenly closer, obliterating her train of thought entirely. His hands were still on her shoulders, and his eyes were unbearably intense as he searched her face. All at once, he leaned down and pressed his lips to her forehead.

"May your labors prosper and your future blossom like the almond tree," he murmured into her hair, the feel of his lips robbing Marieke of breath.

His words were irresistibly reminiscent of the benediction he'd given when they parted ways in Tarandon all that time ago. She wanted to be grateful that he seemed to care, but the words sounded far too much like a permanent goodbye.

Until Zev stepped back, his voice husky in his throat, and his hands reluctant as they released her.

"I hope we'll meet again, Marieke of Oleand."

And without waiting for a reply, he turned and strode away, the bustle of the market obscuring him from sight within moments.

Marieke stared after him, barely able to gather her thoughts. She had to curb a childish impulse to chase after him and beg him to come back.

But both pride and common sense prevented it. It was clear that he'd wrestled with his decision, and his mind was made up as to his course. She knew she couldn't force him to change it. And as the ghost of his touch faded, and her mind reasserted itself, she remembered that she had her own battles to fight.

Bruised heart or not, she wasn't going to sit idle or be complacent if someone or something was still threatening her country. She would lie low for a while as she'd said, but she wouldn't stop looking for answers.

Besides which, she thought, as her eyes searched the crowd which had swallowed Zev, letting Zev go now without a fight didn't mean giving up on him. She was determined they weren't done. Even he had said he hoped they would meet again.

He might not be willing to fight for her—at least right now

—but she remembered vividly his passion when he'd pulled her against him and kissed her. He couldn't pretend to be unaffected, whatever his priorities might currently be.

Marieke's fingers strayed to the place on her forehead where he'd pressed that last, emotion-filled kiss. It was probably her fancy that the skin still felt warm. She stood there for a moment, the market bustling around her as her thoughts encompassed the fate of her country, the lies of the council, the silencing of the last student to ask the wrong—or right—questions, and finally…Zev.

None of it was over. Because she, for one, knew what she was willing to fight for.

# NOTE FROM THE AUTHOR

Thank you for reading *A Splintered Land*. I hope you enjoyed visiting the world of the Sovereign Realms. I would be so grateful if you would consider leaving a review on Amazon—it would really make a difference!

To continue Zev and Marieke's story, check out Book Two —*A Fractured Song*.

If you've yet to read the previous adventures set on the continent of Providore, check out *The Singer Tales* today! This completed series includes six connected but standalone fairy tale retellings featuring strong heroines navigating everything from miniature elves to brutish giants as they chase their own happily ever afters.

Join up to my mailing list at deborahgracewhite.com to be kept up to date on new releases, specials, and giveaways, such as bonus chapters. You'll receive some great freebies, too, including *An Expectation of Magic*, a novella which is a prequel to my completed YA fantasy series *The Vazula Chronicles*.

Plus, you'll receive *Dragon's Sight*, an 8,000 word prequel to my completed YA fantasy trilogy *The Kyona Chronicles*.

Again, thanks for entering the world of Providore! I hope to see you back again.

# ALSO BY DEBORAH GRACE WHITE

The Kyona Chronicles: YA Fantasy

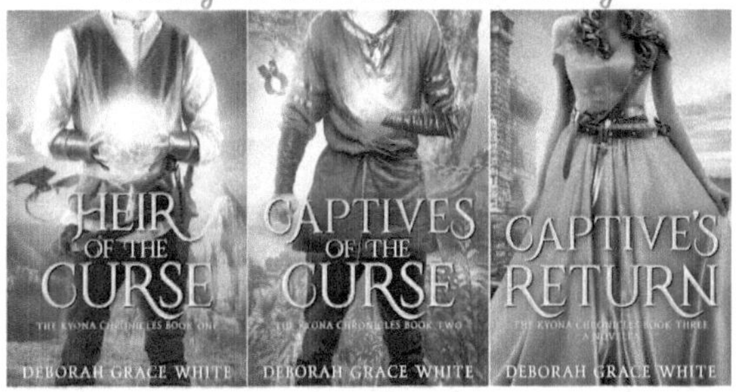

The Kyona Legacy: YA Fantasy

# ALSO BY DEBORAH GRACE WHITE

*The Unlucky Prince: Fairy Tale Retelling*
*(Once Upon a Prince Multi-Author Series)*

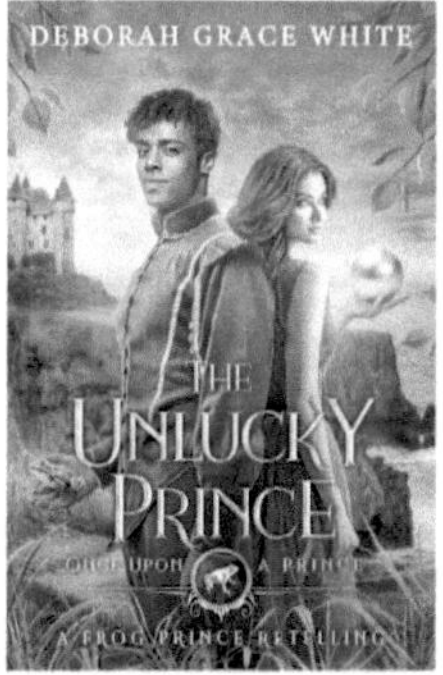

## The Singer Tales: Fairy Tale Retellings

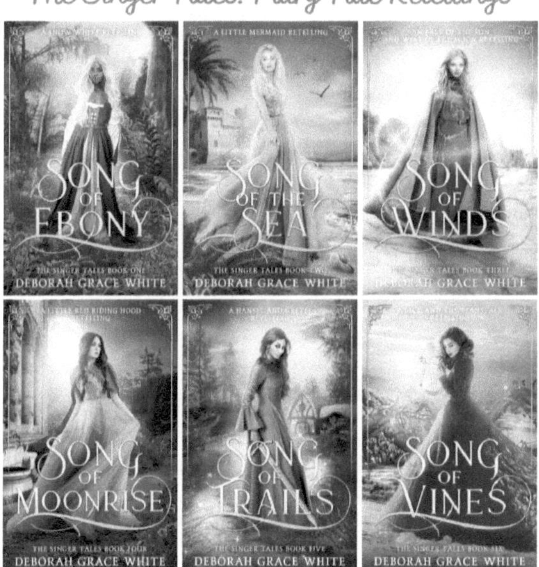

*Island of Secrets & Sacrifice: YA Fantasy*
*(Sacrificed Hearts Multi-Author Series)*

*Heartsong: YA Fantasy*

# Acknowledgments

The start of a new series calls for a new round of thanks to my amazing team!

As always, first thanks to Ray, my awesome husband, every bit as swoonworthy and steady as Zev! Thank you to my beta readers for being so supportive and constructive: Adrian, Alora, Constance, Mel W, Berri, Mum, Steph, and Dad. Thanks to Shae for the thorough and professional proofread. Any remaining errors are mine.

Thanks to Moorbooks for the cover—I just absolutely love how Zev and Marieke turned out! And thanks to Becca for another beautiful map.

To you, the reader, thank you for giving me the privilege of being an author.

And most importantly, to God, who is the source of the only good kind of power there is.

# About the Author

I've been a reader since I can remember, growing up on a wide range of books, from classic literature to light-hearted romps. The love of reading has traveled with me unchanged across multiple  continents, and carried me from my own childhood all the way to having children of my own.

But if reading is like looking through a window into a magical and beautiful world, beginning to write my own stories was like discovering that I could open that window and climb right out into fantasyland.

I cannot believe how privileged I am to actually be living that childhood dream and publishing my own novels. I do so from my hometown of Adelaide, Australia, where I live with my husband and our four little ones.

I've never outgrown my love of young adult stories, so the genre of young adult fantasy was always going to be my niche. Feel free to email me at deborah@deborahgracewhite.com and introduce yourself! Or subscribe to my mailing list at deborah gracewhite.com for free giveaways, sales, and updates.